Praise for *Magical Meet Cute*

"A poignant, timely story abou[...] [...]hen to be soft, and the people you ca[...] —Felicia Gro[...] *Midnight*

"One of the best novels of 202[...] [...], camaraderie and romance and then prepare to spend the next few days in awe." —M.J. Rose, *New York Times* bestselling author of *Forgetting to Remember*

"Smart, timely, and deeply powerful, *Magical Meet Cute* presents a portrait of modern anti-Semitism, while reinforcing the need to thrive and find joy." —Sara Goodman Confino, bestselling author of *Don't Forget to Write*

"This book and its message is an antidote that's sorely needed in today's world, and a powerful reminder of the magic behind our words." —Heidi Shertok, author of *Unorthodox Love*

"Jean Meltzer continues her trend of fearlessly tackling sensitive, mostly uncharted issues with finesse and humor. *Magical Meet Cute* is her boldest novel yet." —Meredith Schorr, author of *As Seen on TV*

"Meltzer's pen weaves charm with flaws in remarkable harmony that will leave readers enchanted." —J'nell Ciesielski, bestselling author of *The Socialite*

"*Magical Meet Cute* is the Jewish joy we all need in our lives right now. It's a funny and playful page-turner, but with so much heart you'll be bursting by the end." —Ali Rosen, bestselling author of *Recipe for Second Chances*

"This book is a masterclass in how to blend heart, humor, and a touch of the mystical, proving Meltzer isn't just spinning clay—she's spinning gold." —Arden Joy, author of *Keep This Off the Record*

"This book is magic—in every sense. It is raw, it is real and very timely." —Maan Gabriel, author of *Twelve Hours in Manhattan*

Magical Meet Cute

JEAN MELTZER

/IIMIRA

/||MIRA™

ISBN-13: 978-0-7783-3441-5

Magical Meet Cute

Recycling programs
for this product may
not exist in your area.

Mira
22 Adelaide St. West, 41st Floor
Toronto, Ontario M5H 4E3, Canada
MIRABooks.com

Printed in U.S.A.

Also by Jean Meltzer

The Matzah Ball
Mr. Perfect on Paper
Kissing Kosher

For My Sisters,

Evelyn Meltzer and Danielle Meltzer Chesney

ONE

It was hard and magnificent.

Faiga Kaplan, otherwise known as Faye to her friends, ran her hands down the long shaft of her latest clay creation. An earthenware vase—at least three feet in length and bearing a perfectly crafted slit for sunflowers at the top—lay on her studio table. Having been painted twice and forged through fire in her kiln, it was now ready for placement in her storefront window. All she had to do was get the heavy, hulking piece of pottery through the first floor of Magic Mud Pottery without breaking it.

Cautiously, she lifted the vase from the table. Peeking out from the sides, carefully managing her balance with each step, she creeped slowly past the tables and chairs of her studio, bumping over the threshold into the hallway, heading through the first floor. She was halfway through the old wooden building, by the center staircase, when she felt something mushy and wet beneath her left foot.

Faye didn't need to look down.

She knew exactly what she had stepped in.

"Hillel," Faye groaned, rolling her eyes to the ceiling.

Carefully, she put the vase down beside the staircase, turning her attention to inspect the damage now seeping through her pink sock.

"Hillel," Faye called out again. "I'm serious. Get in here!"

Hillel, a hairless and toothless Chinese crested, peeked around the corner. Faye had adopted the pathetic-looking creature when he was ten years old. At the time, she had considered it a *mitzvah*, a good deed, in the wake of a dreadful breakup. She thought she could funnel all her love into this poor creature—a dog riddled with back acne and without a home—and he would adore her forever.

"I know you did this on purpose," Faye said, lifting one foot up to display the mess.

Hillel twisted away from her, tail up, his tiny butthole pointed straight in her line of vision. She swore that dog could speak English.

She also knew that his constant accidents had nothing to do with tummy troubles. After all, Faye was a responsible pet owner. She had taken Hillel to the vet a dozen times, run every expensive test to see if there was something physically wrong with him, only to be told that the tiny monster was in perfectly good health. Indeed, the vet had promised her that Hillel would likely live another decade. No, he defecated all over her apartment for the same reason Stuart had called off their engagement. *She was too much.*

"Keep acting this way," Faye warned, narrowing her eyes in his direction, "and I'll send you to go live with Nelly. You can wear frilly doll dresses and be the guest of honor at her Second Glance dog tea parties for the rest of your natural existence."

Hillel strolled past her, unconcerned, before landing on a mess of blankets and pillow squares waiting for him by the storefront window.

Faye had made the tiny bed for Hillel there so he would be comfortable. She figured he could watch the people walking down Main Street, see the customers before they entered her store. It was also the sunniest, and therefore warmest, spot in her building, an absolute necessity for a dog without any fur. She did everything for Hillel. She gave him her best. Devoted her love, time, and energy to his well-being. And what did Hillel do in response?

Crap all over her.

The thought had crossed her mind more than once to return him to the shelter.

Faye never did, of course. No, as it turned out…no amount of snarling, or defecating in high-traffic areas, or trying to bite her with his gummy, toothless mouth, would ever steer her heart away from the four-legged fur demon.

The reason being simple enough. She had made a promise to Hillel. She had stood outside Woodstock Animal Shelter, placed him safely in the front basket of her bike, and told him she would care for him, and protect him—*and never betray his love on a snowmobile in Lapland*—until the bitter end.

Perhaps loving someone to the bitter end had always been her downfall.

Her mind wandered to her ex-fiancé, Stuart, when most applicably her nose wrinkled. The scent of dog feces was beginning to take up residence.

Faye hobbled on one foot up the stairs to the second floor. Finding her way to the bathtub, she set about cleaning up her foot.

For the last three years, Faye had been the sole proprietor of Magic Mud Pottery. She lived above her store and studio in a quaint one-bedroom apartment.

Magic Mud Pottery was one of a handful of old buildings made of wood and painted in bright colors that dotted the bucolic downtown of Woodstock, New York. Set between large trees, and decorated with Pride flags and double-hung windows, it was the type of town that, no matter the season, smelled like burning wood and cinnamon.

Her apartment was small, but as a single woman, she didn't need much space. Plus, she had gotten an amazing price. On the second floor, a cozy bedroom sat towards the back of the building, overlooking a fenced-in yard and garden. In the front, a tiny living room was divided from a half kitchen by a counter. A bathroom rested in between.

As an old building, the layout—but especially the kitchen— was all types of weird. While the oven, stove, and sink were on the second floor, the refrigerator was too tall for the upstairs kitchen alcove. And so it sat downstairs, right behind the front counter, where Faye often rang up customers.

At first, it was a problem. Especially at night, as Faye often liked to sneak downstairs in nothing but her skivvies and have a late-night snack. But Faye quickly realized that most everyone who owned a business in downtown Woodstock lived elsewhere, and so, even though she had invested in curtains, she never bothered to use them.

Beyond all these things, she liked the quirkiness of the building. The fact it was strange and unusual. It reminded her of an apartment she had lived in on the Lower East Side while a young lawyer in Manhattan, with a shower in the kitchen and a bathroom outside the apartment, just down the hall.

Faye was finishing cleaning up when the bell above the front door to Magic Mud Pottery rang out.

"Faiga," a voice called out moments later.

She recognized the voice as belonging to Nelly, who owned the building next door, where she ran the business Second Glance Treasures.

It was a gentle, lovely name for a store that was essentially extra storage space for a woman who had taken the hobby of hoarding to a professional capacity. Perhaps Faye was being too hard on the eccentric octogenarian. But No-Filter Nelly—as Faye sometimes called her behind her back—was a frequent, though not always welcome, visitor.

"One moment," Faye called out.

Quickly, she finished drying off her foot. Spraying down her bathtub and the floor, she popped downstairs. Nelly was standing by the storefront window, arms crossed, her entire forehead wrinkling in displeasure.

"It smells like a porta-potty in here." Nelly grimaced.

Faye huffed. "Hillel had an accident again."

"Again?" Nelly looked towards the dog. "Maybe you should take him to the vet."

"I've taken him to the vet," Faye reminded her *for the ten thousandth time*. Grabbing a towel and some pet odor remover, she bent down to the floor and began cleaning up his mess. "Can I help you with something, Nelly?"

"I was wondering if you're going to Single in the Sukkah tonight?" she asked.

"I'm not planning on it."

"Why not?" Nelly said, following her. *She always followed her.* "Only twenty-four dollars a participant. For a good cause. Plus, you might meet someone."

Faye tossed the turd in the trash. "I'm not interested in meeting anyone right now."

"Why not?"

Faye slammed the lid shut. "You know the reason."

"Because you were dumped by your fiancé of seven years after a snowmobile accident in Lapland?"

Busted.

Faye had first met Stuart Wutz during law school. After a seven-year engagement, the two-week escapade she had painstakingly planned to Lapland was supposed to be a pre-wedding getaway, a chance for them to have some fun before planning for their wedding, three months away, moved into hyperdrive.

Instead, everything about the trip had been a disaster.

Stuart complained constantly. About the cold. About the food. About his hemorrhoids. He nearly caused an international incident when he found out the hamburger he was eating was made of reindeer meat. But it wasn't until that fateful snowmobile ride—when Stuart skidded out on a slick of ice, crashing into a snowy embankment—that their decade-long relationship came to an official end. Bringing her vehicle safely to a stop beside him, racing to check that he was okay, she was shocked when Stuart had stood up and lobbed his own attack.

You're too much, Faye. Everything you do, everything you are… it's just too much. No wonder your own mother couldn't stand you.

The wedding was off. Faye was thirty-one years old, and having given Stuart the best years of her life—the best of her reproductive years, too—back to being single. It was more than betrayal. It was more than a hurt. It was an avalanche of pain that she had barely escaped from. And yet, she couldn't completely blame Stuart for what had happened. He was simply a trigger point in a snowslip that had been building since her youth.

"So, you had one bad experience," Nelly said.

"Not just one," Faye grumbled.

"So, you had *multiple* bad experiences," Nelly said, unfazed. "Lots of people hurt and disappointed you. Because of this, you give up on love forever?"

Faye spun around. "I don't need a mother, Nelly!"

Her words pierced the air and turned into ice.

"Everyone needs a mother," Nelly said, simply.

Faye scoffed, hardening herself against the admission. Against the confession. She had already had a mother in her life, and she sucked. Some nights, she could still feel the pain in her wrist—in her fingers—from where her mom had permanently disabled her.

Faye twisted away from Nelly. "If you're done pestering me about—"

Nelly cut her off. "So come for the synagogue. They always need money."

"How about I just write them a check and spend the night reading a book and eating hard kosher salami by myself?"

Nelly grimaced. "This is fun for you?"

"Yes, Nelly." Faye threw her hands up, exasperated. "This is fun for me. Because I like being alone. More important, I'm better alone. I have no interest in meeting a man, starting a romantic relationship, or getting married. Going to a Single in the Sukkah event would be the equivalent of false advertising."

Faye made her way back through her pottery studio. Picking up her vase, she turned to place it in her storefront window. And that was when she saw it. The vase she had thought was perfect...had a tiny bubble at the bottom.

"Haman's hat," Faye huffed. She tried not to use curse words.

"What's wrong?" Nelly asked.

Faye shook her head. "I must have missed an air bubble before drying."

Clay held memory. If you did something wrong at any part of the process, it would be reflected in the final work. A fingerprint at the edge. A lip all misshapen and wonky. A warp or scratch in the otherwise smooth facade, or worse...the entire thing exploding, shattering completely, when placed into the kiln for firing. Clay, contrary to popular belief, was not an easy material to work with.

"I'm just gonna throw it out," Faye said, attempting to move it out of her window.

"Wha!" Nelly stopped her with both hands. "Why would you throw this out? You've already spent time to make it."

"Because it's awful," Faye snapped back. "No one is going

to want a vase with a bubble sticking out of it!" And because looking at that bubble was a constant reminder of all the things her mother had stolen from her.

Faye was only seventeen years old when it happened. When her mother—in another one of her random and totally unjustified rages—woke her up from a sound sleep because she had accidentally left clay out on the kitchen table. Grabbing Faye by the wrist and pulling her out of bed, she dragged her down the hall to clean up the supposed mess. Faye could still recall the sensation of her hand being twisted the wrong way, the sound of it snapping as the bone broke. But most of all, she remembered screaming for her father to help her.

The abuse Faye had endured as a child changed her. She lost the scholarship to a prestigious art school in Manhattan where she was planning to study ceramics. She became wholly focused on protecting herself, remaining independent... Changing paths, she became a lawyer instead. And when she met Stuart, she thought she had found the safe, unconditional type of love that she read about in her romance novels.

Instead, her clay memory bubbled up and formed blisters all over their love. She became someone unrecognizable. Desperate to keep Stuart happy—desperate to prove she was someone loveable and worthwhile—she lost herself completely. The breakup had been hard, but when she looked at her life now, at Woodstock and Magic Mud Pottery, she was grateful.

What life had taught her, most of all, was that she had to protect herself.

"Come on," Nelly said, attempting to take the vase away from Faye. "Don't be ridiculous. This is a lovely vase! A great vase. Someone is going to want it."

Faye sighed, and met the old woman's eyes. Occasionally, No-Filter Nelly had her good moments. Perhaps that was why, in spite of all their bickering and teasing, she considered the old woman a friend.

"You're right." Faye rolled her eyes.

She had already wasted several nights and not insignificant money on constructing the piece. Small business owners could not afford to throw out a piece simply because it had a small bubble in it.

Nelly smirked, pleased. "Of course, I'm right. I'm always right."

Faye returned to putting her vase in the window. Moving over some ring dishes—she was always making ring dishes—she adjusted her now terribly warped vase so that the bulbous top with the thin slit would be facing outward. Then, she readjusted the gems that lay around it—pink quartz for clarity, blue lapis for prosperity—alongside a collection of antique hamsas, evil eye amulets, and various Hebrew blessings for the home.

After which, Faye went to find her grimoire. She had created it by taking the pages of her siddur—the very same prayer book she had used as a child in Hebrew school—and cutting out the prayers that resonated with her. Pasting them against its natural fiber pages, she had then gone through and written in her own additions, gluing bits of dried flowers to the sides, embellishing the edges with art and calligraphy meant to help beautify the words.

"Which spell is this?" Nelly asked.

"Spell for prosperity," she said, before grabbing a few dried pomegranate seeds and sprinkling them on the storefront window.

She closed her eyes, and called on the Divine Hebrew Goddess.

Faye hadn't always been a Jewitch. For most of her life, Judaism had been an afterthought. She had a limited Hebrew school education and had never celebrated her bat mitzvah. She couldn't speak Hebrew. She had spent one summer at Camp Ahava, as a counselor beside her best friend, Miranda, but she went home early after finding the whole experience way too religious for her. And yet, she always felt Jewish. And she wanted to connect more, to her faith and her identity, but she just never seemed to be able to find an access point.

In the wake of that disastrous breakup with Stuart, Faye had gone to her local bookstore. Perusing the aisles in a listless haze, trying to figure out the next steps for her completely shattered life, she had come across a book entitled *The Jewitch Woman*. The moniker alone was compelling. She had never heard of this concept before. In general, over the course of history, when Jews were linked with witchcraft...they died.

Out of curiosity, she pulled it off the shelf. It was the image on the cover that caught her in its spell. *A Hebrew priestess.* A wild and uninhibited woman leaping through the sky, a crown of stars upon her head, a *tallit* around her shoulders, long brown hair flowing behind her, held a full moon against her beating heart as lovingly as if it were her own child.

Faye took that book home and read it in one sitting. And she related with the words she found inside its pages. This return to the Hebrew Goddess. This idea that she could be like the priestesses of the Holy Temple of Jerusalem, someone powerful and respected—not only a magician, but a healer.

She found her Jewish connection. She didn't need to sit in shul for three hours, speaking a language she didn't understand, to commune with the Hebrew Goddess. She became a solo practitioner. And Faye knew a lot about Jewitch magic. She knew what spells to say to bring prosperity and luck. She knew what to feed a woman wanting a baby, and where to sew knots to keep a child safe. She even practiced her strongest magic in caves, thanks to some words she had gleaned from the Rashbam.

Most of all, Jewitch magic allowed her to rewrite the story of her life.

It gave her a center. It lifted her up, told her she was powerful, reminded her that she had full authority and ability to protect herself. She felt loved by the universe, and the Divine

Goddess, the sacred mother whose light waxed and waned with each new moon. It helped her understand where she had gone wrong with Stuart...and then, it gave her the tools to return to her true self.

With a newfound courage, Faye went to the mikvah on the Upper West Side of Manhattan, and, immersing herself in that sacred bath full of rainwater three times, emerged renewed. From there, she sold her legal practice in Manhattan, moved upstate to Woodstock, New York, and opened Magic Mud Pottery.

It had taken Faye over three decades to find a place where she felt safe.

But finally, she could sleep without nightmares.

Faye finished her spell and turned to place her grimoire back on a shelf. Instead, she nearly plowed into Nelly. The old woman was standing there, invading her personal space once again, with her hand held out.

Nelly nodded to the dried pomegranate seeds. "Give me some."

Faye squinted, confused. "For what?"

"For tonight," she explained. "I want to put some in my bra."

Faye angled her head, concerned. "Single in the Sukkah is being held outside. You're not worried about getting attacked by an owl?"

"It depends," Nelly snarked back. "How big is the owl's—"

"Okay!" Faye said, cutting her off. She dumped all her seeds into Nelly's hands. "Here you go. Don't say I didn't warn you."

Nelly took a few minutes to jiggle and wiggle them into place, while Faye returned to her morning tasks. She went back to her counter, grabbing her phone to take a picture of the vase, before heading back to the computer to upload the details on Etsy.

"What are you going to call it?" Nelly asked.

"I don't know." Faye shrugged. "Almost perfect."

"You should call it *shvantz*."

"Really?"

Nelly shrugged. "It looks like a *shvantz*."

"It does not—"

Faye stopped, cocking her head sideways. Now that Nelly mentioned it, her latest creation had taken on a distinctly phallic shape. A spherical head at the top. A thick shaft, at least thirty-six inches, to place long-stemmed roses in. Perhaps it had been unwise to paint it a rich pink color, which, after being forged in the flames, shimmered in swirls beneath the morning sunlight.

"All your vases look like *shvantzes*," Nelly said, before pointing with one finger towards a maroon vase, the opening of which Faye had designed to accommodate the large and budding leaves of tulips. "Except that one. That one looks like a *pupic*."

The words were, clearly, an open accusation.

Not that Nelly was wrong. Faye might have sworn off love, but she was still a woman. It had been several years since Faye had engaged in a good *shtupping*.

Perhaps it was coming across in her art. "Maybe," Nelly wondered aloud, "you should ask yourself, 'Self…why am I always making ring dishes, and pottery that looks like giant—'"

"Okay," Faye said, rising from her desk. Coming around the counter, she put her hands on Nelly's back and began to physically push the old lady out of her store. For a woman in her eighties, she was surprisingly strong. Either that, or she had grips on the bottoms of her orthopedic sneakers. Faye went with grips. "You've had your say. You can leave now."

"So, you're coming tonight?" Nelly asked, wedging herself into the threshold.

"Not a chance."

"Because I told the cantor you were coming."

Faye released the old woman, anger bubbling over.

Nelly beamed, wide and victorious.

Of course, Nelly told the cantor she was coming. Nelly *always* told the cantor she was coming. Because Cantor Shulamit Amaral was married to Faye's best friend, Miranda. Faye rolled her eyes to the ceiling, and then, telling herself it was a *mitzvah* to support the synagogue, leaned into the old woman.

"You," Faye said, "are a villain."

It was awful.

Faye was less than an hour into Single in the Sukkah, and was already regretting her decision. Her current suitor—Number Three, according to his name tag—was cramming a highlights reel of his lifetime achievements into the five-minute time slot they were allotted.

"And after I finished my residency," he continued, barely coming up for air, "I was offered a teaching fellowship at the local university. It's been a good experience, living and building a medical practice in Woodstock. Plus, I own my own house. Four bedrooms. Three acres. I'm hoping one day to build on an addition, maybe a pool. I've always wanted to build..."

Her eyes drifted to the side of the Sukkah. Cantor Shulamit, a rainbow-colored kippah on her head, was enjoying a slice of babka with apple cider while schmoozing with some of the members of the congregation. She noticed Faye looking and waved in her direction.

At the table next to her, Nelly was leaning in hard to her five-minute speed date. Despite the fact it was the end of September, and cold enough for jackets, she had unbuttoned the top of her blouse.

Number Three cleared his throat. "So, what do you do for a living?"

"I'm a ceramicist," she explained, "and I own Magic Mud Pottery."

"You mean the place downtown with the cauldron in the front window and the little crystals all around?"

"That's the one."

"I know that place," he said, obviously pleased at his ability to find a connection between them. "You hold those arts and crafts classes for kids and their mommies?"

Faye blinked. "It's not…arts and crafts."

A damning silence settled between them. Perhaps Number Three had not meant to be rude, but his words diminished her passion. She couldn't help but sense an air of misogyny in them. As if a craft done by women, for women—*and God forbid, their children*—was somehow less valuable in the scheme of the universe.

This was a teachable moment. She did her best to educate him. "Magic Mud Pottery is a place where people of all shapes and persuasions express their hearts through their hands."

"Of course." He shifted in his seat. "I didn't mean to imply otherwise." His eyes drifted towards the table, embarrassed. "So did you…study pottery in college?"

The question made her wrist ache.

"Unfortunately, no," she said, returning to herself. "Magic Mud Pottery is my second career. Before that, I ran my own very successful law firm in Manhattan."

"Really?" His eyebrows arched up towards the ceiling.

"I sold my firm at thirty-one and came up here to start over."

"Wow." He seemed genuinely impressed. "And what made you want to change your whole life around like that? Were you unhappy with law, or just looking for new ventures to explore—"

"Oh, nothing like that," Faye interrupted him. "My fiancé dumped me during a snowmobile ride in Lapland."

The look of surprise that landed on his face made the entire evening, plus the twenty-four-dollar donation to the synagogue, feel *totally* worth it.

"I'm sorry," Number Three stammered, "your fiancé?"

"Well, obviously, he's not my fiancé anymore. We had been engaged seven years," she said, fully leaning into it now. "All through college and law school—those best reproductive years of a woman's life—and then, when I was thirty-one years old, three months before the wedding, he told me he didn't want to marry me."

She laughed aloud. Maybe too loud. "But after he dumped me and left me to foot the bill *and* call all two hundred and twenty-six people on our guest list to tell them that the wedding was off, I decided it was time for a change. So I came up here, where my best friend and her wife lived, and decided to start over…to focus on the things I really love and care about… to focus on me."

He squinted, still confused. "That's good… I guess?"

"It's very good."

Number Three rubbed the back of his neck. "So, you were going to get married?"

"Correct."

"But he dumped you. And now you live in Woodstock and run Magic Mud Pottery."

"Well, look at that," she quipped happily, "I suppose you can learn a lot about a person in five minutes."

She could also see by the way he was looking at her—like she had snakes coming out of her head instead of hair—that their brief fling was over.

Faye suddenly felt vulnerable, and that vulnerability—the realization that she could be hurt again—made her feel unsafe. She regretted opening up to this man. Even joking, presenting her trauma as an aside, she felt the bubbles in her clay memory rising up and twisting into blisters. All the broken parts of her life, which she had not patched correctly or smoothed over, lingered inside her.

If she continued this conversation, she would shatter.

The alarm on the five-minute timer went off. Number Three raced off to the next table. Faye found that sadness in her heart—the sadness she worked so hard to keep at bay—surging towards the center of her chest. Seeing Number Sixteen—a man old enough to remember the Revolutionary War—shuffling his way to her table, Faye reasoned she had been at Single in the Sukkah long enough. It was late. She wanted to go home. Gathering up her bag, she quickly made her way towards her bike, sitting in the rack in the synagogue parking lot.

Her goal was to slink out without much fanfare. But Faye was halfway through the parking lot when Cantor Shulamit put down her snack, excused herself from her friends, and caught up to Faye.

"Hey," Shully said, "where are you going?"

"Home."

"But the event's not over yet," Shulamit said, genuinely concerned. "You're going to miss all the fun. Plus, you haven't even had a slice of pumpkin-spiced babka. We brought it in fresh from Best Babka in Brooklyn this morning."

Faye smiled politely. Dear, sweet Shulamit. Her intentions were good. Everything Shulamit did came from the purest of hearts. It really was no wonder that Faye's best friend, Miranda—along with the entire congregation of Beth Tikvah synagogue—had fallen completely and totally in love with her. *Everyone loved Shulamit.*

"I'm just not feeling well," Faye lied.

"Oh." Shully frowned before glancing towards Faye's bike. "Well, do you need a ride home?"

"Actually, I'm thinking the fresh air will be helpful. Just tell Miranda I said hi and that I'll call her tomorrow. Maybe we can get together for a Shabbat later this month?"

"That would be wonderful," Shully said genuinely, before leaning in for a long hug.

Faye accepted the embrace somewhat awkwardly, and then quickly skedaddled her way home.

It was approximately three miles from Congregation Beth Tikvah to downtown where Faye lived. Most of the ride was rural. Quiet. The same sense of magic that had provoked her to name her store Magic Mud Pottery now felt palpable. She forgot about Single in the Sukkah and Stuart, focusing instead on the pedaling of her wheels.

Approaching town, most of the storefronts had shuttered. Faye rode past the one business open late—an ice-cream shop called Pinky's—and made her way down Main Street, towards home. The familiar crunch of leaves greeted her arrival.

It was only when one of those leaves found its way into her spokes, and caused her bike to stutter, that she realized she had misinterpreted. Faye braked and stepped off her bike to investigate. As it turned out, the crunching she had felt was no act of nature, but rather flyers. A glance down the street showed her entire neighborhood was littered in white sheets.

Bending down, she picked one up. The words splattered across the top of the page, in crass blue handwriting, were not what she was expecting.

THE JEWS CONTROL THE MEDIA.

THE JEWS ARE RESPONSIBLE FOR COVID.

It was followed by a long list of names and photographs of what were supposed to be Jews.

Faye scanned the images, shock tearing through her body. Flipping the flyer over, she realized that the attacker had not stopped with film executives and government officials. Whoever had made the flyers had also gone through their community, this time including addresses of businesses and homes.

She gasped. An image of her—one she recognized immediately as stolen from the About Us page of her Magic Mud Pottery website—was squeezed between a picture of Cantor Shulamit and Rabbi Devorah Aaronson. And beneath those photos, four tiny words:

JEWS ARE THE PROBLEM.

Her shock dissipated into straight rage. Her stomach twisted into knots. But all the "Best of Anti-Semitism" conspiracy theories were there. The photographs were meant to serve as proof, to provide evidence for some inane belief that Jews, with their space lasers and ability to control the weather, were secretly puppeteering the greater events of the world.

Standing on *her* street, watching those flyers blowing around in the wind, she had only one thought. *How dare they?* How dare they come to her town, to her home, and litter her community with such vile anti-Semitic hatred?

She wanted to throw it away. Give it no thought. Allow it no energy. But it was like passing a car wreck on the highway, everybody slowing down to watch the flames of an automobile on fire. Except this time, the car wreck was here. The fire was in her neighborhood. It had happened in a place she loved, where she had always felt safe, and where she thought…she thought she was welcomed.

TWO

"And did you happen to notice anything else unusual?"

Faye returned her gaze to the young police officer now standing in the front entrance of Magic Mud Pottery. "Unusual?" Faye said, trying to recall the precise moment she turned down her block and saw those flyers. "Not that I can remember."

Her vision drifted back out towards the window, just in time to see another cop car from Woodstock's finest rolling by her business. She had spent the first two hours after finding those flyers waiting for the police. In that time, she had texted her best friend, Miranda, about what had happened, only to learn from Shulamit that several congregants had also returned home to find their front yards peppered with hate.

Her phone vibrated inside her pocket, causing Faye to jump. Shaking off the surprise, she pulled it out to find a text message waiting from Miranda: They're holding an emergency meeting at the shul tomorrow to deal with the flyers. 10:00 AM. Can you make it?

Faye didn't hesitate on a response: I'll be there.

She returned the phone to her pocket, just in time to see the young officer finishing his note-taking.

"So, what happens next?" Faye asked curiously. "What will you need me to do?"

As a lawyer, she imagined that once the people behind the flyers were caught, she would need to give a deposition. Perhaps even testify in a court of law. Instead, the officer closed his sketch pad and placed it into his front pocket.

"I'm not sure there's evidence of a crime yet."

"No evidence of a crime?" Faye was aghast. "It's hate speech."

"It's free speech," he corrected her, "unfortunately."

"Well, what about incitement to violence?" Faye shot back. "What about littering?"

"We might be able to get them for littering," the officer admitted, "but even then, it's only a misdemeanor. A twenty-five-dollar fine, at most. Probably not even worth the paperwork."

Goddess give her strength.

Faye was speechless.

Her eyes wandered over to the name tag on his chest. *Ashton Collins*. Likely not Jewish. Perhaps that was why he didn't understand. Officer Collins didn't have generations of intergenerational trauma, comingled with actual life trauma, triggered in his brain. His entire sympathetic system wasn't now shaking in a stress-induced reaction of flight or fight. Faye took a deep breath and tried to explain.

"Even a littering charge," she swallowed, "would mean these people don't get to remain anonymous. It would mean we know who in our community may be a threat to Jews. It would mean that when I open the door to my home, and my business, I know who I'm letting inside. Don't you think my safety, and the safety of every Jewish person in our community, is worth the paperwork?"

He stared back at her, unblinking.

Clearly, the question was above his pay grade.

"You know what?" Faye said, waving away the entire conversation. "I'll talk to Eric about it."

Eric was the chief of police and a close friend. There was no doubt in her mind that he would see the value in pursuing these anti-Semites.

Faye ushered the young officer out before closing and locking the door behind him. With his departure, Magic Mud Pottery retreated into silence. Outside, the only color piercing the darkness was those flyers blowing around in the wind.

Quickly, she reached for her curtains, drawing the blinds closed.

Checking her watch, she realized it was midnight. She knew she should try to get some sleep. She had promised Miranda and Shulamit she would meet them at the shul first thing the next morning. Instead, she found herself straining her ears, listening for creaks and moans in her building, jumping at every sound.

She focused her intention on making herself feel safe.

After checking every door and window three times, she turned on the alarm in her business and made sure her cell phone was charging. She moved all her crystals into a semicircle around the front door—making both a circle for spiritual protection and a booby trap. Until finally, she returned to her bedroom, got into her pajamas, and stared at her bed.

She couldn't bring herself to get in.

Faye didn't have many happy memories of her childhood. Her house was chaotic, mainly due to her mother. But as a little girl, there was one respite. Her father.

At night, long past her bedtime, Faye would sneak down to the kitchen, meeting her father for a late-night snack. It was a tradition handed down *l'dor v'dor*, from generation to generation. She maintained it long after her father had died of early-onset Alzheimer's.

Heading downstairs, she opened the fridge, finding the kosher salami she had spent the last three months aging. Pulling it out, she was pleased to see that it was finally ready to be eaten. The plastic wrapping had gone all crinkly and white. The meat was hard enough to break teeth. It always took all her arm power, and the sharpest of blades, to cut off a piece.

But it was the way her father had always eaten it.

Faye loaded up a plate and took a bite. An explosion of garlic, salt, and fat, paired with the bitterness of stone-ground mustard, erupted in her mouth. It was perfection. It reminded her of a million nights seeking safety.

And yet, she didn't feel better.

She needed something stronger than salami. She needed magic. She needed drum circles and sacred temple offerings. She needed a coven of Jewitch women, holding hands, chins tilted up to the moon. But it was late, and so she settled on pouring herself a drink.

Faye headed to the coat closet at the front of her store. Opening it, she found the five boxes of kosher wine she had intended to serve for kiddush at her wedding to Stuart. Even though she had plenty of opportunities to drink the wine over the last three years, she could never bring herself to do it. Tonight, however, things felt different.

Stuart wasn't coming back. It was good wine, worthy of being drunk before turning into vinegar. Plus, it was just sitting there, taking up space in her already cramped building...a constant reminder of all the ways she was unlovable.

What the hell. She tore open the box and, after pulling out a bottle, poured herself an extremely large glass. She drank it all down in three full chugs before refilling again. When the first glorious tingles of a tipsy feeling came over her, an even better idea took hold of her. She was going to make drunk pottery.

Grabbing her wine, her glass, and her plate of hard kosher salami, Faye headed to her studio.

Since it was somewhat difficult to eat and sculpt while maneuvering a wheel, she settled on a method of pottery called handcrafting.

It was her favorite way to craft pottery. Ever since she was a small girl, playing with Play-Doh in her kitchen. There was something naturally creative about it. While the wheel, like the etchings and cross-weaving patterns she taught her Magic Mud Mini Warlocks, required a skill set, there was a certain wild and uninhibited freedom that came with sculpting an item by hand.

Gathering her items—clay, X-Acto knives of varying shapes and sizes, water—she sat down at the table. And took another drink of wine. Then, closing her eyes, feeling the clay, holding the weight and heft of it in her hands—trying not think about *shvantzes*—she let it whisper to her.

It spoke of magic. It told her to go with the flow, allow this to happen, that the universe had her back.

She took another drink.

Pressing her thumbs into the clay, she pinched and pulled on the material to soften it, allowing her mind to wander. To the events of the day and the previous evening. To Stuart. To her father. A wellspring of feeling bubbled up inside of her, pressed against her chest—a flood of anger and love, sadness and hurt. She wanted the world to be better.

She took another drink.

Returning from her thoughts, Faye glanced down at the clay in her hands. Strange. She had thought for certain she was crafting a ring dish. But now, she was surprised to see that it had taken on the shape of a man. Two stubby arms and legs, and one awkwardly shaped oval ball, stared up at her. She was just about to reshape the edges—turn it into yet another ring dish—when a word floated up and stopped her in her tracks.

Golem.

She stared down at the semishaped ball of clay. An energy shifted in her belly. Though she had not meant to craft a clay man this evening, it seemed weirdly fitting. Her fingers stroked his square-shaped body.

Not that she was an expert on golems by any stretch of the imagination, but she knew the basics. Golems were a part of Jewish folklore. They were hulking stone men, created by the rabbis to defend the Jewish community against anti-Semitic attacks. They were heroes for people low on hope…which was all crafting a golem in her studio would be. A form of therapy. A need for catharsis. A physical representation of her most secret desires, in order to heal the much deeper pain she was always carrying.

She gave in to that feeling pressing against her chest… And she wished, from that well of sadness deep within her, that she could find love. True love. Great love. The type of love that made you feel safe, and didn't abandon you.

The type of love that protected you, too.

She took a drink before returning to her clay man, shaping the ball that would become his head. She worked hard, crafting it into a vehicle for a proper psyche. And while she crafted, her feelings of powerlessness diminished.

She took another drink, then dipped her fingers into her bowl of water, working out his arms and legs. And as she worked, she felt electricity pouring through her body. Waves crashing in an ocean. An entire world taking shape beneath her hands…

She finished that bottle of wine and opened another.

She worked for another two hours, pulling and tugging on his stubs, using a knife to etch out a six-pack, giving him the most commendable-looking *shvantz* ever…before stumbling over to her craft supplies. She'd had always had a thing for redheads, and so, finding a ball of red yarn, she attached three long strands to the top of his head.

And then, she took another drink. And another. And another. Her clay man began to harden. She analyzed his shape, his form, his perfectly erect penis now pointed her way...and couldn't help but feel that something was missing.

She could hear the universe calling. Like an old crone was sitting there, right beside her at the table, speaking secrets into her ear. What her clay man was missing were words. Incantations. A spell.

Taking her X-Acto knife, she began etching words into his skin. She wrote down everything she wanted in a man, everything she would expect in her perfect golem—*protective, kind, fearless*—and then, because she was more than a little buzzed, she leaned into her list. She included all the things she never had with Stuart. *A reader. Great with children. Loves Scrabble. Enjoys snowmobiling.* She worked frenetically, losing track of time, sweat pouring from her brow, because she could not stop. She would not stop.

As if possessed by some unseen force in the universe, as if she were communicating with the divine feminine itself, she kept building and crafting, electricity coursing through her fingers, energy circulating around the room in wisps and whispers, until every centimeter of her clay man's skin was covered in a powerful discourse of *want* and *words*.

And then, directed by that same unseen force, she closed her eyes. Bringing that golem's head directly against her forehead, she recited the first six letters of the Hebrew alphabet aloud, three times, as the number three—like seven and nine—was considered especially powerful in Jewitch magic.

"Aleph. Bet. Gimel. Dalet. Hey. Vav," Faye said.

Truthfully, it was all she remembered from Hebrew school.

Faye took one deep and centering breath in through her nostrils, to the very place where her *nefesh*, her own soul, had once come to rest, breathing life into her stone effigy, before carefully laying that golem doll back down on her crafting table.

The world seemed to sigh aloud with her in relief. The charge in her belly and throughout the room dissipated. She leaned back in her seat and, blinking with relief, returned from her fugue state. She was soaking wet from sweat. Her back ached from bending over, but her golem was a masterpiece.

Faye washed her hands and, finishing the wine, waited for her clay man to harden.

Strange…the urges that come over a woman in the early hours of morning.

And after two bottles of wine.

Faye threw open the back door to her studio. The yard, with the six-foot wooden fence she had built as a safe space for Hillel and the rose garden against the back, beckoned. It was nearly two in the morning, but Faye didn't care. She tossed her robe to the ground. And then, because she refused to be afraid, because she wanted to strike back against these feelings of vulnerability, she threw off the lingerie she had been wearing beneath that robe, too.

She was naked, the full moon in the sky above her. Her large breasts swinging proudly over the rolls of her voluptuous belly. Her wide hips swaying along with them. She danced, holding that clay man in one hand, humming some preternatural tune as she weaved her way, recklessly, through the grass.

She gave in to it all. The feeling. The absolute pleasure. The dewy grass tickling the bottom of her feet. The cold breeze of a late September evening caressing her most intimate areas. She had only one fleeting lapse into reality. When she heard a car—or a garbage truck, maybe—rumbling down the street.

But then, she remembered that she had a six-foot fence. And that she lived in Woodstock, a place that brought all manner of characters to settle, and for whom wanton nakedness, even in the middle of the night, wouldn't raise too many eyebrows.

All the rest, however, was less than ideal. The best time to do Jewitch magic was after *Havdalah*—the ceremony that closed out Shabbat on Saturday night—and before sunrise. Every good Jewitch knew that the daytime light corrupted spells and sent magical beings scurrying. Sprites and anti-Semites, it turned out, had a lot in common this way.

She had also not checked the astrological charts, or created knots to bind the spell to her will and direction. Though it was during the harvest holiday of Sukkot, the moon in the sky was waning, not full. There were a million better times in her Jewitch tradition to cast a spell, but she settled on making do...self-reliance, and all that. Plus, the will was stronger than any tangled thread.

With both hands, she lifted her clay man up to the heavens, an offering...and tripped on the edge of one of her carefully inlaid graphite stepping stones.

Faye landed face-first in the dirt. Her clay man shot forth from her hands.

"No," Faye cried, and quickly scrambled to save him.

Finding him in the mud, she gently wiped away the dirt from his face. Unnecessary tears gathered in the corners of her eyes. She smoothed out the red yarn she had attached to his head. Checked that all her words, and those first six letters of the Hebrew alphabet, were still correctly pressed into his head and belly.

But then, turning her clay man around—horror. Her mouth opened wide, and a guttural expression of pain released from the very depths of her soul. In the fall, her golem had been injured. A large crack now ran up his perfectly crafted back.

Faye ran her finger alongside the fracture—from the top of his *perfectly* carved ass, all the way to the middle of his left shoulder blade. It made her sad to see her tiny clay hero all sad-looking and broken.

She took him back to her studio and healed the wound with another round of clay...until the break became a raised scar. Finding her balance, she rose to her feet and returned to the backyard. Weaving her way through the grass, trying to be careful not to trip, she came to the row of rosebushes that lined her back fence.

It had been an unseasonably warm summer, and the blooms had come in often, but also late this particular year. The red roses she loved now spread their petals open with full majesty.

She lifted her hand to one of the flowers, feeling its soft petals beneath her fingers, breathing in its fragrant scent...and then, she dropped to her knees and began digging in the dirt with her bare hands. She dug with the ferocity of a wild animal, because she was drunk, and naked, and because when you're drunk and naked at two in the morning, things like burying a clay man beneath your rosebushes make total sense.

She dug until she went deep enough to find the roots of her rosebush, and felt the first few drops of water seeping through the soil. She grabbed her clay man, placing him gently into the hole. She spread the ground back over his body. And then, when he was safely settled in her womb of earth and mud, she sat back on her knees, taking stock of what she'd done.

She swore that somewhere she heard a lone wolf howling.

But it couldn't be...

Wolves always traveled in packs.

A moment of sobriety appeared. She looked down at herself, at her fingernails caked in mud, at the mound of dirt disturbed beneath her rosebushes, and laughed. She laughed so loud and hysterically that it quickly became a cackle. But she kept right on laughing, until she nearly broke a rib, and Hillel began barking from the threshold of the back door.

Faye twisted back to Hillel. "Do you hear that?" she said, totally slurring. "That's the sound of your ancestors calling."

Hillel seemed unimpressed.

Yes, she was being ridiculous. Sculpting a clay man for protection. Burying him under her rosebushes, and during the waning moon of Sukkot. But being ridiculous, as it turned out, made her feel better.

Faye wobbled to an upright position and, finding her way to her bedroom, finally passed out. Not that she needed a man, or some anthropomorphic creature, to appear out of nowhere and rescue her from her life, crafting her future into something better...but the idea of having her own golem, *especially a sexy one*, was titillating all the same.

Faye awoke the next morning to her cell phone ringing and a splitting migraine.

"Hold on," she groaned, blinking her eyes open. "I'm coming."

Stumbling out of bed, with the absolute worst hangover of her life, she only had a hazy recollection of the events of the previous evening. She recalled not being able to sleep, making a golem doll. She remembered heading outside, the cool air brushing against her—*dear God*—naked body. *She was still naked.* But all the rest of the events of the evening were gone. Vanished. Her memory fully dissipating into the haze of what was, *most certainly*, a wild night.

She longed for death.

And for the phone to stop ringing.

Making her way to the living room, Faye found her cell phone on the coffee table.

"Hello?" she whimpered into the receiver.

Her throat was parched. Her body ached. The sun, streaming through the two windows in her living room, was obnoxiously bright.

"Hey," Miranda said, her voice chipper. "I was just calling to see where you are?"

"Where am I?" Faye blinked, then glanced over to a clock. It was almost ten o'clock. In the midst of a terrible hangover, she had completely lost track of time.

"Uh." Miranda was clearly suspicious. "You told me you were coming to the synagogue this morning for the emergency meeting. I was just making sure everything was okay?"

Faye had completely forgotten. "I'm fine."

"It's not like you to forget something."

She needed water. She stumbled back to her bathroom. Finding a cup and filling it at the sink, she chugged back two full glasses. It did little to quench the painful film lingering on her tongue and throat. Almost as quickly as she swallowed, she felt like she was going to throw up.

"You don't sound fine," Miranda said, suspiciously.

Faye lifted the toilet seat, just in case. "I overslept. But I'll be there shortly, okay? Twenty minutes, at most."

Miranda grumbled. Faye clicked off the phone. The rest happened in a mad dash of trying to get ready.

She knew she was not going to be there in twenty minutes. Honestly, if she made it to Temple Beth Tikvah in forty-five minutes, it would be nothing short of a Sukkot miracle. Still, she did her best to sober up, clean up, and take care of Hillel, who, for once, had done her a solid…by not actually leaving a solid on the floor.

Baruch Hashem and Blessed Be.

Heading to the garage, bypassing the dusty and rarely used vehicle she had purchased upon moving to Woodstock, she found her bicycle. Kicking up the stand, she brought it outside. The sun assaulted her once again. She raised one palm to the level of her eye, shielding her vision. The glare made her head hurt even worse. It was also busier than she'd realized.

The streets teemed with people. Volunteers—people from the community armed with their children and black plastic bags—picked up still circulating flyers. Business owners were working hard to put up signs in their windows. *Hate Has No Home Here. We Love Our Jewish Neighbors.*

Perhaps even more surprising was now the addition of news

vans that dotted their otherwise quiet street. Reporters, armed with their cameras and shift crews, interviewed citizens on the sidewalks. Faye had never seen Woodstock so busy.

"Excuse me," a man's voice rang out.

Faye twisted to find an older gentleman. Slightly hunched, he was holding a large trash bag in one hand and wearing a fraying flannel shirt paired with a scowl. He kind of reminded her of a troll—some mythical creature, wrinkled and temperamental, who also happened to be blocking her way.

"Your feet," he said, briskly, before jabbing with one finger towards her legs. "Move!"

Faye glanced down and realized she was standing on a flyer. "Oh," she said, stepping out of the way. "Of course."

The man collected the flyer, and took off for the next piece of litter. Her eyes followed the peculiar fellow. *Weird.* She didn't recognize him from all her years working downtown in Woodstock, but something about how rude he had been made her feel on edge.

Her cell phone started ringing again.

"Yes, Miranda," Faye said, picking it up. "I'm coming right now."

She clicked off her phone and hopped on her bike.

Zigzagging in and out of the crowd, she did her best to avoid the journalists and volunteer street cleaners. The news vans, especially, seemed to have no regard for the laws. It also didn't help that she was rushing, pedaling at full speed with a splitting headache, and totally hungover.

Faye rounded a corner. The sun brightened. She squinted, her line of vision going dark, before passing yet another news van illegally parked. And then, just as her vision returned, a mirage—a man with stunning red hair flowing down to his shoulders stepped into the street.

She attempted to brake, but it was too late. She and her bike crashed into the handsome stranger before they both went flying.

Faye blinked up at the fluffy clouds lingering in the blue skies above her. For a few breathless seconds, she considered the possibility that she was dead. She wiggled her fingers, her toes…and then, she remembered the man.

"Oh my God." Faye scrambled to stand up. "I'm so sorry. I didn't even see you." She knelt down to him, placing her hands upon his chest, a wellspring of panic. "Are you— Oh, oh, oh my."

She sounded like she was having a damn orgasm.

Faye couldn't complete her thought. The stranger, blinking up at her with two wet and confused eyes, was magnificent.

He had hair the color of fire burning in a kiln. Eyes that reminded her of the deepest recesses of the forest in winter. *She forgot about Stuart completely. She forgot about her hangover, too.* The artist in her could feel all the perfectly sculpted lines of his chest, the firmness of his belly…

Though, she recalled from the Krav Maga self-defense class she had taken in college, that could also be from internal bleeding.

"Can you move?" Faye asked, returning her concern to the man. "Or tell me your name?"

His eyes latched onto hers, but otherwise, he said nothing.

She grew concerned. The lack of movement, the blank stare— all of it suggested a much bigger problem. She leaned down closer to him, listening for his heartbeat, trying to see if there was anything erratic happening with his breathing…before realizing she had no idea what she was doing, and that she needed to get him to a hospital.

"Don't worry," she said, trying to be a comfort. "I'm calling nine-one-one. Help is on the way."

She placed one hand on his and used the other to seek out her phone. She was waiting for the dispatcher to pick up when the man sprang to life. Lifting one arm slowly in her direction, he cupped her cheek with his hand. Faye wasn't sure what he was doing—or why he was doing it—but she ignored the instinct to pull away. She ignored everything, falling into him, giving in to the softness of the creases around those green eyes.

"Ay," he said, his voice filled with gravel. "You're beautiful."

And then, this man—this mystery in the body of a redheaded fire demon—promptly passed out.

THREE

She had killed the most glorious-looking creature on Earth.

Faye sat in the waiting room of the ER at Woodstock Hospital, anxiously replaying the accident inside her mind. Granted, he had been jaywalking. But the accident was her fault. If she had been less hungover, not speeding, more careful when zigzagging in and out of traffic on her bike, she wouldn't have hit the most spectacular creature she had ever laid eyes on.

Faye needed a break from her catastrophizing.

"Excuse me," Faye said, heading to the window of the ER. "I was wondering if there was a place I could get a soda?"

The nurse pointed to the double doors. "There's a vending machine past the nurse's kiosk…right before the bathrooms."

"Great," Faye said. "Thank you."

She doubted the soda would help, but she needed something to soothe her upset stomach. In truth, she was wracked with guilt.

Heading to the machine to buy a drink with her card, she tried to focus on the positive. The collision was an accident. She had tried to do her best for the man, too. She had called an ambulance for him. Gotten in her car and followed him to the hospital. And then, hoping to hear good news, she had waited to see him emerge from the ER. She had asked the nurse at the front desk about his status several times, only to be told he was still being evaluated. Now it had been two hours. Faye couldn't help but wonder if the stranger had been moved to the morgue.

Her mother's voice reappeared in her mind. *It's all your fault. You are stupid. Unlovable. You ruin every good thing you touch.*

She needed that soda.

Heading down the hall, through the double doors and past the nurse's station, Faye found the vending machines. She was debating the value of sugar over water in terms of nursing the world's worst hangover when the sound of two voices having a discussion around the nurse's station caused her ears to perk up.

"What do you want to do about the bike accident in room 102?"

"Did you call social services?"

"They said they can't get here today."

"Great."

Her heart sped up inside her chest. They were talking about the man she had hit. Relief. The handsome stranger was alive.

"And you checked his belongings?"

"Twice. Nothing."

"And no one has come by to claim him?"

"Not a soul."

"Well, what about holding him overnight?"

"He's physically fine...other than the fact that he has amnesia."

Her stomach dipped. *Amnesia. Aphasia. Coordination difficulties. Social services.* The words floated by but didn't make her feel better. In fact, she felt worse. A whole lot more terrible.

She hadn't killed the man. Instead, she had gone and given him a brain injury.

"So, we're just supposed to release him with an address to the local shelter?"

"I can hold him till the end of the day, but unless someone comes by to claim him…what else can we do? Our job is to patch 'em up. He's patched up. Let social services deal with the rest."

"I'll get the paperwork started."

Faye had heard enough. Driven by her guilt, she waited for those voices to depart the nurse's station, and then snuck down the hall towards room 102.

She had no idea what she was doing. But she felt compelled—bound, really—to talk with the man. It was her fault she had given him amnesia, and that they were planning on sending him to a shelter, and she wasn't sure what she could do about any of it…but she knew she needed to do something.

She would never forgive herself otherwise.

Slipping inside his room, peering left, then right down the hallway to make sure that no one had seen her entering, she quickly closed the door behind her. The stranger with red hair sat up on his bed, a large pack of ice held across his forehead with gauze, and blinked in her direction.

"Hi," Faye said quickly. Quietly.

"Hello," he said.

That was good. He could talk.

"My name is Faye," she said, glancing back to the door. Any minute, some nurse or doctor could come barging in, and then how would she explain herself? "Do you remember me?"

He did not answer, but his eyes darted around the room, unfocused. It reminded her of her father—of the way he would try to speak, try to find the words to communicate, but couldn't.

She moved closer. "I'm the woman who hit you with my bike. Sorry about that, by the way."

He stared blankly at her.

"I heard the doctors talking," Faye continued. "Apparently, you have amnesia." Obviously, he had some other things going on, too. Some form of aphasia. "I'm sorry," she said, shaking her head. What was she even doing in here? "I'll leave you alone now."

Embarrassed by her behavior, she headed for the door.

"No," the man said.

Faye caught on her step. Slowly, she turned back around. "Excuse me?"

"No."

"I'm sorry," she said, stepping closer to him. "I don't understand."

"Niirrrrrr." The word came out slurred and garbled.

"Oh," she said, putting it together. "You want me to stay?"

He grunted. Still, she got his meaning.

Returning to his side, she grabbed a chair and sat down.

"I suppose I should properly introduce myself then," she said, trying to keep things as normal as possible. "My name is Faye. Faye Kaplan. And I'm a local potter. I run Magic Mud Pottery in downtown Woodstock."

She held her hand out to him. The man didn't take it. Faye patted him gently on the wrist.

"I imagine the doctors explained the situation to you," she continued, "but just in case they didn't—"

She told him he was in the hospital in Woodstock and that the doctors believed him to have amnesia and would be sending him to a shelter until he could remember. "That's why things might seem fuzzy to you right now, and why your language skills are off. I'd love to ask the doctors to give me more information about your condition, but, obviously, there are rules about these things."

In law, they would call it a medical directive.

"Faye," he said suddenly.

"Yes," she said, "that's me."

"Home."

"What?" Faye said, unsure of his meaning.

"Faye...home."

The statement took her back. "No. No, *Faye do not take home.*"

He grunted again—clearly a question.

"Because..." she stammered, touching her heart. "Because you don't belong with me."

He looked so sad at the news.

She thought back to her childhood. To all the people who had never really been there for her, never protected her. As a child, she had worn out the backside of her blue jeans, sitting on curbs outside her home, waiting for someone to save her. The independent streak she'd developed in the wake of all that trauma was born from necessity—a tool for survival.

"Home." The stranger was adamant. "Faye."

"No," Faye repeated, just as resolute. "You belong to someone else. You just don't remember. The doctors are going to send you to a shelter, and then someone will come for you from social services. They will find your people, get you back to where you belong."

"No," he said.

"Yes," she said, lifting from her seat. "Absolutely."

And then, he shouted one word at her. "Remember!"

It came out crystal clear. Loud and powerful. Faye sighed, slumping back into her chair. Despite his limited vocabulary, he certainly seemed to understand what he wanted.

He wasn't wrong. The man was in no place to go to a shelter. Faye couldn't even begin to imagine how anyone, especially doctors, would sign off on a such a thing. Then again, she considered the economics. He was a man without a wallet and a memory—and a voice—which meant he had no ID, no health insurance, and no money to pay for expenses out of pocket.

Welcome to health care in America.

Or maybe it was something else. Maybe the way he looked at her—the lost eyes, scanning the room, desperate for someone to help him—reminded her of herself. She had been abandoned countless times in her life. Perhaps this was the universe offering healing, a way to right the wrongs of her past by saving the life of another.

Faye took a deep breath. "You don't want to go to the shelter."

He grunted.

"I actually agree with you," she said, taking responsibility, feeling the weight of her words—the absurdity of them, honestly—even while she continued to utter them aloud. "I don't think the shelter is the right place for you. I just wish…we could figure out who you belong to. Do you remember anything about who you were before? Maybe a name? Or something about where you lived? Anything that might give me a hint about who I can call…or find? Someone to come pick you up, perhaps. A friend. Or family member. Maybe even a wife?"

She always did stuff like this. She always leaped without thinking. Passionate to the point of recklessness. It had always been her downfall.

"You." He said it definitively.

"You only remember me?"

"You," he repeated. "Home."

Time slowed. Faye swallowed.

He wanted to go home with her. *Obviously*. But even more surprising—she found herself *actually* considering it. Bringing this man home with her, taking him back to Magic Mud Pottery, letting him live in her apartment, nursing him back to health.

She ran through the arguments in her head like she was preparing a legal briefing. On the one hand, despite the faulty language skills, he was clearly capable of understanding the current situation and making choices for himself. She was also the person who'd injured him.

On the other hand, she didn't know this man. *At all.* He could be an axe murderer. A serial killer. A Nazi. Believing in the "inherent goodness of people" felt especially dangerous in the wake of an anti-Semitic incident affecting the town. She needed to be careful. Suss him out. Feel for any kernels of hatred.

"Can I ask you a question?" Faye pulled her chair in closer. "It's gonna sound a little strange. Especially since, well, you have no memory. But you see, the other night, there was an anti-Semitic incident in town. We don't know who did it... and the thing is, I'm Jewish."

"Jewish?"

"It's a religion," she said, before adding, "and an ethnicity. Actually, the question is really complicated because Judaism existed long before our modern-day concepts of race... And you know what? It's not that important. I guess I just need to know...if you hate Jews."

He stared back blankly at her.

"You know," she said, trying to trigger something inside his head. "Do you think they run the media, or are responsible for COVID? Do you believe they sacrifice Christian babies and drink their blood as part of their Shabbat ritual? Do you think that Jews are secretly puppeteering the affairs of our government behind the scenes? Or maybe...you believe that Jews have space lasers? Basically, do you hate Jews? Do you think the world would be better off without them? Do you believe the Holocaust never happened?"

He squinted, clearly confused. "Jews...bad?"

"No," she said, suddenly panicking. "No, Jews are not bad. Jews are not bad, at all."

Great. She had, inadvertently, taken a man with no memory and filled his brain with anti-Semitic rhetoric.

"I just…" she stammered, backtracking, "I just need to know, if I help you…if I agree to do something really unlike myself… something I would never normally in a thousand years do… I need to know you won't one day wake up and remember who you are and hurt me. I need to know I'm safe with you."

It felt like a much larger question than she had originally intended.

"No."

"No, you won't hurt me?" Faye said, needing clarification. "Or no, you can't make that promise?"

"Safe."

"I'm safe with you?"

He grunted.

Almost like a promise.

"So, you really want to come home with me?" she asked.

The man did not hesitate. "Home."

"I should warn you, though. I don't have a big place. You'd have to sleep on the couch. And this isn't for the long term, okay?" She needed to make that clear. "Just until we figure out who you are, or until your memory returns. Hopefully, once I find out more from the doctors, we'll have a better idea on the status of your condition. You okay with that as a general rule between us going forward?"

"Yes."

"Okay," she said, and quickly began developing a plan of action inside her head. "Then here's what I need you to do. I'm going outside to grab the doctors…and when I do, you need to tell them that I'm your wife."

"You…wife?"

"No," she said, shaking her head. "I'm not your wife. It's just…there are laws and things. I don't have any paperwork on me to prove we're married, but if you tell the hospital staff that you suddenly remember me—that I'm your wife—then not only will they give me a full rundown on your condition, but

I'll be able to sign the discharge papers as your spouse and bring you home. They won't send you to a shelter. But it's very important that you tell the doctors I'm your wife when they come in. That we're married. You remember my name, by the way?"

"Wife."

"Close enough," she said comfortingly. "And where do you want to go?"

"Wife," he repeated.

"And who am I again?"

"Wife."

She patted him on the wrist one more time. "Excellent. Very good."

Faye gathered her belongings, and then headed towards a nurse's station outside the man's room. "Excuse me," she said, waving down a doctor. "My name is Faye Kaplan. I'd like to speak to a doctor about the patient in room 102... He's my husband."

FOUR

There were things he could remember.

He remembered how to stand. How to walk. He knew, for instance, that the rumbling in his stomach was the sensation of hunger. Just like the pain spreading through the middle of his forehead was a headache. But he couldn't recall the things that had made him a person.

He couldn't remember his name. Or where he was born. Or what he was doing in this town called Woodstock...though he remembered there had been an accident. Or rather, he remembered with perfect alacrity the woman who had greeted him after the collision.

She was beautiful.

When she had first appeared in his room, he had wanted to tell her that. The thoughts were clear inside his head. He was certain he knew her. She felt familiar. But when he went to open his mouth, express these things aloud, he found a disconnect between his brain and his tongue. The words wouldn't come. And when he attempted to use them—to argue with the doctors or defend himself against the way they were treating him—his words came out stilted. Wrong.

From there, it seemed that everything had gone downhill.

No one seemed to recognize that there was still a person inside of him. It was fine in the beginning—when the doctors entered the room, shone their lights in his face, asked him to touch his nose. But when they realized he couldn't respond correctly, their whole demeanor changed.

They talked over him. Around him. Like he wasn't a person, at all...but another piece of furniture in the room.

He didn't recall what a shelter was, but he knew enough not to trust these people. These doctors with their pens—scribbling out life sentences before casually talking about where they were going for dinner. And yet when he wanted to call out, to shout his frustration, make them understand, he couldn't. Because he was trapped. Abandoned by his memory. A prisoner in his own body. Losing hope. And then, that woman—the beautiful one from the accident—returned. Finally, he felt a glimmer of hope.

She looked him in the eye when she spoke. She asked what he wanted. She talked to him, not around him, even though he couldn't respond. Even though it was *impossible* to get his ideas across—the frustration he felt from being imprisoned within his own body—he fought like hell to make his position known.

Next thing he knew, he was being wheeled towards an exit by a nurse. And Faye, the woman who had understood him, was waiting by a vehicle when they got outside.

"Are you ready to go home, my darling?" Faye said, taking his arm, steadying him.

"Wife," he said.

"That's right, darling." Faye glanced between him and the nurse, playing the role spectacularly. "I'm your wife. Excellent work."

He had not meant to keep repeating the word. But he figured it was his brain working overtime to protect him.

Faye helped him into the car, shutting the door behind him. The nurse departed. Faye slumped in her seat, breathing out all her anxiety in one long and heavy breath.

"Baruch Hashem and Blessed Be," she said before directing her gaze back to him. "We did it. You did a great job in there." He was pleased that she was pleased. "Safety first," she said, reaching over his lap and putting a seat belt on him. "I already almost killed you once today. Oh, but…not to worry. I'm a very good driver. I'll get you home in no time."

His eyes wandered around the car, around the world outside the hospital. And then he caught sight of a man, a large bandage wrapped around his head, sprigs of fire-colored hair jutting out from the top.

"Arhjreh!" He jumped in his seat.

"Haman's hat." Faye clutched her heart. "What's wrong?"

It was only upon inching back in his seat that he realized the strange man in the reflection of the mirror…was him.

And he was a redhead.

It was more than a little disconcerting. He recalled enough to know that the image of the man sitting across from him should have felt familiar, and yet, he was a stranger to himself. "I'm sorry," Faye said softly. "I should have warned you. That's you. And you're fine, okay? It's just a bandage on your head. The ice beneath it is to keep the swelling down."

He tried to get out the word *see*, but all he could manage was a mangled *s*. He wanted to take the bandage off. He was eager to see the full image of himself. Also, the ice had all but melted. He was just about to begin unwrapping it when Faye, once again, seemed to intuit his thoughts.

"Oh, dear," she said, leaning in to inspect the bandage. "Did they really leave you like that? With the ice all melted?" She shook her head. "You poor thing. You must have the worst headache imaginable."

She began taking it off. Slowly, she unwrapped the bandage, her fingertips gliding across his skin.

"I swear," she kept talking. Her voice was soothing, gentle. She made him feel better. "Health care in America nowadays. It's unbelievable. But don't you worry, as soon as we get home, I'm gonna find lots of ice for your head. And Advil, too. Definitely loads of Advil. I promise. I'm gonna take very good care of you."

He believed her.

It was a twenty-minute ride from the hospital to home. Faye filled the silence of the ride by pointing out places as she drove through Woodstock, New York. She started with a private university, just a stone's throw from the hospital they were departing.

"That's where my best friend Miranda works," she explained. "I've known her since I was eight." From there, she pointed out a tourist site, marked by a sign and a small museum of music that lay on a road with three antique shops. "Woodstock is known as the city of peace, love, and rock and roll," she continued. "Do you remember anything about Woodstock? Or does anything ring a bell about what I'm saying?"

He stared out the window, trying to recall. But there was nothing but the present. What he remembered was what he saw. Trees. Forests that stretched beyond the length of his vision. Faye pointed out the window, towards an exit on the road they were driving.

"Down that road is one of my favorite places locally to go caving," she said. "It's called Devil's Cave, and it's a hobby of mine. Can you remember any hobbies you might have had before your accident?"

"Faye."

"No," she corrected him. "I'm not a hobby."

His frustration grew again. That wasn't what he wanted to say.

He was trying to explain that the only thing he remembered about his past was her. He recalled seeing her, thick hair cascading in voluminous curls around her breasts, and the cleavage she had—*holy hell, her cleavage was amazing*—as she bent over.

The thought appeared in his mind without permission.

In truth, sitting so close to her in the car, his eyes wandering back to her skin, her cheeks, *her chest*, he couldn't believe that she was not someone, *something* more to him. It seemed impossible that they were not actually married. That they were, in fact, strangers. She felt so damn familiar.

He was also beginning to wonder if he was some sort of pervert.

The car approached a series of buildings—small houses with knickknacks on shelves lining their porches and signs in pretty lettering etched above the doors.

"That's Pinky's Creamery," Faye said, passing by a small white building with a giant cow out front. "They churn out the best homemade ice cream in all of New York. This is also the start of our little downtown. We have a day care. A bookstore. Several restaurants. We used to be more hopping, honestly… especially with the university nearby…but a lot of businesses didn't make it through COVID."

He didn't know what COVID was.

Faye turned a corner, stopping at a red light. "My store, Magic Mud Pottery, is right over there," she said, and pointed through the front windshield down the street. "I'm a potter. I make pottery. Technically, a ceramicist. And I teach classes… I live above my business. I don't know if I mentioned this already, but it's not very big. My apartment. It's kind of small, and awkwardly shaped, and it's only one bedroom. You'll sleep on the pullout couch in the living room. You do not, *ever*, come into my bedroom to sleep. Understand?"

He searched for the words. "Understand. Faye…not wife."

Faye sighed. "At least we've got that part down."

He noted her reticence.

Reticence.

It was a big word. It must have come from somewhere.

"I suppose," she said, waiting for the light to turn green, "since we're actually going to be doing this, we should give you a name. I can't very well call you *'that guy I hit with my bike'* all week. It's lengthy. Plus, I already feel guilty enough about the whole amnesia thing without the constant linguistic reminder." She turned to face him. "So, any idea what you'd like me to call you?"

He considered her question seriously. Choosing a name seemed like a big deal. An important one, too. He didn't want to get it wrong. Or worse, what if he remembered his name, only to mumble out something like "incredible breasts" by accident? He didn't want to totally freak her out. She had just agreed to bring him home, after all.

A bus rolled up beside them. His eyes wandered to the ad laminated on the side. It was an ad for something called *MadLibidoMax*, featuring the words,

GET YOUR ZEAL FOR LIFE BACK

Beneath the ad came an endorsement from a man named Gregory Pelham. He was holding a tennis racket with his collar turned up and had a swath of gray hair. He looked all types of distinguished. More important…he looked like someone who had a memory.

A fluttery, churning feeling appeared in his belly.

"Greg."

Her head nearly shot off her neck. "You remember your name?"

"No."

He pointed over her shoulder towards the advert. Faye glanced behind her and frowned. The light turned green. "Well," she sighed, stepping on the gas, "I guess Greg will work just as well as anything."

The grand tour of Magic Mud Pottery didn't take very long. Faye led him around the first floor, pointing out the counter, the small kitchen, the back studio, and the garden, before taking him up a set of creaky old stairs to the second floor.

"And this is where you'll be staying," Faye said.

She moved towards a couch pressed up against two windows. A tiny bookcase rested to the side. A coffee table was covered with a vast array of pottery and ring dishes. A hook on the wall, behind a chair in a colorful paisley print, held a collection of hats, scarves, and beaded jewelry.

Faye lifted one of the pillows from the couch to display the bed hidden inside the frame. "It's a pullout," she explained.

"Pull...out?"

The words felt familiar.

"I know it's not ideal," she said apologetically. "Especially for a man your size..." Her eyes trailed the length of his body. "But hopefully, you won't be here too long."

She kept saying that.

Faye inched back out past him. When she stopped again, she was standing behind a counter, in front of a stove and cabinets.

"This is the half kitchen," she explained. "The refrigerator is downstairs, along with some utensils if you want a quick snack. I know it's quirky, or whatever. But I used to live in Manhattan. New York City. The Big Apple. You remember?"

Greg scanned his memory banks. "Smell."

"What?" Faye quipped, her eyes darting around the room. "You smell something funny?" She sniffed the air, followed by a quick once-over of her own armpits. "I don't smell anything weird."

"No," Greg said, and tried again. "Small."

"Oh!" Faye laughed, and got his meaning. "Yeah. My place is small."

Just then, the sound of something click-click-clacking down the wood floors of the hall drew his attention away. Greg looked down to see what appeared to be some type of hairless rat prancing his way.

"Oh," Faye said, running over to pick the animal up. "This is Hillel."

She brought the creature closer. It was not a rat, but some sort of dog. An instinct overtook him. He moved to take the puppy from her hands.

"You don't want to—" Faye stopped herself. "Well, look at that."

The rat-dog nuzzled into his arms.

Greg gave his assessment. "Good."

"Not quite," Faye said. "Hillel can be kind of persnickety with, well, everyone. If you want to know the truth, he's kind of mean. He poops on my floor all the time. But that's just because he's old and grumpy. Thankfully, he's all gums. I mean that literally, too. He has no teeth left. He sucks his food down instead of chewing it. It's actually…kind of sad to watch."

Hillel didn't seem to hate Greg.

When he looked up from petting the dog, his eyes caught on hers. Quickly, she pressed hers towards the wall.

She had pretty eyes.

"On that note…" she said, twisting away from him, waving him down a small hallway. "This is the bathroom. We'll be sharing this for the time being." She flipped on a light. A shower curtain decorated in flowers and a green bath mat greeted his arrival. "There are towels beneath the sink."

She bent down, opening a cabinet to demonstrate.

He liked the way she wiggled. He liked the spread of her hips, and the vastness of her form. He liked how she took up space. That everything—in the room, in the apartment, in the building—smelled and felt like her. *Earthy*. He liked her voice, especially. The way her words took shape and became alive inside of him.

"Home."

"Yes," she said, nodding. "This is your temporary home. *Temporary*, meaning for the time being. Kind of like a sukkah. How appropriate, right?"

He didn't understand.

She returned to giving him a tour of the house. Heading down a hallway, she pushed open a door with one hand. "And this is my bedroom," she said, before adding for clarity, "Where I'll be sleeping...*alone*."

Greg took stock of the space. A queen-size bed filled most of the room. To his left, a closet. To his right, at the front of the bed, was a bureau. Resting on top, between crystals, and photographs of Faye with various friends, was a bundle of dried herbs wrapped up in white yarn. Otherwise, the room was a mess. Clothing—something lacy and silky—lay in a clump on the floor.

"I'm not usually this sloppy," she said, nervously picking up pieces, sweeping away random bits of soil from the floor. "I just...kind of had a rough night."

He wanted to ask her what she meant, but a phone began ringing. Faye raced back downstairs. Greg followed and found her digging through her purse.

"Miranda," she said, pulling out a phone. Twisting away from him, she kept one hand over her mouth and whispered, "Yeah. I know. I'm really sorry. You got my text about the accident?" She glanced back at Greg before continuing. "It's complicated. I don't want to talk in front of him. Yes, *him*. Don't start. There wasn't any other good option."

She hit a button on the phone, turning back to Greg. "I need to take this."

Greg moved to follow her.

"No," she said, putting one hand out to stop him. "Alone."
Greg understood, but she clarified anyway.

"Why don't you just—" she waved around her store, her
apartment, nervously "—make yourself at home. Try to relax.
Take your shoes off. I'm sure you're exhausted after spending
all day at the hospital. I'll be back in just a minute." She headed
through a room of tables, arts and crafts supplies, and towards a
back exit, into a garden. "One minute," she called back. "And
don't go anywhere."

Before Greg could respond, she was gone. Funny…for all
the things he had apparently lost today, he felt her disappear-
ance the most.

FIVE

Faye knew she was about to get the lecture of her life. Standing in her backyard, she took the phone off mute. Miranda was having a conniption.

"Do you know how worried Shulamit and I were?" Miranda said. "You sent one text. One poorly spelled and cryptic text about missing today's meeting at the synagogue because you killed someone with your bicycle...and then, we don't hear from you for six hours!"

"I didn't kill him," Faye cut her off.

"What?" Miranda said, clearly confused. "What are you talking about?"

"I gave him amnesia. Which I suppose is better than killing someone...though probably not by much."

"Excuse me?"

Faye sighed and attempted to boil down the whole sordid story into a palatable three-minute tale. She explained hitting the man with the bike, following him to hospital, learning he had amnesia. She talked about how they were planning to send him to a shelter—completely ignoring Miranda's gasps and grumbles throughout—before just coming out with it. "So, I had him lie to the doctors, tell them I was his wife…and I brought him home with me."

The phone went silent.

Faye wasn't sure if Miranda had dropped it or simply died from the shock.

"Hello?" Faye spoke into the receiver. "Miranda? Are you there?"

"Have you lost your damn mind?" Miranda finally said. Her best friend since she was eight did not bother to hold back.

"What was I supposed to do?" Faye defended her actions.

Miranda bellowed into Faye's ear. "You don't even know this man. There are anti-Semites leaving flyers all over town…and you just welcomed this stranger, this possible white suprema-cist into your home, like you were taking in a lost puppy from the animal shelter?"

"His name is Greg," Faye said, resolutely. "And he's not."

"Not…what?"

"He's not a white supremacist," Faye exclaimed simply. "I spent some time questioning him before I brought him home. I am totally comfortable that I made the right choice."

"You kidnapped the man, Faye."

"First off," she felt the need to point this out, "he asked to come home with me. Practically begged, in fact. Greg had no interest in staying at that hospital, or going to the shelter. Second, he came of his own free will and volition. And I gave him the choice. Whatever lies we entangled ourselves up in, we did it together. You'd be very hard-pressed to prove I committed a felony in a court of American law."

"Well, I'm glad I won't be baking nail files into your babka anytime soon."

"You brought it up," Faye reminded her.

"So now what?" Miranda asked, incredulous. "You're just gonna keep him in your house until you find his real owners? Feed him three times a day and take him on walks like Hillel?"

"The doctors were very optimistic that his memory will return in no time."

"And what if someone is looking for him, Faye? What if someone—right now—is worried sick, missing their husband, brother, father, or son?"

The words caused a stone to land inside her belly.

She shook the thought away.

Goddess willing, he wouldn't be staying with her long enough for anyone to become attached. Faye returned to making her argument.

"Well, they're far more likely to get him back if he's with me than at some shelter. For the Shechinah's sake...the man had no memory, Miranda. No ability to make good decisions or be safe on his own accord. You remember what my father was like when he was dying of dementia? I couldn't just...leave him behind like that."

"This man is not your father, Faye."

"I know that," she said, emphatically. "But he feels like my responsibility all the same."

The universe kept the score, after all.

Miranda continued lecturing. Faye could only half listen. She was wondering about Greg, wondering how he was managing all alone downstairs, hoping that he wasn't getting into too much trouble. She was eager to get off the phone and get back to him.

Not that her feelings were romantic. She was simply being practical. Like with her father, she knew how dangerous it was to leave a man without a memory alone. And then, her eyes caught on the back fence, where an unexpected sight drew her entire focus. The row of pink-and-red rosebushes that lined her back fence had all shriveled up and died.

It couldn't be possible.

She thought back to the previous evening. Granted, her memory was hazy...but she was positive, certain, that as of yesterday evening, her rosebushes had been alive. Thriving, in fact. Now, tiptoeing through the grass, moving closer to inspect, she came across what appeared to be a tiny grave. A small mound of disturbed dirt, like one would make for a goldfish, or a pet hamster...

Her stomach twisted. The memory of the previous evening, burying something, caused her heart to palpitate.

No, there had to be rational explanations for her perfectly blooming rosebushes to have died so suddenly. She laid them out like evidence in a trial. Most likely, her rosebushes had already been in the process of dying, and in her drunken state, she had mistaken one perfectly blooming petal for an entire bush. It was nature. The natural way of the universe. Nothing more.

"I want to meet him," Miranda said, interrupting her thoughts. "Today."

"Not today," Faye said, adamant.

"I am not letting you spend the night with a stranger!"

"Oh, please." Faye scoffed aloud at that one. "You and I both engaged in plenty of reckless decision-making in our younger days. We're both still alive...nothing terrible happened to us. Believe me, this man is completely harmless."

"Faye," Miranda said, cutting her off, "put out the hard kosher salami, because Shulamit and I are coming over whether you like it or not."

"Look," Faye said, feeling the need to protect Greg from the onslaught of her friends and their questions, "the poor man is still struggling to make three-word sentences. He's in no place for visitors. But maybe in a few days when his memory and his vocabulary begin to improve—" It was at that exact moment that a scream, piercing and terrible, erupted from inside her house.

"Miranda," Faye said, twisting back to her building, "I have to go."

"But—"

"We'll talk about this later, okay?"

Faye wasted no time. Clicking off her phone, she raced back inside.

She found Greg squeezed between her bookshelves and the couch, hands raised in open surrender, and Nelly holding him hostage. With a stun baton aimed at his chest, she zapped at the air repeatedly, causing the sound of electricity—followed by Greg's half-hearted grunts and screams—to pierce the entire building of Magic Mud Pottery.

"What on Earth are you doing?" Faye shouted over the zapping.

"I caught him," Nelly said, out of breath, a wild twinkle in her eyes. "I caught the Nazi."

Faye clutched her heart. "He's not a Nazi."

"Then *what*—" Nelly asked, incredulous "—was he doing in your apartment?"

Faye took a deep breath. "I invited him."

Nelly dropped the stun baton, turning directly to Faye in disbelief. "But he's...*a man*?"

"I'm aware of that," Faye said, annoyed.

"In your apartment?"

"Yes," Faye said, exasperated. "In my apartment. *Haman's hat*. He's going to be staying with me for a while..." With the way Nelly was looking at her, Faye might as well have been crawling on the ceiling. "And will you please put that thing away before you hurt yourself...or somebody else?"

Nelly's eyes darted from Faye to Greg, before returning to Faye. Finally, suspicion cleared from her face, and the old woman returned to some semblance of her normal. With a slight shrug of shoulders, Nelly placed her stun baton in the bag she was carrying.

"A man in your apartment," Nelly said, shaking her head, sidestepping Faye to head back downstairs. "No wonder I thought he was a Nazi."

SIX

"I can see why you brought him home." Miranda smirked.

Faye glanced up from the freezer drawer where she was gathering another round of ice for Greg. Miranda, her best friend, had cornered her by the refrigerator downstairs. Her dark curls cascaded around a black leather jacket, while Shulamit, her wife of thirteen years, entertained Greg on the couch, a trill of sunny conversation emanating from her lips.

She was relieved at the sight. It had taken Faye almost two full hours to lay out her arguments to her friends—at one point, even pulling out the rolling whiteboard she used for teaching class. Thankfully, the court of coven opinion had ruled in her favor. A fair resolution was reached between all parties. While Miranda still wasn't ready to trust Greg fully…she was at least willing to respect Faye's autonomy.

Faye finished packing the ice. "It's not like that."

"Oh, come on!" Miranda scoffed. "The red hair. The arms

the size of tree trunks. The fact that he's totally compliant…
Either you have found the world's most perfect man for you,
or just go ahead and admit you've created yourself a golem."

Faye's breath caught in her throat. "What?"

"You know," Miranda continued, "a golem? An anthropomorphic creature made of clay, usually created to protect the
Jewish community from anti-Semitic attacks."

In her two hours of explaining, she hadn't told Miranda or
Shulamit about the previous evening, getting drunk beyond
belief, crafting a tiny man out of clay, before burying it in her
backyard…because *reasons*.

For one, she could barely recall the events of the previous
night. She also didn't want to worry her friends. Shulamit
worked at the shul. Miranda at the local university. They both
had enough to worry about in terms of anti-Semitic dangers
and being targets. She didn't need to add her own troubles, and
sleepless nights, to their list of concerns.

Beyond all these things, Faye prided herself on being independent. Admitting that she was afraid, that the anti-Semitic
flyers had rattled her completely—retraumatized her, triggered
all her intergenerational trauma, the stories she had grown up
with—felt like giving up her power.

Her mind wandered back to her mother.

Her wrist ached once again.

Faye shook the feeling away and settled on getting a grip.
"Honestly, Miranda," Faye said, moving to check on the tea she
had been steeping for all her guests. "Nobody knows who this
man is. He has no ID, no wallet. He's all alone in the world.
The least we can do is be sensitive to his needs right now, and
not make jokes. Greg is, after all, a human being."

"You make it sound so—" Miranda squinted up towards the
ceiling, searching for the word *"—long-term."*

Faye scoffed outright. "It's not long-term."

"You sure?"

"Positive," Faye said, pulling the stainless steel tea infusers from each of the four mugs.

Even if Greg's memory didn't return with some alacrity, Faye reasoned that shortly—within a day or two, at most—someone would come by to claim Greg. A partner. A wife. The gym where he worked as a personal trainer... Otherwise, she would have never agreed to take him home with her.

Faye went to grab the ice, and two cups of tea. Like always, she struggled to keep the left mug steady. Miranda moved to help her.

"I'm fine," Faye said, shrugging her shoulder away.

"Let me help you," Miranda said.

"I'm fine!" Faye snapped back.

In the commotion, Faye's disabled finger slipped. The cup of tea fell to the floor, shattering, sending hot water all over the place. Shulamit, whose voice had been going steadily since Miranda cornered Faye in the kitchen, fell into silence. Thankfully, no one was hurt. But it felt like yet another attack in what had been a truly rotten twenty-four hours. Faye wanted to cry... Instead, she took a deep breath.

Miranda frowned. "Sorry."

"It's okay."

"Can I at least help you clean up?"

Faye snagged a towel and pulled out a trash bin. "Knock yourself out."

Perhaps, she could have come to terms with a broken wrist and disabled finger if it had been an accident. Instead, it served as a constant reminder of all she had lost.

Her scholarship to the New School in Manhattan, where she had hoped to go and study ceramics. The pottery she was so talented at making as a teenager—that all her art teachers fussed and fawned over, providing her the love and attention she never got from her own mom—which was never quite as good. She lived with nerve damage, and pain, and disability, but it was memory which hurt the most.

Faye returned her attention to Greg.

"This is for your head," she explained, handing him the ice pack wrapped in a soothing lavender and bamboo case. "And this is ashwagandha, feverfew, and valerian tea. The ashwagandha is for memory, the feverfew is for headaches, and the valerian is for nerves." She placed the cup on the coffee table, moving over crystals and ring dishes. "Just remember it's hot, okay? Blow on it before you drink…and take tiny sips."

Greg gave Faye the most adorable half-hearted smile. Though he couldn't participate in the conversation fully, Faye knew he was listening. She could tell by the way his eyes followed her around the room, sometimes even catching on her own.

"And how are you two getting along then?" Faye asked, sitting down beside Shully.

"Wonderful," Shully beamed, all sunshine and rainbows. She was medicine for the soul in that way. Faye hoped that her good energy would rub off on Greg and aid his healing. "In fact," Shully said, leaning into him like an old friend, "I was just telling Greg here how we all met."

Greg nodded once in Faye's direction. She became lost in his gaze, in the glimmer of green there, *so intensely beautiful*, until a sound outside caused her to jump.

Nelly was kicking her front door.

"I can see you," Nelly shouted, a large white tote slung over her shoulder, a giant cardboard box in her hands. "I can see you all sitting there!"

Faye sighed and rose from her seat.

Normally, Faye kept the door to the Magic Mud Pottery open during business hours. But today, and even with her store crowded with visitors, she felt safer with it locked. Suddenly, it seemed prudent to know, and have control over, who entered her business. Clearly, the decision had caught Nelly off guard.

Faye unlocked the door, and the old woman breezed past her, placing the cardboard box on the coffee table in front of Greg before turning all her attention to Shulamit.

"Cantor," Nelly said, shaking her head. Her words came out tinged with sympathy. "How are you doing this morning? I can't imagine how nervous you all are over at the synagogue. Terrible. Just terrible."

"I'm hanging in there." Shulamit shrugged. "I think we're all just doing our best to make sense of things."

"Do the police have any idea who's behind it?" Nelly asked.

"Not yet," Shulamit admitted. "But we're meeting Chief Eric Myers later this week to talk about increasing security patrols around the shul."

"I'm not a huge fan of most police," Miranda said, rising from where she had been cleaning, "but he's certainly one of the good ones."

"It's a blessing to have him in our lives," Faye agreed.

Indeed, Eric had sent her a text earlier than morning, letting her know that he was thinking of her and would stop by the first chance he got to check in on her. Though she had long ago decided to forgo relationships with men, the kindness had meant the world to her. Especially because Eric wasn't Jewish.

Shulamit continued. "And on top of all these things, we're working on planning a solidarity rally at Woodstock Town Hall with elected officials and representatives of all the various faith-based denominations in town. The plan is to come together and show that as a community, love is always louder than hate."

"Screw love," Nelly said, plopping down on the couch beside Greg. "I have a much better idea."

"Haman's hat," Faye said, and rubbed her forehead.

"What?" Shulamit glanced between them, confused.

"Nelly found herself a stun baton."

"What?" Miranda raced over from where she had been standing. "Nelly!"

"Don't worry," the old woman said, before narrowing her focus on Greg. "I only plan to use it on Nazis."

The color drained from Greg's face. Faye moved to intervene. "She's kidding," Faye said, touching his arm gently to offer comfort. "She's totally—"

A spark of electricity surged through her body, catching her off guard. She hadn't meant to touch him. Indeed, since bringing Greg home, she had been extremely careful *not* to touch him unless it was to serve as his caregiver, helping him up the stairs, getting him another bag of ice, slinking past his hulking form in the narrow hallways of her home and business, *trying not to let her shoulders skim the magnificence that was his chest...*

Faye lost her train of thought.

"Anyway," Nelly said, pushing the cardboard box towards Faye with the toe of her orthopedic loafer. "Here you go. All the items you asked for, including some I thought of after the fact. Shirts. Pants. Two jackets. Basically, I went through Second Glance Treasures and pulled everything I could find in a size gargantuan."

Faye was relieved. "Thank you."

Nelly was a good friend to Faye. She had grown used to the brittle old octogenarian showing up in her business, nudging her along for her own good, seeking to get her out of her shell. She was kind of like Hillel in that way—brittle, but with purpose.

Unlike Faye's mother, Nelly had always been there for her. Especially when she first opened her store and was still learning the ropes to operating a small business in Woodstock, Nelly was the neighbor willing to stay late, share her hard-earned knowledge gained through experience, and offer all manner of advice.

"I also brought some toiletries," Nelly continued. "Antiperspirant, toothpaste, toothbrush."

Faye grimaced. "Used?"

"Not used," Nelly snapped back. "They were Morty's...before he died. He never got a chance to use them." She sighed at Greg, and then, leaning into him, told him the story. "You know, my Morty…he loved a good deal. If something was on sale, he bought ten of them. Don't you worry, handsome stranger. I've got everything you could possibly need. Razors, creams for every type of itch, catheters out the wazoo…"

Faye doubted that Greg needed catheters.

"What do I owe you?" Faye asked, heading off to find her pocketbook.

Nelly waved the offer away.

"Come on," Faye said, pulling out a wad of cash. "All of this stuff costs money. I insist."

"You taking it off my hands is a favor," Nelly said, just as adamant. "More room at the store and more space in my basement."

Faye put her cash away. There was no point arguing with Nelly when she made up her mind about something. The old woman was, to be fair, as stubborn as Faye in this regard. Perhaps that was what they both enjoyed about each other. But unlike Faye, Nelly had eighty years of experience in getting her way, and, being closer to death than to fifty at this point, had simply decided she had no more *fackacktes* to give.

"You finally cleaning out the house?" Miranda asked.

Nelly shook her head. "I need space for a new project."

"A project?" Shulamit clapped her hands together. "That sounds fun! What kind of project?"

Faye expected Nelly to say something typical. Some hobby one would expect from a cranky old octogenarian. Like scrapbooking or playing mahjong. Instead, Nelly crossed her arms against her chest. "I'm going Nazi hunting."

She said it flatly. Point-blank. Her words as remarkable as if she was describing making a cup of coffee in the morning. Except they weren't talking about coffee. They were talking about Nelly setting up some Simon Wiesenthal–style war room in her basement, trying to track down the people responsible for the anti-Semitic attack.

"I can't deal with this today," Faye said.

"We should deal with this," Miranda grumbled under her breath.

"You know what?" Faye decided for everyone that the best course of action was simply to settle on one thing they could always agree on—food. "Who wants dinner?"

Miranda popped up from her seat. "Great idea."

"On it," Shully said, following her wife.

"You think I come for the company?" Nelly teased.

The rest was a ritual they had performed many times together. Shulamit raced upstairs, bringing down plates, forks, knives, and a cutting board. Faye reached into her fridge, pushing past coleslaw and potato salad until she found the hard kosher salami she had been working through. Nelly readied the rye bread and salad, while Miranda pulled out condiments, a mixture of mayonnaise, mustard, red chili peppers, red peppers, and red onions.

Despite the fact the kitchen was upstairs, when her friends were over, they always ate downstairs in the main foyer, around the couches and coffee table arranged for visitors. And sometimes, if the room was set up for it, in the back at one of the long tables for classes. There really wasn't enough room upstairs for all four of them.

"Who's cutting the salami?" Miranda asked.

"I'll do it," Faye said, reaching for the knife, before an even better idea crossed her mind. "Actually," she said, twisting towards Greg, still sitting on the couch. "Why don't we let our new guest do it?"

The whole room fell into an awkward and concerned silence.

Normally, the task of cutting the salami for a sandwich took all her arm and back power. Even then, the pieces often came out lopsided. Some thick. Some thin. It also didn't help that her finger was disabled...

She couldn't help but feel it was the right choice. First, the man was a beast. Surely he would have no trouble slicing hard kosher salami with a bread knife. And if he did have trouble, if his coordination went all wonky on him, she would be right there to guide him back to safety.

But mainly, there was a certain level of trust that went into handing a knife to a total stranger. It represented something epic, and important, that all of them would witness together. Besides, if he did try to kill them all…it would be four against one.

"Are you sure about that?" Miranda asked quietly.

"I'm sure," Faye said, before pointing the knife towards Greg. "If you're up for it, of course…"

Greg nodded. Rising from the couch, he made his way over to the counter, his mass causing all her friends to split like the Red Sea. Faye handed him the knife, and he turned to the meat waiting on the cutting board, pausing for his next instruction.

Faye leaned into him, whispering. "Press down," she explained, demonstrating with her own hand over his own. "Hard. Cut through…as thin and as equal in size as possible, okay?"

She stepped back from Greg.

And then, magic.

He sliced through the first piece without any problem. Hearing the familiar sound of his favorite snack being prepared downstairs, Hillel emerged from Faye's bedroom where he had been napping, tapping his way downstairs in order to garner a treat.

Faye clapped her hands together, ecstatic. "Perfect," she said, and truly meant it. "Would you like to keep trying?"

Greg nodded again. Faye stepped back, and allowed him to continue unaided. Soon, it was raining hard kosher salami. Miranda inched her way over.

"Well, Faye," Miranda said, leaning into her to whisper, "are you still going to tell me that you didn't create a golem?"

"Will you stop already."

"Alright," Miranda acquiesced, before meeting her eyes directly. "But promise me you'll call at the first sign of trouble, okay?"

Faye promised, before her eyes wandered back over to Shulamit. She was standing in the living room, her hand inadvertently rubbing her lower belly. "Oh," Faye said, quickly scooting around to one of the cabinets, "I almost forgot."

She had been so busy with Greg, she had completely forgotten about the fertility spell she had prepared for Shulamit. Faye pulled the red velvet pouch from a drawer and handed it to Miranda. "Hang this in your bedroom, on the wall directly across from your bed."

"You know we're doing IVF, right?"

Faye angled her head sideways. "The point is to set your intention, to make sure that the divine energies of the universe are aligned to your deepest desires."

Miranda and Shulamit had been trying to get pregnant for months. After three failed rounds of IUI, they were finally ready for IVF. Faye reasoned that in addition to modern medicine, everyone could benefit from a little Jewitch spiritual help.

"Thanks, Faye," Miranda said, taking the pouch.

Her friends humored her spiritual practice more than they ever took part in it themselves. But as her magic was firmly rooted in her Jewish tradition, and her friends were all on the more liberal side of the Jewish family prism, they saw no opposition between their faith and a little Jewitch magic.

"It's no easy matter to create life," Faye said.

Miranda let the comment linger in the air, before her eyes wandered back over to Greg. "I mean, so you claim..."

Faye shook her head. "You are out of control."

"You love me," Miranda teased back. "Also, when you're done with making us babies... I would also like you to make us a golem. I have a ton of yard work I need to get done, and a painting I want hung in my office at the university."

Faye forced a smile. "I'll get right on that."

Miranda took off to check on Shulamit. Faye returned her gaze to Greg. He was still at the counter, almost finished with his task of slicing enough hard kosher salami to feed all five of them for dinner. In the process, his back and arm muscles were *seriously* testing the strength of his shirt. Goddess give her strength. He really was magnificent.

Her mind began to wander into strange and fantastical territory, and she found herself humored by one thought. If he were a golem, one that she had designed and created...would it really be so bad?

SEVEN

Greg stepped out of the shower and planted his feet firmly on the soft cushion of a bath mat. Dripping wet, he wiped away the steam from the mirror with one hand. Once again, the image caught him off guard. The man staring back at him with long red hair was still a stranger, but fully naked now. He took a moment to analyze the shape of his form. He wasn't just big— his eyes fell to between his legs—*he was big all over.*

"You okay in there?" Faye shouted through the door.

"Oh…kay," Greg responded, eventually.

"There's a towel and pajamas for you on the toilet," she explained, before adding, "Dry off with the towel. Then put your clothes on. Take your time, okay? No rush getting dressed. Just…make sure you get dressed."

Greg left behind his penis and focused on getting dressed. Doing as Faye had instructed him, he dried himself off. Put on the pajamas she had left him. It was a matching plaid set. He pulled on the underwear and pants. Then he went to work on the shirt, a long-sleeve button-down, when his brain suddenly glitched out. He stared at the buttons, trailing across the material like a path all the way up to his neck, and for the life of him… couldn't remember what to do with them.

Weird.

He tried to figure it out for himself. He grabbed at the edges, found the slits, attempted to wedge the tiny plastic circles in between them.

Thankfully, his coordination was okay. He was able to walk, cut hard kosher salami, take a shower. But every now and then, similar to the words in his mouth, he got stuck. The impulse was there, along with the sense that this was something simple, something he should remember—it would sit on the edge of his brain, teasing him with possibility—but instead of his brain communicating with his body, he would freeze.

Of everything in the world that should be difficult, he wasn't sure why it was suddenly buttons that had become the enemy. He stared down at his hands. Maybe it was the size of them in comparison to shiny plastic circles. Perhaps he simply didn't have the dexterity. *Dexterity. That was a big word, too.* Either way, he gave up on the buttons. He opened the door and stepped out.

The room had changed. The couch had shifted into a bed. The coffee table had been moved, pressed up against a rack full of hats, scarves, and jewelry. Faye stood over a pullout couch, smoothing sheets.

"Oh," Faye said, twisting around to greet him. "Your…*chest.*"

Greg glanced down at himself.

Yes, he did indeed have a chest.

Though he wasn't sure why she was bothering to point it out.

He wanted to explain what had happened in the bathroom, describe the way his brain had glitched out, but the effort would require more than one-word answers. It required a full story. He had the vocabulary, but not the ability to speak his thoughts and feelings. The frustration he had felt in the hospital reemerged. A heaviness formed in the pit of his stomach, and then, Faye, like always, worked her magic. Without him saying anything, without him needing to utter one single word, she left the bedsheets and came over.

"Here," Faye said softly, reaching for the collar of his shirt. "Let me help you."

She ran her hands down the material. In the process, his body sparked. Greg latched onto her eyes. She had beautiful eyes. Earthy, like the tea she had made for him, and the forests that surrounded Woodstock. She was so incredibly comforting.

"You know," she said, talking while she worked, "it's normal. All the difficulty you're having right now. With words. With certain actions. Your memory is just working extra hard to come back to you. Still, I imagine you're very frustrated."

Greg nodded ferociously. "Yes."

She sighed sympathetically as her hands lingered on the second button. "But I want you to know, the doctors told me it should resolve eventually. One day—" her eyes lifted like a smile up towards him "—your words will come back. Your memory, too. And then…we'll be able to get you home."

Greg caught on the word. "Home."

"The place where you belong. The place where people love you."

Home felt like Faye.

"Faye," he said, adamant.

"I'm not your home," she said gently. "I'm just the person you remember. But no need to feel embarrassed about any of this. Believe it or not, I'm adept at helping people with memory problems. My dad went through something similar when he was diagnosed with early-onset Alzheimer's. Laces, buttons, zippers—all of it became calculus for him. Not that you have the same disease. *Baruch Hashem and Blessed Be.*"

Greg did not remember his own father. But the way Faye

talked about hers, it seemed like an important relationship. Perhaps this was why she was so adamant about getting him home. Perhaps, there were people—parents and others—who were waiting for him.

"Home," he repeated. "Father?"

The question caused her to stop once again. She took her hands off his buttons. "Father," she said, simply. "A mother, maybe. You could also have a partner. Or a wife. Maybe even children. And those people, who make up your home, are probably worried sick about you right now. They probably are wondering where you are. I'm sure we'll find them in no time."

The news made his stomach turn, but he wasn't sure why. Faye finished buttoning up his shirt. "All done," she said, before adding, "Would you like to try it for yourself now?"

"Yes."

She returned her hands to his chest, unbuttoning his shirt. When his chest was once again exposed, she nodded for him to begin. He followed what he had seen her do, smoothing out the shirt, making sure the plastic circles were aligned with the tiny slits, before aiming to close the first one.

Faye stepped back, giving him space to work. And when he had trouble with the first one, she didn't just jump to intervene. Instead, she waited patiently—without the yoke of judgment attached—for him to figure it out, remember for himself.

"Believe it or not," Faye said, watching him work, "I also have trouble with buttons."

Greg got the words out. "You...do?"

"Yep." She held up her left hand, revealing a large scar down the center. "My wrist was broken when I was seventeen. Unfortunately, it was never able to get set back the right way. Now, my pointer finger doesn't behave correctly. It does its own thing...with or without my permission."

She began to wiggle her fingers. One of them did not move with all the rest.

"It's actually affected my career," she said, almost to herself. "Ever since my wrist was broken, I've never been able to make pieces in quite the right way. Or, at least, the way I see them in my head. A lot of times, they're lopsided, funny…the lips come out weird and misshapen, or a warp appears where I didn't have the ability to smooth out a bubble in the clay. But we make do, right? We make the best out of what we are given."

Curiosity overcame him. He reached for her hand. She jumped a little, unsure what he was reaching for, but then allowed it. Turning her hand over, finding the scar, he ran one finger down the tiny white line. He didn't like seeing her hurt. It made his own heart ache in ways that were indescribable.

"How?" he asked.

Faye pulled her hand away. "Long story."

He wanted to hear it, but instead, she pulled her long sleeve over the damage, and flitted away from him completely. Heading back over to the couch, she returned to working on the sheets. *Conversation over.* Greg stared down at the six buttons he still had left to close.

"It's okay," Faye said, glancing back at him. "I'm right here."

"Here," he repeated.

"Just a stone's throw away…if you need any help."

He needed Faye.

He liked when she was close, when her hands touched his shirt, when her fingertips brushed his skin. He liked the way she made him feel, like his body was on fire. Things made sense when Faye was around. He wished he could tell her that.

"Faye," Greg said.

She looked up from the bed, both eyebrows raised in his direction.

He focused on the words. "Thank…you."

Her whole face edged downwards. She swallowed. "You're most welcome."

Their eyes caught once again. She pushed a curl behind her ear and looked away.

"Before the accident, believe it or not… I had a full scholarship to a very prestigious art school in Manhattan."

He didn't understand.

"I was going to study ceramics at the college level," she explained. "I had won lots of competitions for my work. Not just competitions for teenagers, but across the country, against artists and professionals. I was interested specifically in modular concepts for functional tableware."

Her hands trailed over to a vase sitting on the nightstand. She lifted it up, and then broke it into three distinct pieces, turning that vase into three separate drinking glasses. It was, quite frankly, the coolest thing he had ever seen in his entire life. At least, the life he could remember.

"Ma…gic," he got the word out.

She corrected him. "Mathematics."

He didn't agree with her. It seemed to Greg that wherever Faye went, she sprinkled enchantment. Faye snapped two of the drinking glasses back together, and took the third one to the sink in the kitchen behind him, filling it up with water.

"I loved the complexity required to get something just right," she explained. "All the angles and edges had to be planned and made in alignment, so that a piece could move, or interact with another piece, without them damaging each other. It had to be perfect."

"Perfect?"

"Without mistake," she explained, her voice lilting with the memory. "But after the accident, I couldn't create those perfect pieces anymore. That one disabled finger changed my art irrevocably…and my life."

Greg frowned. Granted, without a memory, he had no idea what made a piece of art perfect versus merely acceptable. But he couldn't help but feel she was being way too hard on herself. He had seen Faye's pottery all over her home and business. Perhaps she was no longer making vases that turned into cups, but she was still enormously talented.

"Ta...ta," Greg said.

"I'm talking too much?" she said, frowning with her whole mouth.

Finally, he got the word out. "Tal...en...ted."

It was slow, and difficult, but he was able to express the sentiment clear enough. The corner of her eyes creased downwards. "You think I'm talented?"

He nodded. "Yes. Very."

The room fell into silence once more. Her eyes caught on his, and in her gaze, he felt stable. Faye was the terra firma beneath his feet.

"Anyway," she said, stepping away from his bed. "I hope this is okay for now."

"Oh-kay," he confirmed.

"I know it's not the Ritz-Carlton or anything," she said nervously. "But hopefully, you'll be comfortable here for the time being. And really, I don't imagine you'll be here for more than a few days. I'm sure we'll figure out who you are...and get you home in no time."

Greg considered her words. "Okay."

"Great." Faye seemed relieved. "Then if there's nothing else you need, I'll just let you get some rest."

With that, Faye disappeared. The door to her bedroom shut behind her...followed by the sound of something clicking into place. Greg turned back to *his* room, now uncomfortably silent, before glancing down at his pajamas. Three buttons were still left undone.

Quickly, he moved to close them up, and then, crawling into bed, he got under the covers that Faye had so carefully laid out for him. She had done everything possible to make him comfortable. The bed was warm. There was water to drink at his side. His buttons were fastened securely on his shirt. And yet the feeling that something was wrong, that something had been unraveled inside of him, remained.

Faye locked the door to her bedroom and sat down on her bed. A thousand thoughts spun through her mind. She had not meant to share such intimacies with a stranger…with Greg. She had not meant to word-vomit all over him. She had especially not wanted to see his *absolutely spectacular* chest.

Goddess give her strength.

The man was built like a challah.

She lay back on her bed and took a deep breath. She waved away the heat from her cheeks, and then, grabbing a pillow to spoon for comfort, laughed at herself. She was being ridiculous. There was no reason to feel nervous around Greg. Yes, he was her type. He had an undeniable sweetness about him, excelled at slicing hard kosher salami, and thought she was talented… but he was also unattainably attractive.

And yet, the way he was looking at her…

The feeling that sparked in her body as he took her hand, one finger drifting down the skin on her wrist…

She had to pull away.

Honestly, she wasn't sure why she was even worried about it. It could never happen. She would never allow it to happen between them. Because one day, his memory would return. Or the people who loved him would come looking for him. And then, *just like with Stuart*, he'd leave all his crap behind in her apartment…and move on with his life.

Unless, of course, he was a golem.

Faye didn't know much about golems. The decision to create one had simply been an act of self-care in the wake of an anti-Semitic attack, a way to feel less vulnerable against invisible enemies…also, a dream for something better in her life. Unconditional love. A partner who would function like one of her modular pieces of pottery, allowing her to move independently as needed, then snap back together, without damaging her forever.

The long day had clearly gotten to her.

Rising up, she settled on sleep. Heading to her dresser, she opened her drawer full of pajamas. With Greg down the hall, she debated wearing something modest for bed, sweatpants along with a bra and a T-shirt. But she always got hot at night, and so she settled on something more comfortable. A silk chemise that covered *just* enough, and a robe that she hung on the back of the door.

She began to change, straightening up her room as she went, her mind wandering back to the question at hand. Greg was not a golem, because golems did not exist. They were creatures of Jewish folklore, totally fictional. And yet, now that she was able to fully give Miranda's earlier accusation some energy, she had to admit that the synchronicities between Greg and the golem doll she had created were strange.

Curiosity got the best of her. Finding her phone, she opened it to the page for an AI research assistant. She knew it was silly, searching for information on such fantastical beings…but really, what was the harm? It was late. She was stressed out. Might as well have a little fun before heading to bed. She typed in her question. What is a golem?

The AI chatbot began scrolling with text. In Jewish folklore, a golem is an anthropomorphic creature that is created from inanimate materials, such as clay or mud. The golem is usually crafted with a distinct purpose in mind. Historically, golems have been used for labor and manual tasks, defense and guardianship, such as protecting a Jewish community during times of anti-Semitism, as well as aiding in magic rituals. The most famous golem of all was The Golem of Prague, attributed to Rabbi Judah Loew.

She liked all that.

Especially the bit about aiding in magic rituals.

She sat down on the bed and, staring at those words, found her mind wandering. In truth, the idea of Greg being a golem was more than just a little bit titillating. She imagined all the things he could be useful for around Magic Mud Pottery. Practical things like carrying heavy boxes of clay, setting up the back studio for her Magic Mud Mini Warlocks. Emotional things like defending her from night terrors and guarding her store from anti–Semites. *And sex.* She imagined that having sex with a golem would be mind–blowingly fantastic.

Like a vibrator with a fully functioning tongue and two perfect hands.

She was getting into this Greg being a golem thing.

She typed another question. How do I know what my golem's purpose is?

The AI responded: A golem's purpose is determined by its creator. It is important that the creator gives clear direction to the golem in terms of instruction. Otherwise, the golem may become dangerous.

Faye stared down at the last line of text.

Dangerous.

That sounded…foreboding.

What do you mean by dangerous?

The AI did not hesitate: The golem goes berserk.

WHAT?

The AI continued. Without a sense of purpose, the golem becomes distraught, disruptive, and violent. It begins to disobey the commands of its creator, wreaking havoc on the people and communities it was designed to protect. In the most extreme cases, the golem goes on a rampage, killing the creator, often accidentally, by crushing them. In this way, the golem is a cautionary tale about usurping God and the natural order of the universe. Human beings are not permitted to create life from clay.

Faye swallowed.

The actually sounded *really* freaking bad.

Her heart sped up inside her chest. A new worry formed like some primordial bubble oozing up from the sludge… She completely freaked out. Because she knew it. She totally freaking knew it. Whether Greg was a man or a golem, he was going to hurt her. He was going to leave her. Either by remembering who he was, and returning to his old life…or crushing her to death beneath his massive body. *Maybe he would even kill her during sex.*

Screw that.

She was not going to die making the O-face.

Rising from her bed, Faye tossed the phone down. Grabbing her robe, she went to storm down the hallway. She was going to demand that Greg—this man, or this golem, it really didn't matter anymore—leave her apartment. Indeed, she had her hand on the doorknob, and was just about to unlock it and throw it open, when she stopped. Her eyes caught sight of one of those anti-Semitic flyers, lying on the floor of her bedroom beside her laundry hamper. She must have brought a copy upstairs with her last night.

She bent down to pick it up, and the fear that had been dimmed in the wake of Greg's appearance suddenly returned. Her name was on that flyer. Her picture. Her address. Her eyes fell to the window, and the darkness she found there, the knowledge that there was someone in town who hated her enough to target her directly, was terrifying.

It was like being with her mother all over again.

Faye stepped back from the door. Putting that flyer away in a drawer for safekeeping, she crawled into bed. And then, knowing Greg was at the end of the hall, she turned off the light sitting on her nightstand. The room fell into darkness, and she told herself that she had done the right thing.

She needed to sleep without spells or alcohol. She needed to dream without waking up to real-life nightmares. Whatever dangers were at home with a man the size of a giant, or some supernatural sentinel, paled in comparison to the threats that now lingered outside. As much as Greg needed her…she also needed him.

Greg couldn't sleep. Instead, he tossed and turned beneath Faye's covers, before finally giving up, staring up at her white ceiling. The problem wasn't simply an issue of insomnia. With Faye having disappeared into her bedroom, the house suddenly felt too quiet. Too silent. And with the luxury of space, images without explanation—without memories attached, either—assaulted him.

He saw a cityscape before him, heard the sound of honking horns. He could hear children laughing, recall the feeling of snow landing on his tongue, but the images were nothing more than pictures in his mind, nonsensical. Confusing. They didn't bring comfort or understanding, only the sense that he had forgotten something integral and important. Perhaps he had forgotten his entire reason for being. But a woman's voice appeared. Soft and pleasant, it whispered over the images, *justice, justice.*

Greg sat up in his bed. It was too much. Without Faye to guide him, he felt very lost. He tore off his bedsheets and stomped back down the hall, knocking on her door.

"Yes?" Faye shouted through the wood.

"Can't."

"You can't sleep?"

He grunted an affirmation.

She was quiet for a few moments. "Have you tried closing your eyes?"

He hadn't tried that.

Greg returned to his bed, closing his eyes. After a few minutes, the silence assaulted him again. That anxious and unsettled feeling returned. Rising from his bed, he made his way down the hall once more. This time, Faye opened the door and stuck her head out.

Through the crack, he could see she had changed. Now, instead of the normal clothes she had on at the hospital and during the day, she was wearing lingerie. *Lingerie.* He remembered the word. His eyes wandered down to her breasts, where the flimsy silk material did little to cover her ample cleavage.

"Yes?" Faye whispered.

"Still...can't."

Her lips edged down to the floor in a frown. *Bored.* That was word he was looking for. He didn't like staring up at the ceiling with nothing but strange images and weird voices spinning inside his head. It made him feel...well, he couldn't remember what the word was, but it felt like a tickle. An uncomfortable tickle. Not at all like the kind of tickle he got when he saw Faye wearing *lingerie.*

He tried, once again, to explain what was happening inside of him.

"Book," Greg said.

Faye squinted. "You want to read a book?"

No, he did not want to read a book. He tried again. *"Booooooook."*

"Okay," Faye said, moving to shut the door. "I understand. Let me just put on a robe."

He gave up. Faye shut the door. When she reappeared, she was wearing a robe, clutching it around her breasts. She slunk past him in the hallway, leading him back towards the living room to the small bookcase situated on the wall beside his bed-not-bed.

"I have them organized by topic," she explained quietly.

He wasn't sure why she was whispering. They were the only two people in the house. Well, aside from Hillel. He glanced over his shoulder to see the rat-dog curled up into a swirl beside his pillow. Perhaps she was being quiet for his sake.

"Self-help is on the top," Faye said, pointing them out. "Spirituality, philosophy, and nonfiction are on the second shelf. And fiction is on the third row. Romance, mainly...but there's also some thrillers, mysteries...and the rest, everything else scattered about, are board games."

"Scrabble," he said, surprising himself.

Faye blinked. "You remember Scrabble?"

"No."

He didn't remember. He also had no idea why he had said that word.

It was awful not understanding why certain words and actions came to him, when others seemed lost and forgotten. His cheeks burned hot. His chest ached in an unbearable sort of pain. He was losing hope, too...when his eyes latched onto hers. They were soft. Sympathetic. *She understood.*

"Anyway," Faye said gently. "Those are all my books. Feel free to just look through and read whatever interests you, okay?"

Greg wanted to thank her, express his gratitude. But all he got out was a grunt.

Faye didn't mind. She wished him a good night, and after the slightest touch of his wrist, returned to her bedroom. The door closed behind her. He heard the familiar *click* of a lock being turned, before the apartment fell back into silence. He turned to her bookshelves, desperate to fill up that void, and reached for a book on the first row.

Self-help. It seemed like a good place to start.

YOU ARE THE MOUNTAIN
By Dr. Richard X. Simmons
A guidebook for reclaiming your best self.

Page 146

It is important to remember that what you believe will become reality. You are the mountain. If you envision the path ahead of you as filled with rocks, and crags, steep cliffs, insurmountable obstacles—if you believe that the journey ahead is always hard—it will always be hard, and you will find your dreams unattainable.

If, however, you wake up with confidence, tell yourself that it is not the mountain standing in your way, but that you, yourself, are the mountain—majestic and attainable—then all that you wish for, believe in, and desire will become yours. You create your reality. And your thoughts will either aid you in achieving success, or guarantee your failure.

EIGHT

Faye awoke to the aroma of something familiar cooking in her apartment. Blinking her eyes open, she tried to place the scent—something like butter and eggs, but also, burning. All at once, she sat up in her bed and threw off her covers, just in time to hear the fire alarm in her upstairs hallway going off. There was no one in the house but Greg…and he was cooking.

She pulled on a robe and, tearing open her bedroom door, raced down the hall to stop him. "Greg," she shouted. "No. No cooking. We don't use the stove when we don't have our memory."

It was too late. Faye arrived just in time to find a horror show.

Dirty pots and pans littered every corner of her upstairs kitchen. Broken eggs were splattered like modern art all over the floor and counter. She stepped on a shell, feeling the slimy bits wedging between her toes.

Greg searched through the cabinets, pressing his fingers past towels and blankets, ignoring breakfast sitting on the stove. At least, she assumed it was breakfast...because all she could see was salt. An entire container, a mountain of Morton's, rested in the pan and was fully burning. Dark smoke billowed into the air.

Greg twisted around, totally overwhelmed. Hillel, who had been watching the entire scenario unfold from the windowsill behind the couch, quickly jumped off and ran away.

"Okay!" Faye said, quickly taking charge of the situation. "It's okay."

She kept her cool. She turned the stove off, removing the eggs and salt, dumping it in the sink. She grabbed a chair, turning off the smoke detector. She would deal with the cleanup, all the eggs and pots and pans—also calming down Hillel—later. For now, she needed to help Greg.

"It's okay," she said, taking his hands in her own. Leading him to the couch, sitting down beside him, she could see he was upset.

Greg couldn't remember why the room was singing. But he knew that he had messed up. He knew it as soon as he saw Faye racing from her bedroom, her face all contorted with *apprehension*, before tossing his eggs in the sink.

He felt bad, seeing her so concerned, and that his breakfast was ruined. He was trying to make sense of what had happened—of where he had gone wrong in believing he was the mountain.

"First," she said, still holding his hands. "Are you okay?"

"Okay," he confirmed.

She sighed, relieved.

He was grateful for her patience with him, even though he still wasn't sure where he had gone wrong. He had no trouble the previous evening slicing hard kosher salami. He had successfully handled a knife and helped Faye make dinner. He assumed that making breakfast would be just as easy.

Instead, much like those buttons that gave him and Faye

trouble, he had miscalculated the effort required. It turned out that while he remembered some things about making eggs, he had forgotten others. For example, he knew there were eggs in the refrigerator downstairs, but he had forgotten how delicate they were...dropping two, and crushing three more, on the way to the stove upstairs.

He remembered that you scrambled eggs in a pan, but he had forgotten to add butter or oil, and so they started to burn. He was just in the process of attempting to salvage them with the addition of salt when the room began screaming. The sound caused him to jump, and he dropped the canister he was using. Next thing he knew, Faye was there. Breakfast was ruined. And Hillel had run away from them both.

He wanted to explain all that, but he couldn't form the words.

"Hey," Faye said sweetly. "It's okay."

"Sorry."

"I just want to double-check," she said, her eyes scanning his form. "You're not hurt, are you? Nothing's broken, bruised, or bleeding?"

"No."

He was surprised at himself. For the first time since waking up in the hospital, he was answering questions easily. His thoughts shifted from the space in his head to his tongue without a significant pause or delay. It felt good, being able to communicate. He wondered if the book he was reading had helped the connections between his brain and his mouth.

"You were hungry?" Faye asked.

"No."

He did it again. He told her how he felt. They were simple words, obviously, but he was grateful for them all the same. It felt like the first step in what would eventually grow to be a victory.

"I don't understand," Faye said. "If you weren't hungry, why were you making breakfast?"

"Breakfast…for…you."

She squinted. "You wanted to make me breakfast?"

"Yes."

The idea had appeared to him upon waking. After all, he had spent the night at Faye's. He had seen her in her lingerie. Though it wasn't in Dr. Richard X Simmons's self-help book, it felt like making her breakfast was the right thing to do.

"Greg," Faye said, gently. "That's really sweet of you. I appreciate you being so thoughtful…but what on Earth made you think you could cook me breakfast?"

Greg reached for his book, *You Are the Mountain*, and opened it to the page he had bookmarked.

Faye squinted, leaning in. "You were reading this book?"

"Yes." He pointed to the line he had been reading.

Faye read the sentence aloud. "'It is important to remember that what you believe will become your reality.' So, you read this book, and thought…if you believed you could make eggs, you could make them?"

"Yes." Greg nodded before adding, "Self-help."

"Self-help?"

"Help me," Greg explained. "Help…with words."

"Oh," she said, her features relaxing. "I understand."

For all that frustration sitting inside of him, there was one person in the world who could speak his language.

Faye put the book to the side. "The thing is," she explained, "there's a lot of good advice in that book. There's a lot of good advice in many of my books, honestly…but, while we're still getting you back to some level of health, I think it's best if you take everything with a grain of salt."

"Salt?"

"It means…don't believe everything you read."

"No…believe?"

It was such a strange concept. What was the point of books, of words, of having and using a whole big and beautiful language, if not to express something important? But maybe he just hadn't come to that shelf of ideas yet. Maybe some books were simply stories.

"No…understand," Greg said.

"Like the flyers."

"Flyers?"

Faye got up from the couch and went to her bedroom. When she returned, she was holding a small white paper, folded up and crumpled, more words—but this time, also images—splattered across the front. "These flyers," she said, sitting back down next to Greg. "They're not true. In fact, they say all sorts of horrible things about the Jewish people."

"Jewish people?"

"About me," she said, meeting his eyes directly. "They put my name, address, and photograph on that flyer. They put the names of my friends on that flyer…and then, they spread these untrue stories all over town, trying to hurt us."

He remembered Faye and her friends talking about it a little last night before dinner. He remembered Faye asking him about it in the hospital, too. And those words, the ones that were too long and confusing to utter aloud, reappeared inside his mind… *justice, justice.*

The whisper was getting louder.

He took the flyer from her hands. He inspected the pages, reading the words—*these untruths*—for himself. A rumbling appeared from the depths of his belly, a quake forming beneath the mountain.

Faye was so good. She had been so good to him, taking him home, speaking his language. He liked her friends, too. Shulamit had talked to him like a person, filling him up with stories. Nelly had brought him over clothes, and toiletries. And Miranda…well, he understood the instinct to protect her friend. He felt protective of Faye, too. His curiosity morphed into anger.

"These people...bad."

"Yes," Faye confirmed. "They're bad."

"Where?" He rose from his spot.

"Where are they?" she repeated, before sighing heavily. "Well, that is apparently the question of the hour."

"No understand."

"They hide," she explained. "Kind of like cockroaches...in dark places, undercover. They do these things anonymously, so that they can't get caught. So that they can continue to spread their lies and propaganda about Jews."

"No understand!"

His anger morphed into rage. *It wasn't right.* These people, just going around town, spreading lies and untruths about Jews. *About Faye.* She deserved better.

"I don't want you to be upset," she said.

"Ang...ry."

"I know," she said quietly. "I'm angry, too. But I don't want you to worry, Greg. I have an alarm on my business. I once took a Krav Maga class in college. And our police, along with the FBI, are working very hard to find the people who are responsible for these flyers. In fact, my very dear friend Eric is the chief of police in Woodstock. So, you see...we have nothing to worry about. You're perfectly safe here."

He wasn't worried about himself. He was worried for Faye. It was her face, and name, and address on the flyer. And though there were no direct threats on the paper, he felt for certain that it was one all the same. *Insidious.* That was the word that popped into his brain. The people who left these flyers knew exactly what they were doing. They didn't just use language to make erroneous claims. They twisted it into something ugly and maniacal.

"Sorry," Greg said.

"No." Faye shook her head. She was very adamant. "You have nothing to apologize for, okay? You didn't make the flyers, and it's not your fault what happened with breakfast. *It's my fault*. I should have gotten up earlier. I should have made sure you were safe. But going forward, how about you and I make a deal?"

"Deal?"

"A promise to each other," she explained. "It means that the words we say, the meaning we give them, have power. When we both agree to something, we don't backtrack or change our minds later. We do what we say. Always."

Greg considered her proposition thoughtfully. "Okay," he agreed. "We promise."

She shifted closer to him on the couch, and the rage he had felt dissipated into the warmth of her presence. He liked how it felt to be close to her. He liked how she looked, too. The messy hair. The wrinkled lingerie peeking out from beneath her robe. He would promise Faye anything…if it meant she would stay.

"So how about we promise," Faye continued, "that for the time being, when you read a book, before attempting anything you find there…you come and talk to me first. If it's something new you want to try, like cooking a meal or whatever, we'll figure it out together, okay?"

"Promise," Greg said, gripping her hands tighter, feeling the tether between them—between their two worlds—strengthening like a cord. "No cook. Take books…mound…"

"Grain," she corrected him. "I think you mean grain."

He looked towards the sink, where breakfast was now drowning in a tub of water.

"Mound," he said, succinctly. Clearly.

"*Guh-raaaaaaa*—" She moved to help him, mimicking the word for him in her own mouth, but then, she stopped. Her eyes drifted towards the sink, where a mountain of salt—*not a grain*—was waiting to be cleaned up.

"Wait," she said, her chin cocking. "Did you just make a joke?"

Greg smiled, but did not use his words. It seemed more fitting just to raise an eyebrow.

For the next week, Faye kept Greg close to her. Both physically and spiritually, she tethered him to her hip, creating an invisible cord between them, binding them together.

She gave him simple tasks throughout the day to aid in his coordination—closing boxes, sweeping the front foyer. During meals, and through the daytime hours at Magic Mud Pottery, they practiced speaking together. She set up appointments with a neurologist and speech therapist, even though, despite her best efforts to get Greg in sooner, it would be three months before their first appointment.

From there, she supplemented traditional healing methods with alternative ones. She made him magical teas and baladur cakes meant to aid his memory. She placed crystals under his pillows and left rosemary in his pockets. And every night, after she made up his makeshift bed on the couch and retired to her own bedroom, locking the door behind her, Greg read a book. He read and read with a passion that impressed her...but also, periodically, made her think back to that golem doll.

JEWISH MAGIC THROUGH THE AGES
By Rabbi Avraham Frankel

Page 76

The study of Torah, and subsequently, Jewish law is considered one of the most honored pursuits within the Jewish tradition. For centuries, and even in many communities still to this day, there isn't a more honorable pursuit for a young man than to become a Talmud chacham, a person who is considered an expert in the Talmud and Jewish law.

In fact, so important was this quest for learning, that between the third and sixth centuries we find many texts which contain instruction for both increasing memory and decreasing forgetfulness. Some items that increased forgetfulness, and were to be avoided, included eating olives, drinking bathing water, and mending clothes while one is naked.

There were also ways to aid memory. Chief among these were an incantation to Sar HaTorah, an angel of revelation associated with memory, and Poteh, the prince of forgetting, a name frequently uttered by mothers before sending their children to school.

In addition, a Baladur mixture was often used as a tool to aid in memory and retrieval. The Baladur, which appears in both early Jewish and Muslim medical literature, was to be made as a paste and eaten in conjunction with a hearty breakfast.

NINE

The universe was working in his favor.

Greg stood in the kitchen, and under Faye's guidance, worked hard to complete the baladur mixture for their breakfast. Over the last week, Faye had been making him the tiny magic cakes in order to help induce the return of his memory. Having both observed her and read a book on the topic, he was excited to try his hand at aiding her in one of her magical recipes.

With mortar in hand, and his pestle waiting on the counter, he collected the ingredients. "Cloves," he said, practicing his words as he grabbed each item. "Long peppers, dates…ginger, muskat nuts…"

Faye stopped him. "Don't forget the galangal root."

"Ga…langal root," he repeated. "Almost forgot."

He reached for the ingredient.

It was incredible how much he was progressing. He still wasn't capable of speaking complex words and sentences, but he was able to form words with multiple syllables. And while he still needed to take his time, life was feeling less frustrating.

"That's what I'm here for." Faye took a seat at the counter.

Greg began grinding the mixture. While he had seen Faye do it every morning, it was reading *Jewish Magic Through the Ages* that really solidified the meaning behind the process for him.

Jewitch magic was done within the sphere of Judaism and Jewish law. There were also two components to the magical act—the physical and the emotional. It was important that each act be done with intention, and that the paste he was making all be measured in equal quantities.

After the paste was complete, he would pour it into a cake batter that Faye had waiting on the side. Then, he would dump that batter into muffin tins—seven in total, as seven was a special number in Jewitch magic—before using a branch of a rosemary leaf to write the name *Sar HaTorah* into the top of each. Finally, the cakes would be baked at three hundred sixty degrees for exactly twenty-eight minutes.

Faye folded her chin into the palm of her hand. "I appreciate you humoring me with these rituals, being so open to my Jewitch beliefs and magic."

"Not humoring you," he said, pouring his paste into the cake batter. "You make me…believe."

Faye seemed tickled. "I make you believe in magic?"

"No," Greg clarified. "You are…magic."

Her lips parted.

Greg smiled and returned to his cake mixture. "Now you're… speechless."

His joke did the trick.

She laughed, tossing her whole head back.

"You comedian," she said softly.

He didn't remember what that was. "Comedian?"

"It's a person who makes jokes for a living."

"Sounds like—" Greg raised one eyebrow playfully "—a funny way…to make a living."

This time, she nearly spit out her magical tea. He loved seeing her that way, happy and open. It made his heart soar.

"Goddess give me strength," she said, catching her breath. "That is either the best, or worst, dad joke I have ever heard."

"Dad joke?" He didn't know what that was, either.

She attempted to explain. "A dad joke is like a corny, punchy pun. It's funny but also makes you roll your eyes."

Greg put the muffin pan in the oven, setting the timer for twenty-eight minutes. "Why…do dads make them…and not moms?"

The question stumped her. "I don't actually know."

"Did…your dad?"

"My dad?" Quiet for a moment, she drifted away, looking towards the wall, her eyes not meeting his own. She always did that when she talked about her family. Finally, she found her words. "My dad wasn't very funny."

Faye got up and started straightening up around the house.

"I wonder," Greg mused. "About…my dad."

He was surprised how sad saying the words aloud made him feel.

"You still don't remember anything, huh?" Faye asked sympathetically.

"Pictures," he explained. "Words. But no…link."

"I'm sorry, Greg."

He was sorry, too.

The bell above the door downstairs rattled before someone began knocking. Faye glanced down at the watch she was wearing. "Someone's here early," she said, and rose to head downstairs. "Guess I should go deal with that."

Greg stopped her. "Let me," he said, taking off his apron. "You watch…the cakes."

He wanted to do it. It was good for Greg to be practicing

his speaking skills with other people. Plus, it made him feel useful to be able to help Faye out around Magic Mud Pottery. Thankfully, Faye agreed.

Greg hopped down the stairs and found a woman peering through the glass of the front door. A small girl was wrapped up in a coat beside her. Greg unlocked the door.

"I'm so sorry," the woman said, clearly flustered. "I know it's super early, but are you guys open right now?"

"We open at ten," he explained. "But why don't...you come inside."

She sighed, relieved. "Thank you so much. You have no idea how much you are saving me right now."

The little girl followed her mother. Three tiny fingers found their way inside her mouth, and he watched her eyes trail up— all the way up—from his knees to his head. It wasn't the first time a little kid had that reaction to him. Greg was just beginning to understand that he was big. *Really big.* The long red hair also didn't seem to help. He went out of his way to be gentle with her, offering her a tiny wave of friendship, before returning his attention to the mom.

"And what...can I help you with today?" he asked.

"I need a gift for my mother-in-law," the woman explained. "She's coming this morning, and I totally forgot it was her birthday."

He did his best to help her out, showing her vases, ring dishes shaped like hamsas, bowls, and candle holders, every shape and color. Still, the mom couldn't decide.

Greg had an idea.

"Actually," he said, waving her to the back studio, "let me show you...one of my favorite pieces."

Like her Jewitch ritual items, Faye had pottery all over the store. It was crammed on shelves. It sat on tables and countertops. It lived in bathrooms, laundry rooms, and on metal shelving in her garage. But his favorite piece was a rounded jar he had discovered while helping dust Magic Mud Pottery. It lived behind something Faye called a *Seder plate*, a Jewish ritual item used on Passover.

Apparently, Faye had hidden it there because she hated the rusty color and the large bubbles that exploded like soapsuds and encircled the exterior. She said that it was supposed to be smooth, free from gurgles and eruptions, but it was Greg's favorite piece in the store. It reminded him of Faye. A one-off. Rare. Earthy with its rounded shape and distinctive form.

Greg pulled the jar down from the shelf. "This is my favorite."

"It's beautiful," she said.

"It's a… Faiga Kaplan original."

"Wow."

It was also a sale.

Faye came down from upstairs, just in time to handle ringing her up. With the woman occupied at the counter, Greg turned his attention to the little girl. He kneeled to her eye level, an attempt to make himself a little less scary.

"Hey," he whispered.

He reached behind the counter, where Faye kept some lollipops for her younger students, and pulled one out for her. The sweet treat did the trick. They were suddenly best friends. She tiptoed over to him.

"I'm Greg," he said.

"May," she said, and opened her candy, taking a lick. "You're big."

"I am," he admitted.

"How did you get so big?"

"You really want to know?" he teased her.

She nodded.

He pointed to the candy she was eating. "Lollipops."

"Whoa."

When he glanced back up, Faye was standing over him. The

customer was ready to go home. "Come on, May," the woman said, offering her hand. "We gotta go pick up Grandma at the airport."

The little girl skipped out behind her, stopping at the door. "Bye, Greg!" she shouted. "Don't forget to eat your lollipops."

With one last chime of the bells above the front door, they were gone.

"I can't believe you sold that piece," Faye said quietly.

"I told you…it was good."

"Hm," she said. "Seems like you made a friend, too."

He found his eyes lingering on the door as it closed behind them, thinking about that mom, and that little girl, especially. Something about them felt familiar. His head began to hurt. Pound. On instinct, he rubbed his temples and closed his eyes.

Faye laid one hand on his arm. "You okay?"

"Yeah." Greg returned to her.

"You seemed far away." Faye asked curiously, "Did you remember something?"

"Just a feeling."

"A feeling?" she pressed him.

"Like I've…forgotten something…important."

He rubbed the back of his neck, the ache in his head spreading into his shoulders.

People often came into Magic Mud Pottery looking to buy gifts for loved ones. Ring dishes for weddings. A vase for a bouquet of flowers to give to a lover. A figurine for a teacher, a librarian, or a friend. Each time it would happen, his heart would break. A pain would appear, so raw it felt like a cavity directly into his soul.

He knew he was missing something important, something he should have remembered…but for the life of him, he couldn't remember what that was. He was like a book, half-read but unfinished. Only partway to understanding his full story.

"We'll find them," Faye said suddenly.

"How do you know?"

She wiggled her nine working fingers playfully. "Because I'm magic, remember?"

He believed her.

"Actually," Faye said, "I have something for you. Give me your left hand."

"Why left?" Greg asked.

"Because it's closest to your heart."

From her pocket, she withdrew a red string bracelet. A series of knots, seven in total, spread out across the design. She took his wrist in one hand, turning it over.

"Now, this is very old magic," Faye explained. "I know it looks like a simple red bracelet, but it's been braided and knotted for extra protection. And it will keep the evil eye away and bring you good luck. It will also make sure all the energies of the universe are working to support you. I'll knot it around your wrist, and you wear it until it falls off. How does that sound to you?"

Greg cleared his throat. "You...made this?"

"It really wasn't too much trouble." She shrugged. "I've been making friendship bracelets ever since my one summer working as a camp counselor at Camp Ahava. This time, I just infused it with some Jewitch magic."

She tied the bracelet around his wrist, knotting it at the place where his veins pulsed hot.

Greg caught on the term. "Friendship bracelet?"

"It's a thing that kids do," she quipped breezily. "To show that they like each other."

"Because we're friends?"

"Yes," she said, her eyes drifting up towards him, "we're friends."

Greg made sure his words were clear. "I love it."

"Good."

Despite his uncertainty about life, he found his gaze wandering towards her lips. They were pink and succulent, angled in his direction, totally kissable. Quickly he shook the thought away. Yes, Faye had become his whole world. The anchor that grounded him. But he could have people out there, a family that was missing him. A wife, children. He needed to remember and return to who he had been.

And yet, the desire to kiss her kept reappearing.

TEN

Faye was distracted that afternoon. Despite having two new orders waiting in her Etsy account, she couldn't seem to focus enough to leave the computer downstairs where she was working, and begin packing up orders. Instead, she found her thoughts lingering on Greg.

"Hey," Greg said, appearing from the studio. She had given him the task this morning of unboxing items, new clay and a restock of paints for her upcoming classes this week. Now, he was standing in the hallway, holding one rectangle of stoneware clay wrapped in plastic. "Where should I…put this?"

"You know the drawers where all the tools are?"

"Yes."

"It goes in the cabinet with them," she explained. "Just open it up, and you'll see all the rest of the clay waiting."

"Got…it."

Greg turned to leave, and inadvertently, her eyes caught on

his backside. A flicker of desire coursed through her body before Faye shook it away. She and Greg were just friends. She was helping him get better, heal…nothing more. There couldn't be anything more with a man who didn't have a memory. And yet, every day they spent together, their intimacies grew. She shared secrets with Greg. Lowered her walls. Sometimes, they even read together.

It wasn't good. She was especially concerned about the way her heart had begun to leap when he walked into a room. How just the sight of him offering her that cheeky and adorable grin caused her entire body to vibrate with wild swings of joy. She recognized the ache for something more with him, which she had to stop, eradicate, push down and away inside of her…because love was dangerous for Faye.

It turned her into someone else.

And then it betrayed her.

Her wrist and fingers began to ache. She attempted to rub it out, stretch the tendons and nerves so they would click back into place, but it was no use. Rising from her spot at the computer, she went to find some ibuprofen before loading up on ice.

Her mother might have broken her wrist when she was seventeen years old, but the pain lingered. A reminder. A warning. Faye would be wise to listen to the stories her own bones were telling her. There was no happy ending with Greg. Or any man, for that matter. Unless, of course, Greg wasn't a man at all…but a golem.

Returning to her computer—ice on her hand—she had to admit it was strange. Greg had been with her nearly a week, and no one had come to claim him. When she had first brought him home, she was certain that there would have been some inkling of his past. Missing posters hung up around town. A story in the local news. But despite checking every morning, there was nothing.

Like the man had just appeared out of thin air.

It wasn't possible. And yet…the man did seem to have golem-like qualities. She began to lay them out like evidence inside her mind. He had red hair. He was a reader. He was aiding her in magic rituals *and* helping her around the house doing chores and labor. And today, he had proven that he was good with children.

She thought back to the AI chat. The one that warned her that golems eventually went berserk and became dangerous.

Berserk.

It was such an extreme word. It would have been nice if the AI chat could have come up with something a little tamer.

An email notification chime rang out on her computer, causing her to jump. The ice she had been using to decrease her pain fell to the floor. Faye bent down to pick it up. Either Greg, the man, would leave her…or Greg, the golem, would go rogue, begin disobeying orders, and eventually cast destruction over her and all of Woodstock.

If the past was a fair indication of one's future, it sounded about right.

She needed to get back to work on her Etsy orders. One was from a new client in Tennessee, ordering a ring dish for an upcoming engagement gift. She was to paint the words "Mazal Tov," along with the image of two grooms under a chuppah, across the top. *Simple enough.* Plus, she always appreciated an order that allowed her to pull out her paintbrushes.

The other order was for her most recent piece. The one that Nelly had said looked like a *shvantz.* It was also from a name she recognized. *Sam Jones.*

Faye had never met Sam Jones. She sent all the pieces he ordered to a PO box about an hour away. But they had corresponded a few times by email, and she had even once personally invited him to visit her store. Surprisingly, her biggest fan declined. And after that, she buried her curiosity, not wanting to look a gift horse in the mouth as Sam had become a very good client over the years.

Faye had built a nice life for herself in Woodstock. Granted, she wasn't rich. But she was smart with her money. She lived beneath her means. She invested wisely. She had savings from selling her legal practice back in Manhattan. Still, as it went with small businesses, things were not always easy. She wished her Etsy store would do better. She wished that people, outside of folks buying ring dishes as wedding presents, would take note of her work. That people would understand she was a ceramicist, an artist…

But not every story had a happy ending.

The sound of Greg groaning loudly in her studio brought her back to reality. "Greg?" Faye called out. "Everything okay?"

"Okay," he responded from the main room. "Just…stepped in poop."

Faye grimaced. "Sorry! Do you want me to come clean it up?"

"No," Greg called. "Got it."

Greg was so sweet, so helpful…*so red*. Faye shook away the thoughts. Leaving her computer, she went to begin packing up her vase. She was halfway finished with bubble wrapping when the bells above her front door chimed out. Faye glanced up to see Chief Eric Myers, her friend from the police department.

The sight of him standing there in his uniform, gun holstered at his side, this symbol of safety and justice, relieved all the worry she had been feeling regarding those flyers.

"Faye," he said, moving to embrace her.

She hugged him back. "Eric."

Eric was a good man. Easy on the eyes, too—even though, with blond hair, he wasn't really her type. She had even tried to set him up with one of the single mothers from her pottery class, but the *shidduch* never happened. And though she knew she had disappointed Eric with her rejection, they were able to remain friends.

"I would have come sooner," he said, apologetically, "but I've been so busy with the investigation."

"Oh, Eric." Faye waved away his concern. "Of course. I can't even imagine. The fact you even texted me…it was well above the call of duty."

"You were my first thought," he said, shaking his head, distraught. "Honestly, Faye. It just kills me what happened. It makes me so damn angry. These bastards, coming to our town."

"I know. It's horrible."

"And I just—" he placed both hands on her arms "—I've just been so damn worried about you."

"Can you stay for a while?" She twisted back towards the counter where the teakettle lived. "Or can I get you something? A snack…or maybe a cup of magical tea for protection?"

"Actually," Eric said, pulling out something from his pants pocket, "I came to bring you a gift."

"Me?" Faye glanced down to see him holding a tiny velvet bag.

"Well, go on," he said, nudging her. "Open it."

Inside was a stunning piece of black tourmaline.

"Oh, Eric…" Faye touched her heart.

"For safety, right?" Eric had done his research. "And protection."

"This is amazing!"

"So, you like it?"

"It's perfect," she said, moving to kiss him on the cheek. "Just like you."

They were standing awkwardly close to each other, teetering on the balls of their feet, all nervous energy, when Greg appeared from the back studio, holding a bag full of Hillel's poop. "Oh," Faye said, stepping back from Eric, feeling weirdly caught. "Greg! You're here."

Eric squinted, confused. "You...have a visitor?"

"A friend," Faye defended herself.

She wasn't sure why she was suddenly so nervous. Greg was a friend. *Not a boyfriend. Not a golem.* There was no reason for anyone to act strange.

"Greg," Faye said, waving him over. "This is my friend Eric. Remember I told you about him? He's the chief of police here in Woodstock."

Greg jumped in to help with the explanation. "She hit me with her—"

Faye cut him off. "He'll be staying with me for a while."

For once, she wished Greg's language skills weren't developing so rapidly.

"Well," Eric said finally, moving over to Greg, "it's nice to meet you. Any friend of Faye is a friend of mine."

Eric went to shake his hand, but Greg—likely because he hadn't read a book yet on social cues and etiquette, but also because he was holding a bag of Hillel's freshly expelled excrement—stared down at it, awkward and unmoving.

"Okay," Faye said, stepping between them—taking the bag of poop away from Greg in the process. Quickly she tossed the poop in the trash, then washed her hands before returning to the two men and whispering in Eric's direction, "I'll explain later."

Eric's chin dipped back, clearly confused. Faye tried to steer the conversation back to the investigation. "Eric was just stopping by to check on me," she explained to Greg. She was talking so quickly, unsure why her words were going full-speed. "He's been very busy trying to find the people behind the flyers." She spun back to Eric, attempting to catch her breath. "Please tell me there are leads."

Eric frowned. "It's still an active investigation," he said, placing his hands on his waist, "so unfortunately, I can't go into too many details. But I can tell you what we just sent out in a press release this morning. We believe the flyers are tied to a group called The Paper Boys."

"The Paper Boys?" That name sounded familiar.

"They're an anti-Semitic group that has various cells across the country," Eric explained. "It seems that they've started a cell here in Woodstock and the environs. The FBI has been brought in, and we're doing everything in our power to figure out who these people are…and bring them to justice. But that's really all I can tell either of you for now."

She had no idea what Greg might be thinking, but she knew what she was thinking—this was so much scarier than just flyers. The idea that there was a group, *radicals*, that necessitated an entire federal investigation, wasn't just dreadful. It felt unbelievably unfair. Surreal, even.

She had spent her whole life feeling unsafe. And now, despite all her best efforts to reclaim her power, keep some semblance of control in her life…someone had come along and stolen her sense of security all the same.

"I appreciate you sharing that Eric," she said. "Truly. And I appreciate you taking time out of your busy schedule to come check on me."

"Of course—" Eric said, glancing back towards Greg. "Well, if there's nothing else I can help you with around here—"

"Actually," Faye said, an idea forming, "why don't I walk you out to your car?"

Leaving Greg behind in the shop, Faye grabbed a cardigan and followed Eric outside. Pulling her sweater taut against the impending chill, she felt for the black tourmaline she was now carrying in her pocket, and settled on getting to the heart of the matter.

"So," Faye said gently, "I should probably explain about that." Eric played coy. *"About?"*

"Greg," she said simply. "The red elephant in the room."

She was concerned that Eric would think she and Greg were

dating. They weren't dating. Obviously. But having moved a stranger into her home, and business, she didn't want her friend, but especially her ally the chief of police, to get the wrong idea. Especially since Faye had told Eric two years earlier that she preferred to remain single, thus ending any chance of romance between them.

Beyond the personal reasons for following him outside, there were also practical matters to contend with. Eric was a police officer. He might have insight, and information, that could offer some clues to Greg's mysterious past.

She began to explain the situation, telling him about hitting Greg, learning he had amnesia, bringing him home, nursing him back to health.

Eric listened intently, patiently, his face surprisingly devoid of any trace of shock or disbelief. She imagined it was a skill that came with years of police work—the ability to remain cool and collected, no matter what *meshugana* story he was hearing.

"I was just wondering," Faye asked, hopeful for good news, "if you've heard anything. If anyone has reported a missing red-headed giant in Woodstock? Or, if something has come over your police channels? If he looks familiar..."

Eric considered the question. "Unfortunately, no," he said, thumbing his lower lip. "And I definitely would have noticed a missing person's report come in, especially with everything that's been going on in Woodstock lately regarding The Paper Boys. But we've also had a lot of strangers coming to town recently—federal agents, folks from the Anti-Defamation League, journalists. I suppose it's possible he could be one of them."

"And would there be any way to check if maybe he was one of these people?"

"Not really." Eric frowned. "Feds don't exactly share information with local police departments, especially during active investigations. Same thing with journalists. They usually keep a pretty low profile. ADL, though... I can put a few calls in.

But I imagine someone working in a nonprofit would have noticed if one of their people had gone missing."

"Right." She pressed her lips together. "It is strange, though, right? That no one has come to claim him yet. That he just randomly appeared here without explanation. I mean, it's been almost a week, and not one person in the world is looking for him? Not some friend, family member, or even an employer? It seems unbelievable."

Eric crossed his arms against his chest. "There is another option, of course."

Hope filled up her chest. "Yes?"

Eric spoke pointedly. "It's a con, Faye."

"What?" She blinked, surprised. "No…"

"You were a lawyer, right?" he asked. Clearly, the question was rhetorical. "So, let's lay out the facts of the case. He jumps in front of your bike."

Faye corrected him. "I hit him with my bike."

"And then," Eric continued, counting off the evidence with his fingers, "he has no ID on him, nobody knows who he is, you get to the hospital, and this man, this total stranger…conveniently happens to have amnesia. And then, with you feeling all types of guilty, he begs you to bring him home. He basically gives you no option but to bring him home."

"His doctors didn't seem to think he was faking his condition."

"And now he's living with you," Eric said. "Freeloading off you, I might add…and surprise, surprise, no one has come to claim him. Has he even expressed an interest in figuring out who he is?"

"Well, no…but he only started being able to put cohesive sentences together recently."

Eric shook his head. "You're too nice, Faye."

"I just… I find it hard to believe that this is all an act."

"Look," Eric said gently. "Let's say that everything this Greg guy told you turns out to be true. Is this really the right time in your life to be inviting strange men into your home? There's so much happening right now in Woodstock. There's so much going on with The Paper Boys. The flyers are likely just the beginning. Don't you think you should reserve space in your life, in your apartment, especially…for a man that you actually know and trust?"

Her eyes fell to the cement sidewalk. That was the thing. She trusted Greg. Since their first meeting in the hospital, he had given her no reason not to trust him. And yet, she couldn't deny that Eric had made some good points. Perhaps she had been naive, given into magical thinking—*allowed herself to believe Greg was some sort of golem*—when there was a far more logical option.

"So, what do I do?" Faye asked, throwing her hands up. "Other than hiding all my checkbooks and credit cards, obviously."

"I have an idea," Eric said suddenly. "Why don't you bring him by the police station?"

Faye balked. *"The police station?"*

"Sure," he said, breezy and casual. "We can run some prints. See if this guy has a record. Once we get them back, and providing he's in our system, it should be easy to figure out where he came from…and what his true intentions are."

"How long does that normally take?"

"Usually, twenty-four to forty-eight hours. But I've heard if you know someone in the department—" he nudged her playfully "—maybe like the chief of police, we could probably get it done in a few hours."

"Right. I should have known."

A dreary wind worked its way through her body. It was a good idea, bringing him down to the police station, letting them use their channels to figure out who he actually was. Still, something about it wasn't sitting entirely right with Faye. Greg was her friend. In their limited time together, he had given her no reason to distrust him. It seemed wrong to drag your friend down to a police station and run their prints.

Unless he wasn't her friend at all. Maybe his sweet nature—*like reading all her books*—was part of the con. Perhaps Greg wanted her to fall for him, drop her guard, so he could empty her bank accounts, and take off for the next mark.

She couldn't believe she had been so naive.

"I'll talk to him," Faye said finally.

"Good," Eric said. "In the meantime, you have my cell phone number. You call me…first sign of trouble, okay? Better yet, call me before there's any trouble. I'll be right over."

She nodded and hugged him again.

Faye waited for Eric to depart fully, taking off in his police cruiser, before turning back to her store. Entering inside, she resigned herself to laying down the law. *She was not going to be the target for some criminal.*

"Greg?" Faye called out. "Can I speak with you for a—"

His head appeared from behind the counter. "Hey."

"Oh." She blinked, surprised to see him at the refrigerator. "What are you doing?"

"Getting you more ice," he said, holding up the bag she had been using for her wrist. "It was…melting."

Her willpower faltered. Her heart twisted. He was so thoughtful. *Or he was a con man, trying to win her over.* Truth be told, she wasn't entirely certain.

"Why?" she asked, her voice unsteady.

"Because," Greg said simply, "you took…care of me."

She felt her heart being squeezed between two impulses. The fear that he would hurt her sitting beside the desire to keep him close.

But Eric was right. She needed to get back to her life. The life she had built. The life she had designed, free from vulnerability, with high walls and clear boundaries—a sanctuary for the terra-cotta soldier that lived inside of her—but when she tried to have the conversation with Greg, it was Faye who couldn't find the words.

EMBRACING YOUR EGGSHELLS
Real-Life Wisdom for Adult Children
by Dr. Jenna T. Bray

Page 16

What is an adult child? An adult child is any adult who has grown up in a dysfunctional or toxic home environment where the primary caregiver could not fulfill the child's need for love, stability, or safety.

As an adult child, you likely grew up feeling unsafe. Your house was always tumultuous, the love of your parents uncertain. The trauma you experienced as a child continues to play out in your adult relationships. Even when you are aware of such patterns, you find yourself engaging in the same roles of your childhood—you acquiesce, you feel guilty standing up for yourself, you have a need for extreme perfectionism—all in an effort to prove that you are worthy of the parental love that was withheld from you as a child.

You deserve to be with people who bring out the softness in you. You deserve to be in relationships where you are safe, where you have clear boundaries, and they are respected. You deserve to be in relationships where your needs are met. But first, you must untangle the unhealthy knots that have bound you to these patterns.

ELEVEN

It was the same nightmare she always had.

Faye was back in the house she grew up in in Passaic, New Jersey. The cramped detached row house, whose lawn was always too high and blinds always closed tight. Lost inside, she pressed her hands up against dusty walls, traversing a maze of never-ending hallways, trying to get out, trying to escape…all while her mother's voice, demanding and terrifying, screeched for Faye to come find her.

She awoke in a cold sweat, her wrist hurting.

Anxiety coursed through every cell in her body. All the feelings of her childhood, all that chaotic and consistent trauma, returned in full force. Despite her bravado, she felt exposed. Vulnerable. She swore she could hear someone, *something dangerous*, shifting about down the hall. She was going to throw up.

Tossing off her covers, she sprinted from her bedroom, down the hall and to the bathroom. She was so mired in her own fear, in staving off yet another nocturnal panic attack, that she barely even noticed Greg, still awake at the end of the hallway, reading a book. Hillel resting patiently on the windowsill above the pullout bed.

Locking the bathroom door, she double-checked that it was secure behind her, jiggling the handle erratically, before turning on the sink in her bathroom, letting it run ice-cold. She put her whole face beneath the freezing water. The shock on her skin, the feeling of it stinging her cheeks, brought her back to reality.

Lifting from the water, she grabbed a towel, leaning back on the bathroom wall. She reminded herself these feelings were not *real* feelings. They were memories, words etched onto an epitaph somewhere, triggered in the wake of an anti-Semitic attack. *And Greg possibly being a criminal.* She couldn't help but think it.

She also couldn't believe she had ever thought he was a golem.

She stood there, feeling numb—escaping into the familiar safety of her own dissociative tendencies—when Greg knocked on the door.

"Faye?" Greg called out.

She'd been in the bathroom with the water running for several minutes, and he was worried that she had full-on drowned in there.

When she didn't answer, he knocked again. "You...okay?"

Still, no answer.

He stepped back from the door, and a new type of tickle appeared in his chest. "Faye!" The words came out strong and clear. "If you don't answer me right now, I'm coming in."

No response. He peeled up the sleeves of his T-shirt, ready to charge shoulder-first into the wood. Finally, the water turned off.

Faye opened the door and looked up at him with a half-hearted smile. "That was a very good sentence."

He considered her statement. "Must have been...the nerves."

"Nerves?" she asked, curiously.

"I was...worried about you."

He suddenly understood the tickle, the anxiety for her safety, because it went away at the sight of her safe. And yet, looking at her before him, he got the feeling that something was wrong.

Her cheeks were flushed. The tips and edges of her hair, along with the top of her nightgown, were soaked through. Her nipples—two perfect little stones—were erect and visible beneath the drenched material.

"I didn't mean to worry you," Faye said. "I had a bad dream. A nightmare, actually."

He angled his head curiously. "But why are you all wet?"

"Sometimes," she explained, stepping out into the hall one inch, "the water helps me calm down. Or, in the very least, keeps the feelings associated with the nightmare from getting worse."

He didn't like seeing her afraid. He didn't like hearing that her dreams were so bad, she had to practically drown herself in the bathroom sink to stave off the negative feelings. Granted, he didn't know all of Faye's backstory, but it seemed to him that she was such a good person. Unique, with a type of fearless courage that came from trusting your gut that he couldn't help but admire. She deserved better than to spend all night being terrorized by specters.

He wanted to tell her these things, but he noticed a shiver run through her body.

"Let me get you a robe," Greg said.

Faye nodded. "That would be great."

Quickly he made his way to her bedroom. Grabbing the robe off a hook by the door, he returned to her, helping her slink her arms through. When another shiver passed through her, he rubbed his hands up and down the length of her form—her ample and beautiful body—before bringing her over to his makeshift bed.

From there, he grabbed the extra blanket she always left him, laying it on her legs. He pulled apart her modular vase, creating a glass, then went to the kitchen to pour her a cup of warm water.

"Here," he said, handing it to her.

She drank. "Thank you."

Her hands were shaking. Greg sat down beside her, and the room fell into silence once more. Her eyes drifted towards nothing, landing in darkness, spacing out. Greg thought back to the book he was reading.

"Do you…have them a lot?"

Faye returned from wherever she was. "What?"

"The nightmares," he said.

She shifted in her seat. "I used to get them a lot, but not as much since moving to Woodstock. I guess… I've just had a lot on my mind recently. Between the flyers, and…well, other things."

He couldn't help but get the sense that he was the *other thing*.

"What was it about?" he asked. "The nightmare."

"Honestly, it's always the same dream for me. I'm in the house where I grew up in New Jersey. But it's not actually my house. Instead, it's just this horrible fun house maze…and my mother is calling my name."

"Your mother?" Greg didn't understand. "Shouldn't that be a good dream then?"

"Not for me."

He looked down to see her rolling her wrist.

"Is your wrist hurting?" he asked.

"Hm?" she asked.

"You were…stretching it out, I guess."

"Oh." She stared down at her own left hand. "I didn't even realize."

Faye often talked about her father. He came up in bits and pieces during their last few days together, such as the tradition of eating hard kosher salami, or being there for him when he was dying. And yet, having become more aware of the relationships missing in his own life...he noticed the ones missing from hers.

"You don't...talk about your mom a lot."

"My mom was sick," she said quietly.

"Sick." Greg tugged on his ear, wanting to understand. "Like your dad?"

"No." She pulled the blanket closer to her. "Sick, in her mind."

Greg still didn't completely understand. Faye tried to explain.

"The truth is," she continued, "my mom never stayed in therapy long enough to get one clear diagnosis...or any help for her disease. But she would get angry. There were times when she could be kind, where she could be loving, where she could act totally normal... But then, she would go through these episodes, tearing through the house, yelling and screaming. That's how I broke my wrist. She was holding on to it, dragging me down the hallway. I just was...never safe growing up. Never protected. By anybody."

His heart ached at her words. He couldn't imagine how someone who was supposed to love you, and protect you, could be so cruel.

"You know," she said, shaking her head, "the worst part about my mom is that she didn't just disable me physically. She disabled me emotionally, too. My whole life—even when I've gone to therapy, changed my entire life by moving to Woodstock, staved off love for my own protection—I've never been completely free. I'm just the by-product of her choices, this person she made me. I think that's what hurts the most. She changed me. I was someone else once, someone whole and unbroken, and then she made choices—cruel choices, totally unnecessary choices—because she couldn't control herself, her rage, and her anger. And those choices changed the person I was meant to become. That woman...ruined me."

He couldn't help but think back to her pottery, the way she was always complaining it wasn't good enough, perfect enough...that it wasn't worthy of being loved or valued. He couldn't help but sense that she treated herself in the same way.

"Where is she now?" Greg asked.

"Florida." Faye shrugged. "I check in on her every now and then, do my due diligence as her daughter, make sure the Medicaid is going through in the assisted living center where she lives. Occasionally, I'll even call her on a holiday. Rosh Hashanah. Yom Kippur. Maybe one day I'll even get that apology. But otherwise, we don't have a relationship. It's not healthy for me to have a relationship with her."

Greg nodded, and thought back to the book he had been reading. "You deserve to be with people who bring out the softness in you."

Faye blinked. "What?"

He continued. "You deserve to be in relationships where you're safe. Where you have clear boundaries, and they are respected. You deserve to have your needs met. But first, you must untangle the unhealthy knots that have bound you to these patterns."

Her lower lip fell to the floor. A look of shock spread across her face. And then her eyes darted over to the nightstand, where the book *Embracing Your Eggshells* was sitting open. Reaching back, she grabbed it, opening to the same page he had been on when he had put it down.

"You were reading this book?" she asked.

Greg answered honestly. "I thought it was about making breakfast."

For the first time that evening, she laughed. Seeing her relax made his heart happy, before she angled her head sideways. "And you remembered all that?" Faye squinted. "Just from reading it tonight? You remember these words?"

"You highlighted it."

Indeed, she had covered the words in a yellow marker, scribbling notes all over the side like *REMEMBER THIS* and *SCREW STUART!!!* Greg had no idea who *Stuart* was, but he decided to obey her command. He committed those words to his memory.

It wasn't all that difficult. For one, his mind was currently functioning like a sieve. Without a memory, he had plenty of space to fill up with the magic of books. Plus, he had been eating a lot of baladur cakes. Mostly, however, he valued his relationship with Faye. If the words were important to her, then of course they were important to him.

"Who's Stuart, by the way?" Greg asked curiously.

Faye seemed confused. "Stuart."

"His name was—"

She cut him off. "I don't want to talk about Stuart."

He left the conversation at that.

Faye returned to staring down at his book. "It's actually kind of remarkable that you can do that, though. Remember what you read so succinctly." She shook her head. "Most people don't have that type of eidetic memory."

Eidetic. He liked the word. But also, he couldn't help but notice how those beautiful and soft lips had morphed back into a concerned frown.

"Is that a problem?" he asked seriously.

"Not necessarily."

"But you seem…worried."

"It's just," she stammered, "I'm concerned that you're not actually remembering things, developing back to your original personality—whatever that was—but just becoming a repository of my books. It's great that your aphasia is diminishing…

but the whole point of bringing you here was to help you remember your past, get you home."

Home.

He thought back to the families he had met when they visited Magic Mud Pottery, and his heart returned to that strange place between an ache and a fear.

"Actually," Faye said, shifting in the seat closer to him, "Eric did offer us another option."

"Another option?"

"We could go down to the police station, run your prints… find out if you have a record."

She began to explain. If he had a record, if he had done something bad—*not really bad, obviously, she didn't believe all that*—just something as simple as not paying a bunch of speeding tickets… "Then the police might have your real name and real address on file. Wouldn't that be great, Greg? We could figure out who you are…and just like that, you could go home."

It sounded like a reasonable next step, but he was having difficulty agreeing.

"Eric is your friend?" Greg said quietly.

"Yes." Faye nodded. "Eric is my friend."

"And you trust him?"

"I trust him, completely."

"But," Greg said, meeting her eyes directly, "he doesn't have a red bracelet."

She cocked her head sideways. "What?"

"A red bracelet." He lifted his left wrist to remind her. The red string dangling there, connected to his heart, connecting him to Faye. "If Eric is your friend, and you trust him…why doesn't he have one?"

She swallowed. "I guess…because you're special."

Their eyes met, and an electric tension filled the room. A flicker of desire passed through him, and he wanted to kiss her.

He wanted to take these swirling, breathless feelings and find refuge in her own heady craving.

And yet he couldn't kiss her.

Because Greg didn't know who he was.

He could have people out there that he had forgotten—a wife, maybe even children—and his mind wandered back to the book he was reading. If he wanted a better future, he had to untangle the knots of his past.

"Okay," Greg said finally.

Faye blinked, surprised. "Really?"

"Yeah." He forced a smile. "Let's go…figure out who I am."

She threw her arms around him in a tight embrace. And he held her there, her warmth pressing against his own, the scent of her filling his nostrils, causing those pleasurable feelings, alongside the rising tide of questions, to work their way through his body once more.

Faye locked the door to her bedroom.

She had done it. She had talked to Greg about going down to the police station, running his prints. It gave her some small measure of relief. If Greg was a con man, he was about to be found out. And if he was simply a man with amnesia, one who was beginning to tear down her walls and work his way into her heart…

Honestly, she didn't want to think about that option.

But she could hear her own heart beating wildly inside her chest. It sounded like some siren song, a sea Gorgon tempting men to her shorelines before turning them all to stone. It was lonely being a monster. Until finally, crawling into bed that evening, she found herself wondering—would living with a golem really be that bad?

TWELVE

Faye sat on the bench in the lobby of the police station and tried not to appear nervous. Greg was somewhere in the back room with Eric getting his fingerprints taken, and it was taking *forever*.

In the process of waiting, her mind wandered. She envisioned Greg, the con man, sneaking around Magic Mud Pottery while she was sleeping, opening a dozen credit cards in her name. She imagined that Greg was innocent of all charges, but that the fingerprint analysis had revealed his identity. She foresaw his family arriving to Magic Mud Pottery, his perfect wife, his four beautiful redheaded children…before her mind drifted to having sex with Greg. His hands trailing her body. His massive form on top of her as he plunged an equally impressive beast into her willing body…

Seeing someone walk by, she resigned herself to less steamy thoughts. It had all been a fantasy, anyway.

Finally, Eric emerged from a hallway. Greg wasn't with him. Faye rose from her seat.

"Well," Eric said, finally. "I have good news and bad news."

Faye frowned. "What does that mean?"

"The good news is—" Eric paused dramatically "—that your friend Greg appears to be totally clean. He has no record, at all. Clean as a whistle. Spotless record, in fact. Not even an unpaid parking ticket."

Faye could hardly contain her excitement. "That's great news!"

She no longer had to worry about going home and closing all her bank accounts.

"Now, before you get too excited," Eric said, "I want to be clear on something. The fact he has no record doesn't mean he's not a criminal. It only means he hasn't been caught, yet. You understand the difference, right? He could still have bad intentions towards you, your business…your livelihood."

"I understand," she said swiftly.

"But otherwise—" he shrugged and threw his hands up "—I have no idea who he is."

"Wait," she said, shaking her head. "Does that mean…"

"He's not in any file. I even went back and ran his information through a few lesser-known databases, and nothing. I'm sorry, Faye. I was really hoping I could help you out on this one. Get this Greg character out of your hair. But unfortunately, I've exhausted the channels I have available here."

The entire police station began to spin around her. Because it didn't make sense. Surely, Greg must have been in the system somewhere. One of those childhood programs run in the eighties to fingerprint children in case they went missing. A new fear arose, which quickly replaced any thought of Greg being a con man.

He was a golem.

The evidence formed like a lineup inside her mind. His red

hair. His perfect freaking body. The way he did chores and assisted with her magical rituals. The fact he had no history, no backstory, no memory. Because he wasn't a man, at all, but some supernatural creature she had summoned from some other dimension…a creature that would eventually come to destroy her and everything she loved.

Yet even as she thought these things, she realized how absolutely batshit absurd it all sounded inside her brain.

Because golems didn't exist.

They were folklore. Fiction. Just some made-up Jewish story. She was being ridiculous, seeing monsters where there were none, turning into her mother. Her hand wandered up to her mouth, where she began to chew on one finger, a nervous habit she had developed in childhood to self-soothe when her mother couldn't meet her needs. Now, as an adult, it appeared during times of high stress. She needed to get a damn grip.

"So, what do I do now?" she said, half talking to herself.

"I suppose you still have options," Eric said, listing them off. "You could start investigating who he is yourself. Put out flyers. Ask around town. See if anyone knows him. I'm happy to also put out some feelers on my end, too."

She stopped chewing on herself. "I would appreciate that, Eric."

"But, Faye." He rubbed the back of his neck. "I don't mean to overstep any boundaries here, and I appreciate that you hit this guy with your bike and you felt you owed him something… but don't you think you've done enough for Greg at this point? Don't you think it would be better for both of you if you just hand him off to a social worker?"

It would be better for her, definitely.

But it wouldn't be better for him.

She placed herself in his massive size thirteen shoes.

He deserved better than to be treated like a criminal. *Or a golem.* He was a decent, and kind, *human being* who deserved to be protected. Everyone deserved to know that someone in this world would have their back.

She wouldn't leave him.

Even though she knew that eventually, he would leave her.

"Where's Greg now?" she asked.

"In the back," Eric said, pointing towards double doors.

"Does he know?"

"I told him the basics," Eric admitted.

Her heart broke for him. She imagined Greg sitting somewhere, all alone, wondering where he was, wondering when he would be able to go home. All at once, she forgot about him being a golem and simply wanted to go to him.

"I really appreciate your help today, Eric."

"Of course," he said, touching her arm. "And I'm assuming I'll see you at the Say No to Hate Rally next Sunday?"

"I wouldn't miss it for the world," she said, before adding, "Also, Miranda voluntold me to be there early to help with setup."

"Great," he said, before a flush of red appeared on his cheeks. "Because Shulamit asked me to give a speech, and I was hoping you'd be there. I could use the support, honestly. I'm not exactly a guy who likes to be the center of attention."

"Oh, Eric." Faye touched her heart. "Of course I'll be there."

They hugged, and his arms lingered around her. She found herself breathing him in, grateful for his friendship, for his protection. The affection she had for him felt both stable and real, and she began to wonder if she had been wrong, all those years before, rejecting Eric and his advances...before she pulled away from him, and went to collect Greg.

Greg didn't feel great that afternoon.

Sitting on a bench outside a series of offices within the police station, he stared up at the fluorescent light blinking annoyingly above him. He wasn't sure what it was about the last four hours that had made him feel so off-kilter. Only that he felt raw. Like turning the water too hot before getting in the shower, it scalded him.

He still didn't know who he was.

In his four hours of waiting, he had grown hopeful. He had come to believe that Eric, these helpful police people, would solve the mystery of his story. Instead, it was even worse news. The fingerprints they had taken had not yielded one single clue.

But now, there were new words in his head. Words he had not learned from Faye or her books, but from Eric. Like the possibility of Greg being a con man. Like the way Eric mentioned, more than once, that he and Faye had dated. And even though Eric kept smiling at Greg—promising all the ways they would "get this thing sorted"—nothing about their interactions in the back of the police station felt friendly.

Maybe she didn't tell him because she felt he wouldn't understand. He couldn't blame her. After all, he couldn't remember if he had ever been in love. Or engaged. Heck, he couldn't even remember if he'd ever had sex.

He assumed he had, based on the instinctual feelings that arose inside him whenever Faye was around, but without knowing for certain, he felt almost like a nonentity. *A non-person.* The whole world had a past. They had people who cared about them and loved them. But sitting on a police bench surrounded by strangers, Greg had never felt more alone.

He didn't know what to do, or where to go next, when he saw Faye coming down the hall. She was wearing a surprisingly wide smile, practically beaming, which should have made him happy. It usually made him happy. But he just couldn't seem to work his way out of the pit he had found himself at him. Everything felt dark. Dank. *Depressing.* That was the word. He thought about giving up.

Faye must have understood, though. She always somehow managed to intuit his deeper meaning—because her feet slowed upon approach. The carefree smile she was wearing faded entirely. She sat down on the bench beside him, and a long silence settled between them.

"I'm sorry," she said.

The knot in his stomach caused him to choke. "Yeah."

"I can't even imagine," she said, shaking her head. "I can't even imagine how disappointed you are right now."

"I thought maybe…maybe I would find someone…"

Greg swallowed, trying to find the words. But this time, there were just too many floating around inside of him. There wasn't a way to take this intensity of feeling—all the sadness and pain, all the loss that he was experiencing—and boil them down into simple sentences. The frustration he had been dealing with since being diagnosed with amnesia returned, and from there, twisted into hopelessness.

"We're not done fighting, Greg."

"But—"

"Look," she said, taking both his hands inside hers. "I am not giving up, okay? *We* are not giving up. Yes, we're disappointed at the results we found out today. But there's still so much more we can do. Now that you're feeling better, now that your language skills have improved, we can begin becoming more proactive. We can make flyers, talk to people around town… We're going to get you home, Greg. We are absolutely going to find your family. This isn't the end…this is just an early chapter in a very long book."

He met her eyes directly. "A book?"

She nodded. "Old Jewish saying, 'God made man because he loves stories.' And that's all this is, Greg. That's how stories work, with ups and downs, false peaks, and wild climaxes. We took one path, and it led us to a dead end. But we are not at the end of this book, okay? We are just at the beginning of figuring out who you are, and I promise… I will be with you, every step of the way, until that happens."

He believed her. Even though he didn't completely understand her. Even though he still had so many questions, about himself, *about her*, about who he had been and what had brought him to Woodstock, and the way a person can lie to you without speaking any words…

Until all he really wanted was the comfort of one safe place and a person he knew.

"Faye," he said desperately. "Can we go home now?"

She didn't hesitate. She rose from her spot and, searching for her car keys in her pocketbook, twisted towards the exit. "Okay then," she said, as if it were a simple matter. "Let's go home."

"I like this photo where you're smiling," Faye said.

Greg stopped cutting hard kosher salami and glanced back towards Faye. She was sitting at her computer, working hard to finalize the flyers they would be using in their search to identify him. Above an image of him smiling, wide and toothy, were the words, *Do You Know This Man?*

Greg cocked his head sideways. "You don't think I look… weird?"

"Weird?" Faye asked curiously. "No. Not at all."

He couldn't help but think it. Staring at the image of himself on the screen, his mouth seemed far too wide for his face. Like someone had built a six-foot fence between his ears. He never realized how many teeth he had. "Maybe," Greg offered up, "I'm just not used to…looking at myself."

Upside, it seemed his language skills were getting better. He still had occasional pauses in his speech, but he had moved on to almost full sentences and complete thoughts without too much problem. The books were helping. The baladur cakes, too, it seemed. And Faye. He wouldn't be doing half as well as he was without her serving as his caregiver.

"Hm," Faye said, and then exchanged the photograph with another image. This time his lips were closed, pressed together in a thin line. The lines on his forehead furrowed intensely in the direction of the lens. "Well, what about this one?" Faye asked.

He couldn't help but compare himself to the mug shots he had seen all over the walls of the police station. "I look...scary."

"You do not," Faye exclaimed, before on second thought grimacing in the direction of the computer. "You know what, let's just stick with the one where you're smiling."

"Good call."

Faye returned to her flyers, while Greg finished making dinner. Bringing over a charcuterie board full of hard kosher salami, he knew he had fixed the meal just the way Faye liked it. With rye bread, and two types of mustard—one grainy but sweet, one spicy enough to burn the skin off the roof of your mouth. He preferred the spicy one himself.

"Oh," Faye said, as he slid down next to her. "You didn't have to do all that."

"You were busy."

"I know," she said, gathering up items to make a small sandwich. He watched her pop one into her mouth before her eyes went wide. "You know what would go great with this right now?" He didn't know. "Wine." She ate another piece of salami.

"Do you...have?"

"Oh," she said, wiggling her fingers towards the front closet. "I have five boxes of the best and most expensive kosher red wine overwhelming my front closet. Haven't seen the floor of that closet in three years, in fact."

Greg didn't understand. "So, why don't you drink it?"

"It's a long story. Complicated, too. I did break into the stash recently, but that was a whole drama. I'm taking it as a sign from the universe that I should never drink again."

Her cheeks flushed red.

"They were from my wedding," she said quietly. "A few years back, I was engaged to be married."

He thought back to the name scribbled all over her self-help books. "Stuart?"

"Stuart," she admitted, and popped another piece of salami into her mouth.

She went on to explain it. How they had been together for seven years. How he had dumped her on a snowdrift in Lapland. How she had come back to their shared apartment in Manhattan to find he had absconded completely.

"He left me to call everyone, you know?" Faye said, shaking her head. "All two hundred and twenty-six guests…and tell them that the wedding was off. And every single one of them asking the questions, 'Why? Why, Faye? What did you do wrong? What happened?'"

She shivered, as if the memory still injured her. And it broke Greg's heart. Faye deserved so much better than to be betrayed by all those people she loved.

"Anyway," she said, returning to herself, "it's been three years, and I know, I know… I should either drink the wine, or give it away. But, for whatever reason, I can't seem to let go of it. I suppose that's always been my downfall in life. I hold on to people who should be let go."

Greg had heard enough. If Faye wanted wine, he was going to get her some.

"What are you doing?" Faye asked.

"Getting you wine."

He went to the front closet, opened it up…

Haman's hat.

Faye hadn't been kidding. He could barely make out the coats and jackets shoved haphazardly behind five large wine crates.

"I know," Faye said, burying her head in her hands. "It's a disaster zone."

"Only one way to fix that then."

He reached in and pulled out a bottle of wine before waving it in her direction. Faye lifted her head. "You know what," she said, finally. "You're right. Let's drink some damn wine!"

The next bit, Faye had to help him with. Finding her way to a drawer in the counter, she pulled out a strange-looking torture device. "Wine opener," she explained, and then showed him how to use it. The cork popped open, and Faye went to pour two glasses.

"Sniff," she said, bringing it up to her lips, "and sip."

"Sniff and sip," he repeated.

Greg took a sip. It was good. Kind of acrid-tasting, though. He much preferred her magical teas. But when he looked over, Faye had her eyelids closed in sheer delight. "Oh God," she said, slumping into her chair. "I forgot how good that was."

"You like red wine?" he asked, sitting back down beside her.

"This isn't just any red wine," she said. "This is basically the best kosher red wine that money can buy. It was going to be a *really* nice wedding. What do you think of it?"

He stared down at his glass. "Okay."

"You must have been a beer drinker," she said. She put her glass of red to the side, nodding to the salami. "You're not hungry?"

"Actually," he said, treading carefully, "I was hoping to talk to you about something."

"That sounds awfully serious."

He nodded. "Why did you think I was a con man?"

"Oh," she grimaced, "that."

"Eric mentioned it."

He had learned about being clear with your needs in the self-help book he was reading, but he could see by the way splotchy red patches were suddenly forming all over her face that she was feeling under attack. *This was normal with adult children. A form of self-preservation. It was important to make her feel safe.*

"I'm not mad, Faye," he said gently. "I understand. I'm a stranger. I have no…backstory. No history. And based on what you have shared with me regarding your mother, and your ex-fiancé, I understand the need to protect yourself. You have a right to protect yourself, to ask questions, to ask me anything you would like. But I would like to know…if there is a way I could make you feel safer."

She was quiet for a long time. "I don't think so."

He nodded, affirming her feelings. "Still, I would like to try."

"I know."

Silence passed between them, before Hillel—waking up from his nap—finally tapped down the stairs. Greg gave the little guy a snack, and then the dog settled himself on the couch to watch Faye and Greg continue their conversation.

"He really does like you," Faye said quietly.

"I like him."

Her eyes floated back to his. They drifted there together. Until finally, Faye felt safe enough to share her story with him. "I didn't actually think you were a con man until Eric showed up and put the thought into my mind. Honestly, my biggest concern when we first met was that you were the person who left the flyers."

"And that would be bad."

"That would be very bad," she admitted. "There's no room in my home or my business for anti-Semites." He made a mental note of this fact. "But then, we were getting along, having no problems. You were so perfect, and wonderful—"

He caught on the word. "You think I'm perfect?"

She shifted. Stopped. "More perfect than me."

She always did that. Put herself down. He swore, she was incapable of accepting a compliment. It was like holding up a mirror to someone, telling them all the ways they are beautiful, only to have them say *see*…then point out each flaw, line, and scar.

"I like who you are, Faye."

She scoffed, like she didn't believe him. "How do you do that?"

"What?"

"Always manage to say the right thing."

He considered her question honestly. "I read your self-help books."

She laughed outright. The room fell silent once again, and he was suddenly fully aware of the heat in her body, the way her thigh and her arm were pressing up against him. It caused his own skin to flush red with hot desire in return.

"So," Faye said, raising an eyebrow. "What else did Eric tell you?"

"He also mentioned that when you moved to Woodstock... you dated."

"He told you that?"

"Honestly," he rubbed the back of his neck, "it didn't feel very friendly."

"Freaking Eric," she said, shaking her head, "I should put a binding spell on that tongue of his." A silence shifted over the space. "I'm so sorry, Greg. I'm sure Eric didn't mean to make you feel uncomfortable. He must have just assumed...that since you were living here, you were privy to that information. I'm sure it was just an honest mistake."

He wanted to believe her, but there was still something about Eric that rubbed Greg the wrong way.

"I'm grateful for your honesty, and clarity," Greg said. "And for what you have shared with me so far. I hope that one day, you'll feel comfortable enough...to share the rest of your story, too. I know we're focused on figuring out who I am, but I would like to understand you better. In the meantime, I will continue doing what I can...to make sure you feel safe."

Her eyes softened. "I appreciate that, Greg."

He became aware of how close they were sitting. How their legs and their arms—even their breaths, the pace of their chests shifting up and down—moved in perfect rhythmic timing with each other, until his eyes wandered from a freckle sitting at the roundest bit of her cleavage and up to her lips.

The urge appeared again, to kiss her, to take her in his arms, to feel her body pressed up against his, two souls merging. An ache so strong, so powerful inside of him, he found himself leaning forward. Faye did the same, one hand landing on the top of his thigh, causing that flash of desire to turn into a full-kiln burn...

Hillel dropped his chunk of hard kosher salami onto the floor. With one loud *kerplunk*, followed by a scramble off the couch to save his treat, the spell was broken. Faye quickly shifted back to her computer screen, adjusting her hair, her dress... while Greg stood up, and just as speedily adjusted himself.

"I suppose we should get back to these flyers," Faye squeaked, her voice trilling into a high pitch nervously.

"Right," Greg said, looking at the ceiling. "Flyers. Anything else I need to do?"

"Nope," she said, her eyes pinned to the monitor. "Tomorrow, we'll start handing them out around town, beginning our investigation. Just like one of those detectives in my crime novels. Samantha Beacher always solves the case, you know? And in this case, we already know you're not a criminal. We know you're not a bad guy...so, we're making good progress. Great progress, in fact! No doubt, we will get you out of here...and back home in no time."

She wasn't looking at him. Greg took the hint. Her walls firmly erected once again—the near-kiss between them rightfully interrupted. He left Faye to finish the flyers while he headed upstairs to start a new book. Because he needed to take his mind off Faye, and the heat still raging unquenched in his body, and because only a man with a past could have a future with a woman.

LIE TO ME
A Samantha Beacher Mystery

Page 16

The bodies had been discovered by a maid.

Samantha Beacher stood at the edge of the crime scene, her eyes trailing past the bloody footprints, towards the room where the bodies of Mr. and Mrs. Blecher—beloved parents, upstanding business leaders, generous philanthropists—lay bludgeoned to death. Their eight-year-old daughter, Missy, was missing.

"Pretty gnarly, right?" Cass, her friend and head of forensics, appeared beside her.

"Did you look in their mouths?" Sam asked, ignoring the obvious.

Cass blinked, confused. "Their mouths?"

"For the rest of the message…"

She had spent years in therapy to avoid bringing her own trauma to a crime scene. The emotions could easily cloud her judgment on a case, but now, the coffee she had drunk on the way over turned inside her stomach.

Moving on instinct, she grabbed a pair of vinyl gloves from a box. Bending down to Mrs. Blecher, opening her mouth, she dug one hand past her teeth, and tongue, till her fingers were into her esophagus. Finally, she felt the tiny paper edge of a wing, pulling out a small origami swan.

"It can't be," Cass gasped.

Sam opened the swan. Inside, the killer had written the words RE-MEMBER ME.

Sam had been assigned to hundreds of murder investigations, but this one was the first case since being a rookie to make her hands shake. She knew this butcherer. Intimately. There was no doubt in her mind that this was the handiwork of the Origami Killer.

The only thing she didn't understand was how. The man who had murdered her own parents, then kept her chained inside a dark cell for nine days, had been executed ten years before.

"Get a photo of that," Sam said, tossing it down to the floor.

She removed her gloves, glancing down at her watch. It was seven thirty on a Monday morning. The house had been empty all weekend. Missy Blecher only had five more days to live. Sam wasn't going to waste any more time. Leaving the forensics to Cass, she turned to exit the Blecher estate.

"Where are you going?" Cass called after her.

"I'll call you later," she said.

A child was missing, after all, and the clock was ticking. And Sam had learned twenty years earlier—chained up in the prison of a sick and twisted deviant beneath the Earth—that the only way to solve a mystery was to unravel it piece by piece.

THIRTEEN

If Samantha Beacher could do it, so could Greg.

For the next several days, Greg and Faye scoured the downtown environs of Woodstock. They handed out flyers with his photo on them. They went to every coffee shop, gas station, hotel, and gym, and talked to strangers they passed on the street. But despite the myriad of mysteries resolved in the novel he was reading, *Lie to Me*, the only thing Greg had managed to accomplish after all their hours of pounding the pavement together was getting a cramp in his foot.

"Are you sure you don't recognize him?" Faye asked, standing at yet another hotel counter, speaking with the concierge.

"I'm sorry, ma'am." The concierge frowned.

Greg analyzed their latest suspect. He was tall and skinny—totally inconspicuous on the surface, which made Greg immediately think he was guilty of some nefarious crime. It was always the innocent-looking ones in his Sam Beacher novels, the ones you never would suspect, who had basements full of missing children.

"Can you just check one more time for me?" Faye asked.

Greg could hear the despondency in her voice. "Listen, you," Greg said, moving to intervene with a line from his book. "You think I don't realize what you're doing here?"

The desk attendant blinked. "What?"

"I've got your number—" Greg said, his eyes drifting down to young man's name tag. "*Clark*. And you might have everyone around here fooled, but I know what you've been doing, late at night, when you think no one is watching."

Clark swallowed. "I… I… I always wash my hands after."

"Okay!" Faye suddenly interrupted. "I think we've had enough investigating for one day."

Faye grabbed Greg by the arm and, thanking the young concierge for his help, quickly pulled him outside.

"What—" she asked, raising both eyebrows in his direction "—was that?"

Greg shrugged. "It worked in your Samantha Beacher novels."

"Not everything is how it is in books."

"I know that," he admitted, shifting his weight on the balls of his feet. "But I'm feeling a little desperate right now."

The frustration he used to have with speech now reappeared with every dead end. While he could finally express himself fully—only experiencing the occasional glitch—he still had no idea who he was. No one had come for him. No one seemed to recognize him. His memory had not returned, and Greg was losing hope.

Faye chewed on her lower lip. "There is another option."

The charge in his chest returned. "Really? Well, that's great news!"

"Hold on," she said, raising one hand to stop him. He could see she was choosing her words carefully. "There are a few motels on the outskirts of town. I didn't originally mention them because, well... I didn't think you would be staying at them. They're kind of sketchy."

Greg squinted. "Sketchy...how?"

"Like they once found three decapitated bodies in the swamp behind them sketchy."

"That's horrible."

Still, they were running out of ideas. His eyes fell downwards, to the sheet of paper Faye was carrying. They had checked every location on her list, run his fingerprints. They had even taken one of those DNA tests, spitting into a tube before mailing it off to California, to see if Greg had lost relatives somewhere...but they wouldn't get the results back for several weeks.

It felt like an unnaturally long time to a man without a memory.

"I suppose we should get going then," he said finally.

Faye nodded. "I think that's the right call."

The sky twisted into golds and purples around them, dusk settling, as they made their way back to her car. And on the drive beyond town, Greg thought back to the novels he'd been reading. It was always darkest before the dawn. There was always a series of tests and challenges, of growth amid rising stakes, before eventually, the final resolution.

Faye wasn't kidding when she called the stretch of motels beyond town sketchy. Had it not been for a few lone cars, and the sporadic hum of a half-broken neon sign glowing VAC NCY, Greg would have assumed they had all been abandoned.

"We should split up," she said.

"Absolutely not." Greg did not hesitate.

Even if he hadn't been in the middle of devouring yet another Samantha Beacher mystery, serial killers would have still been on his mind. The last thing Greg was going to allow was Faye wandering about this murder trap alone. He had promised her back in the hospital to keep her safe—and after everything she had done for him, he was not about to go back on his word.

"We can cover more ground if we split up."

"No," he replied firmly. "We go together."

"Greg." She said his name with a huff, clearly frustrated. "I appreciate your concern here, but I am a grown woman who can spend fifteen minutes—"

He cut her off. "Samantha Beacher is always getting kidnapped."

Her eyebrows lifted into her forehead. "Samantha Beacher isn't real, Greg! It's just a made-up story, with fun plot twists and wild turns, meant to entertain. You're being ridiculous."

He threw the argument right back at her. "Just because a book is fun and fictional...doesn't mean there's nothing real to learn inside of it. You said it yourself...you have to read everything with a grain of salt. You have to look at the world through a lens of nuance and discernment. Well, here's my grain of salt, Faye. Bad things exist. Bad people, too. You're not getting murdered on my watch."

"I thought we were worried about me getting kidnapped?"

"Faye!"

He did not find her joke funny. He looked over to see her rubbing one eyebrow, a clear sign that she was getting stressed. "Greg," she said, finally. "I appreciate what you're saying...but there is no Origami Killer."

With that, she tore off her seat belt and started down the block. "Meet you back at the car in fifteen minutes," she shouted back at him.

He crossed his arms against his chest, slightly annoyed. It seemed unfair to win an argument by just leaving.

It was pointless.

The first motel yielded no results. Instead, all he managed was to get trapped in a conversation with some old dude—eyebrows like caterpillars—who told him that he had once been possessed by a demon. The second motel was also uneventful. It was padlocked shut and the interior covered in spooky cobwebs.

Finally, he found his way into the last motel on his side of the strip. Upon entering, he was surprised to find it in an almost suitable condition. The lobby was clean, devoid of any strange smell or cockroaches scampering across the counters. The carpeting, a paisley pink-and-mauve print on the floor, had been freshly vacuumed. All the electricity, like the lights in the sign out front and on the ceiling above him, was working.

The only thing that detracted from the entrance was ongoing construction. In the center of the hallway, a young man, wearing oversized jeans splattered with paint, stood on a ladder. A toolbox by his feet, his head was hidden within the open tile of a drop ceiling…and he was talking to himself. Greg approached him.

"It couldn't be a hotel in Miami, right?" splatter-pants said, then banged on a pipe repeatedly. "Not the Fontainebleau in South Beach. Or the Mandarin in Cocoa Bay, right? No, you had to die and leave me this cesspool of bedbugs and bad plumbing to deal with. *I'm leaving you the dream, Shelby.* The dream. Ha!"

"Excuse me?" Greg called out.

"One minute."

Shelby—at least, Greg assumed the man's name was Shelby, based on the conversation he was having with himself—continued ignoring him. Greg glanced over to a clock on the counter. He only had a few more minutes left before he needed to get back to Faye.

"I just need to ask you a quick question," Greg said.

"And I said—" Shelby appeared from beneath the tile "—I'll be with you in a minute."

Shelby disappeared back into the drop ceiling. Greg sighed. Stepped closer. Laying both hands on the ladder, he looked up at the young fellow. "I just need to know if you've ever seen me before?"

"I've seen you," Shelby shouted back.

"You barely even looked at me."

Shelby huffed, and bent down to meet Greg. "Well, let's see," Shelby snarked, waving his wrench around like a wand, "you've got flaming red hair, you've clearly never missed leg day…and you look like some dude who just escaped from a romance novel. So, yeah. I'm positive I've seen you before. Happy?"

Shelby went to dive back into his hidey-hole. This time, Greg had the wherewithal—and apparently, speed—needed to stop him. On instinct, he reached out and grabbed the man's arm, holding him there for the last question.

"Do you happen to have an extra key to my room?"

Shelby rolled his eyes, annoyed. "You lost the key?"

"I've lost a lot of things."

Shelby huffed and considered the request. "Room 13," he said finally. "You can find an extra key on the back wall of my office. Only…take…one."

"Thank you," Greg said, and raced to grab the key.

"And bring it back when you find the other," Shelby shouted, before dipping back into his hole, mumbling between curse words and profanities. "If you haven't noticed, we are not exactly drowning in cash around here!"

Greg made his way towards room 13. A *Do Not Disturb* sign still hung on the knob. He took a deep breath, bracing himself for what he would find inside. Thankfully, upon opening the door, everything seemed normal enough.

The place was tidy and inconspicuous. The bed was made. The trash by the door was empty. There weren't any strange items lying about like a collection of origami animals made from human skin. He was slightly relieved at the innocent nature of what was apparently his room—that Faye was right, that his books were not always situated in reality—when his eyes drifted towards a black leather duffel bag on the floor.

Jackpot.

Heading to the bag, he opened it up, digging his fingers around. But pulling out each item for inspection, all he found was clothes. No photos. No notebooks. Just clothing, which, given the size on the tags, must have belonged to him.

Still, it was progress. He had a room. He had a bag. It must have meant something.

Trying to jog his memory, he brought the clothing up to his nose, inhaling the scent. He hoped it would remind him of some person or place—the place where he had come from—but despite nearly suffocating himself on the material, he came up empty. His mind was a blank. There was nothing.

Giving up on the duffel bag, he decided to focus on the rest of the hotel room. He checked the drawers in the bureau. *Empty.* The closets, too. *Empty.* In the bathroom, a toothbrush, toothpaste, and dental floss lay on the sink counter. But otherwise, the space was devoid of any personality. The only thing Greg could ascertain about his past was that he practiced good dental hygiene.

He supposed it was something.

He turned back towards the door to find Faye, and tell her what he had found…when an instinct came over him. Almost like a whisper, without words, the tingle of a memory. Slowly, he turned back to the bed. And then, bending down on one knee, he ran one hand between the mattress and the box spring, and felt it catch on something. Pulling it out, he found himself staring down at a large manila envelope.

Greg dragged one hand down his face.

Nope, that didn't seem good.

A strange sense of foreboding overcame him. He was torn between the urge to open it up, and the sense that he should just forget about it completely. And yet, he wanted to know the truth about out who he was. He sank down to both knees, opening it, laying out each item, one by one, on the carpet in front of him.

The first was a new phone—a flip phone, in fact—still in its original plastic packaging. He blinked, confused, until a memory from the novel he had been reading returned. This was not a normal phone but *a burner phone*. The type of phone criminals used, because it came with prepaid minutes and could be discarded after use.

His heart sped up inside his chest. *This was not good. Not good at all.* Still, he didn't want to panic. Maybe there was a perfectly logical explanation for a man to be staying in a sketchy hotel, with just a bag full of clothes and a burner phone hidden beneath his mattress…

He returned to that manila envelope, and pulled out a wad of cash.

Okay. That wasn't great, either.

Again, he took a deep breath and tried to remain rational. He reminded himself that Eric had run his fingerprints. The police had checked his identity against countless criminals in their systems, and Greg's had come back clean. *He wasn't a bad guy.* Even with the cash, and the burner phone…it was all still speculation. He had no direct evidence that he had been involved in something nefarious. *Samantha Beacher always needs evidence to solve a crime.*

He tossed the cash to the side and, taking a deep breath, continued. He pulled out the last item, finding it at the very bottom of that manila envelope—and all at once, his heart sank. His world, his life with Faye, came crashing down around him. Because there, hidden inside his hotel room, alongside a burner phone and that wad of cash, was a single anti-Semitic flyer. On the front, written in bright blue ink and circled as if the note was important, were the words,

THE PAPER BOYS—WOODSTOCK, NY

He didn't want to believe it. That he was one of them. *A Nazi. A Paper Boy. A bad guy.* Some hateful and despicable human being, who had come to Woodstock with the goal of spreading vile anti-Semitic propaganda. But the evidence, as he had found it, seemed to suggest that he was...and a physical pain rolled through the center of his chest.

He clutched at his heart, wanting it to stop, but it all began to make sense. Why he had appeared on the day after the flyers. Why Eric had rubbed him the wrong way at the police station, even though Faye was adamant that he meant well.

Why no one from his real life—parents and partners, employers, or friends—had shown up. The realization hit him hard, and all at once. Greg was a found person who, as it turned out, not a single person in the world was missing.

FOURTEEN

Greg stood frozen to the carpet in his motel room, staring down at the flyer. A thousand new words, which he couldn't recall ever learning, floated up into his brain. He was a *skuzz-ball*. An *evildoer*. A *miscreant* and a *malefactor*. He was the worst of humanity. *A Nazi*. A person who spread vile and hateful rhetoric. A *propagandist*.

It felt like the floor beneath his feet had turned to quick-sand. It dragged him down, his head spinning. All at once, he was assaulted by some memory, disjointed sounds and images. *Car horns blaring. Doctors, shining a light into his eyes at the hospital.* And that voice, whispering in his head, *justice, justice…*

The voice was getting louder.

He didn't understand it. But he knew, beyond a shadow of any doubt, that he didn't want to be one of these people—a bad guy. A Paper Boy.

And yet the evidence was overwhelming.

He also needed to get back to Faye. Scrambling to put back the items, Greg hid them beneath his mattress. Leaving that hotel room, he functioned in a daze.

Faye was already waiting in the parking. He was torn between impulses—to tell her the truth, to lie—until his mind wandered back to something Faye had said to him. *There was no room in her life or business for an anti-Semite.*

"So," Faye asked, clapping her hands together. "Any luck?"

"What?" Greg blinked back to reality.

"Did you find out anything juicy?" she asked. "Anything that would make a Samantha Beacher novel look pale in comparison?"

His heart lurched into his throat. He didn't want to lie to her, but he also couldn't very well tell the truth. He was caught in her gaze, in her thick curls swirling around those cherublike cheeks, and she looked so lovely. He thought back on their time together, all the things she had done for him, all the ways she had helped him, the promises they had made to each other—the red string still dangling from his wrist—and he didn't want to hurt her.

He didn't have time to think this plan through. He simply took one look at Faye and decided that whoever he had been in the past no longer mattered. She had changed him, made him a good person. *If he had been a Nazi, he wasn't one anymore.* Now his only desire was to protect her. To keep her safe. *Safe from him, especially.*

"Listen, Faye," Greg said, trying to hide any sign of anxiety. "I appreciate everything you've done for me so far. I really do. Taking me in when I didn't have anywhere to go, nursing me back to health, feeding me all those delicious baladur cakes, teaching me Jewitch magic...but I was thinking about it just now. Maybe it's best you take me to a shelter."

Her chin dipped back. "You're not comfortable on the pull-out couch?"

"It's not that."

"Because we could always switch it up," she offered. "Take turns. I don't mind the—"

"I'm fine on the couch, Faye."

She looked confused.

He was, too.

"Is this because we had a fight?" she asked.

"What are you talking about?"

She attempted to clarify. "I ran off without taking you and your fears seriously."

He had totally forgotten about their fight. In truth, it seemed so spectacularly insignificant now, given what he had learned in the hotel room. Especially because, *plot twist*, it turned out he was the one who was dangerous. He rubbed between his temples, at the spot where a headache was beginning to develop inside of him, and tried to explain again.

"It's not about you, Faye."

"Well, I don't believe that for a minute." She laughed.

"It's not about you."

His eyes caught on hers. And he could see it there, in the depths of them—the way the whites began to water—that he was hurting her. That he was breaking her, in some form or fashion. It was hurting him, too. He was surprised at how raw the thought of leaving her left him. And yet he couldn't stay. He wouldn't stay. Because it was wrong. Because he might wake up one morning, remembering who he was—and hurt her.

He had to prevent that, no matter the cost.

"What I'm trying to say is that you've done enough for me, okay? You've given me enough of your time, enough of your life. You've been more than kind, more than generous. But you have a business and a life to get back to. You have friends and…and Eric. And you've done enough for me, okay? You don't owe me anything else. So please, just take me to a shelter."

Her eyes drifted down to the asphalt. Her nine working fingers tapped on her purse.

"I need to tell you something," Faye said finally. Quietly. "Before you go…"

"Okay."

"The night before I hit you with my bike, I was drinking."

"Drinking?"

"Drunk," she admitted. "For the first time in three years, I broke into that wedding wine, and I drank two bottles…and then, I did some *really, really* weird things."

Greg couldn't help but be curious. "What sort of…*really, really* weird things?"

"It doesn't matter," she said, quickly. "The point is, I was all alone at Magic Mud Pottery, the flyers had just happened, and even though I have fought so hard to be this person who is never vulnerable…the truth is, I was afraid."

His heart broke. He hated that someone had made her feel that way, that *he* had made her feel that way. He wanted to take it away. Make it better. But all he could manage to do was stand there, collapsing under the weight of his own shame.

"I'm so sorry, Faye," he stammered. He meant it. "You have no idea how sorry I am."

She nodded, her eyes drifting off into the darkness surrounding them. And he could see this was hard for her. It was in her face, the pained expression, the way every beautiful laugh line scrunched up around her nose. God, her nose was adorable. And he hated that it had to be like this, that the universe had brought them together in such a spectacularly awful fashion— but he would never regret meeting Faye.

Faye took a breath and continued. "But since you've come to live with me, I haven't been scared. I've been able to sleep peacefully most nights. And when I've had a nightmare, you were there for me…with hard kosher salami, just like my father. So, I guess what I'm trying to say is, if you really want to go to a shelter, if you really can't stand me that much, if I'm some sort of sea Gorgon that you're eventually going to have to kill with a cap of invisibility, and a shield made of mirrors—"

"Wait, what?" Greg didn't understand where her words were coming from. "What are you talking about?"

"Just let me finish."

He stopped talking.

"What I'm trying to explain to you," she said finally, "is that if you really want to leave me, I'll respect your wishes. I'll drop you off at the shelter, and I will never bother you again. But please don't feel you need to leave here on my account, because the truth is, I like having you around. I feel safer when you're there. And I don't want you to leave, Greg. So, I'm inviting you—I'm asking you—to stay with me for as long as you want."

"Faye…"

Her name caught in his mouth. Because he was torn. Wavering between the knowledge that he might not be safe for her—that he might be one of those awful, bad people—while simultaneously acknowledging that he made her feel secure. He made her feel safe. Above all else, she was asking him to stay.

He didn't know what the right choice was. He didn't know what was good, all the ways to take things with a grain of salt, understand the nuance—but he knew that he didn't want to leave her. He glanced down to his hand, his wrist, where that red string was still knotted. It hadn't fallen off yet.

"Okay," he said simply.

"Okay?" Faye asked, her eyes going wide. "You're going to stay?"

"Yes."

A tiny whoop of victory escaped her lips. The brightness in her eyes returned, which remarkably made Greg feel lighter, too. *It was going to be okay.*

The universe was working in his favor.

It was on that car ride back to Magic Mud Pottery that he

made an important decision. He didn't know for certain if he
was a Paper Boy, or a bad guy, but he was going to find out.
And if he had been the person behind the flyers, he would
spend the rest of his life working for divine retribution, combating anti-Semitism, earning his forgiveness.

He glanced over the console at Faye, the woman who understood him, and made a second, silent promise to her.

He was going to protect her.

There was a lightness that followed them the rest of the evening. The same routine they had always done together—pulling
out the bed inside the couch, trying not to trap Hillel beneath
the frame in the process—was dotted with sideways glances,
and flushed cheeks, both of which lingered too long. And when
it was time for sleep, when Faye retired to her bedroom, and
Greg went to the edge of his mattress to find another book,
she closed the door behind her.

Except this time, he didn't hear it lock.

UNDERSTANDING ANTI-SEMITISM
By Howard Beier and Jared Cohen

Page 115

Jew-hatred has existed for thousands of years and is evidenced by numerous instances of anti-Semitism throughout history.

In the Russian Empire during the 19th and early 20th century, attacks on Jewish communities were so commonplace that the word "pogrom" came into existence in order to describe them. These pogroms included mass beatings, burning of buildings, rape, and the murder of Jews.

Today, the devastation of pogroms on the Jewish people has been largely forgotten in the wake of The Holocaust, where six million Jews were systematically murdered, including one point five million Jewish babies, infants, and children. Yet, a comparison of both in Jewish history shows disturbing similarities.

In both instances, the annihilation of Jews was seen as a solution to "The Jewish Problem." All Jews were targeted in these attacks, including women, babies, and children. And, perhaps most troubling, both events could not have occurred without the cooperation of non-Jewish neighbors and those within the general population.

FIFTEEN

"Well," Miranda said, nursing a cup of warm apple cider, "at least we got nice weather for the rally."

Faye angled her head up to the sky. Despite weather forecasters predicting a forty percent chance of rain for Sunday, the clouds had parted. Warmer temperatures had returned. It was a glorious October morning in upstate New York, and everyone had pulled out their chunky sweaters and smiles for the occasion. Instead of needing to squeeze their Say No to Hate Rally into the local high school gymnasium, it was able to go on as planned in front of the large rotunda of Woodstock Town Hall.

"Excuse me?" Shulamit said from the podium. "Can everybody hear me okay?"

"We can hear you," Miranda shouted back.

Shulamit gave two thumbs-up to the crowd before proceeding. "I wanted to thank everyone so much for your patience. In just a few minutes, we'll be starting our Say No to Hate Rally!

Please, grab your signs, get comfy…and don't forget to leave a message of unity on one of our display boards. Today is all about celebrating and acknowledging love." With that, Shulamit headed to the side of the stage to talk to a waiting pastor.

"She really is the best of all of us." Miranda sighed.

Faye had to agree. For all the bad of the world, it was nice to know that people like Shulamit still existed. Not even the worst anti-Semite could frazzle her love of humanity, and her desire to make the world better.

"And," Miranda said, nudging her friend playfully, "now that I finally have you to myself…"

Faye tsked her teeth. "Stop."

"I'm just saying, it seems like things between you and Greg are going *really* well."

Faye had been keeping her friend abreast of the situation over the last few weeks. She texted her updates on his improvement regarding his speech, news about their search, all the dead ends they hit together. She supposed that Miranda— like all her friends, really—was waiting for some great reveal regarding his identity. When it didn't happen, they were all surprised. But the fact Greg was still living with her, and without a defined date for his departure, clearly shocked Miranda to the core. For three years, after all, Faye had been adamantly staving off relationships.

"I'm sorry." Faye grimaced. "I know I've been MIA recently, but I've just been so busy between the store and helping Greg—"

"Hey." Miranda cut her off right there. "You don't have to explain yourself to me. I mean, I was sort of hoping you missed hanging out with your best friends in the world because you were having amazing, incredible, nonstop sex with this magic golem you created…"

A shiver ran down Faye's spine. "He's not a golem."

"Of course he's a golem." Miranda laughed. "I mean, look

at him! He's hot. He's huge. He's redheaded—which is totally your kink, by the way. He's also still living with you…"

"He's living with me because we haven't figured out who he is yet."

"Right." She grinned. "And you won't figure out who he is…because he's a golem."

Faye fell silent. She knew her friend was just joking, but it bothered her all the same. Her eyes drifted back to the stage, where Greg was now carrying a speaker beneath one arm. Her mind wandered back to the clay effigy she had created. She had given him bulk, size…

She had given him size everywhere.

Quickly, she shook the thought away. There was nothing remotely supernatural about what she and Greg were experiencing together.

His language skills had improved because she and Greg had been working for weeks on his speech. He was able to cook baladur cakes and help around the store because in addition to practicing his words, they had worked to reteach him important life skills, tasks he had forgotten alongside his accompanying amnesia. As for his ability to read and then regurgitate books like some sort of supernatural AI chatbot…okay, she had to admit, that one was weird.

But she wasn't a doctor.

This was likely all…totally normal. Evidence of progress. Improvement. He was getting better. Which meant that Greg, *the man*, would eventually leave her. She wasn't so far gone as to not realize the implication of that, to feel the weight of her own baggage, her own clay memory, about to shatter beneath the pressure.

Greg put the speaker down, and his eyes scanned the crowd, landing on Faye. He lifted one hand to acknowledge he had seen her, and she waved back…before Shulamit set him on yet another task. Watching him depart, she knew that Greg was growing on her, inching his way past her terra-cotta walls...until there were moments that she almost wished he was a golem.

Some force in her life that would protect her. Some creature who would love her unconditionally, but also, never leave. She was certain it would be easier to be crushed to death, trampled beneath the foot of some stone giant that would eventually go *berserk*...than to have her heart broken once again.

"I'm kidding," Miranda said suddenly.

"What?" Faye returned from her thoughts.

"He's obviously not a golem," she clarified, "and I didn't mean to sound insensitive. I know that this whole experience must be hard for Greg. You, too. How is everything going, by the way? Where are you in the search for his true identity? I'm amazed at how much his language skills have improved."

Greg had spent some time talking to Miranda and Shulamit when they had arrived early to help set up for the rally.

"He's doing better," Faye said. "His speech is almost entirely back to normal, save for some leftover remnants and glitches. Otherwise, I can't really say there's been any downside to having Greg live with me. He's been helpful around the store. Hillel loves him. Unfortunately, poor guy... In terms of the search, we're kind of at a standstill. We've decided to take a bit of a break from hunting for the time being."

Miranda raised one eyebrow. "Oh, really?"

Faye brushed off the insinuation. "We're just trying to be less proactive and more mindful. We're actually going caving this afternoon."

"Oh my Gawd!" Miranda got excited all over again. "Please tell me you are going to have hot all-night sex with Greg in a cave!"

"Of course not," Faye spat back. "There are bats."

Miranda snickered.

"Anyway," Faye said, attempting to clarify once again. "We'll still be doing Jewitch rituals, focusing our intentions, all of that good and helpful stuff. But as we've exhausted all earthly resources at this point, the only thing I can think to do now is step back. Let him relax a little. Let his mind relax a little, too. My hope is that letting go of any pressure associated with remembering will actually aid his memory in returning."

"Soooooo—" Miranda pursed her lips together "—kind of like when folks finally stop trying to get pregnant…they get pregnant?"

"Exactly," Faye quipped, "just like that."

Miranda smirked from behind her cider.

Her best friend was acting coy.

"What?" Faye said, looking around her.

Seriously, she didn't understand what Miranda was standing there smirking about. And then, Faye finally put it together.

"No…" Faye said.

"Why do you think we wanted Greg to move the speakers?"

"Miranda!" Faye shouted her name. "You're pregnant!"

She threw her arms around her best friend. Miranda and Shully had been trying for a baby forever, and now it was finally happening.

"*Shhhhh,*" Miranda shushed her, leaning in to whisper. "It's not common knowledge yet. Plus, Shully still has to let the synagogue know. But we both wanted to tell you. We *were* going to tell you together at the Rosh Chodesh Women's Circle—but clearly, you were too busy entertaining the redheaded hottie who gives you salami."

Faye laughed. "So, I've turned you into a believer of Jewitch magic then?"

"Well, I'll tell you this much," Miranda said, shrugging her shoulders at her own disbelief. "I would not have paid for three rounds of IUI if I had known that all we needed to do was nail a red pouch full of some weird-ass stuff to our wall. I don't know, Faye. Maybe you should close Magic Mud Pottery and just do spells for people. We got babies coming, talking golems… What's next? You gonna single-handedly bring down The Paper Boys with a hex?"

Faye laughed, and hugged her bestie again. "I'm so happy for you, Miranda."

Just then, a blustering wind appeared from the north, causing kippahs to go flying off of heads, and papers to go soaring off the podium.

Perhaps there was part of her that never believed in her own power. When she considered the last three years, she had done many spells…but much like prayers in her childhood, they often went unanswered. And yet, Greg had appeared in her life, seemingly out of nowhere. Shulamit and Miranda were finally pregnant. She supposed she could look at the events as coincidence…but what if she really could bend the natural world to her will?

It seemed impossible, given her backstory. She was not an educated Jewish woman. She had a shoddy Hebrew school background and could barely read Hebrew. But maybe, when it came to embracing the divine Goddess that lived inside of her, none of that mattered. She was powerful enough simply because she believed, and because when she did magic…it connected her to six thousand years of Jewitch women who came before.

It was a lovely thought. As lovely as the knowledge that Faye would soon have a little baby in her life to spoil.

Faye pulled back from Miranda just in time to see Greg approaching from behind.

"Greg!" Faye said upon his return to her side. "You'll never believe it. Shulamit is pregnant!"

"That's amazing," Greg said, and moved to hug Miranda as well. "Congratulations."

"Thank you." Miranda beamed. "We're due in April."

Faye gasped excitedly. "A Passover baby!"

"Let's hope not," Miranda said, shaking her head. "Can you imagine? Passover cake for every birthday, for the rest of her natural life. She'll write memoirs about me, for sure. Seriously, Faye. Do you think you could work one of your spells to get her in around the late February time frame— *Oh my Gawd!*"

Faye jumped, clutching her heart. "What? What is it?"

She had no idea what Miranda was freaking out about. And then, she spotted a tiny gray-haired woman pushing her way through the crowd. Clad in a black leather pageboy cap, with a tiny German flag sticking out of the side, was Nelly.

"I'm sorry," Greg asked, glancing between the three of them. "Is something wrong?"

Faye grimaced. "Most definitely."

Indeed, No-Filter Nelly had completed whatever *meshuga* look she was going for with the addition of lederhosen, black combat boots, and a T-shirt bearing the emblem of a German flag inside a heart.

She looked ridiculous. Like some tourist who had lost all their luggage at the Frankfurt airport on Christmas morning and had no choice but to buy their entire wardrobe from the gift shop of their hotel. Worse still, she had the audacity to be storming their way.

"This can't be good." Miranda shielded her face with one hand. "Oh God...she's coming over here. Faye...do something!"

Faye threw her hands up. "What do you want me to do?"

"I don't know," Miranda said. "Just...make sure people know we're Jewish."

Faye glanced to a family of five—the women all wearing long skirts and black stockings—standing beside them.

"Shabbat shalom." Faye smiled.

It was Sunday.

The family looked askance at each other. Then, not trying to make things even *more* awkward, mumbled back the familiar refrain. Faye returned her line of sight to the fast-approaching Lufthansa jet heading in their direction.

"There you are," Nelly said, infiltrating their inner circle. "I've been looking all over for you."

"Why?" Faye deadpanned. "You planning to lead us all in a bright-and-early goosestep this morning?"

"Hush," Nelly said, ignoring her jab. "Don't you see what I'm doing here?"

"Not really," Miranda admitted.

"I'm infiltrating," Nelly explained, before leaning in to whisper, "Everything I'm wearing...*is German.*"

"Should I ask?" Faye rolled her eyes over to Miranda. "I really don't want to ask."

"You should ask," Miranda squeaked.

Despite no one asking, Nelly answered the question anyway. "Remember when I told you I was setting up a VPN in my basement?"

Faye covered her mouth. "You didn't?"

"I did," Nelly shouted happily. "I set one up, and I went on the dark board—"

"You mean the dark web," Miranda corrected her.

"Whatever!" Nelly snapped back. "My point is, I found them. The group claiming responsibility for the flyers. *The Paper Boys!* And now, I've been listening to the online chatter. Did you know they got a local cell operating here in upstate New York? Can you believe it? The audacity of these people."

"We've all seen the news, Nelly."

"Well, that's why I'm dressed up like this," Nelly explained, pointing to herself again. "I'm infiltrating. Going undercover! They'll see me wearing this Nazi gear, think I'm one of them, and invite me to one of their meetings. Once I'm in good with them, I'll figure out what they're planning next. And then we can finally use our stun batons to bring those Nazis to justice."

Faye wanted to respond, but she couldn't. Her lower lip had fully found its way to the sidewalk beneath her feet. Even Miranda, not one to ever miss an occasion for snark, was shaken into silence. Nelly had always been a bit eccentric, but now her antics were veering into dangerous territory.

"Nelly," Faye said calmly, "you really should leave the investigating to law enforcement."

Her whole face wrinkled up around her nose. "Why the hell would I do that?"

"Because that's their job," Faye snapped at her. "And because half the people in this town know you as the eccentric old Jewish lady who runs dog tea parties out of Second Glance Treasure. You're gonna get yourself killed."

"Nelly." Miranda attempted a less hostile takeover. "This isn't a game, okay? This isn't a Netflix documentary, either. This is a vile and hateful anti-Semitic group that has committed really terrible crimes against innocent Jewish people all across America. I know you mean well...but you really don't want to be drawing so much attention to yourself."

"But that's exactly what I want," Nelly said, exasperated. "I want the Nazis to contact me. I want them to find me." And then, without warning, Nelly snapped her feet together and attempted to give the one-arm salute. "Heil Hit—"

"Nelly!" Faye grabbed the old woman's arm before she had a chance to cause a riot.

Nelly pulled her hand back, annoyed. "At least I'm being proactive. That's more than I can say for the lot of you."

"Do you not see us all here at the peace rally?" Miranda asked, incredulous.

"Blah." Nelly spat out the word. "All this peace and love nonsense. You think these *alter cockers* care about peace and love? You think they're gonna eat some pumpkin-spiced babka, hear a speech from the cantor, and suddenly realize they shouldn't hate Jews? You're all living in a dream world. A la-la-lovefest fantasy land. Shame on you when—*as Jews, especially*—you should know better."

With that, Nelly was off, pressing through the crowd,

screaming about how much she loved visiting Germany in the 1930s.

Faye sighed. "Do you think Germany would take her?"

Miranda snickered. *"Faye."*

"You know you were thinking it."

Miranda laughed. Faye did, too. And then her eyes caught on Greg. He wasn't joining in on the fun. Instead, his gaze was fixated on Nelly. The old woman had approached a group of middle school boys, who were now cornered by the back of the stage.

"That woman will be the death of me." Faye sighed before adding, "One of us should probably go keep an eye on her."

"If you want," Greg said, intervening, "I'd be happy to keep an eye on her."

"You wouldn't mind?" Faye asked.

"Of course not."

"Thank you," Miranda said. "Truly."

Greg wasted no time chasing her down. Faye found her eyes following his perfectly sculpted back where muscle met shoulder blades...when a sight towards the edge of the crowd drew her concern. A man was lingering at the boundaries of the rally.

He was old and alone. Practically scowling. Plus, he was wearing a coat far too big and puffy to be applicable for the warm weather. She didn't want to jump to conclusions, but her mind wandered.

She didn't understand why he would come to the rally and stand off at the edge. She didn't like the way he behaved, eyes scanning the faces of the crowd, as if he were taking a census. And then, a memory returned... She recognized this man. He was the same man she had seen sweeping up flyers the morning after the anti-Semitic incident.

She swallowed, and immediately bit back the thought. Once again, she was being extreme, seeing anti-Semites where there were none. Golems where only men existed. Delusional. Prone to fantasy and fits. Just like her mother. Still, she made a mental note to mention the man to Eric as soon as the rally was over.

Greg pressed through the crowd with only one thought on his mind. *Nelly had information on The Paper Boys.* He needed to speak with her. He caught up with the octogenarian smack-dab in the middle of interrogating a group of middle school boys waiting to sign a unity poster.

"Let me ask you each a question," Nelly said, pointing a blue marker at each of their heads. "You have two movies to watch on Friday night. The first is *Schindler's List*. The second one is *Triumph of the Will*. Which one do you pick?"

The boys looked awkwardly at each other.

"Hey, Nelly," Greg said, stepping between them, "I was wondering if I could speak to you for a minute."

The boys took their opportunity to escape. They sprinted off into the crowds and back to their parents. Nelly was not pleased. Crossing her arms against her chest, she fixed him with a frosty gaze. "You spare the rod," Nelly said through pursed lips, "you'll spoil the anti-Semite."

"I don't think those kids were part of The Paper Boys."

"You don't know that," Nelly defended herself. "Maybe they're not with The Paper Boys, but kids know things. Kids hear things. It's always the ones that seem nice on the surface that cause the most trouble." She allowed the comment to linger in the air. "You can talk now?"

"I can talk," Greg confirmed.

She wrinkled her nose at him, but otherwise didn't seem all that impressed.

"They don't get it, you know?" Nelly said, finally. "Faye, Miranda, even the police… I try to tell them what I found, what I've been doing, but they treat me like a joke. Do you think I'm a joke, Greg?"

"Not at all."

"But they sent you to babysit me?"

"Kind of," he admitted. "But also, I was sort of hoping to talk to you alone. I'd actually love to hear more about what you've learned regarding The Paper Boys."

Her eyes went wide in shock. "You would?"

Of course, what Nelly didn't know was that his interest in The Paper Boys was as much for personal reasons as anything else.

"I knew you were a smart one," Nelly said, rubbing her hands together. "So, when do you want to do this?"

Greg was confused. "Do…what?"

"Come over and see my war room," she said excitedly.

"Whoa." Greg raised both his hands up in the air. "That's not exactly what I meant."

"Well, we can't talk here."

"Why not?"

"Eyes and ears, Greggy boy," Nelly said, leaning in to whisper, nodding to the crowd beyond the row of hedges where they were speaking. "You never know who's listening. That's the thing about these Nazis. They hide in plain sight. We can't talk here, 'cause then they'll know what I'm up to, capiche? It'll blow my cover."

It seemed a tad extreme. Greg couldn't help but think it. He took stock of the crowd surrounding him, families eating ice cream, couples waving American and rainbow-colored flags. Still, Nelly was the only person in his world right now that seemed both willing to answer and capable of answering any question he had relating to The Paper Boys.

"What's the problem?" Nelly said.

"I'm just not sure how to get away from Faye without looking suspicious."

Since his accident, Greg hadn't spent one second away from Faye. Other than when they were sleeping, of course. Or in the bathroom. But even then, she was always just down the hall. Like Hillel.

Plus, there were practical matters to contend with. For one, how could he explain leaving her for any extended length of time? It would raise questions. Uncomfortable ones. He had read a book about finding a missing person. But he hadn't yet read one that would help him disappear.

"Lie," she said simply.

"I can't just lie to her."

"Why not?" Nelly shrugged. "I lie to Faye all the time. She's none the wiser."

"Well, maybe I can just tell her I'm going over to your place? Explain to her that I want to learn more about The Paper—"

"What's the matter with you?" Nelly grabbed him by the collar. "Don't you have any sense of self-preservation? What do you think Faye will do if you tell her you want to come see my war room?"

"I have no idea."

Nelly spat out the words. "She'll ground you, Baby Bird. Put you on lockdown. Lock up that nest of hers like we're all back in COVID. And you know what that means, don't you? No hunting down The Paper Boys. No stunning those bastards into oblivion, either. You see what she's like. *She's got no vision.* You'll never have it make sense to her. And she'll never allow you to go running into the danger zone, either."

Nelly had a point. Still, Greg couldn't help but hesitate. Something about sneaking out, lying to Faye—especially after everything she had done for him—felt all types of wrong.

"You're struggling," Nelly said. "I can see you're struggling."

"I suppose I am," he admitted.

"Come closer then," she whispered sweetly. "I want to explain something to you. I realize you have no memory left, so let me tell you a story. It's a true story. You like stories, don't you, Greggy?"

"I love stories."

"Good," Nelly said, her voice creaking with age, "because we Jews are a storytelling people. It's very important, the transmission of memory, you know? Not just telling a history, blind facts, and all that…but feeling as if that history is your own. So that you become responsible for it. So that it seeps into your DNA, into your bones, until it becomes your memory, too. You understand, right? The way a memory, or a story, can feel like it happens to you."

"I think so."

"So I got two grandkids in Boca," she continued. "Two beautiful and perfect grandchildren who I love very much… and every time I go to visit them, they draw me a picture, and ask me, 'Grandma? Do you like my artwork? Are you going to keep it forever?' Do you know what I tell them, Greg?"

"That you love it?"

"Smart one," she said, pinching his cheeks. "Every single time, I tell them, 'Oh, yes. Grandma loves your artwork. Grandma is going to keep this drawing on her refrigerator forever.' And do you know what I do the second I get home from visiting them?"

"You put it on your refrigerator?" Greg assumed innocently.

"I throw it straight in the trash," Nelly said. "Nobody has time for those scribbles."

"Haman's hat."

"My point is, Greg," Nelly said definitively, "I love my grandkids, but I don't tell them the truth. I let them live in their sweet delusional little fantasy world, give them better than reality…because if I told them the truth, they would cry, and get upset, and not understand why Grandma hates their most special artwork. I lie because they will never understand why I don't want a house full of crayon drawings that they spent three seconds on. Capiche?"

Greg considered her words. "You're kind of a terrible influence, you know?"

She shrugged. "I know who I am."

I know who I am. The words brought his entire debate back down to its essential question. He hated the idea of lying to Faye. But he had questions—about who he was, if he was a bad person, the real reason why he had come to Woodstock. And for all his baladur cakes, he was no closer to answers. If he had been a Paper Boy, he felt the urge to right the wrongs of his past, too.

"I'll try," he said finally. "But it might take some time."

"Well, Baby Bird." Nelly expelled the words in a huff. "When you find a way to fly the nest without Mamma Bird watching, come and find me. But don't take too long. I can't wait forever. And neither will the anti-Semites." With that, the old woman was off, disappearing back through the hedges and into the crowd.

It was your typical sort of peace rally. Faye followed along politely beside Miranda in the audience.

After the nondenominational prayer, there was a poetry reading by a local student. A synchronized dance done with large feathers and sparkle bodysuits by the SilverSmiles Dance Company, a dance troupe made up of residents from the nearby assisted living center. A moving and heartbreaking speech from a Holocaust survivor, aided by her daughter. Until all the examples of why anti-Semitism was bad for the greater society were exhausted, and they brought out representatives from local and federal government.

Finally, it was Chief Eric Myers's turn. Faye gave a little more gusto to her applause than usual.

"Hey," Greg said, reappearing at her side.

Faye was surprised to see him so soon. "Hey," she said back. "Everything okay?"

"Yeah." Greg pointed with one thumb towards the parking lot. "Nelly decided to leave. Apparently, she didn't understand how old ladies in feathers were going to stop *The Paper Boys*... and also, too many people here recognized her."

"*Oy.*" Faye rubbed an eyebrow in frustration. "Well, I appreciate you looking after her."

"Of course," Greg said, and then nudged her playfully. "Anytime."

She appreciated him so much.

Faye turned her attention back to the stage, where Eric was just beginning. Hands on the podium, lips angled directly into the microphone, he gave no hint of anxiety regarding his performance. His eyes panned around the audience. His voice never wavered. In truth, she was impressed. She had no idea that Eric could be such an eloquent speaker.

He spoke about what led him to become a cop, and eventually, chief of police. He professed his love for law enforcement and the people of Woodstock. At one point, Faye felt her hand inadvertently drift over her heart. The man was straight-up mesmerizing.

"Believe me," Chief Myers said, "I have the full resources of the law at my disposal, and we will prosecute these offenses swiftly and to the highest level of the law. Let this serve as a warning to anyone here thinking about engaging with, or participating in, these acts... You will be found out, and you will serve serious time for any crimes you commit within my jurisdiction."

It felt good to have someone like Eric in her community.

"What happened over the holiday of Sukkot," Eric continued, "was not just an attack on the Jewish community, but on everyone in Woodstock. It was an attack on our values and our beliefs and our ability to live free, in any way that we please. A Hasidic proverb teaches, 'Love is the most reliable cure for wounds of the soul.' Last week, someone papered our town with hateful propaganda and rhetoric. But today, we are all one family. We are all one community. We are all Jews."

His words caused the entire crowd to explode in simultaneous uproar. Eric embraced Shulamit warmly before heading to each person on stage, shaking their hands.

The final act was a wild rendition of "Hava Nagila," played by the local high school jazz band. The song had the intended effect. Moments after the trumpets began blaring, people were grabbing hands. Forming a circle in the middle of the town square, everyone at the rally began to dance. Faye was just about to grab Greg's hand and join her friends when she saw Eric moving through the crowd, waving her down.

"Oh, Eric," Faye said, rushing to greet him. "You were spectacular. Just incredible. I had no idea you were such an eloquent and passionate speaker."

Eric blushed. "Thank you, Faye. That means the world... coming from you."

His words touched her, along with those piercing blue eyes, before his attention flicked back to Greg. "Greg," Eric said, offering his hand. "How are you?"

"Good," Greg said.

"Still here, though?"

Greg cocked his chin back. "Excuse me?"

Tension sat in the air between them before Eric retreated. "I'm sorry," Eric said. "I didn't mean that to sound rude. I just meant... I'm surprised you're still here. I thought you two would have figured out who you are by now. Memory's not back yet then?"

Thankfully, Greg relaxed with the apology. "Unfortunately, no."

"I'm sorry to hear that," Eric said genuinely. "Hopefully, one day soon then?"

Greg nodded. "Hopefully."

"Actually," Faye said, twisting back to Eric, "I was wondering if I could speak with you for a minute. Privately." She glanced over her shoulder back at Greg. "You don't mind, do you, Greg?"

His eyes flicked back to Eric. "Not at all."

"Great," she said, and moved with Eric, out of earshot of the rest of the rally goers. "I was wondering if you heard any more news?"

"You talking about Greg?"

"No." Faye waved away his concern. "Not Greg. Greg has been nothing but a perfect gentleman. I was just wondering if you've heard any more news on people in our community, strangers who might have come to our town with ill intention. It's just..."

Eric squinted. "What brings this up?"

"There's this guy around town I've been seeing. He's just... giving me a bad feeling."

She went on to explain it. Their strange interaction the day after the flyers. The way he had been lingering and watching the crowd. Eric listened intently, and after she was finished recounting her story—which, even she had to admit, seemed totally innocuous on the surface—he placed his hands on the divots of his hips and grew serious.

"Well, I don't know, Faye," Eric admitted. "There's not much to go on here."

She shook her head. "I know... I sound completely bonkers."

"Tell you what," he said, finally, "I'm going to investigate it, okay? I'll let my guys know to keep an eye out—on your place, especially—and if we see this perp loitering about, we'll bring him in for questioning."

She put her hand on his arm. "I appreciate that."

"Of course," he said, returning the touch, both their hands lingering. "Anything for you. Really, I hate that you're going through all this."

With one final embrace, Eric took off, pushing back through the crowd. Cops often didn't have the best rep in America, but Eric was, undoubtedly, a beloved and respected member of their community.

SIXTEEN

"Wow," Greg said.

Faye hadn't been kidding. Devil's Cave was nothing short of remarkable. His eyes drifted up to a hole in the ceiling where he could see the sky. A white cloud floated by before the sound of rustling leaves filled the tiny rotunda of stalagmites and stone they were standing inside. It was like being on the inside of one of Faye's circular vases.

"Beautiful, right?" Faye said, stepping beside him.

His eyes caught on hers. "Beyond."

"I told you it would put everything into perspective."

He nodded. "Makes nearly killing myself on a rock totally worth it."

He was kidding, of course. The cavern was only a short distance from the original entry point. The pathway flat and mostly clear. Indeed, the most difficult part of the beginner cave she had taken them to was the long hike through the woods from the parking lot.

As for the rock he had slipped on, that was also his own fault. He had been distracted on their hike up to the cave together. His mind was on Nelly and The Paper Boys. His eyes kept trailing over to Faye. Though she had warned him that the rocks beneath their feet had become slippery due to a stream just beyond the path, he hadn't been paying attention.

"Thankfully," Greg reminded her, "you were there to keep me from breaking an ankle."

"Not me." She held up her left hand, tapping on her wrist. "The red bracelet."

He laughed. "Indeed."

"Should we get started?" she asked.

Greg nodded, took off his backpack, and handed it to her. Faye got to work, laying both backpacks on the floor, pulling out and sorting items.

"How did you discover this place?" Greg asked.

"When I first moved to Woodstock," she explained, "I was looking for things to occupy my free time. I tried out a whole bunch of hobbies. Cheese-making. Pickleball. Archery. But, for whatever reason…caving is the one that stuck. I guess it makes sense, being a ceramicist. I come here a lot for Jewitch rituals, too. When I need strong magic."

"Hopefully, this will work then."

The first item she laid out was a candle, which she had infused with flax, and with her fingernail alone, engraved with seven circles. Next was a small brass knife and a bowl, where she combined soot, water, and oil. Finally, she pulled out a mirror, laying it on the ground between them.

"First, you take the candle." Greg did as instructed, and she lit it, the flame flickering upwards to the hole in the ceiling. "And now, you say the following. 'Adam, Chavah, Abthon, Absalom, Sarviel, Nurial, Daniel…'"

Greg repeated, "Adam, Chavah, Abthon, Absalom, Sarviel, Nurial, Daniel."

"And now—"

"Sorry," Greg interrupted her. "I'm just confused. Who are all these people again?"

"Oh." Faye tipped her chin. "I actually have no idea."

"Really?"

"All I know is these names were used in a fifteenth-century Jewish divination ritual in Germany."

That sounded legit enough for Greg. "Let's hope it works then."

"Agreed," she said, and returned to her instructions. "Now, you repeat seven times, 'Gerte, I conjure you here with these seven names I have mentioned, to appear in the wax of this candle, carefully prepared and designated for this purpose, and to answer whatever question I may ask of you.'"

He did as instructed, the flame growing wild between them, the wind rustling in the trees just beyond, as if she were kicking up into a storm. The room in the energy shifted. "And now," Faye said, "cast your eyes onto the flame. And ask the universe your question."

Greg swallowed. "Who am I?"

"Tell me what you see in the light."

His eyes narrowed. The image of Faye dwindled, disappeared, until all he could see was the flickering light of the flame, stretching into eternity. And then, out of the fire, stepped a woman.

Her face was fuzzy, but he could make out the outline of her features. Straight hair down to her shoulders, a green turtleneck. She waved him forward. In his mind's eye, he stepped closer, and she felt so familiar. Someone he recognized. Except, he didn't know who she was. For the life of him, he couldn't remember—but his heart ached in her presence. And that voice reappeared, melodic and soft, whispering a message. *Justice, justice.*

Greg squinted, unsure of the meaning. "What?" he called out to her.

"What do you see, Greg?" Faye asked him.

"A woman."

"Tell me about her."

Greg felt tears coming to his eyes. "She's kind."

"Yes."

"And she's good." He said it again. "She's so damn good… it's remarkable."

"This is great," Faye said, her voice rising into a fevered pitch. "Just keep going with it. More!"

"I think… I think I might be falling in love with her."

The woman transformed inside his mind and grew in clarity. The straight hair twisted into thick curls. Her angular features became round and pleasant.

"Who is she, Greg?" Faye asked.

He knew. "Faye…"

"Tell me."

"Faye."

"Ask for her name, Greg. Demand she tell you!"

"Faye!" Greg finally shouted. "Stop! It's you."

The sky above them rumbled. A breeze found its way into the cave. The light in the candle flickered out, smoke dancing upwards between them. Greg blinked awake. The spell had been broken. And, as was the tendency with Jewitches and magic, in the wake of the ritual…another one had been cast.

Faye paused for a breath and then, rising from her spot on the ground, began quickly blaming everything on a faulty Jewitch ritual. "It's just a silly old divination space. It doesn't mean anything."

She began to pace—back and forth, like Hillel sometimes did

when Greg put him in the laundry room—endlessly banging into walls. Greg tried to draw her back to the circle.

"Faye," he said. "Please sit down."

She was not listening. "I mean—" she waved her hands in the air as she spoke, talking to herself, to the universe, *to everyone but Greg* "—these things usually take two or three times at least to get an answer. I don't think we really need to analyze it more than that."

Greg tried again. "Faye."

"It can't happen, Greg," she said, spinning around, pointing between them. "You, me...*us*! It can't happen."

Greg didn't hesitate. "I know that, Faye."

He said it with the full finality of a funeral.

He said it resolutely, too.

She turned back to him. "You do?"

"Yeah?" he said, shrugging his shoulders. "This experience we're having together, it's temporary. It's not going to last forever. One day, I'm going to remember who I am. I'm going to return to my normal life, whatever that is." *He really hoped it wasn't as a Paper Boy.* "And given all the impossibilities of this situation, I think you're right."

She blinked three times. "I am?"

"Yes," he said, waving her back to the circle. "Look, I'm not gonna lie. I do like you, Faye. I think you're remarkable. And, if I'm also being honest in this space, I am attracted to you, too."

"You are?"

"I think you're...stunning."

"Stunning." The word fell from her mouth in a whisper.

"Honestly," he said, rubbing the back of his neck, "that doesn't even feel like the right word, because it's so much more than that. It's the way you see the world, like a kaleidoscope, like the beautiful vases you make...not like some mass-produced vase you can buy in a market. And I love your sense of humor, and your books, and your magic cakes, too."

She laughed a little, before her face went all squishy again.

"And I don't know," he continued, shrugging his shoulders, "maybe there are a million women like you on the planet, a million people who have all these shining shards made up inside of them. But I don't know a million other women, Faye. I just know you. Because you're the woman who found me."

The tiniest little breath escaped her lips.

"All of which is to say," Greg said, before holding up his left hand, showcasing his red bracelet between them, "we're friends. I'm not gonna hurt you. I want the best for you, okay? But I'd like to know your story. I'd like to understand you better."

She swallowed. "Okay."

"So, why aren't you with Eric?"

"What?" Faye nearly spit up the word.

"Eric," Greg repeated. "Chief Eric Myers."

"Why would you even ask that?"

"Well, for one," Greg explained it simply, "both when he came to the store to check up on you, but also at the rally… I think it's pretty darn clear that he likes you. It also seems to me that you enjoy his company, too. Whenever he's around, you two are always sneaking off together to whisper, touching each other. So, I guess I want to know…what's holding you back?"

She swallowed. Pressed her eyes to the wall.

It took her a long time to come around and answer him.

"Poor sweet Greg," she said finally, softly. "You haven't yet read about women with snakes instead of hair, who turn men to stone upon approaching?"

Faye could see Greg didn't understand.

"Medusa," she said, clarifying her previous statement. "It's an ancient story, from Greek mythology, about a beautiful woman who was turned into a monster. Well, technically…a sea Gorgon. But the point is, Medusa had a head full of hissing snakes instead of hair, and she lived on an island, in a cave just like this one… And she was so horrifying to behold, that whenever any person approached her shorelines, had the misfortune to even look upon her for an instant…they immediately turned to stone."

"Huh," Greg said. "Sounds like a lonely life."

"I suppose it was," she said, quietly.

She sighed, and searched for her courage. Damn those self-help books. Damn all those Jewitch rituals. Was Greg even a real person? Or was she simply talking to some blank slate of a man who had filled himself up with *her* books?

But then she caught on his eyes. Those same eyes that had persuaded her to take him home from the hospital. Like his lips—all those mornings together, practicing words—until Greg could speak those most thoughtful and beautiful sentences. Her gaze drifted down to his hands, so large and masculine. She felt safe with him, didn't she?

"He said I was too much." The words fell from her lips.

"Who?"

"My fiancé," Faye explained, filling in bits and pieces of the story. "Stuart. We had been dating for ten years, engaged for seven, and then, three months before our wedding…he dumped me during a snowmobile ride in Lapland."

Stuart's words echoed in her head. Just like she could recall every line in his face as he screamed at her. *You're too much, Faye. Everything you do, everything you are. No wonder your own mother couldn't stand you.*

"I'm so sorry, Faye," Greg said.

"Thank you."

Greg inched in closer. The red string on his wrist, still bound and knotted, dangled like a promise between them.

"So," Greg said. His voice was clear, matter-of-fact. "Because of what happened with Stuart, you've given up on any chance of happiness with Eric?"

"No," Faye said. "That's not it at all."

Her wrist was aching, acting up. She looked down to see the pointer finger on her left hand spasming without her. The pain in her hand stretched its way up to her neck, back, before landing in her chest.

"I told you a little bit about my mother," she continued. "That she was sick, toxic...explosive. So, in order to prevent her from going off on one of these awful and violent rages... I would try to be the perfect daughter. I would try to be better than perfect. I would walk on eggshells, constantly, all to avoid triggering her."

She began to describe some of her memories from growing up. How she once scrubbed the kitchen floors for hours, just for her mother to come in and start screaming that she had made the floors wet. That she would bring home good grades, try to excel in after-school activities and clubs, only to have her mother scoff, then exclaim her teachers must be idiots. And finally, she told him more about how her mother had broken her wrist.

"I had this scholarship to art school," she said. "I was getting out, you know? Going off to New York City to live out my dream. And because I was going to be this great and famous ceramicist, my work was all over the house. I would try to clean it up, so that my mom wouldn't get angry...but I'm seventeen. I'm not perfect."

She had never been perfect.

She had never been good enough.

"One night," she continued, "I left one of my modular designs sitting on the kitchen table. Minor infraction, I suppose... in most homes. In most homes, parents would be proud of their kids for being talented, or taking initiative. For working so hard that you get a full scholarship to one of the best fine arts programs in America. But in my home, it meant that at three o'clock in the morning, my mom would come into my room and tear down my covers..."

She swallowed over the words, over the memory, the ache in her wrist becoming unbearable.

"My mom could be violent," she said. "Growing up, I remember being spanked. Slapped. My hair pulled. But this night, my mom goes berserk. She loses control of herself completely. She grabs me by my left wrist, and yanks me out of bed. Next thing I know I'm getting dragged down the hall, my legs banging into side tables, my head knocking over trash bins...and, of course, I'm screaming, 'Mommy, it hurts, Mommy, stop'... and then, *snap*...she broke my wrist."

Tears began gathering in the corners of her eyes. She didn't want to cry, admit vulnerability, show her weakness, but most of all, she felt shame. For what had happened to her. That she couldn't be better. If she had just been good, loveable...her mother wouldn't have hurt her. *Hated her.*

"Where was your dad?" Greg asked quietly.

"My dad?" She was caught off guard by the question.

"Didn't he hear you yelling?"

Faye moved to defend him. "He was in his office."

Greg squinted. "At three o'clock in the morning?"

She stammered, "It was in the basement."

She looked away, pressing her eyes towards the wall of the cave. Because her father loved her. *He loved her.* Even though he never protected her. Even though he let Faye take the brunt of her mother's rages. *She needed to believe that her father loved her.*

"You don't understand," she said. "My mother was toxic. She was...cruel. My dad was just trying to keep the peace."

"Keep the peace," Greg scoffed. "Faye...you were a child."

"Don't be mad at me!"

"I'm not mad at you," he said, shaking his head. "I'm hurt for you, Faye. I'm angry for you, too. I'm angry that these people, who were supposed to love and protect you, failed you so miserably."

The weight of all the pain she was carrying began to bubble over.

"I told my mother that something was wrong," she continued. "I begged her to take me to the hospital, but my mother told me I was being ridiculous. She had yelled at me to go sleep, stop pretending. She sent me to school. And I buried how much it hurt. I kept my mother's secret...for five long days."

"Faye..."

He pulled away from her, rose from his seat, clearly wanting to comfort her. She held out one hand to stop him. "Don't."

"I just want to give you a hug."

"No," she said firmly.

She didn't want to be touched. She didn't want to be held, because she knew that if Greg wrapped his arms around her, he would say the right things. He would tell her it wasn't her fault, that she deserved better. *And then, he would leave her.* She had given him her story, the truth of who she was, her worst and darkest moments. That had to be enough.

Faye sucked back her tears. Taking a deep breath, she got ahold of herself.

"It wasn't until I went over to Miranda's house that I said anything," Faye explained quietly. "We were sitting at the kitchen table, doing homework together...and her mom saw I was having trouble. She went to look at my hand, saw the blue-and-purple welt there, and took me to the hospital."

Her mother had splintered the bone in three places. Faye was in a cast for months. She probably should have gone to more than one session of physical therapy, but of course, her mom couldn't get it together enough to make sure that her bones healed properly. Her hand never healed right. Her finger was permanently disabled. And from there, she lost her scholarship.

"Becoming a lawyer was never my dream," she said sadly. "But it provided financial independence. It allowed me to escape from my mom and her rages. I suppose her jealousy, too.

Until, one day in college, my father called to tell me that he was dying. I returned home to help, because I loved my father, and he loved me…and because, how could I leave him unprotected with my mother. It was during law school, at the point where he had lost both the ability to recognize me and to speak, that I met Stuart."

"He replaced your father," Greg said softly.

She nodded. "Looking back on it, I can see how he was just a fill-in for the things I needed. It wasn't a good relationship, you know? We were toxic for each other from the start. But I held on, refusing to let go of him…because I never believed that I would find better. And because watching him walk away would prove this thing that I always felt. This bubble left inside my clay memory by my mother. That no one would ever love me."

"Faye," he said, scooting in closer. "Look at me."

She met his eyes directly.

"You are not the bad that you endured, okay?"

She rolled her eyes. "What book is that from?"

"It's not from a book."

He seemed almost insulted.

She found herself staring at her left hand, her one disabled finger, and her sadness, coupled with rage, returned.

"You know, sometimes I look back on it," she said. "And I see the irony of wanting to spend my life creating modular pieces. Pottery with pieces that can move in relationship with each other, without damaging one another. And there are lots of people out there who are modular pottery. They're modular people."

Greg shook his head, confused. "I'm sorry. I don't…completely understand."

"You see how Miranda and Shulamit are," Faye explained. "You see how they support each other, nurture each other, make each other better…but they still have their own interests, their own goals, their own dreams."

"They're partners."

"Partners." She nodded. "That's right. That's another word for it, too. Because they're both healthy people, so they can be in a healthy partnership with each other. But I'm not a healthy person, Greg. When I get into a relationship with someone, I don't become a partner. Instead, I morph. I go back in time, and I become that scared little girl again, wondering what I did wrong, constantly worried about being perfect, giving up all my dreams and interests in the process…out of some desperate and pathetic need to keep this one person, this fill-in for my mother and her love, from leaving me.

"So, you see, Greg," Faye continued, "it's not about Eric. It's not about Stuart. It's not about you, or any man. In fact, even if the most perfect man in the world, my *bashert*, plopped down in front of me, like manna falling from the heavens… I still wouldn't date him. And I'm going to tell you why. I'm going to tell you the exact same thing I said to Eric two years ago, too."

"Lay it on me."

"I have no interest in partnering with another human being. I have no interest in some great romance, or falling in love. *I will never get married.* Because I like who I am. I like who I've become since moving to Woodstock, running Magic Mud Pottery. I like that my life, where I eat, the hobbies I take on, what friends I see—are my choice, and mine alone. I'm in control. It took me three years to remember Faye Kaplan after Stuart… and it'll be a cold day in hell before I ever risk losing her again."

He was quiet for a long time. "Fair enough," he said finally.

They lingered there together, unmoving, the space caving in around them. And then, Faye stood and wiped her hands clean of dirt. Outside, the skies were darkening. They needed to be getting home.

"We should probably get going," she said.

Greg nodded, and they began gathering up supplies, and she resigned herself to one thought, one focused intention, which she played on repeat inside her mind. Whatever longing for Greg was inside of her was irrelevant. Whatever wants or dreams she had for a chance at true love had to be ignored. It could never happen. *It would never happen.* Because Greg was a man without a memory...

And she was a woman with too much.

Faye was quiet on the way back to the car, but the silence, along with the long hike through the woods, allowed him time to reflect on what she had just told him. The story she had shared had bothered him to no end. But even greater than his anger at the injustice she had endured, he hated how she saw herself.

Greg didn't see her broken bits as flaws. If anything, it was the opposite. She was like that one vase in the store she had hidden behind the fancier and more elaborate-looking Seder plate. She saw herself as warped and damaged, undeserving of love and attention. Yet it was all the bubbles in her clay memory, the scratches and scars...that made her unique.

Faye went to throw the bags in the trunk.

"This Medusa lady," Greg asked. "Did she have many suitors?"

"I wouldn't call them suitors," Faye said, "but yes, many men came to the island where she lived."

"And all of them turned to stone?"

"Every single one except the last guy," she informed him. "Perseus."

"And what happened to him?" Greg asked.

"Well, there are different versions of the story, but all of them end the same way."

"What's that?"

"He killed her," Faye explained succinctly. "He went to her island, with a cap of invisibility he had stolen from this goddess Athena and a shield made of mirrors, and when she saw her own reflection, she turned to stone. Or fell asleep. It depends on the version you're reading. But after which, he cut off her head."

Greg grimaced. "That's horrible."

"Yeah, well," Faye mumbled, "nobody loves a monster."

She closed the trunk and angled to leave him, heading for the driver's side. Greg stopped her again. "You know," Greg said, "I think you're telling this story all wrong."

Faye scoffed. "Oh really?"

"The way I see it…poor Medusa was just minding her business, trying to have a nice beach vacation…and all these jerks with swords and shields keep coming around and bothering her. No wonder she needed snakes for hair. It sounds to me like she was a woman who settled on protecting herself."

"Actually," Faye corrected him, "she was punished with snakes for hair."

"It's a feminist retelling." Greg smirked.

Faye lifted her hands in open surrender.

Greg continued. "Now, personally, I like to believe that the problem wasn't with Medusa, at all. Maybe what Medusa needed more than soldiers, more than cowardly men with weapons in their hands and something to prove, more than yet another *Stuart* in her life…"

She shook her head. "I knew you were going there."

"Will you let me finish, please?"

She waved him forward.

"Thank you," Greg said, continuing his tale. "What Medusa really needed in her life was not a weak man, some enervated creature who couldn't even hold up the crown she was wearing… but a snake handler."

"A snake handler?" She laughed.

"Heck yeah," he mused thoughtfully. "And that's how my version of the story is gonna end. Not the story that Perseus, a clear Chad, by the way, took back with him to the seawall and told all his buddies to make himself look good. My story is gonna end that Medusa and... Give me another name, Faye."

"Harry," she said.

"Medusa and Harry," he said, imagining their first meeting, "famed snake handler, saw that beautiful crown full of serpents, hissing...and realized, right away, that he was staring at a Deity. And so, he did what men do when they're standing in front of supernatural beings. He dropped to his knees and lowered his eyes, which immediately saved his life. And because he was worthy, because he was not at all afraid of her power... she welcomed him into her cave."

"Very nice." She clapped emphatically. "Excellent story."

"Hold on. I'm not done here."

"Alright."

"And so, Harry," Greg continued, very dramatically, "lay down by her side that night. He pressed his head upon her bosom, feeling the sweet caresses of those snakes as they wrapped around his skin, feeling them pulling him into her. And it was only then, sinking into each other, merging into one, with the tide rising around them, and the sea lapping at their feet...that he pressed his lips up to her ears, and whispered these words." Greg wrapped one arm around her waist, pulling her close enough to whisper in her ear. "Don't you see, my love? There's no difference between a monster and a Goddess."

"Greg!" Faye nearly fell out of her sneakers. "Have you been reading my romance novels?"

"No," he asked, curiously. "Should I?"

"It's just..." Her voice caught in her throat. "That was really good!"

He smiled. "I'm glad you liked it."

"I loved it," she admitted.

"Good," he said, finally releasing her. "Because remember what you told me. You got to take stories with a grain of salt. You got to learn to look at them with discernment and nuance. Don't believe everything you read. Or hear. And sometimes, what that means is...you gotta take a story that someone has told you your whole life and look at it from a new angle."

It took her a moment, but she laughed. They faded into silence, and her eyes flicked upwards in his direction. He latched onto her, the heat rising in his chest as that desire to kiss her returned, a fire burning inside of him...which he was growing more certain would never be quenched.

THE ROGUE PRINCE
A Prince Caspian Hardwood Romance—Book I

Prince Caspian Hardwood wore many costumes.

At times, he was a scourge pirate, traveling the high seas, striking fear into the hearts of many a maiden. Once, he played a beggar, a man without name or reputation, who had taken to lingering on the steps of a church, just beside a nunnery. He traveled all throughout the realm, passing through ports and villages, taking on odd jobs, using strange names, careful to hide any hints of his true and royal lineage. But otherwise, Prince Caspian Hardwood was certain that his reputation had not preceded him.

Nor was his uncle—the new King Damian Hardwood—any closer to tracking him down.

Perhaps, had it not been for the Lady Magdalene, he would have absconded from the realm completely. Boarded one of those pirate ships for some new land across the sea, where his uncle and the threats to his life could not reach him. But Magdalene—his one true love, the only woman who had ever fully besotted him—was still in danger. She had been imprisoned in the castle of the new king, under lock and key.

Yes, there would be many maidens. Many beds he would lay upon. Many dangerous travels in his adventures towards her freedom. But Prince Caspian Hardwood was biding his time, searching for clues, gathering up allies—preparing for the day when he would restore the kingdom he loved most to safety, rescue the beautiful Magdalene, and make her his queen.

SEVENTEEN

"*Haman's hat!*" Faye yelled.

Greg put down the romance novel he was reading in the foyer downstairs and glanced at the clock on the wall. It was late. Long past the time when Faye normally went to sleep, but she was working on something in her studio. He heard the wheel begin to start again. Satisfied that Faye was okay, he returned to his book.

Prince Caspian wrapped one arm around her waist. Her jawline tightened. "You, sir," she said, her gaze drifting southward, "have an unusually large sword."

He wasn't expecting that twist in the story. He moved to adjust himself when his gaze fell on Hillel, perched on the sofa armrest beside him. The dog was staring at him, clearly judgy. "Don't give me that," Greg said, and reached over to give the guy a good scratch behind the ears.

After all, the little guy didn't even have balls.

Meanwhile, Greg couldn't read one page of that romance novel without his mind circling back to Faye.

He was beginning to wonder if there was something wrong with him.

He kept having these intrusive thoughts, instincts that would appear in his mind without permission, which he would have to tamp down by reminding himself that it couldn't happen because he might be a Paper Boy.

Faye would walk past him during business hours, and he would think about grabbing her ass. She would bend over the dishwasher after breakfast, and his eyes would drift to her cleavage. Granted, he had been eating a ton of baladur cakes since coming to live at Magic Mud Pottery…but that wasn't the reason his pants felt tighter.

And frankly, the romance novels weren't helping.

The worst of those intrusive thoughts came at night, though. After spending time together, he would head up to bed, his mind tumbling. It wasn't just sex that he wanted. Sex felt way too tame compared to the fantasies now rolling around in his head, partially inspired by Prince Caspian and his exploits.

He envisioned ravaging Faye, the escapades he was reading about serving as a guide to giving her pleasure. He wanted to make her ripple with desire, explore her inner thighs with his tongue, before sinking his erect manhood inside of her…

Yep. He was definitely some sort of pervert.

Greg took a few moments to see if Faye would shout out again. When she didn't, he returned to his reading.

"It's not the size of the sword," Prince Caspian said, angling his weapon into her belly, "it's what a man can do with it, and believe me, my lady… I have been known to battle all night."

"Mother—" Faye shouted.

Greg stopped reading. From his vantage point in the foyer, he couldn't hear the rest of what Faye was grumbling, but she was obviously distraught.

Closing his book, he went to discover what was happening in the back studio. He found Faye sitting at her pottery wheel, wearing a green apron over pajamas, covered in clay. To her side, a dozen different sketches and drawings were laid out across the floor.

Greg raised an eyebrow. "You okay?"

"I'm fine," she huffed, still pedaling.

She didn't seem fine.

"I just…" she said, shaking her head, partly talking to herself. "I don't even know what I was thinking."

He grabbed a chair to sit down next to her.

"I thought I could try it again," she said, nodding to a square vase that had been completed and was now drying on a back table. "Modular designs. I sketched it out and everything, like I used to do as a teenager…but of course, I can't get the second piece right. It's supposed to be a *Havdalah* set, a set you use at the end of Shabbat. All the pieces, for the candle holder and the wine and the spice box, need to come together."

He analyzed the bowl she was working on. "It looks great to me."

"Well, it's not."

She stopped pedaling, letting the whole thing crumple into clay at the bottom of the bowl.

"Why'd you do that?" Greg asked.

"What?"

"Destroy it?"

"Because it's not right," she said, before adding, "For a modular design, it needs to be perfect. The pieces, the edges, everything needs to be in alignment, or else it won't work."

Greg rubbed his chin. She was always doing that. Undervaluing herself. He didn't see the warps, fingerprints, and misshapen lips that she was always complaining about. But he saw how she destroyed things before she ever gave them a chance.

"You ever think about leaving it as is?" he asked.

"Leaving what as is?"

"Your pottery," he said, nodding back towards the wheel. "Make your modular pieces, whatever the final product looks like. Make it to the best of your ability, and if a piece doesn't fit right…if something doesn't come out just perfectly, so be it."

"Nobody wants messed-up pottery, Greg."

She was torturing herself for no reason.

He picked up the sketches she had made of her Havdalah set. Analyzing it for himself, he had to admit it was a clever design.

"Do you want to make modular designs, Faye?"

"What I want," she grumbled again, "is ten working fingers."

She was so damn stubborn. He couldn't help but think it.

"Actually," Faye said, suddenly, "maybe you can help me."

Greg put down her sketches. "What do you need?"

"I'm thinking…maybe you can be my hands."

He didn't understand. She rose from her seat, gathering another apron, tying it at his waist before directing him to the seat at the wheel. "We're gonna do this *Ghost*-style," she explained. "It's an old movie about a potter. But in our version, you're gonna be my hands, and I'm going to direct them, okay?"

"Okay."

She moved to take a seat behind him, her legs wrapping around his, her breasts pressed up against his back. His mind circled back to the romance novel he had been reading, and his body responded. She was, in every sense of the word, painfully close.

"All you need to do is follow my lead," she said.

Greg cleared his throat. "Okay."

She pressed her hands around his and began to pedal the wheel. He could feel the pressure building, and he worked to obey—taking note to mimic each touch, feeling the wet clay being shaped beneath his hands, guided by her own. His body began to respond when her hands drifted lower.

"Oh," she said, sitting back.

The pottery crumpled beneath them.

Greg closed his eyes. Great. Now she would know he was a pervert. What kind of sick and twisted deviant gets aroused making modular pottery with a woman? Still, he felt the need to explain. "I've been…reading your romance novels."

She rose from her spot. Also, fairly noted, moved away from him.

"No worries!" she quipped, her voice moving into that high-pitched trill that always happened when she got nervous, before she started chewing on one finger. She stopped, though, when she realized it was covered in clay.

"I just…" He pointed to his own back. "You were very close. And then your hand was…"

"I didn't realize it would be there."

"Right."

"It's very…" She made a weird gesticulating motion with her hands. *"Tall."*

He squinted. "Tall?"

Now he was getting worried that there was something wrong with his penis.

"I just mean," she said, backtracking, "it was an unexpected thing."

He had to know. *"Bad?"*

"Nooooo," she said, shaking her head, very adamant. "Not bad at all. Excellent, in fact."

"Well, that's a relief."

The room fell quiet once more. Her wild eyes drifted back to him. The red flush in her cheeks had now spread to her breasts. And those intrusive thoughts returned, to kiss her, to make love to her, to merge with her, body and soul…

The wise thing to do would be to head upstairs to their respective beds alone. Except she was so damn beautiful. Not just her physical being, but her soul. He had committed every curve, hair, bone, and breath to his core memory—but standing so close to her, clay beneath both their fingernails, it was those hidden and invisible pieces that he longed to explore. He considered it a strange affair indeed that she worried about being too much, because he found himself having the opposite problem—he always wanted more from her.

"Would you like a snack?" Faye asked suddenly.

"Actually," Greg said, grateful for the reprieve, "I'd love one."

"Great." She sighed, her shoulders relaxing. "Then why don't you just let me finish cleaning up back here. I'll meet you out in the front foyer in ten."

He shook off the sex haze he had found himself in and moved to do as Faye had instructed. He took off his apron. Washed up. Headed to the kitchen, gathering up supplies to begin making the charcuterie board for Faye and himself. Ten minutes later, as promised, she returned to the downstairs foyer area.

"Oh," she said, glancing at the board. "You're almost finished."

"I know how you like it." He grinned.

She took a spot across from him at the counter. "Listen," she said, pushing one curl behind her ear, "about what happened back there…"

Greg moved to interrupt her. "You don't have to… I know it can't happen, Faye."

"Right."

"I just…" He shook his head, hating himself for not having more control over his own body. "I'm sorry. It won't happen again."

At least, he was going to try to keep it from happening again. In fact, he was going to stop reading romance novels and pick up a book on quantum physics instead. He would spend the rest of his life reading about math equations…and not thinking about Faye.

"Do you want it thick tonight?" Greg asked.

"Hm?" she said, sitting up taller.

"The salami," he said, pointing towards the board.

"Oh." She looked away. "Thick. Thick is always...good."

He began slicing the way she wanted, before her eyes drifted back to his romance novel sitting on the couch. "So, what do you think of it?" she asked curiously.

"Truthfully," he said, catching her eyes, "I love it."

"Really?" She seemed surprised.

"Honestly, I was kind of sad I was getting to the end, and then I looked back on your shelf and realized it was only the first book in a six-book series about The Rogue Prince. The news basically made my night."

She laughed. "Well, I'm glad you appreciate my stories."

He finished layering the meat on the charcuterie board before twisting it back her way. "For you, my lady. For I shall not have anyone in this kingdom claim that I came but did not give my queen her fill..."

"Amazing how you can do that," she said, popping a piece into her mouth.

"Wise words deserve to be recalled."

"What book is that from?"

He caught her gaze. "Not everything I say is taken from a book."

"Hm." She considered his words before adding, "Noted."

A noise appeared in the distance. Greg craned his ears towards the window. It sounded familiar. Something like a car, rumbling down the street at top speed...yet, given the time of night, it didn't feel innocuous.

"What on Earth?" Faye said, heading towards her storefront window to inspect.

Greg peered past her, through the glass, into the darkness of the alley. A car was loitering in the alley across from him. He squinted, trying to discern who was inside the vehicle, when the voice that lived inside of him returned.

Justice, justice…

It echoed inside of him.

Justice, justice…

And then, it became a full sentence.

Justice, justice…you shall pursue.

The rest happened in a flash. An instinct that came over him, The Rogue Prince unsheathing his sword even before the threat had fully been unleashed, because he knew exactly what was about to happen.

"Faye, get down," Greg said.

"What?" Faye said, twisting towards him.

"Get down," he shouted. "Now!"

Dropping the knife, he jumped over the counter and sprinted towards her with only one thought on his mind—Faye was in danger.

He slammed his body against hers, taking her down to the ground. A blur of voices and shouting from the street beyond, their bodies thumping and then falling together—before there was a crash, and they were both caught in a downpour of glass.

He shielded her with his body. Felt the shards come down around them, blades against his back, skin, and head. All while that voice in his head, the one he had heard since waking up in Woodstock, screamed inside of him and refused to abate. *Justice, justice, you shall pursue. Justice, justice, you shall pursue.*

Greg lifted off Faye, checking her body. Running his hands down her face, scanning her form to see if there was blood or injury. *Pupils clear. Limbs moving.* She was safe.

"Greg," she said, her voice quavering.

He stroked her cheek. "You're okay."

"You're bleeding," she said, lifting one hand up to touch a spot on his forehead.

"I'm fine," he said. His only concern was her. "I'm fine, Faye."

Quickly, he assessed the situation. Someone had broken the front window of Magic Mud Pottery. Shards of pottery alongside shattered glass now spread out through the front foyer. The voice returned. *Justice, justice, you shall pursue.*

"Wait here," Greg said, standing up.

"Greg," Faye shouted after him. "No. Don't—"

But he could not stop. *He would not stop.* He raced out the front door and onto the street. The voice got louder. *Justice, justice, you shall pursue. Justice, justice, you shall pursue.*

His entire body on fire, a red-hot fury filled his core. He took off running down the street, his head on a swivel searching the darkness. He was halfway down the block when a blue sedan, burning rubber, came into view. Greg squinted, trying to see the license plate through the darkness. He had only enough time to make out the first four letters and numbers.

HX34

He committed it to memory.

Greg would have run after that car forever, but when he glanced back, Faye was standing in the middle of the street. Her hair disheveled, her pajamas scuffed and torn, she held a brick in one hand and an uncrumpled piece of paper in the other. He raced back to her. She handed him the note, tears in her eyes, her words scattered, hands shaking. Written in red ink over the image of a stick-figure woman being hung from a noose was a simple message:

NO MERCY TO JEWS

He did not hesitate. Wrapping one arm around Faye, he pulled her close to him. She buried her head in his chest, and a wail escaped her lips. He had never heard anyone sob so loud. He didn't even know that such hurt, such pain, could be possible. And it killed him, broke him as a man in ten thousand ways, to feel her shivering inside his grip.

"I'm here," he whispered.

"Greg," she cried. "Oh, God… Greg."

"It's okay, Faye. They're gone."

She couldn't stop crying. The words that had propelled him to action, that had finally appeared in their completion, screamed out inside his head. *Justice, justice, you shall pursue. Justice, justice, you shall pursue.* Greg still didn't know who he was, but he decided that who he had been no longer completely mattered. Because like The Rogue Prince setting off across a kingdom to rescue his maiden, he knew what he had to do.

Justice, justice, he would pursue.

EIGHTEEN

The next morning, Faye stared out over the aftermath of destruction. Shards of glass covered the floors, counters and couches. Her storefront window, the place she had always taken so much pride in decorating, now lay in pieces. Her home. Her business. Her sense of security. All the things she had worked so hard to achieve, destroyed.

Sadly, she wasn't the only one shaken. In the wake of the attack, Hillel had disappeared, planting himself in the upstairs bathroom, where he hid behind the toilet and refused to come out. Even Greg—the man who had so heroically saved her from the shattering glass—seemed to have trouble relaxing. He kept pacing around the front foyer, looking out the broken window onto the street, searching for something to occupy himself while they waited for the police to arrive.

"Here," Greg said, offering her a cup of tea. "I was able to find some kava kava without glass shards in it. I thought it might help you relax."

"Thank you," she said, taking it from him.

He kneeled in front of her, placing one hand on her knee. "How are you doing?"

"Fine, physically," she confirmed, before nodding towards the cut on his forehead. "How's the head?"

"Oh, you know me," Greg said, attempting to brush off her fretting with a joke. "I can take a knocking."

"At this rate," she said, returning the favor by attempting to keep things light, "we should start worrying about permanent damage."

"Hm." Greg twisted back to the foyer, hands angled on his hips as he surveyed the damage once more. "I wish I could start cleaning up for you."

"We need to wait for the police," Faye said. "There may be evidence worth gathering."

She hoped there would evidence worth gathering.

She had called them first thing after the attack, but apparently, she wasn't the only location that had been hit throughout the night. Across Woodstock, reports were coming in regarding a rash of overnight anti-Semitic violence.

These unknown assailants, *The Paper Boys*, had hit multiple locations. Not just Jewish ones, like her business and Shulamit's synagogue, but any place Jews were participants in daily life—from the local high school to the Jewish cemetery. They broke windows and kicked over gravestones. They spray-painted hateful anti-Semitic messages on brick walls and sidewalks. They left threats, wrote the words *Holocaust 2.0* across buildings, promised more destruction to come.

It didn't feel like America, but rather like she had woken up and found herself living inside the stories of her ancestors. She thought of the pogroms of the Russian pale. Of Kristallnacht in Germany and the unofficial start of the Holocaust. Of the massacre of October 7. The promise of *never again*—the words uttered her whole life by Jewish clergy and Hebrew school teachers—suddenly felt like a lie.

Or maybe—she couldn't help but think it—Jews had never been safe.

Maybe all that hatred she was now experiencing had always been there, bubbling under the surface. Perhaps anti-Semitism could embed in your genes, get handed down *l'dor v'dor*, generation to generation, the same way as intergenerational trauma. She didn't want to feel this way about her neighbors. She didn't want to think that people in her community secretly harbored beliefs that led them to hate her...but she was staring out at her home and business, and it had been destroyed.

She didn't want to give The Paper Boys this much power, but it was affecting her all the same. Her emotions veered out of control *because she felt out of control*. Her body reacted without sense or logic. She couldn't focus. All morning long she had been constantly distracted. One moment she wanted to sob hysterically. A second later, she was angry, on her feet and spewing a litany of hateful curses...

She wanted justice, to return the favor of feeling unsafe, until she had convinced herself that there wasn't a righteous person left in this world, and that the entire Earth, and all of humanity, should just burn like Sodom and Gomorrah—when her eyes would wander back to Greg. Greg, who had been there for her. Greg, who was still here for her.

He had shielded her last evening in the onslaught of glass. Used his own body to cover hers as the shards rained down around them. She couldn't help but think back to her father. And Stuart. She was so used to people disappointing her, abandoning her when she needed them the most. But Greg had shown up for her. He had put himself in harm's way in the process, too. It was all so very heroic, and she had to admit... a *little* romantic.

"You really should sit down," Faye said. "I don't want you getting a headache."

"I'm fine," Greg said, heading to the kitchen.

"Greg." Faye put her cup of tea down to show she was serious. "You don't have to play being the hero, okay? It's normal to be *rocked* in situations like these."

"But you misunderstand," he said, pulling out some hard kosher salami, grabbing the knife, and laying down the cutting board. "I'm not rocked. I'm furious." He cut a slice before offering it to her. "You want?"

"No," Faye said. She had no appetite for breakfast. "But if you're hungry, we can order in some food while we wait for the police."

"Actually—" Greg laid three slices out on a paper towel "—I was going to take them upstairs to Hillel. See if I can coax him out. Poor guy hasn't come out from behind the toilet for hours."

She watched him depart up the stairs. He was a good person. Thankfully, they still existed.

Moments later, Nelly came bursting through her front door. "These goddamn Nazis," Nelly said, spitting out the words to an old Yiddish curse. "May they have Pharaoh's plagues sprinkled with Job's scabies!"

For once, Faye found it hard to disagree with her neighbor.

Greg found Hillel shivering behind Faye's upstairs toilet. Pulling the salami from the paper towel, he crouched down— trying to make himself lower than the little creature—before waving his favorite snack towards the little guy. "Hey, Hillel," Greg said, pitching his voice higher. "It's okay. You can come out. I promise…no one is going to hurt you. Not you or Faye."

Hillel sniffed at the air but otherwise refused to budge.

Greg sat back on his knees. He needed to figure out next steps.

A sound from the first floor drew his attention away. Nelly

had arrived and was speaking with Faye. *Jackpot.* Greg craned his ears towards their voices.

"I was just at the synagogue," Nelly said.

"How's Shulamit handling everything?" Faye asked.

"How do you think?" Nelly sputtered, upset. "'We need to combat this hate with even more love.' Ridiculous! What we need is duct tape, stun guns, and a whole lot of old-world chutzpah."

Hearing Nelly, a plan sparked to mind. Leaving Hillel behind with the salami, Greg proceeded down the stairs.

"So," Nelly said, "what do you need help with?"

"Nothing right now," Faye explained. "We're just waiting for the police."

"Actually," Greg said, bouncing down the stairs, landing in a loud thump in front of them, "I have an idea."

"Oh," Faye said, surprised. "Okay."

"I was thinking that Nelly could take me over to Home Depot while you wait for the police. We're going to need to buy some wood planks and nails to get that boarded up. It's already almost eleven. I don't want the day to get ahead of us, and we really should get this place secure by nightfall."

Nelly squinted. "You're gonna leave Faye—"

He cocked his head sideways, pressing his lips together, and attempted to communicate his thinking with his eyes. It took Nelly a minute, but eventually, a flash of recognition crossed her face. "Oh. Ooooooh. Right. Home Depot. Good idea. Yep, I should...totally drive you over there. Straight there and back. What do you say, Faye?"

"I don't know," Faye said, wrapping her arms around her body. "I'm sure the police will want to question you, too, Greg. You're the one who saw the car and license plate, after all."

"I can write it down for you," Greg said, heading to the counter to find a pen and paper from one of her drawers, scribbling out the letters HX34. "And you can text Nelly if they show up. We'll come right back if they do, obviously. But really...we should get the window boarded up by nightfall."

He knew he wasn't wrong. Still, Faye was hesitating.

"You know," Nelly said, walking towards that broken window, "a bird once flew into Second Glance Treasures. I tried to get him out. Used a broomstick, opened every window and doorway...and you know what that bird did?"

Faye attempted to stop her. "I really don't care to—"

Nelly kept going anyway. "He flew around and around, smacking himself headfirst into walls, tiny blue and brown wings fluttering about, blood splatter everywhere. Who would have thought just one little bird could make such a mess. My store looked like a goddamn crime scene. Took me three weeks to clean it all up, too. Forget about The Paper Boys, coming back at nightfall, hell-bent on finishing what they started. It's the birds... The birds are the ones that will really *fakakte* your day up."

Faye's mouth had formed into the shape of an O. "You know what?" Faye said, throwing her hands up. "I can't deal with this right now. You're right. Why don't you and Nelly go down to Home Depot. I'll stay here and wait for the police."

Greg wasted no time in escaping. Grabbing his jacket, he followed Nelly out to her car and climbed into the passenger seat. She had just sat down, and was still working to get her key in the ignition, when he got right down to business.

"I'm ready, Nelly," Greg said, all hesitation in his voice now gone. "Take me to your war room."

NINETEEN

Faye glanced down at her watch. It had been over an hour, and Greg still hadn't returned with Nelly. She debated calling the old woman, demanding they return, when a sight across the street caused her heart to begin palpitating. The little old man, the one who had been at the Say No to Hate Rally in the dark jacket, had now taken up a position on a bench outside of her store.

What was he doing?

She didn't like it. She didn't like the way this stranger always showed up in the wake of anti-Semitic events. She didn't like how he stared at her store, unmoving, like he had ill intent. She debated her options. Going out there, confronting him directly. Or, better yet, she could just call Eric. She retrieved her cell phone when the pitter-patter of tiny feet pulled her attention away.

Hillel had wandered out from his hidey-hole. Relieved to see him, Faye crouched down to the tiny animal. Hillel responded by giving her a good nuzzle into her wrist. It was a surprisingly sweet gesture from an animal who spent most of his time revenge-pooping all over her floors.

"Don't worry," she said, comforting the creature. "Greg will be back soon."

It seemed that both of them were feeling his absence.

Faye shook the thought away. Rising from her spot, she glanced back out the shattered window to find the old man had departed. The street returned to quiet. Faye moved away from the window, careful not to step on any glass, and waited. Each second ticked by more slowly than the previous one. And so, she made more tea. Tried to set her intention. Tried to relax with deep breathing exercises and meditation. She found her way back to her studio and picked up the drawings of the modular Havdalah set she made. It would never come out the way she wanted. Because pieces couldn't exist without hurting each other…

The bell at the front of her store rang out an arrival. Quickly, she put her papers back down and rushed to see who had entered. Eric, fully dressed in uniform, was standing in her foyer. His police vehicle was parked right outside her business.

She had never been so happy to see him.

"Eric," Faye said.

"Faye," he said, rushing over, embracing her. "I came as soon as I could."

Feeling the warmth of his arms around her—the safety he provided—caused a levee to break inside of her. She hated crying in front of other people. It made her feel silly, vulnerable. It reminded her of growing up with her mother, no one ever coming to protect her. But the tears came anyway.

"It's okay," he said comfortingly. "I'm here."

"I'm sorry," she said, pulling away from him. She grabbed a tissue to blot back her tears. "I'm just…so overwhelmed right now. I can't believe this happened."

"You have every right to be upset," Eric said, releasing her.

He stepped back, eyes scanning the room. Fists on his hips, he took in the full extent of the damage surrounding them. "Look at this place." Eric spat out the words. "Goddamn criminals. Goddamn monsters. I swear to God, Faye…"

His voice trailed off. He pressed his lips together. She could hear the anger in his voice, and surprisingly, it soothed her nerves. It was comforting to know that Eric, a member of law enforcement, was taking this crime seriously.

"Can I get you a cup of tea?" Faye asked. "Or perhaps coffee?"

"Coffee would be great."

She headed to the kitchen to begin making it, flicking away a piece of glass that had inadvertently fallen inside the mug. She was finding glass everywhere. In the meantime, she tried to call Nelly and Greg, tell them to come back, but nobody answered.

"Here you go," she said, handing the mug to him. "Though I can't promise it won't come without injury."

"Thanks for the warning," he said, their fingers brushing on accident. "You're being a good sport about all this."

She shrugged. "What choice do I really have?"

They spent a few moments going through official business. Eric took her statement, then collected the brick, along with the note, in a plastic evidence bag. He took photos of the damage—the broken window, her pottery scattered across the floor, a hamsa broken and bent out of shape by the couch.

It was kind of Eric to come himself.

"I really appreciate this, Eric."

He glanced back over his shoulder, playing coy. "What?"

"You're the chief of police," she said, simply. "I know that this, coming to my store, doing all the legwork on a crime scene…isn't usually in your purview."

He returned to sketching some notes in his pad. "You're

right. Normally, I would let someone more junior handle this part. But you're my friend, Faye. I care about you. Even when I don't like the decisions you make… I'll be here for you, too."

She nodded. "I know."

He finished scribbling, putting his notepad in his front pocket. "So," he said, glancing around her store, "where's Greg?"

"He went to the hardware store to get some wood planks to board up the window."

"Ah." Eric seemed displeased. "I was hoping to question him, too."

"I'm sorry," Faye said, reaching for her cell phone. "I tried calling him and Nelly to come back, but I guess they're having trouble with reception." She wasn't sure why a trip to Home Depot to buy some wood was taking them over an hour.

"Those big box stores can often be dead zones," he offered.

"Yeah."

He considered his options before waving off her concern. "It's fine. I think I have most of what I need here."

"Oh," she said, suddenly remembering. "I do have something for you." Faye rose from her spot on the couch, standing up to find the note that Greg had left scribbled on the counter. "Greg went after the attackers last night."

"You're kidding me."

"I know," Faye said, shaking her head. "I told him not to, but I think he was just so pumped up on adrenaline at that point… he wasn't thinking clearly. Anyway, he was able to get a quick peek at the car along with the license plate."

"He did?"

"Well, actually…it's only the first four letters and numbers," Faye qualified. "But basically, it was a dark blue four-door sedan. I figured it might be a good start in tracking down whoever was behind this." She handed the evidence over to him.

Eric stared down at the note. "This is great, Faye."

"Really?"

"Definitely." He beamed, clearly impressed. "I'm gonna take this right back to the station and run it against our files. See if we can come up with an owner for this vehicle. Honestly, Faye…this might just be the break in the case we need."

It made her feel better. He made her feel better.

"And there is—" she swallowed a little over the words "—there is one other thing. I'm not even sure I should mention it."

Eric leaned in. "Okay."

"I saw that man again."

He squinted, confused. "What man?"

"The weird one," she said, feeling foolish for even mentioning it. "The one that has been lurking about, showing up whenever there seems to be anything happening with these Paper Boys. I saw him after the flyers, and at the rally, and this morning, I looked out my window…and, well, he was just sitting on the bench across from the street, watching my store."

"Did he do anything else?" Eric asked, concerned. "Threaten you? Say something weird or inappropriate?"

"No." She shook her head. And then, realizing once again how paranoid it all sounded, brushed off her own fear. "I'm sorry," she said, apologizing for her behavior. "I'm just so mixed up nowadays. Ignore me. With everything happening as of late, I'm not thinking clearly."

"Hey," Eric said, touching her arms gently. "You don't have to apologize to me ever. I'm here for you, alright?"

"I know."

"I'm always here for you, okay?" He met her eyes directly. "Whatever you need, Faye… I've got your six, okay?"

She believed him. He moved to hug her again, and his arms lingered there around her. She took note of how good he felt. The heat of his skin, the comfort he was providing. And yet, her mind wandered to Greg. Deep down inside, despite both their attempts to keep things friendly, it was Greg that she wanted more than anything.

★ ★ ★

Greg stepped out of Nelly's vehicle and found himself smack-dab in the middle of the woods. A modest home with birch tree shingles and strange angles greeted his arrival. On the front door was a mezuzah.

"This is where you live?" Greg asked.

"Last fifty years." Nelly sighed. "My husband was an architect. This was our dream home."

It was beautiful. The peaceful surroundings, which so seamlessly blended in with the building, stood in stark contrast to the war zone he had just come from. Nelly waved him forward, one hand on her hip while she proceeded up three front steps and they both went inside.

With the flip of a switch, the lights around the living room and foyer went on. The same angles, the sharp sloping lines that made up the aesthetic of the outside of the house, now found their way indoors. Unlike Second Glance Treasures, crammed full of items, covered in dust, her house wasn't messy.

It was, however, filled with art.

From the foyer to the living room, sitting on consoles and coffee tables alike, were all manner of statues, paintings, and sculptures. Greg recognized the pink vase with a large circular opening at the top sitting front and center on a table in the hallway.

"Isn't this one of Faye's pieces?" Greg asked.

"You here to talk about my art collection or learn about The Paper Boys?" Nelly said.

"Paper Boys," Greg admitted.

"Good," she said, her hand encircling the knob of a closed door, a keypad at the side. She turned to enter in numbers. "Because we don't have much time."

The door beeped, followed by the sound of whirring, bolts unlocking, and some machine grinding across a tread, before finally, the door popped open. Greg followed Nelly down a dark set of stairs and landed in her war room. Nelly had not been kidding. What the old woman had created in her basement was more than mission control. It was the goddamn epicenter for the antics of The Paper Boys across America.

Track lighting glowed green, yellow, and purple, each denoting a different and ongoing investigation in its respective corner of the room. On the wall in front of him sat a large map of Woodstock. To the right of that map, the state of New York was separated into counties and towns. To the left, another map of the United States of America. Connecting the maps were hundreds of red strings, each one pinned to a newspaper, or a photograph, or a note.

Greg twisted towards a pool table being used as an actual table in the center of the room. A large metal machine, clunky and old, sat beside spray paint and laminate paper. "Is this a machine to make fake IDs?"

"Yeah." Nelly squinted. "How did you know?"

"I don't know."

He considered the question. It hadn't come up in Faye's books, he was certain. But somehow, as soon as he saw it sitting there, he knew what it was. *Strange.* From there, his eyes moved to a pile of yellow shirts with green lettering—five in total—folded up at the corner.

Greg picked one up. On the front, in dark green lettering, were the words *Nazi Hunters.* Beneath that, the tiny image of a gecko scrambled across the front.

"You got T-shirts made?" Greg asked.

"Well," Nelly said, pulling it away from him, "I thought Faye and the rest would be the ones down here, helping me out. If I had known it was only going to be you… I wouldn't have spent so much money getting a bulk order."

"What's with the gecko?"

"Mistake on a previous order," Nelly explained. "I got a good deal if I used these T-shirts instead of new ones."

He supposed that made sense.

"Here," she said, tossing him a shirt in his size.

Greg put it on. "Now what?"

"Now—" she pointed to a large and well-used ottoman positioned in front of a projection screen "—you take a seat. Settle in for a little presentation."

Greg did as instructed. The lights went off. The movie projector went on.

"Let's start with the basics," Nelly said, flipping to her first image. Five black-and-white photographs with names and ages in large block lettering appeared. "The Paper Boys are an underground network of individuals across America connected by one shared fact...their virulent anti-Semitism. It's led by five main figureheads. Those figureheads are the public face of the organization and run the bulk of their websites, organize demonstrations, coordinate attacks on social media...along with PaperBoy TV."

Nelly flipped to an image of one primary computer with arrows to other computers.

"But that's not even the worst of it. The Paper Boys may have five main figureheads, but the bulk of their followers work alone...or in small local cells within their communities."

"So, they work anonymously?"

"That is correct," Nelly confirmed. "Each cell operates independently from the other cells. Sometimes a cell is small. A group of three or four people. A cell can even be as small as one single person. Sometimes it's larger. But they all function the same. They work to spread disinformation and fear around Jews...and to recruit others to join them in their antics."

"But what do they want?" Greg asked. "Why go to all this trouble?"

"What all anti-Semites want," Nelly said. "To spread their hatred of the Jewish people to a wider audience. For their beliefs to take hold, and ultimately, lead to violence."

He had seen that violence for himself last night.

The lights in the room returned.

"I need your help, Greg," Nelly said. "I've made headway into the cell operating in Woodstock. I found them online. Followed their chatter. Found out that they meet in a place that serves buffalo wings."

"Buffalo wings?"

She lifted one finger into the air. "Without blue cheese dressing."

"Okay."

Greg didn't understand how this was relevant.

"So," she said, smugly, "I went ahead and checked with every single restaurant in town, and there are only three restaurants in all of Woodstock that serve buffalo wings without blue cheese dressing. But here's my problem… I can't go into them. People know me. They know I'm Jewish. They'll google my name, and bam, we're done for. Also, my hip has been acting up…"

"I'm sorry to hear that."

"But nobody knows you, Greg," she said, grabbing him by both knees. "You're a blank slate, a tabula rasa, a total unknown. Which means…you can go in and infiltrate The Paper Boys. You can find out who's behind these attacks, and bring them to justice."

Nelly didn't have to wait long for a response.

"Okay," Greg said. "Count me in."

Faye swept another round of shards up and into a garbage bag. She had been cleaning for close to an hour, trying to sort through the mess of broken glass and pottery to see what was salvageable. It didn't feel like much.

On top of everything, her wrist was aching. Absolutely killing her. It was like everything in her body was suddenly inflamed, working in hyperdrive. All the trauma of her past, meeting up with her present, until she couldn't seem to focus on anything but keeping busy.

And yet, unlike all those nights being abused by her mother—those nights where her father would just disappear—Greg had been there. He had jumped into action, risking his own safety in the process to protect her.

Like a bona fide golem.

She couldn't help but think it.

He had to be a golem, because men like Greg didn't exist. At least, not for Faye.

She was still thinking about all the ways it could never work out between them, when the bell above the front door rang out.

Greg had returned.

She exploded into tears, and Greg didn't hesitate. He dropped those wood planks by the door, rushed over, and wrapped his arms around her.

"I'm sorry it took so long."

"It was only an hour," she stammered.

Technically, one hour and thirty-six minutes, but she didn't want him to know that she had counted every single second. That she had been afraid, even in broad daylight, with Eric stopping by to visit. That every sound had made her jump, brought her back to her childhood, brought her back to the feelings of being a victim...

She was not herself. Maybe she would never be able to find herself again.

"I'm sorry," she said, pulling back from him. "Last night has just gotten me so spun up."

"You have every right to be upset."

He was a golem. He was a man. She was a woman, stuck in the past, unable to move on in her present. She didn't know who she was anymore, only that the feeling of his arms around her wasn't enough. She needed him. She needed to forget about what had happened, to escape from this cruel and heartless reality, to believe that she was deserving of better.

"I'm never going to be okay again."

"You are."

"I'm so afraid."

"Listen to me," he said, his voice firm. "I am going to protect you."

"You can't," she stammered. "Nobody can."

He took her by the arms, his nostrils flaring. "I will protect you, Faye."

It felt like a promise.

Her lips parted. The breath in her chest quickened. She was screaming with need, and suddenly, all the reasons she had for avoiding a kiss went right out that broken window. And she was going to give in to it, allow herself to be soft and vulnerable, wanting him to take her in his arms and bring her up to her bedroom, never letting her go again—when a bird, a bright and happy cardinal, landed on a shard of broken glass in the window, chirping its happy song in their direction.

Faye pulled back. "We should probably get that window boarded up."

Greg grimaced. "Yeah."

Pulling apart, they jumped into action. Picking up boards, gathering nails, trying to lessen the damage of that broken window. Putting all thoughts of romance—like all those complicated conversations and questions simmering beneath the surface—in the background.

FEARLESS: A MEMOIR
One Woman's Quest to Climb Mount Everest
By Sandra B. Klatz

Page 160

At forty-six years old, all the things I had been told growing up about what my life should look like, fell apart around me. I was divorced. My career was in ruins. I didn't have relationships, friends and family to fall back on in my darkest moments, because I had never been taught how to nurture them. But most importantly, I had never been taught to nurture the relationship with myself.

So, there I was, alone in my living room, about to pop open another bottle of wine, pour my heartache and my fear into another oversized glass of red, the news serving as wallpaper on the background, when a story came on about a group of local climbers heading to Everest. There was something about the mountain that called to me, the freedom of it, the escape…but mainly, the challenge of taking on something new, something no one had ever expected of me. And I found myself wondering, "What would my life look like if I had never been afraid? What would it look like if I could free myself from self-criticism and judgment?"

TWENTY

It broke Greg's heart seeing Faye over the next week.

Despite the good front she put on for him, and when customers came into the store, he could tell that something was wrong. She was distracted. On edge. At night, she couldn't sleep. More than once, Greg had looked up from a book he was reading to find Faye racing to the bathroom, having just awoken from a nightmare.

She didn't get a break during the day, either. She was always picking up her phone, looking at the news, checking to see if something else terrible had happened. Her eyes drifted to corners, and out onto the street, scanning for some unknown assailant lurking in the darkness. Her wrist bothered her constantly.

Greg did his best to comfort her. He was there when she couldn't sleep, offering up conversation and hard kosher salami. He got her ice. Tried to take on more responsibility when folks came into the store. But nothing really seemed to help. Once, he had even lain down in bed beside her, rubbing her back until she finally felt safe enough to sleep.

She wasn't safe, though. Nobody could feel safe when they were constantly under attack. As for Greg, all he felt was rage. All he could think about was tracking down The Paper Boys. *Justice, justice, you shall pursue.* The words ran constantly in his head.

Greg was sitting on the pullout bed upstairs and reading a memoir called *Fearless* when he heard Faye sigh. Looking up, he saw she was sitting at the kitchen counter upstairs, a dozen different sketches laid out around her. He glanced over to the clock sitting on the nightstand. It was late. Once again, Faye wasn't sleeping.

It didn't bother him, of course. He liked having her in the room with him. But he could tell by the way she kept sighing, shuffling papers around, scribbling notes all over the pages with her colored pencils, that something was wrong.

Faye sighed again. Loudly.

Greg got the hint and put his book down.

"Everything okay?" Greg asked.

"Yeah," she said, twisting on her chair to face him. "Just trying to figure out what I'm going to do with the new storefront window."

She had been debating what to do with the window for several hours.

"You can always just go with what you had," he reminded her.

"I know," she said. She turned back to her papers, pursing her lips, obsessing over her new sketches once more.

He couldn't help but think that what she really needed right now was a break. Some space to clear her head. Figure out, like Sandra B. Klatz in the memoir he was reading, what the issues really were that were leading to her indecision. He debated offering up a snack, or a walk outside with Hillel…when his eyes landed on that Scrabble board at the very bottom of her bookshelf.

He wasn't sure why he was drawn to it. Maybe it was the bright red box, or the fact that it had letters on tiles splattered across the front and edges. He had come to find he had a real affinity for words and language. He leaned across the mattress, pulling it out.

"Up for a game?" Greg asked.

Faye twisted back around. "Scrabble?" she asked, her eyes drifting to the board he was holding. "You remember how to play it?"

"Not at all." He grinned back her. "But I figured, I know a good teacher."

She laughed, a moment of freedom from her worry, before stretching out her back and hands. "Add a snack to that offer," she said, "and you have a deal."

Faye laid out a six-letter word on a double word score: *softer.*

"Excellent," Greg said, writing her score down on a tiny pad with a pen. "Eighteen points."

She appreciated him being a good sport, but it wasn't her best word. Beyond being distracted—she still hadn't decided what to do with her storefront window—Greg was absolutely killing her in the game. She glanced back down at the board.

"I can't get over how good you are at Scrabble," Faye said.

"You think?" Greg said.

"*Scarp, butte, bulwark.* Those aren't everyday words."

Greg laid down the word *defense.* "Twenty-seven points."

"That's it," Faye said, throwing her hands up. "I admit defeat. You win!"

He inhaled. "Game's still not over."

It might not have been over, but it certainly felt like it was heading that way.

She watched Greg move around his tiles when a memory

returned. She thought back to the night she had created her clay effigy, scribbling the words *loves Scrabble* onto one leg. The recollection was foggy, but there. Her eyes wandered down to the board. *He had asked her to play Scrabble.*

It could have just been coincidence, but it was so damn weird. Another impossibility in a long list of oddities associated with Greg. Her fears, like all her anxieties, returned swiftly.

He was going to hurt her. Destroy her. Because the world was unsafe. *It had always been unsafe for Faye.* An anxious sense of spinning returned to her chest again. She touched her heart, certain that it had stopped beating. Greg immediately took notice.

"Should we do some breathing?" he asked.

She nodded. Closing her eyes, she breathed along as he counted. "One," he said. "Two…"

He counted to seven. A lucky number in Jewitch magic. A number that reminded her of the knots, that little red bracelet, still dangling from his wrist. He brought her back to herself. The smooth intonation in his words. The warmth and size of his hands. *Panic attack avoided.* She opened her eyes and found herself situated back in reality.

Because Greg was a man.

A man who would eventually leave her…

She didn't know which option was better, honestly.

She wished she was braver, that the evil of the world didn't constantly make her feel so damn vulnerable, but she had no control. She wished she did, but like always, she was at the mercy of other people's choices. Choices that left her changed, and usually not for the better. She braved a glance back to the sketches sitting on the counter.

"You want to talk about it?" Greg asked.

She couldn't even pocket her surprise. "How…how did you know?"

"I can read you," he grinned, "like a book."

She laughed. Goddess, how she loved all the ways he could make her smile.

"It's stressing me out," she admitted.

"The window?"

"Everything."

She needed to make a decision.

If it had been one thing, she would have been better equipped to deal with everything. But it was all her layers of trauma. Her past, bumping up against her present. It was Greg, bringing that softness out in her, at the same time she needed to be stronger than ever.

No wonder she kept thinking the man was a golem. The way her life was going, he had to be inhuman.

The window was just the icing on the cake.

It was one more thing on a list she didn't feel at all capable of handling. And she was overwhelmed. Ordering the glass, needing to plan out the stenciling and images with the sign people. The simplest option was to just go with what she'd had—the name of the store, a tiny cauldron with a wooden spoon floating above it—but she was hesitating.

"When do you have to decide by?" Greg asked.

"Ideally, by the end of this week."

He pressed his lips together. "Not much time."

Of course, she could delay. Put it off for a few more days and weeks. The wood beams nailed up across her storefront window were effective. But she hated looking at them. They were a constant reminder of what had happened, and every time she glanced their way, it made her stomach churn. She just wanted those boards gone...and yet she was hesitating on what to replace them with.

"Can you focus on what you're feeling?" Greg asked.

"Powerless," Faye said, throwing her hands up. "Hopeless. Vulnerable. The total lack of recourse I have in defending myself, in confronting these Paper Boys for myself."

"Shulamit is hosting another rally," Greg offered up.

"I don't know if I'm in a loving mood this time," Faye admitted, out of ideas.

"You could always join up with Nelly." He smirked.

"Ha!" She scoffed outright. "Please, I'm already stressed out enough."

She ran one hand through her curls. He laid out another word on the board: *steward*.

Faye shook her head at the seven-letter word. "You're killing me here, Greg."

"I only play with worthy opponents."

"Hm." She shifted in her seat.

He was so good to her.

In every interaction, in every moment—perfect. *Like she had crafted him from clay.* She shook the thought away once more. No, it was so much more than simple magic. It was something he had said, all the way back on one their first nights together. *You deserve to be in relationships that bring out the softness in you.* He brought out the softness in her. He reversed time, turning her back into the clay that she was certain had already hardened.

Granted, he had regurgitated his wisdom, like many bits and pieces of his personality, from one of her books...but still, it meant something to her. She could feel bile gathering in the back of her throat. The taste of acid, enveloping her. Because she knew what she felt. Finally. She found her damn words.

"I'm tired of apologizing for surviving."

Greg sat back, his gaze pinned on her.

But that was exactly it. The feeling that she had been holding inside of her. The feeling that began with her mother. That there was something wrong with her. That she had to hide. She hid her mistakes from her mother so that the woman would love her. She hid her real feelings from Stuart so that he wouldn't leave her. And she hid her Jewish identity from a bunch of anti-Semites…so that they wouldn't throw a brick through her window.

And, at the end of the day, none of that making herself smaller mattered. Because nothing about what these people had done to her, chosen for her, was fair. Or right.

Just like it had never, ever been her fault.

But she was exhausted from a lifetime of making other people feel comfortable. And suddenly, she was done. Straight-up finished with all these less than deserving people arriving to her shoreline. Damn the silence. Damn the consequences. She was ready to live her life without constantly interrupting herself to say that she was sorry.

"I wish I was braver," she said finally. "I wish I could drink that wine in my closet, and have a relationship without losing myself, and make broke-ass pottery with my disabled finger, even if it's not perfect, even if it's not right…because who gives a flying broomstick as long as I'm happy! But I don't do these things, Greg. I don't know how to do these things, because despite all my protestations about being brave, and independent… deep down inside, I'm a damn coward."

There. She had admitted her truth. She had told Greg one of her biggest secrets. She waited for him to be disgusted, to shift in his seat, grimace and come up with some excuse for both of them to go to bed. She waited for him to leave her, prepared herself for it, rallied that terra-cotta soldier that lived inside of her. Instead, Greg moved closer to her. He shifted the game board off to the side, so that their legs and arms were touching on the mattress.

"Perhaps," he said, his gaze boring into her soul, "both Shulamit and Nelly have found what works for them. Shulamit holds a rally. Nelly buys a stun gun. They're both experiencing the same sort of fear, the same sense of powerlessness…but they each rely on different items in their emotional toolbox to deal with the situation."

He had a point.

Even though he had probably stolen it from a book.

"So," Greg said. "What do you need?"

His question rattled her.

She thought back to all those nights, hiding from her mother. She thought about her dad, too—the way she was there for him when he was dying—even though he had failed her so often throughout her youth. And she thought about Stuart. How she never got to tell him that he was awful, wrong, *that she deserved better*, after he dumped her on a snowdrift in Lapland.

She gave others what she had always needed from them— love and affection, security and protection, a place to land when things got bad—while never demanding the same for herself.

Her thoughts wandered to The Paper Boys, these invisible assailants, who had the audacity—*the cowardice*—to throw a brick through her window in the middle of the night. And the only thing she could think, the words that came up from her belly in a rage, were simply…

Hex. Them. All.

"I want to take my power back," Faye said suddenly.

"And what will help you reclaim your power?"

"Art," she said. "Art makes me feel better. And caving, obviously. Connecting with nature. But I don't know if making a vase and a trip underground is going to suffice right now. I don't know if pottery is big enough, loud enough, for all these feelings bubbling around inside of me."

"So, what will be big enough to handle all those large feelings?"

He reached over to remove a piece of hair that had fallen across her face. She allowed the intrusion, the palm of his hand brushing against her cheek, the weight of his support, sinking into her like they were sinking into the mattress.

"I want to…no, I *need* to make a statement, to say something… to make it clear that this is not okay. I want to respond."

"But you're hesitating?" he asked.

"Yes," she said. "Because I'm afraid. I'm always afraid, Greg."

"What would it look like if you weren't afraid?" Greg asked.

"Not afraid…"

She scoffed at the idea. The concept. Because Faye was The Great Pretender. She acted strong, played at independence… but, she was a coward. She had built up this whole new life in Woodstock, trying to return to herself, trying to live out the dream that had been stolen from her, and yet nothing had really changed.

But then, there was Greg. The man who had come into her life—who may very well have also been some sort of Scrabble-playing, book-reading golem—and he hadn't yet run away from her. He shifted closer, his eyes impossibly serious, his lips dangerously close to her own. "Don't think it through," he said, enveloping her in his gaze. "Just go with your heart, with your gut. The first thing that comes to mind. If you could separate out your fear from the thing you wanted to do—it doesn't mean you have to do it, obviously—but what would it look like to free yourself from self-criticism and judgment?"

She would kiss him.

It was the first thought that came to mind. The thing she had been wanting to do since forever. But there were so many barriers to a happy ending. There were so many ways it was likely to go wrong—and she returned her thoughts to the window.

"Seriously," Faye said, shifting to sit up in her seat once more, "I really need to do a re-read on my self-help books."

"They were quite useful," he admitted.

"I swear…you're better than therapy."

The room fell into silence once more. And Greg gave her space. Space to be free from judgment, space to be free from fear. He let her take up all the air, all that emotional energy, without complaining he was suffocating. And Faye was grateful, for this man, for this person—*for this totally not a golem*—

who had read all her books and used the words he had found there to change her.

Change. It didn't always have to be scary.

"I would change the window," she said.

"Okay."

"I would put something on that window that really speaks to my beliefs, my pride in being a Jewitch woman…and a giant screw-you to all the anti-Semites and all these people trying to run me out of my home and my business."

The words came, free and clear.

Greg let her have the space to keep going with them.

"And then," Faye said, rising from her seat, growing more animated with each passing moment, "just to show I wasn't afraid, I would throw a giant party. I would invite the entire neighborhood, all the people I love and trust, all the people I don't know, too… I would make it open to everyone, and I would bake cupcakes with Jewitch stars on them, and give away all my ring dishes, and serve all that expensive and fancy kosher red wine that never got drunk from my wedding—because screw Stuart, too!"

After which she would have totally amazing and completely reckless sex with Greg.

But, *obviously*, she left that part out.

Greg waited patiently for her to finish. He lay there on the squeaky mattress beside her, never overstepping her boundaries, always a comfort—and God, how she wanted to kiss him, but she turned her head back to the ceiling instead.

"Is this when you tell me I have my answer?" Faye asked.

"No." Greg grinned devilishly. "I would never do that."

"But it's what I should do, right?" she said, sitting up again. "Separate out my present life from my fear. Live my best and proudest Jewitch life. Say *screw you* to the anti-Semites."

He shrugged.

She tossed a throw pillow at him. "You are no help."

Greg laughed and caught it. They were so close to each other now. They were so comfortable with each other, too. It seemed impossible. They were impossible together. And yet, she wanted him to touch her. She wanted him, in every single way.

"Whatever *you* decide, Faye," he said, submerged in her eyes, "I'm here for you."

Faye nodded. "I know."

But what would happen when Greg wasn't there? If she allowed these feelings, and he left her—like Stuart, like her father—forever. She didn't want to think about these things. She didn't want to think about how much losing him for good, for forever, would hurt. But she knew if she needed anything in her life right now, it was courage. Perhaps one courageous act would make taking on another easier.

"Okay," Faye said, after a few thoughtful beats. "I know what I want to do."

THE JOYS OF JEWITCH COOKING
By Priestess Dina Lovejoy

VANILLA MAGIC CAKES

Vanilla is a magical ingredient that both tastes great in baked goods and has calming properties. Use this basic recipe for cupcakes whenever you're looking for a super sweet treat that will help soothe your nerves. Or, include it in a party where blessings of prosperity are needed. The beauty of this simple recipe is that it can be modified to elevate and include other magical ingredients, such as cinnamon, cocoa, pomegranate and more. Allow your inner Hebrew Goddess to guide you and you really can't go wrong!

INGREDIENTS

2 Cups Flour
½ Teaspoon Baking Powder
½ Teaspoon Salt
½ Cup Butter, Softened
1 Cup Sugar
2 Eggs
1 Cup Yogurt
1 Teaspoon Vanilla Extract

DIRECTIONS

1. Preheat oven to 375 degrees
2. Line a muffin tin with paper
3. Combine flour, salt, and baking powder in bowl
4. Cream butter, yogurt, and sugar together, then beat in eggs one at a time
5. Pour flour into wet mixture, beating well
6. Stir in vanilla
7. Divide evenly and bake for 18 minutes
8. Cool before decorating

TWENTY-ONE

The grand reenvisioning of Magic Mud Pottery was even better than Faye had imagined. Once word had spread about the reveal of a new window and a party, her neighbors had responded. Despite it being the lunch hour, folks closed their own shops to join Faye and show support. There were cupcakes, red wine, and best part of all, she had nearly sold out of ring dishes.

"Quite a turnout," Greg said, appearing beside her.

"Indeed," Faye said.

She was feeling surprisingly good about things. Even though she knew what she was about to do might cause trouble, she felt freer than she had in weeks. Her eyes drifted to the top of Greg's shirt, where three buttons were still left undone, revealing the most gloriously sexy sprigs of bright red chest hair. She could imagine running her fingers through all that manliness...

"How are you feeling about things?" Greg asked.

"Good," she said, returning to herself. She twisted towards

a table, grabbing a bottle of red wine and two plastic cups. "Would you like to make a toast with me?"

Greg took the wine from her and lifted his glass. Faye did the same.

"To life," she said, simply.

"Baruch Hashem and Blessed Be," Greg said.

They both took a drink.

A warmth flushed her cheeks, though it seemed too soon to be coming from the wine.

"Faiga!" a voice called out from behind her.

Faye turned around to find Miranda with Shulamit by her side.

"You made it," Faye said, giving her bestie a hug. She wasn't sure with Miranda's teaching schedule if she would be able to get off.

"Of course we made it," Miranda said.

"Wouldn't miss it for the world," Shulamit said fondly. "And look at this turnout!"

Faye had to agree. Even though the victory wasn't hers alone. "Well," Faye said, resting one hand on Greg's arm, "I can't take all the accolades. Greg here has been an absolute lifesaver. Not only did he support me through getting the window fixed and choosing a final design…but he was instrumental in helping get the word out, and setting up for the party. He actually made all the cupcakes."

"Really?" Miranda asked, surprised. "I had no idea you were a baker, Greg."

"I read a cookbook," Greg said, before adding, "And I have lots of experience making baladur cakes. It was an easy transition from there."

"No doubt." Miranda smiled.

Just then, Nelly appeared on the stoop of her shop. Faye was clearly in a good mood, because upon seeing her, she lifted on her tiptoes and tried to wave her over. Sadly, Nelly didn't see her.

"Can I get you ladies a glass of wine?" Greg asked before winking at Shulamit. "Or perhaps some water and a cupcake?"

"You know what?" Miranda said, raising both eyebrows. "I would love both...if it's not too much trouble."

"None at all," Greg confirmed.

"Actually," Shully said as she slinked past them, "if you don't mind, I see a few congregants. I should probably go over and say hi."

With that, both Greg and Shulamit departed. Faye and Miranda were finally alone. Faye couldn't contain herself any longer. "Miranda, I have to tell you something. I really like him."

"Noooo."

"Like." Faye grimaced. "I'm having feelings. Big ones."

"Well, yeah, Faye!" Miranda said. "I think it's fairly obvious."

"I don't know what to do."

"What do you mean *what to do*?" Miranda asked, incredulous. "You need me to buy you a book on the matter?"

"Really?"

"Better yet—" Miranda began edging into hysterics "—I'll buy Greg a book on the subject. In fact, I'll bring him a whole library's worth of books about pleasing a woman...turn him into the best lover you've ever had."

Faye crossed her arms against her chest. "I'm being serious here, Miranda."

"And so am I," Miranda said, not missing a beat. "Listen, Faye... I know you have this tendency to believe that you're not deserving of love and happiness, so hear me when I say this—you are a great woman...and Greg is a great guy."

"I thought he was a golem?"

"Who cares if he is!" Miranda said. "I mean, he's amazing, Faye. He's amazing for you. Let's consider the evidence here. He's read all your books. He cleans up after Hillel. He enjoys hanging out with your friends, and better yet, your friends actually like this one. He brings you hard kosher salami whenever you ask for it. I mean, who wouldn't like someone like Greg? The only thing that shocks me about this situation is that you two haven't done it already." She backtracked. "You haven't had sex with him, right?"

"I thought it would complicate things."

"Well, it can't get more complicated than a brick through your window."

She wasn't wrong.

Her friends had never really liked Stuart. They tolerated him, obviously...invited him to events that she was invited to, but otherwise, respected her decision to marry him by keeping their mouths shut.

It wasn't until after the breakup that their real feelings came out.

Stuart never made any type of real effort. He stared at his phone when they came over to her apartment in Manhattan. *He had no hair.* But mainly, what they disliked about Stuart was the way Faye changed with him. She took care of everything—the groceries, the bills, the cleaning—while Stuart couldn't even get it together enough to buy her a birthday gift.

"You know, Faye," Miranda said gently, "not every man is Stuart."

"What's that supposed to mean?"

"I'm just saying," Miranda replied, "what if Greg's memory never comes back? What if you just have this hot redheaded tabula rasa, with huge muscles and a giant heart, eager to help you out in *every which way* for the rest of your natural life?"

"I really doubt that's going to happen."

"Well," Miranda said simply, "if it does happen, try to keep what I said in mind. Not every man is Stuart. *Thank God.* Besides, you always deserved better than him, anyway."

Just then, a sight at the corner of the crowd drew Faye's attention away. On a bench, across from her business, was that old man she had been seeing all around town. Once again, he appeared to be scowling, wearing that same puffer jacket that appeared far too warm for the weather.

Her nerves returned. Her mind wandered into worst-case scenarios. She scanned the crowd to see if Eric had arrived… and then, on second thought, she gave up on the idea entirely. She was tired of feeling this way. Always afraid. She was ready to confront her fear.

"Excuse me for a second," Faye said. "There's someone I need to talk to for a minute."

"No worries," Miranda said, lifting her glass of red wine. "I'll be right here, all alone…getting sloshed before noon."

Faye grabbed a tray full of cupcakes decorated with Jewitch symbols and made her way down the street, taking a seat beside him. A cool breeze passed over them before Faye twisted in her seat and offered him a cupcake.

"Would you like one?" she asked, smiling at the old man.

He peered at the offering.

"Cupcakes," she explained. "The ones with purple icing are chocolate, and the ones with strawberry icing are vanilla."

He grumbled and, rolling up the sleeve of his coat so as not to make a mess, reached for a chocolate.

"My name is Faye." She offered her hand. "Faiga Kaplan."

"Ruben."

He shifted the cupcake he was eating from one palm to the other, extending his hand. Faye went to shake it. In the process, her eyes drifted down to his left wrist, where a number, faded and black, was etched into his skin.

The words she had been meaning to say caught in her throat.

"Good," he said after his first bite. "You make them?"

"My friend made them, actually."

"I like them," he said. "My wife…she used to make cupcakes. Haven't had one for years, since she died. Forgot how good they were."

"I believe I've seen you around town," Faye inquired, "though

I don't think we've ever had the chance to meet. You live in Woodstock?"

"Few towns over."

"Ah." Faye nodded to her store. "I own Magic Mud Pottery."

"I know," he said, before adding, "I've been keeping an eye on it for you."

She was surprised. "You have?"

"I've been keeping an eye on the whole town," he said proudly. "Ever since these flyers came...damn Nazis."

Suddenly it all made sense to her. The old man appearing at various Jewish events throughout town. The way he lingered, eyes constantly scanning the crowd, like he was a sentry on patrol duty. He wasn't there as a Paper Boy or to spread nefarious intent. He was there as a Jew, and a Holocaust survivor, to protect others from the horrors he had faced.

"Also," he offered up, pointing the last of his cupcake towards Second Glance Treasures, "the little one is awfully cute."

Faye squinted, confused. "The little one?"

"The little one with the short gray hair, one who owns Second Glance Treasures. The little one...who throws all those dog tea parties. Sometimes erotic parties, too, I heard."

Faye could hardly believe her ears. It seemed her wily old friend had a secret admirer. "Nelly," Faye informed him. "Her name is Nelly."

"Nelly," he repeated dreamily. "A beautiful name for a beautiful woman."

"I'd be happy to introduce you to her," Faye said. "I happen to know that she's single...and very much on the market. I'm sure she would be thrilled to meet you."

The man shifted in his seat nervously. The question had clearly caught him off guard. After a long pause considering the idea, he waved it away entirely. "Not yet," he said firmly. "First, I gotta protect the town from these damn Nazis. After that, there will be plenty of time for romance."

She patted the man on the wrist. "Well, I look forward to that day."

He nodded stoically, then returned his attention to scanning the crowd. Leaving him, Faye went back to Miranda.

"What was that all about?" Miranda asked.

"Nothing," Faye said innocently. "Just someone with a major crush on our Nelly."

Miranda's eyes went wide. "Noooooo."

"Yep," Faye said, nodding to the man on the bench. "He likes the little one. He's heard about her dog tea parties, and erotic ones, too…and still, he likes the little one."

"Well." Miranda laughed, shaking her head at the thought. "It's nice to know that, no matter what, love finds a way to happen."

Faye raised her glass to that sentiment. "Indeed."

She had always been so certain that love was a weakness. A vulnerability that had to be tapped down. A thing that would eventually destroy her. But what anti-Semitism, and Greg, were teaching her…was that love could be a balm, too.

She didn't know how her story would end. Perhaps the dreams she crafted for herself, etched onto the body of a golem doll, would never come true. But today, in the present, without concern for the past and without thinking about the future, she was ready to be fearless.

"I have news," Nelly said, pulling Greg into Second Glance Treasures. She bolted the lock on the door behind them so they could talk privately. There was a glimmer of excitement in her voice. "The Paper Boys are meeting *for sure* tonight."

His mouth went dry. "Where?"

"Not entirely sure," she admitted. "But based on previous chatter, I believe it's one of the three locations that serve buffalo wings without blue cheese dressing. Now, what I was thinking is we send you in undercover."

Greg knew what to do. He had learned all these lessons from his books.

He knew about going undercover, searching for clues and evidence from Sam Beacher. He knew about pretending to be someone you weren't through The Rogue Prince. And he understood anti-Semites, how they thought, how they operated, the lingo and terms they used in their beliefs, from the nonfiction books he had read.

"So," Greg said, filling in the blanks, "I go to each of those locations. See what I can feel out. See if I can make contact with these people directly."

"Now we're talking."

"How do we start?" Greg asked.

"Meet me outside Pinky's ice-cream joint at seven o'clock tonight."

"What about Faye?" Greg frowned, concerned.

Nelly squinted. "What about her?"

"How am I going to sneak out without raising her suspicion?"

He thought back on their time together. For as long as he could remember, they shared hard kosher salami together at night. Now, they paired it with playing Scrabble. It would be weird to suddenly claim that he just wanted to go to sleep. What if she got up in the middle of the night, and saw he wasn't there?

"Well, figure out something, Baby Bird," Nelly snapped back at him. "Because tonight's the night!"

With that, she unlocked the door, pushing Greg back outside. He dragged one hand down his face, and considered his options. Because Nelly was right. Time could not be wasted. The Paper Boys had to be found and held accountable for their actions. The words—*justice, justice, you shall pursue*—played like a song on repeat inside his head.

He settled on dealing with specifics later. For now, he was

eager to get back to Faye. He found her, along with Miranda, talking to Chief Eric Myers.

"Eric," Greg said, offering his hand. "How you doing?"

"Good," Eric said.

"It's nice of you to come," Greg said.

"Unfortunately, I can't stay that long," Eric said casually. "But even with as busy as I am down at the station, I wouldn't miss the chance to support Faye." He threw one arm around her, pulling her towards him, speaking to her directly. "I'm glad I can be here for you."

Greg forced a smile.

Eric was saying all the right things, but still, the man rubbed Greg all types of wrong.

It drove him bonkers the way Eric was always touching her... but he did his best to acknowledge those feelings as jealousy, and then let them go. Besides, he had bigger anti-Semitic fish to fry, and having the chief of police in front of him was to his benefit.

"So," Greg asked, "what's happening with the investigation?"

"Well, unfortunately, Greg..." Eric inhaled deeply, as if the question itself was both bothersome, and unbelievably stupid. "Because it is still an active investigation, I'm not at liberty to discuss specifics."

Greg refused to let it go.

"But what about the license plate?" he asked.

"What?" Miranda said, confused.

Faye stepped in to clarify. "Greg saw the license plate the night of the attack."

At the news, Miranda's eyes went wide. "You're kidding me. That's amazing!"

Greg agreed. He would have thought that the license plate would have provided a break in the case, but Eric seemed to have difficulty remembering. He squinted in Greg's direction. "Oh, right," Eric said, finally. "A green sedan with four—"

"A blue sedan with four doors," Greg interrupted him.

"What?" Eric said, annoyed.

"It was a blue sedan with four doors," Greg corrected him. "The first four letters of the license plate were HX34. Faye gave it to you when you stopped by. You said you were going to run it? Faye mentioned that it might be the break in the case that you need. So, any word on that?"

A pause teetered between all four of them, before Eric blew all the air out of his chest. "Unfortunately," Eric said, "we ran what you gave us, trying to find a comparable vehicle in the area...but nothing came of it."

"Nothing?" Greg almost couldn't believe it.

"Well, what about the FBI?" Miranda brought up. "Surely they must have federal databases they can explore that local police don't have access to."

Eric raised both hands up in open surrender. "We've done all that," he explained. "At this point...it's out of my hands."

"Oh," Faye said sadly. "That's so disappointing."

"I know," Eric said, his eyes falling to her gently. "Honestly, I was so hoping it would solve this thing once and for all. But when it just brought us back to a bunch of dead ends... I figured that Greg must have been mistaken."

Greg dipped his chin back. "Mistaken?"

"Not for nothing, Greg," Eric said. "I appreciate your help in this matter, and that you were there to protect Faye when Magic Mud Pottery was attacked. But you're also not exactly the most reliable witness out there, considering you don't have a memory. Truthfully, I doubt that anything you would say... would hold up in a court of law."

He didn't like it. The way Eric wasn't taking him seriously, brushing him off, treating him like he was incompetent simply because he was living with a temporary disability. He attempted to keep his cool, but the words stung. The frustration he had experienced in the hospital—the way the doctors had treated him like furniture—returned.

"Actually," Faye said, tipping her cup of wine in his direction, "Greg has an excellent memory. Basically eidetic. In fact, what we have learned about Greg since he's come to live with me is that he is a man of many talents. One of which is to pick up a book, any book, and remember parts of what he read word for word."

Eric squinted. "You're kidding me?"

"Hm," Faye said, her eyes drifting back towards Greg. "It's really...quite remarkable. Also a talent that, having been a lawyer myself, could be easily proven in any court of law. Indeed, a jury would gasp aloud at seeing what he's capable of...such a brilliant and smart man."

His eyes lifted from the sidewalk, meeting hers.

"But that's not my point in telling you this," Faye quipped, twisting back to Eric. "My reasoning is much simpler. Because if Greg says he saw that license plate, on a blue four-door sedan, and that the first four letters were HX34... I'd stake all my money, along with all the magic in the world, on believing him."

He couldn't hear the rest of the conversation, because he was fully focused on Faye. Faye, and her kindness. Faye, and her words. Faye, the woman he wanted, but couldn't have, because he might be a Paper Boy. And the words in his head returned, a song with one chord repeated, over and over again.

Justice, justice, you shall pursue.

Faye tapped on an empty wine bottle with a metal spoon.

"Excuse me," she said, standing in front of Magic Mud Pottery, bringing the crowd to attention. "If I could have your attention."

The crowd quieted, turning towards her. Faye scanned their faces. Eric had to leave early but all her friends were there. Miranda and Shulamit. Nelly. Greg, too. Their presence, lifting her up, making her feel stronger.

She was ready to reclaim her power.

"First," Faye said. "I wanted to thank all of you for your support over the last six weeks. Some days, it's easy to forget how much good there is still left in the world. But when I look around at this street, and this block—at all my neighbors, friends, and chosen family who have shown up for me—I know that hatred and white supremacy will never win."

A round of applause exploded from the crowd. She waited for them to quiet before continuing. "I've been thinking a lot about combating anti-Semitism lately, and the truth is, I don't know if I will ever be able to change the mind of a white supremacist. Anti-Semitism is not a Jewish problem. It's a problem that affects the Jews. But I know what I can control. I can model Jewish pride. I can be strong and courageous in the knowledge of my identity. And maybe by doing these things, I can inspire others to feel strong and courageous in speaking up, too."

Faye reached for the rope holding up the tarp across the window.

"I will not be afraid," she said. "I will not be silenced. I will not shutter my business or leave Woodstock, either. And from this day forward, I want everyone in Woodstock to know that Magic Mud Pottery is owned and operated by a proud *Jewitch* woman."

She pulled on the rope, and the tarp fell. A gasp went up from the crowd, before applause and cheering, both loud and raucous, rang out from the crowd.

Faye turned back to the glass, taking in the shape and make of her new storefront window. The old cauldron with a stirring spoon was gone. Now, in its place, was the image of a Jewitch woman standing upon the ground, tefillin wrapping around her arm, tallit blowing in the wind, a full moon above her, and the sky above filled with six-pointed Stars of David.

Beside her, above a raging fire, were the words *MAGIC MUD POTTERY* written in an enchanted script.

But the pièce de résistance—her final *screw-you* to the anti-Semites or anyone still at risk of missing her message—was a note, in big block lettering, right at the bottom of the glass.

**THIS STORE IS PROUDLY OWNED AND
OPERATED BY A JEWITCH WOMAN**

**"LET ALL WHO CAST STONES, BE CURSED.
AND ALL WHO SHAPE CLAY, FIND WELCOME."**

TWENTY-TWO

"Look at that," Faye said. "I can see wood."

Greg glanced up from the bag of trash he was taking out to see that the closet—once overrun by boxes of wine—was now nearly empty. Only a single box, and a few bottles, remained. Jackets hung neatly from a rack. Scarves and mittens were piled up on a shelf.

"I'm proud of you, Faye."

She twisted in her spot to face him. "You know what?" she said. "I'm proud of me, too."

With that, she swung the door to her closet shut.

Greg nodded solemnly, and took out the trash. Tossing it in the bin outside, he tried to come up with reasons for leaving her behind at night to go track down The Paper Boys with Nelly. But everything he landed on—like getting kidnapped by pirates in *The Rogue Prince*—wouldn't work with Faye.

Returning to the foyer, he found Faye locking the front door.

"Is that the last of it?" she said.

Greg examined the space. The tables had been put back in both the studio and the garage. The glass wine bottles had been cleaned and loaded into recycling. "I think so."

They were alone. The quiet spread out across the foyer, and her eyes caught on his. Her hips, like her breasts, were angled in his direction. And she looked so free in that moment. So happy, too. He loved seeing her like this, full up with all the joy she deserved. He fell into her gaze, her swinging, shifting angles, until all reason was lost.

A heat flushed in his chest…and loins. A feeling so intense, a craving, sprang from the deepest well of him, because the way she was looking at him…also felt like hunger.

He swallowed, unable to form words, his body responding. And Faye closed the distance. All the desire he had been pushing down, squelching nightly because it was wrong, because he didn't know who he was, because he didn't want to hurt her…disappeared under the spell of his own throbbing need.

Faye met him with her own frenzied hunger. Her words disappeared into moans, her hands reaching behind his neck, greedy fingers pulling at his hair, while she kissed his mouth. Gentle kisses were followed by forceful ones, swirling tongues like these swirling feelings, because he shouldn't be doing this. They shouldn't be doing this.

And yet he kissed her, and kissed, and kissed her…drowning out the noise inside his head, forgetting all about his past and his future, softening like clay beneath her touch, because hearing those soft moans of pleasure escaping her mouth, his instinct as a man fully took over.

"Faye." He groaned her name.

"Yes," she whispered back.

"We should stop."

"We should," she said, wrapping her legs around his waist. His erection grew, because she was magnificent. He pulled at the buttons of her dress—a reminder that he didn't know who he was, that he should stop this—and yet he tore open her dress all the same. Nuzzling his lips into the space between her breasts, he felt her weight, her heft, the splendor of this one brilliant creature, bucking beneath his grip.

"You're magnificent," Greg whispered.

"Yes," Faye moaned.

"Perfection."

"Greg."

The name brought him back to reality. "But we shouldn't…"

His tongue found her nipple, and he covered her bare skin with his mouth. She shivered—*he felt her shiver*—and so he drew her closer to his body, two tectonic plates shifting towards an earthquake.

"You have no idea…how badly…"

"Greg," she whispered, meeting his eyes. "Let's go to the bedroom."

His heart ached. A thousand reasons why he shouldn't, *why he couldn't*, floated through his brain…before he obeyed, lifting her up, angling those thick thighs around his waist, his manhood engorged with blood, pressing against her, pressing into her, desperate for the wet heat that was lingering there—for some release, craven and preternatural. While she kept kissing him, tearing at him, the heat of his need meeting her own arousal. He carried her up the stairs, careful not to trip over Hillel, and kicked her bedroom door open.

There was no hesitation anymore. No fear shared between them. He released her, placing her feet carefully upon the ground. And she tore at his shirt. Her hands reached into his waistband—not even bothering with his buttons anymore— her fingertips grazing the tip of his desire, causing him to melt, before she lifted up his shirt, taking it off and throwing it to the side, where it landed on the ground in one crumpled lump.

Her eyes rolled over his form, his naked chest, the painfully obvious bulge in his pants.

He moved to step forward, touch her once more, when her gaze shifted upwards, over his shoulder, towards the mirror that was situated behind them. Faye squinted, her chin jutting out, before she stumbled back.

And just like that, the spell was broken.

TWENTY-THREE

It was impossible.

But it was there, staring back at her in the mirror. Greg had a large scar running down the center of his back. Her mind drifted back to the night she had made that golem doll, and a hazy recollection appeared. She had dropped the clay figure, cracking its back, and had to return to her studio to patch it.

"What?" Greg asked, confused.

"You have…" she stammered "…a scar on your back."

"I do?" Greg twisted around, trying to see in the mirror. But the way it sat, right in the center of his back, made it difficult. "That's weird," he said, shrugging simply, innocently, totally unaware of the storm now raging in her mind. "I wonder how I got it."

"You don't remember?" Faye asked.

Her throat felt parched. Her tongue felt unfamiliar inside her own mouth. Of course he didn't remember…*because he was a goddamn golem*. Some supernatural creature, summoned from another realm, walking around in a person suit. It was a story that Faye had heard a thousand times, and that the AI chatbot had promised her never ended well for the creator.

Death. Destruction. The golem would run amok... Punishment for having the audacity to believe that she deserved better. Her mother's voice. Her misshapen pottery. Her own unlovable self. Men, constantly, leaving her.

That's what Faye saw in the mirror.

"You know what?" she said, trying to act normal. "Could you maybe wait here for a minute?"

Greg blinked, confused. "What?"

She began to button up her dress, followed by inching backwards towards the door. "Just wait here." She forced a wide and innocent smile. "I promise, I will be right back."

She made her way towards the stairs, nearly tripping over Hillel in the process. "And if you don't mind," she shouted back at him from the top of the stairs, "could you maybe put your shirt back on, too?"

"You want me to get dressed?" he shouted back.

"Yes, please." Her voice was saccharine sweet.

It took Greg a moment to answer. "Okay."

Faye turned on her heel and sprinted down the stairs. Racing onto the street, she bolted towards the front door of Second Glance Treasures.

"Nelly?" Faye said, entering the store. "Are you here?"

No answer.

She tried again. "Nelly, please!" she shouted out from between overstuffed racks of women's clothing. "It's important. I need to ask a favor."

"Are you out of your mind?" Nelly finally appeared from a doorway in the back. "Coming into my place of business screaming your head off. I'm eighty years old. You trying to keep me from making eighty-one?"

"I'm sorry," Faye said, out of breath. "I didn't mean to scare you."

"Well, why are you screaming then?" Nelly said, perturbed. "And why do you look like you were just mauled by a bear?"

"What?" Faye squinted.

Nelly waved towards her dress. Faye glanced down. The top of her dress was buttoned up wrong...leaving her bra, and one of her breasts, significantly exposed. "Oh, *Haman's hat*," Faye said, and quickly turned around to fix herself before facing Nelly again.

"Looks like you had an interesting afternoon," Nelly said dryly.

"It's nothing."

"Uh-huh."

Nelly smirked. Faye didn't have to get into this with Nelly. More important, she was desperate. She needed the old woman's help.

"Listen," Faye said quickly, "what are you doing right now?"

"What do you think I'm doing?" Nelly balked. "It's five o'clock. I'm closing up the store and getting ready to go home."

"I need a favor from you."

Her whole face wrinkled up around her nose. "What type of favor?"

"I need you to take Greg off my hands for a bit," Faye said, before clarifying, "Actually, not just for a bit...but most of the night. All night, if possible."

Nelly's chin dipped back. "All night?"

"There are some things I need to do." She spat out the words. "And I just, I just can't do them if Greg is around. I know it's a huge ask on you, but if you could maybe babysit him, keep him company, keep him out of my hair, for as long as humanly possible... I would be so appreciative."

Nelly crossed her arms against her chest, obviously ready to drive a hard bargain.

"Dinner," Nelly said finally.

"What?"

"The thing is," Nelly explained, "I've been having this hankering for buffalo wings. Buffalo wings *without* blue cheese dressing. Now, normally, I would go and get these buffalo wings myself. But I suppose, since you're so desperate and all, I can take Greg along with me…providing you pay."

"Hot wings?" Faye asked, confused. "I mean, okay."

"So, you'll pay for it?"

"I'll pay," Faye agreed without a fight. "I'm happy to pay for dinner. And anything else you two want to do tonight."

"Looks like we have a deal." Nelly beamed. "When do you want me to take him off your hands?"

"Now," Faye explained, wasting no time heading back towards the door. "Right now."

Greg wasn't sure what was going on. But he did as Faye requested. He put his shirt back on, zipped up his pants, and waited in the bedroom for her. He thought about what had happened—what had almost happened—and the way her face contorted, fearful and confused, when she saw that scar on his back.

He didn't understand it, her interest followed by her reluctance. If he had done something wrong in the way he was touching her…but he couldn't help but feel that something had shifted, instantaneously and irrevocably, between them. Because it wasn't just a scar, he realized, most sadly. It was his past. The person he had been before—the person who would eventually leave her—inscribed on the skin of his back.

Of course she stopped him. *He should have stopped it himself.* How could he kiss her, be intimate with her, when he still didn't know who he was? He resigned himself to tell her that, explain how he would never kiss her again, touch her again, give in to these simmering and overwhelming feelings…when Nelly appeared at the top of the stairs, Faye trailing behind her.

"Faye wants me to take you to dinner," Nelly said.

Greg squinted at them. "Now?"

"Yep."

Faye wasn't looking at him. Instead, she was holding on to Hillel in a sort of death grip, while he fidgeted and struggled.

Greg glanced towards Faye. "Are you coming with?"

"No."

Both women answered at the same time.

He got the hint.

Still, heading downstairs, slinking past her, he needed to make sure she was okay. "Everything cool between us then?" he asked.

"Fine," she said quickly. Too quickly.

It was no use. Greg nodded. She was right to be mad at him. He was mad at himself for giving in to his desire, not thinking about the consequences—not thinking about his promise to Faye, most of all. He had not kept her safe. The least he could do now was respect her wishes. Give her time to heal and process what had happened. Maybe do a Jewitch centering ritual. Leaving Faye behind, he followed Nelly out of Magic Mud Pottery—and towards her car.

"What the hell did you do to the woman?" Nelly spat out the words as soon as the doors closed on her vehicle.

"Nothing." Greg raised his hands in open surrender. "I swear, Nelly. Nothing."

She fixed him with a cynical gaze. He grew concerned about feeling the brunt of her wrath. Nelly was super protective of her friends, after all…

Instead, she slapped the steering wheel, totally delighted.

"Well, whatever you did—" Nelly beamed "—it worked."

"It did?"

"Faye raced into my store *begging* me to take you off her hands. She even agreed to pay for dinner. How on Earth did you manage it?"

Greg slunk in his seat, not at all pleased with her assessment. "To tell you the truth, Nelly," he said, "I don't know what I did wrong. Or right. One minute, she was closing the store, and we were laughing, and talking. Next thing I knew, we were kissing. I started unbuttoning her dress. We made it up to her bedroom, and then—"

"Wait, wait, wait," Nelly said, interrupting him. "You and Faye were going to do the old horizontal hora?"

He had never heard it described that way before. "I guess."

"Ha!" Nelly laughed. "Well, that makes sense then."

"What makes sense?"

"Like the old Yiddish proverb, 'No one sees the hump growing on their own back.'" Greg didn't completely understand. "Anyway," Nelly said, nodding towards his feet. "We got bigger anti–Semitic fish to fry tonight. Look under your seat, Baby Bird."

Greg looked under his seat. Feeling around, he pulled out a bag. "What's this?"

"Supplies," Nelly said soberly. "Go on. Open it up."

He did as instructed. Opening the bag, he found a fake ID, five hundred dollars in cash, and a burner phone.

"You know what to do with that stuff, Baby Bird?"

"Believe it or not, Nelly," he said, putting the items into his pockets, "I know exactly what to do with them."

"Excellent," Nelly replied. "Then here's how this is gonna work. You're gonna be on your own for most of it. Take cabs, walk, talk to folks, keep your head down."

"I can handle that."

She reached into her pocket, pulling out a slip of paper. On it were the names of three bars, followed by addresses.

"My number is programmed into that phone there," she continued. "You go to each of these locations. Feel 'em out. Make contact. Use your gut. I'll be monitoring from my war room if you got any questions, any problems. But the minute you find something we can use as evidence…don't delay. Text me. Understand?"

Greg nodded. "Perfectly."

"Good." Nelly grinned, turning the key in the ignition. "Then let's go hunt us some Nazis."

With that, they were off to their first location in their shared quest for truth. And to keep the people they cared about safe. *Justice, justice, you shall pursue.* The words echoed in his brain, a driving force, his one focused intention, and became his new mantra.

That evening, Faye waited. She stood on the second floor, by the upstairs window, to watch Nelly and Greg driving away from Magic Mud Pottery. She waited for nightfall, for her neighbors to close their shops, turning off the lights and heading for home. For the quiet to come, when the only sound was the humming of streetlamps and Hillel snoring—before finally heading downstairs.

She tiptoed out to her back garden. Falling to her knees, she began to dig. Scooping up mounds of dirt with her bare hands, too anxious to care about ruining her nails or the pajamas she was wearing, she uprooted earth, tearing and clawing, before pulling out the golem doll from his grave. He was covered in mud.

Quickly, she cleaned him up, pulling clumps of mud from those three strings of red emanating from his head. Her mind fought with itself, *because it was impossible*—casting a spell, performing *real* magic—but as she wiped away dirt, each word she had forgotten reappeared on his clay skin, bringing with it a thousand new memories.

A hero. Greg had saved her from an anti-Semitic attack.

A reader. Greg had read all her books.

Loves Scrabble. They had just started playing.

On and on, the evidence appeared before her—in the yarn,

in the language, in the words she had scribbled on its skin, which now existed. A thing she had wanted so bad—a secret so deep she had kept it locked away inside of her—it had bent the universe to her will.

And then, she turned the doll over.

A cry escaped her lips. Abject horror spread throughout her body. Because there, on his back—in the same exact size and shape as Greg's scar—was the crack that she had patched.

She threw the doll to the side, not wanting to touch it. *Screw that.* She barely wanted to look at it. But there was no question in her mind now. No sense of uncertainty. All the evidence she had—all the evidence she needed—was there, splayed out in its lifeless clay body upon the grass.

She had done it. Real magic. The type of magic that mortals were always punished for. The type of magic that humans, but especially women, were never meant to possess. The type of magic that the AI chatbot had told her would destroy her. Until every muscle and fiber of her human being was forced to acknowledge the truth. In the wake of an anti-Semitic attack, over the waning moon of Sukkot, Faiga Kaplan had created a golem.

Or, in her case—Faye couldn't help but think it—a *Gregolem*.

TWENTY-FOUR

Greg stared down at his half-eaten plate of hot wings. He had been at Hacksaws Bar & Grill for over three hours, and aside from a serious case of indigestion, he had not garnered much. He had no new information regarding The Paper Boys. He had done his best to talk to folks at the bar. He had even made conversation—sometimes awkwardly—in the men's restroom.

He had a sense upon arrival that Hacksaws would be a bust. Clearly a family establishment, with kids shoved into booths and chocolate cake sundaes bearing birthday candles, it was not the type of place where one could easily muse with friends about committing a hate crime. By midnight, the place was shut down. Greg paid for his wings and took off, choosing to walk home over taking a cab.

He needed the long walk to clear his head. But even with the fresh air, he still felt off. His mind returned to Faye as he replayed snippets of her inside his mind. The way she tasted.

The way she felt under his hands—the way she had wanted him to make love to her—before she completely shut him out. All he wanted to do now was make things right by her. The problem was, as he stepped into Magic Mud Pottery, nothing was normal.

Faye was home, but instead of greeting him, she was in her bedroom upstairs—the door closed, a light peeking out from underneath it. He told himself it was a blessing in disguise, and used Faye's disappearing act to hide the burner phone, cash, and ID that Nelly had given him at the bottom of a wicker basket by his bed. And then, not wanting to leave things unsaid, he headed to her door to speak with her.

It was panic.

Sitting in her bedroom with the door locked and a chair moved in front of it, she stared at that golem doll on the bureau across from her. Covered in a layer of soil, words etched haphazardly all over its body, its dead eyes—two horrifying little O's—stared back at her, unblinking. It was so unbelievably creepy. She couldn't believe she had ever found the damn thing comforting.

All she wanted to do was throw it in the kiln downstairs and burn it alive. Smash it into a thousand pieces with a hammer. She even considered calling Shulamit and begging her to bury it in a *genizah* somewhere… But as much as she wanted to destroy the thing outright, she was afraid that doing so would lead to bigger problems down the line.

She debated calling her friends—Eric, too—but who the hell would believe her? They would claim she was delusional. Or worse. Point to her own broken nature, her own baggage, the things she made up in her mind. But this wasn't like her mother, prone to fantastical delusions, believing her own worst fears were coming to fruition—this was reality. Her reality. She needed someone who would help without judging her.

She needed an expert opinion.

She scrambled to find her phone and was opening the AI research assistant when a knock on her door caused Faye to jump. She threw her cell down, caught. Her entire body froze as she waited, staring at her door, praying that the lock was enough to keep a soulless clay man walking around in a person costume from entering.

"Hey, Faye," Greg said quietly. Gently. "You up?"

Faye pressed her lips together and said nothing. Maybe, if she stayed quiet long enough, he would think she was sleeping and go away. She heard the squeak of the hallway outside, and thinking he was leaving, breathed a sigh of relief.

"I know you're up, Faye," Greg said.

"I'm not," she shouted back.

"Your light is on," he said, pointing out the obvious.

Great.

Next time, she was going to craft a less aware golem.

"Can we talk?" Gregolem asked through the door. "Just for a minute. I just… I want to apologize for what happened."

Unbelievable. Gregolem was, once again, saying all the right things, being sweet and adorable…and it made her heart ache. It broke her into ten thousand pieces because there was some part of her, like the part that had created him, that still wanted him. Someone she could love—who would love her in return, unconditionally—and who wouldn't betray that space in her heart by leaving her.

But then, she reminded herself that Gregolem wasn't real. She had created *this thing* now living in her house with words, clay, and magic. More important, her AI chatbot had confirmed the worst of the stories she had heard in her youth. Golems were dangerous. They always eventually freaked out, destroying the very communities they were meant to protect, killing their creators in the process. *Perseus approaching her shores with his cap of invisibility and his shield made of mirrors.*

"Faye," Greg whined outside her door.

"What?"

"Please," he said, again. "It will only take a minute."

She rose in a huff, heading to the door, opening it just an inch so that her Gregolem doll, still sitting on the bureau, wouldn't be visible.

"Yes?" Faye asked.

"I just wanted to talk—" Gregolem squinted, his thoughts interrupted. "Are you okay?"

"I'm fine," Faye said confidently.

His eyes rolled down her body. "You're covered in dirt."

Faye glanced down. In her panic, she had forgotten that she had spent thirty minutes digging up her garden.

She feigned innocence. "I don't know what you're talking about."

"You've also got—" Greg pointed at his own head "—a dead rose, or something, in your hair."

She went to find it, feeling a small dried-up bud sitting at the top of her curls. Pulling it down, tossing it to the ground, she huffed, and pretended it was totally normal.

"Were you doing a ritual?" Greg asked.

"What?"

"While I was out," Greg said curiously.

It felt like an accusation.

There also wasn't a chance in hell that she was ever going to tell Greg the truth about his existence. After all, she couldn't very well *tell* the golem that he was a golem. He could freak out, go on a rampage, killing everyone in Woodstock. He had already broken her damn heart. Next step was cutting off her head completely.

"Is there something I can help you with, Greg?"

"Right." Greg rubbed the back of his neck. "I guess I just wanted to say that I'm sorry about what happened this afternoon. I'm sorry that... I let myself get carried away. But I wanted you to know that it won't happen again. Regardless of how I feel… I understand why we can't act on these feelings. And I'm sorry. You've been good to me, too good…and you deserve a person who can be with you, honestly and fully. Where you don't have to worry that one day he's going to leave you."

Her mind wandered with his words. Her body responded, too. Because seeing him there, his gentle voice speaking so sweetly, she wanted him to be real. But like his perfect, impeccably carved body—too many green flags always equaled red.

"It's fine, Greg," Faye said quickly.

"You sure?"

"Of course." She forced a smile, lying through her teeth. "And you're right. We can't let this happen again. You're, *obviously*, a human being with a past…with family out there that loves you. Even though, no matter what we do, you can't remember." Her words came out high-pitched. "But still, *clearly*, a human being!"

"Okay…"

"Human," she repeated, nodding her head up and down extremely slowly. "Yep! Total flesh and blood, right there."

He shifted on the balls of his feet, the floor making groaning noises beneath his weight. "Well, since we're both up then—" he glanced once down the hall "—would you like to play Scrabble?"

Un-freaking-believable.

No, she did not want to play Scrabble with a golem.

No wonder he always won.

"Not tonight," she said, and moved to shut the door.

"Or, if you're hungry," he said quickly, attempting to keep the conversation going, "I can make you a plate of hard kosher—"

"Greg," Faye interrupted him. "All I want to do is go to sleep, okay?" And then, just so he would get the full gist of her meaning, she added one word. *"Alone."*

The floorboards stopped squeaking beneath his feet. His entire face—*his beautiful, sweet face, the face she had come to know and trust*—morphed into sadness. In truth, seeing his upset awoke the same inside of her. Yes, there was a part of her that wanted to believe what she had created, what they were experiencing together, could remain good. Stable. But she had already made that wish with Stuart…and look where it had gotten her.

"Alright," Greg said softly. "Well, I appreciate you opening the door to talk to me."

"Of course."

"We're still friends, right?" He held up one hand, displaying the bracelet still knotted on his wrist.

She looked away from him. "Friends," she repeated. "Definitely."

Satisfied by her promise that things would go back to normal between them, Greg departed back down the hall.

Faye closed the door, locking it behind her, before dragging her chair, the mirror, the laundry basket, and part of her nightstand in front of it. Grabbing that creepy-ass golem doll off the bureau, she hid it in the very deepest recesses of her closet, behind a pile of old clothing, before returning to the safety of her bed. Turning off the light, raising her covers above her head, she opened the AI and typed her question out: How do I get rid of a golem?

The AI began to scroll: In Jewish folklore, the golem is an anthropomorphic creature made from clay and mud, designed to serve the will of their creator. However, in many stories, the creator eventually loses control of the golem. As the golem begins to act on its own accord, it becomes dangerous. Some methods for destroying a golem are to satiate the golem, dismantle the golem, or give the golem an impossible task.

Faye committed those words to memory. Her resolve so strong, her intention so fiercely focused, that she almost missed the last sentence as it appeared on the bottom of her screen: It is worth remembering that the golem is a fictional creature, and that none of these techniques should ever be attempted in real life.

TWENTY-FIVE

Greg did his best to put on a good face the next morning. After all, he didn't want any lingering tension to remain between them. But arriving downstairs, stepping into the kitchen, he was pleased to see that Faye seemed back to normal. Better than normal, in fact. She was working hard at what could only be described as a breakfast buffet.

A shot of freshly brewed espresso rested by an Italian press on the counter. A fruit salad—watermelon, strawberries, and honeydew—filled one of her pottery bowls. On the table before him, beside a stack of pancakes and waffles that rose to the ceiling, were three omelets and ten breakfast burritos.

"Good morning," Greg said, surprised.

Faye spun around, wide-eyed and beaming. "Good morning." She smiled. She was wearing an apron, holding a spatula in one hand. "I thought I would make us breakfast."

★ ★ ★

For three days, Faye fed Gregolem.

Between classes and Etsy orders, she filled him up with every manner of edible item. She ordered Thai food and Indian food, made him scrambled eggs with hard kosher salami, chased him up the stairs with bowls of ice cream, and at night left full-sized candy bars, along with family-sized bags of Doritos, hidden within the covers of his bed. But after three long days of begging him to take just one more bite, the only thing she had managed to do was make Greg violently ill.

"Ugggggh," Gregolem moaned from the bathroom.

Faye stood outside the door. "You okay in there?"

"I think... I might be dying."

He wasn't dying. Dying was a privilege reserved for *living creatures*. No, what she was doing was sending her Gregolem back to the primordial sludge from which he had been created. *Nothing less. Nothing more.*

Turning from the door, she did a happy little hip-hop and a skip back down the hall towards her living room, until she came face-to-face with Hillel. Four paws planted firmly on the ground, head cocked sideways with his tongue hanging out, he was looking at her all judgy.

"Oh, don't give me that," Faye said, crossing her arms against her chest. "He would have likely crushed your sweet little hairless body beneath his massive paws eventually."

Hillel responded by refusing to move.

Faye sidestepped the creature, taking a seat on the couch. She was not going to be made to feel guilty by a Chinese crested.

Faye listened to the groaning for a few more minutes, until all at once, it ceased. The entire house went quiet. Faye perked up, one hand over her mouth. *This was it.* She waited with bated breath to hear movement, to hear something—but nothing came.

She had gotten rid of Gregolem.

She thought she would be happy. And yet, sitting on the couch in her apartment, silence abounding, the strangest thing happened. A wellspring of feelings, hot and uncontrollable, rushed up from her core. Despite her best efforts not to cry, her cheeks flushed red. *Because she would miss him.* She would miss playing Scrabble with him, and eating snacks at night, and all the conversations they shared about books and Jewitch magic. Suddenly, all she could think about was how she had just made a terrible mistake.

Faye jumped to her feet and rushed towards the bathroom door. "Greg." She began to pound the wood with her fist. "Are you there?"

The toilet flushed, followed by the sound of running water. Seconds later, Greg exited bathroom.

"Whoa," he said, surprised at the sight of her. "I didn't realize you were right there."

Faye stammered. "I... I...thought you were gone."

"Are you okay?" Greg asked, squinting in her direction.

"I'm fine."

"You look like you've been...crying."

A long and very awkward moment of silence settled between them before—Baruch Hashem and Blessed Be—Hillel came prancing down the hall.

"He was worried about you," Faye said, quickly, using the hairless creature as her excuse. "Hillel. He thought you were... sick. He was an absolute wreck, honestly."

Greg bent down to pet the creature. "I'm okay, little guy," Greg said, sweetly comforting him before rising again. "Just too much of *everything*."

Greg looked so unbelievably sweet. She was losing her resolve, forgetting all the reasons why she had to get rid of him. So she reminded herself of what would happen if she continued to play the weakest link in their relationship. He would stop obeying her. He would become destructive. *He would go berserk.* This was no time to get complacent.

She shook off the feelings, returning her resolve to the task at hand.

There must have been something she had done wrong in her reversal spell. Perhaps she had misunderstood the AI's directions. Or maybe she was not supposed to satiate Greg with food, but with something else…like sex.

All at once, she began unbuttoning her blouse.

"What are you doing?" Greg asked, his eyes drifting downwards.

"What does it look like I'm doing?" she said, pulling one boob from her shirt like she was planning on breastfeeding him. "Let's have sex."

Greg squinted. "What?"

"You, me," she said, nodding towards the bedroom. "Eh?"

His entire face froze in a look of abject horror…or fear. She couldn't entirely be certain.

Granted, it was quite possibly the most unromantic request for sex ever. There was nothing attractive, at all, happening between them at that moment. Greg had just appeared from the bathroom after being sick. The bra she was wearing was older than Nelly's grandchildren. But Faye was desperate. And Greg was a golem. So really, the time for both good decision-making and modesty had passed.

"Come on," she said, nodding towards the bedroom. "Let's just get this over with."

"Faye." His chin dipped back. "I don't want to have sex with you."

Now she was the one insulted. "Excuse me?"

"I mean," he stammered, but attempted to close her shirt *all the same*, "of course I want to have sex with you. Obviously, I'm totally attracted to you."

"So, what's the problem?"

"The last time things got heated between us," he reminded her, "you completely freaked out."

"I remember."

Like she was the one with amnesia.

"And," he said, definitive as ever, "you were right, okay? Having sex is a terrible idea for both of us. I respect and care about you too much to do something that might hurt you in the end. Once we figure out who I am, once we know for certain, we can reevaluate these feelings. Believe me, I hope we get the chance."

Fabulous.

She was being rejected by a golem.

Because, clearly, she was a sea Gorgon that not even a soulless vessel wanted to tap.

"Fine," she said, throwing her hands up. "Fine. *You do you.*"

She spun away from him, back to her bedroom. Slamming the door behind her, locking it firmly, she buttoned up her blouse. And then, forcing herself to get a grip, she gave up on satiating the golem...and resigned herself to disassembling him instead.

Well, that was odd.

Standing in the hallway, rubbing the back of his neck, Greg tried to make sense of what had just happened with Faye. He also debated his options—talk to her, or leave her alone—but frankly, she seemed all types of unhinged.

He thought back to the book he had been reading. Perhaps these oddities in her behavior were a misguided attempt to gain control in an uncontrollable situation. It would make sense. She had been through so much in her life. Not just from her mother, and Stuart, but then, to be revictimized by The Paper Boys.

No wonder she was acting weird. She was triggered. All those bad feelings of her past, all those memories, coming back to haunt her.

He stared at the closed door. Faye had returned to locking herself in the bedroom. And while he hated leaving her alone at night, he consoled himself with one simple fact. Everything he was doing was for her benefit.

Finding his supplies in the wicker basket where he had hidden them, he texted Nelly that he was heading out to Jumbos—the second bar on their list of potential meeting spots for The Paper Boys—and would be in contact soon. He was not at all surprised when Nelly texted back immediately.

Good, she wrote, followed by a series of little lightning emojis. Cause those Nazis ain't gonna stun themselves.

TWENTY-SIX

Greg had a good feeling.

Unlike Hacksaws, which was clearly a family establishment, the bar known as Jumbos lay in the middle of a thicket of trees in a building the size of a trailer. It also had fewer windows, and far less appeal. After paying cash for the cab, he dug his hands into his pockets and entered.

Inside, there were only a few patrons. A man played a game of pinball towards the side. A few barflies pounded back drinks at the bar. Greg took a seat beside the ones at the counter and ordered himself a beer. And then, like he had read about in all his novels—like The Rogue Prince and Samantha Beacher would often do when they were undercover—he attempted to read the room.

He waited. He watched. *He learned.* And then, he worked to mimic the language, attitude, and behaviors of the people he was meeting. He kept things cool. He made casual chitchat and friendly conversation, until finally, a kid in the back, who had spent most of the evening in a booth staring down at his phone, came up to the bar and ordered buffalo wings.

His hair stood on edge.

He watched the young man out of the corner of his eye, analyzing him. There were no outright signs of white supremacy. No inappropriate tattoos of swastikas or red laces tied into combat boots. If Greg had met the man at Magic Mud Pottery, he would have welcomed him inside with open arms.

The kid was still waiting for his wings when Greg made his move.

"Hey," Greg called to the bartender. "You got any blue cheese dressing to go with these wings?"

"Sorry," the bartender said. "Only ranch."

Greg shook his head, mumbling beneath his breath. "Who the hell doesn't serve blue cheese dressing with buffalo wings?"

His words did the trick. The kid turned to face him. "Ridiculous, right?"

They spent a few more minutes shooting the breeze, bonding over the sheer audacity of a chef who would serve hot wings without the proper sauce, when Greg nodded to the seat across from him. "You up for company?"

"Got nothing better going on," he said. "My friend was supposed to meet me here, but his kid got sick at the last minute. Wife started harping on him, you know?"

"I'm sorry to hear that," he said, offering his hand. "I'm Greg, by the way."

"John," the man said, taking his offer of friendship. "Nice to meet you."

Greg doubted that John was his real name. He knew from Nelly, and his crime thrillers, that The Paper Boys were likely to be using aliases.

They continued talking. At first, about cars. And then, about women. Periodically, John would look to the television screen over the bar—the one playing the news on mute—and begin ranting about something. But mainly, Greg let the man talk. He let him word-vomit every one of his thoughts, never disagreeing with him, never arguing...because Greg wanted John to feel comfortable and safe around him. Finally, after two more hours of Greg putting on his best show, John was the one buying him drinks.

"So," John said. "You working?"

"Laid off." Greg frowned. "Three months now."

"Damn," he said, shaking his head. "Sorry to hear that."

"Thanks for the beer, by the way," Greg said, before adding, "Company decided to...*restructure*."

"They're restructuring alright." John shook his head. "God-damn Jews."

Greg's chest went taut. His stomach roiled. He was disgusted by this man and his words—but he focused on maintaining his cover. Indeed, he found it surprisingly easy to both lie and be believed.

"You know, it's funny you say that," Greg said, tipping his beer towards John. "About a month or two ago, I found this flyer."

John shifted in his seat, leaning closer. "A flyer?"

"Basically, what it said was that, even though we don't see it, the Jews are responsible for everything bad happening in the world right now. Like they got super powers, you know? They control the government, the media. Heck, according to what was in those papers, they even created COVID."

"You don't say?"

"I swear," Greg said, finishing off his glass. "And maybe I wouldn't have believed it, you know? But then, in this flyer... they got all these pictures, names and addresses, and lo and behold, right there, right there in front of me in black and white—the evidence. All these Jews in power. Can you believe it? Right under our noses the whole time, and I had never seen it before that moment."

John nodded. "It's scary when you realize how much they control."

"Like magic," Greg said. "Like witchcraft."

"That's exactly it, man." John slapped his hand down on the bar.

"Though what I can't figure out—" Greg shook his head, pressing his lips together "—is what they all want in the end."

"What they want?" John scoffed at the question. "To destroy white America, obviously. To turn us all gay—little boys wearing dresses. Black people leading this country... The end of America, my friend. The end of what we are. Hell, look at what they did to Disney."

"Damn," Greg said, shaking his head. "When you put it like that, it does sound scary."

It was a lie, of course. Personally, Greg didn't think that boys wearing dresses or Black people leading the country was ruining *anything*...but he was playing a role.

The irony was John himself. He was so warm and friendly. So incredibly welcoming, too. Beyond all the drinks the young man had bought him, John was offering him something. A sense of community, a feeling of belonging, a place to lay all his failures and fears. A friendship, created around something so evil and vile, it made Greg feel physically sick.

"I just wish there was something I could do," Greg said after a few fateful minutes.

John leaned in closer, dropping his voice to a whisper. "Well, you know...there are some folks in town who are like-minded and such. If it interests you, if you're serious about stopping the scourge against white America, I can see about a meeting. We could always use good folks fighting for the cause."

Greg forced a smile. "I'd like that very much."

Faye heard Greg creeping up the stairs of Magic Mud Pottery at three o'clock in the morning. Closing her eyes, listening

to him moving around beyond her door, rage built up inside
of her. It was worse than she thought.

Faye was losing control of her golem.

Now, not only was he disobeying direct orders, refusing to
have sex with her…but he was sneaking out. She had no choice
now. She had to get rid of him.

The next morning, bright and early, she waited to hear the
shower on the second floor running. And then, knowing that
Greg was occupied, she found that creepy-ass golem doll, hid-
den in the recesses of her closet, and raced down the steps.
Heading to her studio, she tossed that clay figure onto a table.
Grabbing a hammer, she brought it down onto its belly.

The sound of it dissolving into pieces beneath her swings was
wonderfully cathartic. And so she kept going. She kept swinging.
A modern-day Lizzie Borden. Until finally, with sweat dripping
from her brow, and fully out of breath, she tossed the hammer to the side.

Greg was still upstairs moving around.

"Faye?" he called out. "Everything okay down there?"

"Fine," she shouted back.

Clearly, destroying the damn thing with a hammer was not
enough.

She debated her options. Perhaps golems were more like
Estries, female Jewish vampires that could also shape-shift. In
order to get rid of Greg, she would need to cram his mouth
full of dirt and decapitate him.

It sounded messy.

Instead, she grabbed a shopping bag, collecting up the pieces
of her golem doll, before heading to her garage and jumping
on her bike.

She rode for as long and as fast as her pedals would take her,
not even noticing the November cold, until she was far beyond
the environs of downtown Woodstock. Surrounded by trees
and nature, she began tossing out shards.

Handfuls of dust flew into the wind behind her. Pieces of that golem doll—like the memories that came with it—dissipated into nothing. She was certain that she had never felt more free, more alive in her own power—when sirens sounded behind her.

Glancing over her shoulder and seeing a police vehicle, she quickly pulled off to the side. A momentary panic filled her chest. Getting pulled over by cops was never a good thing, but how the hell would she explain summoning, and then needing to get rid of, a golem.

Haman's hat. Could a reversal spell on a supernatural creature be the equivalent to a crime? She was already sweating, losing her cool *and* her grip on reality, when Chief Eric Myers exited the vehicle.

"Oh, it's you," Faye said, breathing a sigh of relief.

She probably shouldn't have said it with such gusto. It was unfair to expect Eric—an officer of the law—to cut her some slack simply because they were friends.

"It's me," he repeated.

She tried to play innocent. "Is everything okay?"

"I'm afraid," Eric said, grabbing the handlebars of her bike, holding her there, "that someone reported a madwoman, riding around on her bike, littering all over Woodstock."

Faye guffawed. "You're kidding me?"

"Afraid not," Eric said. "Unfortunately, I'm gonna have to take you in."

The color drained from her face. Granted, she knew it was wrong to litter—but extreme situations, and all that. Also, her pottery was made from clay and mud—totally natural and earthen elements. Surely, returning them back to the ground, back to the forest, wouldn't damage the delicate ecosystem around Woodstock.

"I'm kidding," he said.

Faye laughed. "Of course."

"You should have seen your face."

In truth, she didn't find the joke very funny. But considering what she had done—the fact that Gregolem was now living in her apartment, about to wreak every manner of havoc on her life and community—she felt the need to keep things friendly between them.

"What are you doing, though?" he said, reaching his fingers towards her bag.

"Oh," she laughed, pushing the bag away. "It's nothing. Just a…a…"

"Just a Jewish thing?"

Faye squinted, unsure of what to say. It was, *technically*, a Jewish thing. She was trying to get rid of a golem. But still, his comment felt totally off base. There were a thousand things she could be doing right now on a bicycle in the woods… Why land on that? And then, Eric—*Baruch Hashem and Blessed Be*—clarified.

"You know," Eric said, trying to explain his thinking, "like that thing you do…on Rosh Hashanah."

Faye had no idea what he was talking about. "Rosh Hashanah?"

"When you all go to down to the river?"

It took her a minute. "Oh," she said, touching her head, finally putting it together. "You mean *tashlich*?"

"That's the one," he said, beaming with pride that he had gotten it correct. "Is that what you're doing?"

"Kind of," Faye lied.

Eric laughed, shaking his head, before finally getting serious. "Well, actually," he said, "I'm glad I caught you, because there is something I wanted to talk to you about. Now, I don't want you to take this the wrong way, Faye…but I wanted to talk to you about your new window display."

She blinked. "My window display?"

"What on Earth were you thinking?"

Her chin tipped backwards. "I'm sorry," she said, somewhat

flabbergasted, "what exactly is the problem with my window display?"

"You're advertising to everyone that you're Jewish."

"So?"

"So, you're making yourself a target," he said. "You think it's funny to antagonize them?"

"I don't think it's funny at all."

"Because it was stupid, Faye," he said finally. "Stupid and childish."

Her entire face contorted, flabbergasted into silence.

But also, she didn't think that mentioning the fact she was a Jewitch—on her business—should be a danger. Or necessitate a warning. People put up Christmas trees and Christmas lights *all the time*, and none of them had to go to bed at night wondering if they would wake up to a rock through their front window.

It was exactly the same.

Judaism was not *just* a religion. It was a culture. A people. Her ethnicity. And even though she used more nontraditional parts of her tradition to find her spiritual center, it didn't make her less Jewish.

She had a right to celebrate who she was without fearing blowback. She had a right to live out of the Jewitch broom closet. And she wanted to say all these things, argue with him, tell Eric to shove it—but she was stunned, absolutely floored, into silence.

And so she said nothing.

The Great Pretender. The Great Lie she kept selling everyone around her. Including herself. That she was brave, fearless, that nothing could hurt her. That she could survive, and survive, and survive...

She hated that she said nothing. Despised herself for it—like with Stuart and her mother. Like with her father, too, if she was really getting honest with herself. All those moments when he was dying, all those times where she wanted to say, *Why weren't you there?*

But she also reasoned, she had no choice.

Not just because Eric was a police officer and a man in power, but because she was a Jew. And this was how she survived being a minority in America. Maybe also a woman. She diminished. She downplayed. Because, contrary to popular belief, it wasn't just the Holocaust etched into her memory, handed down *l'dor v'dor* from generation-to-generation.

It was grade school, where a boy threw pennies at her on the way to lunch, before telling her that there would never be a Jewish Miss America...because Jewish girls were all ugly. It was college, where she had to hide her feelings, and sometimes her confusion, about Israel, where she couldn't even discuss it without another student, sometimes a professor, pointing at her and outright calling her a genocidal maniac.

It was online and in the news. Every drive-by one-star review that had appeared on her Yelp page, people who had never even visited her store, trying to put her out of business. It was every meme shared on Facebook that diminished the atrocities of Hitler, or yellow stars, or concentration camps, to prove some larger, grander point... #JewsAreNotAMetaphor

It was Air France Flight 139, when all the Jewish passengers were separated out from the rest, then held hostage in a warehouse in Uganda, only Israel coming to save them. It was the cruise ship *Achille Lauro* where Leon Klinghoffer, a Jewish man in a wheelchair, was shot and pushed overboard. It was journalist Daniel Pearl, kidnapped in Pakistan, being forced to say, "I am Jewish, I am a Zionist," before being beheaded in front of cameras. It was Tree of Life Synagogue in Pittsburgh, where on a Shabbat morning, eleven people were shot, point-blank, while they prayed.

It was looking at someone who wasn't Jewish, who had

maybe never met a Jew before in their entire life, and wondering, *What do they really think about me?*

She hated that she felt this way. Despised that there was always this voice buzzing around in the back of her head, these memories, that constantly kept her wondering. But when she looked at her life, at Woodstock—a town known for peace, love, and rock and roll, littered with anti-Semitic flyers—at the history of Jewish people, both past and current, all those tragedies, mountains of bodies, one stacked on top of another like black-and-white photographs taken in a concentration camp, at her books, an entire industry making money from the Holocaust and dead Jews, but very few bestselling books that celebrated the living ones—*how could she think anything else?*

And then, Eric—perhaps sensing that he had gone too far—pulled back.

"I'm sorry," he said softly. "I didn't mean to come off as harsh."

"I know that."

"It's just…" He shook his head, sighing heavily. "I don't want to see you get hurt, Faye. These people you're messing with, these people you're antagonizing…they mean business. And it would kill me, Faye, if something bad happened to you because of it."

"Well, what would you have me do then?"

He pressed his lips together. "I think you should take it down."

"Down?" She couldn't believe what he was saying.

"Just until this whole thing blows over…" he clarified. "Just until…these Paper Boys are no longer a threat."

She shifted on the balls of her feet—all those memories she was holding like a sieve inside of her spilling out. Memory upon memory, until they all began to blur together, and she could no longer tell if she were the receiver of the story, or the one telling the story. But she began to wonder if Eric was right. Perhaps she had been naive in faking courage. She wasn't brave. She was scared of everything...getting hurt most of all.

But Eric cared about her. And unlike Greg, he was human.

"I understand," she said softly. "And I do appreciate your concern, Eric. I realize it comes from a good place."

Eric nodded. "It does."

He hugged her, and she accepted it, fully.

"So," he said, finally dropping the topic. He angled his body towards his police car. "Can I pop your bike in the trunk, maybe give you a ride home? If you weren't fully aware of this...it is, actually, freezing out today."

Faye laughed. He wasn't wrong that it was chilly. She moved to take Eric up on the offer, when on second thought, she decided against it. A ray of sunlight appeared, and with the warmth shining down on her, the thought of a bike ride home felt comforting. Necessary.

"Maybe another time."

"Of course."

Eric touched her on the arm one last time before departing.

Greg was in the middle of unpacking a box of new clay when he heard the front door to Magic Mud Pottery open. Faye was standing in the threshold, her hair a mess, her skin all sweaty. Her eyes wandered once over his form, unblinking.

"Oh," she said. "You're still here."

"I'm here," he said, rising from his spot, wiping dust off his hands. "You okay?"

"I went for a bike ride."

He glanced out the window, where leaves were blowing around in the wind. "In this weather?"

She shrugged. And then, without any further explanation—without another word—she dragged herself past him to her bedroom, where she locked herself in once more.

TWENTY-SEVEN

For the next few days, Faye was weirdly quiet. Greg tried not to take it personally, but all the words they once shared, all the beautiful language that had once been the foundation of their relationship, dissipated.

Instead, they became mired in their own thoughts, each keeping to themselves, two travelers on the same path, but neither one acknowledging the other. Until one night, after yet another dinner that they had each taken separately, Faye emerged from her locked bedroom. Greg looked up from the book he was reading.

"Hi," he said, surprised to see her.

"Hey," she said, stepping forward. "How are you doing?"

He put his book down. "Good."

"I was wondering—" she ran one hand through her hair "—if you'd like to play Scrabble?"

"Scrabble?" He was surprised by the offer, surprised that

they were suddenly and just like that back to normal. "Yeah," he said. "Scrabble would be great."

"Great."

Faye set up the board. Greg pulled out the letter *A* from the blue velvet bag, denoting that he would go first. He tossed it back into the bag, pulling out seven letters, laying them on the wooden tile holder, before sliding around combinations, trying to find the best word. He was just about to lay one down when Faye stopped him, putting her hand on his.

"I have a better idea," Faye said.

"You do?" He swallowed. He could only imagine what better idea was in store.

"I'm getting a little bored of regular Scrabble." She beamed wider. There was mischief in her eyes that made him think of romance. "Have you ever played eight-letter Scrabble?"

"Eight-letter Scrabble?" he asked curiously.

"It's one of my favorite ways to play."

There was something about how she was smiling at him, all wide-eyed and bordering on hysterical, that felt off-putting. Still, he tried to look on the bright side. He was happy that Faye had finally decided to speak with him. He had missed their long conversations together, talking life, Jewitch magic, and books.

"Okay," he said, clapping his hands together. "How do we play eight-letter Scrabble?"

"Well, how we play this game is…you have to make an eight-letter word."

Greg angled his chin. "I'm confused."

"You have to use all your letters, making an eight-letter word."

"But I only have seven letters."

"Right."

She kept right on smiling. In truth, it was creepy as all hell. Greg dragged one hand down his face. "Faye," he said, trying to explain his logic to her, "there is no way to make an eight-letter word with seven letters."

"Yes, there is."

"No, there isn't."

"Well, that's the only way I know how to play eight-letter Scrabble."

"Then I don't want to play eight-letter Scrabble."

"Fine." She crossed her arms against her chest, defiant. "Then we can play ten-letter Scrabble."

"Do I want to venture a guess here?"

"It's very similar to eight-letter Scrabble," she admitted, pointing to the board. "Except you have to make a ten-letter word."

"How about we just play regular Scrabble?" he asked. "Like always."

"I don't think so."

Greg huffed his resignation. It made no sense. She made no sense. What the heck was going on with her? "Are you messing with me?" he asked.

"Of course not," she quipped back.

"Then why are you acting like this?"

Faye was the epitome of calm. "Because I want to play eight-letter Scrabble."

"That's not how you play Scrabble." He was getting frustrated. Losing his cool. He touched his forehead, where a migraine was quickly beginning to develop, and tried to regroup. "I feel like I've entered some parallel universe."

"Please," she said almost desperately, before pointing down at the board. "I just… I really need you to try, Greg."

He stared down at the board. Because he wanted to please her, to make her happy. But the task she had given him was impossible, and he didn't particularly like the feeling of being set up to fail. Tired of the game—both hers and the one on the board—Greg glanced down at his watch before rising from his seat.

"Where are you going?" Faye asked.

"Out."

"Out where?"

"Just out," he said, attempting to avoid the question.

Faye followed him. "Well, what about our game of eight-letter Scrabble?"

He twisted in his spot, meeting her eyes. Was she being serious right now? And then, without her permission—without bothering to sneak off or offer up an explanation—Greg made his way outside and began the long walk towards Jumbos.

Faye stared down at the Scrabble board in front of her. Freaking AI. Useless AI. She should have known better than to trust one empty vessel to help her get rid of another. But seeing Greg through the window walking towards Goddess knew where in the late evening hours, she realized what was happening. She understood it fully now.

Faye was losing control of her Gregolem.

He was becoming destructive, going berserk, *disobeying direct orders*. She had no more time left to mess about with new technology. What Faye needed was an expert. Someone with old-world wisdom, who could read ancient texts in their original languages. Someone who had spent their life studying the Jewish supernatural.

Obviously, that person wasn't Shulamit…but, as these things tended to go in the Jewish professional world, she figured her friend might know someone. Picking up her phone, she bypassed Miranda and dialed Shully's cell phone directly.

"Hey," Shulamit said, picking up on the first ring, "Miranda isn't here right now."

"No, it's not that…" Faye did her best to sound sane. Totally normal. "Believe it or not, I have a question for you, actually."

"Oh," Shulamit sounded surprised, "okay. Hit me."

"Well," Faye said, the tension rising in her belly with every syllable, "I'm thinking of starting a new pottery series, and I'd like to get some real research done before I begin. I've consulted Google and an AI, of course...but I'm just not finding what I need—the good stuff, you know, the meaty stuff you would only find on the most esoteric pages of the Talmud. Anyway, I was wondering if you happen to know any experts on...well, on golems?"

TWENTY-EIGHT

"You play?" John asked. Greg glanced up from his beer to see John angling a cue stick at him. He had been at Jumbos for the last two hours, once again nursing a round of beers and buffalo wings with his new fake friend, hoping to be introduced to the next tier of leadership.

"Not sure," Greg said, staring down at the cue. He couldn't remember ever playing pool. He certainly hadn't read a book on the topic.

John looked askance. "What do you mean…*not sure*?"

Greg backtracked. "I mean…" he said, grabbing the pool stick and squaring his shoulders, all confident energy, "I can try."

"That's the spirit," John said, clapping him on the back.

Bending over, Greg took aim. One red ball landed straight in a corner pocket.

"Damn." John balked. "You hustling me?"

Greg pointed out the obvious. "If I was hustling you," he said with a knowing smirk, "I would have missed the shot."

It took John a minute. "I see," he said, waving one finger at Greg. "I see what you did there."

Greg found himself being forced to play two more rounds with the man—John talking his ear off the entire time—before Greg glanced down at his watch. It was getting late.

"So, you told me you had some friends you wanted me to meet?" Greg asked.

"They're coming," John said, missing his own shot in the process. "Mike has some sort of parent-teacher meeting...and Lewis doesn't get out of work till nine."

Greg nodded sympathetically, a pretense of understanding. It was a twist that he wasn't expecting. Hearing that these people were raising families, attending school functions, and holding down jobs surprised him.

He half expected them to all be unemployed neckbeards, the type of folks keyboard-warrioring from their mothers' basements all day, trolling folks for their *lolz* in the comments. He did not expect fully functioning members of society, voting members of the public, who also raised children. It made the threat feel even more insidious.

"You got kids?" Greg asked, attempting to learn more about these people.

"Nah," John said. "You?"

"Me, either."

"Probably better that way," John said, after a few thoughtful minutes. "I mean, the way our country is going... I really can't imagine bringing kids into this mess. This fucking world...it's such a goddamn tragedy, you know? They're destroying everything. Fucking Jews. Fucking hate them. I wish I could just... go back in time, finish the job that Hitler started."

"Totally." Greg pressed the word through his lips.

John was so extreme. Not just his beliefs, but the language he used. Greg couldn't help but think it.

Everything with John was life or death, the end of the world, or a great battle for salvation. He talked about Jews the same way he talked about beer and buffalo wings. He *loved* the beer at Jumbos. He *hated* the cook, because he took it as a personal vendetta against him—some slight against the spinning of his universe—that the buffalo wings were never served with blue cheese dressing.

At times, John got so worked up in his own digs and rants, all Greg wanted to do was snap at him to *simmer down*. But talking to John was a bit like talking to an anti-Semitic brick wall.

He'd read enough books at this point to understand that it wasn't *only* anti-Semitism affecting John. Perhaps he had mental health challenges, or a low IQ, or even was on the dark triad of sociopathy. But Greg had his own theory—an explanation much simpler. John had no ability to discern issues.

He was like a sieve, some empty vessel that downloaded information but was incapable of sorting through it. He didn't question the things he read, didn't sort information into fact or fiction. Beyond that, he was lazy. He word-vomited things he had seen online, repeated memes like they were facts, never dug up a research article or checked out a book—because anything backed by approved sources was somehow already tainted.

And yet he was a self-professed expert on *every single topic*.

He was beyond annoying. And exhausting. And Greg was beginning to think that he was nowhere closer to meeting The Paper Boys—that John was simply a wannabe, someone jumping on a bandwagon, instead of a person with a real connection to the cell currently operating in Woodstock—when two men appeared at the door.

John put his cue stick down and raced to introduce them.

The first man, going by the name of Mike, appeared to be in his late thirties. Also, clean-cut. Black hair pressed down, he was wearing jeans and a casual, almost preppy-looking sweater. He looked like a dad—like someone just coming from a PTA event, having a serious discussion with a teacher about the education of his children. But he stood in contrast to his companion, Lewis, who was much shorter, and smaller, than all of them—but who wore his intimidation out front in the form of a bald head and a string of anti-Semitic tattoos on his neck that peeked out from the collar of his shirt.

The next few minutes were tense. Mike and Lewis were clearly less trusting than John. Their eyes rolled over Greg's form as they made small talk between them. Greg knew they were trying to suss him out, figure out his deal, decide if he could be trusted. Finally, the three shook hands, and Mike, perhaps as a form of a peace offering, nodded towards the pool table. "You up for starting a new game?"

"Sounds good to me," Greg said.

They began to play. Everyone taking a turn—drinking beer, keeping things casual. After another hour, Mike began to trust Greg.

"John tells me you're going through some hard times," Mike said.

"Yeah," Greg said, lifting off from his shot. "Lost my job three months ago. Been looking ever since…but no such luck."

"And where you staying in the meantime?" he asked. "I haven't seen you around."

"I'm over at the Woodstock Lodge."

"That dump over on Highway 89?"

"That's the one."

"Damn," Mike said, all friendly-like. "I'm sorry to hear that."

Mike was calmer than John. Cooler, too. Greg matched his energy, when suddenly, John broke into one of his diatribes. "Freaking Jews," John said, shaking his head. "That's what they want, you know? To keep everyone in poverty so they get richer."

"Hey," Mike hushed him, slapping his cue stick out of the way with one hand. "What have I told you about going on and on about that shit. Not here, alright?" John slunk back, and then, Mike pulled out his phone. "You got a social media page?"

"I got a phone," Greg said.

Mike was incredulous. "What? No Facebook?"

"What can I say?" Greg leaned back over the pool table to take his shot. "Never quite got into the social media thing."

"What about an ID?" Lewis interjected.

Greg shrugged simply. "Didn't bring it with me."

An awkward silence spread out across the four men.

"You see," Mike said, finally leaning in to whisper, "we got to be careful who we talk to, who we let into our inner circle. There's a lot of eyes and ears out there, heat we're not looking to take… Now, my friend John here says you seem like a good guy. The problem is, we got no way of knowing that."

Greg let the suspicion, like the question, linger in the air. And then, blowing all the air out of his chest, he acted like he was being forced to spill the beans. "Listen," Greg said, "you're right. I'm not exactly who I say I am. And I'm not trying to be dodgy here, not giving you my name and all that. It's just…if you want to know the truth, I actually got a few warrants out for my arrest."

"What kind of warrants?" Lewis interjected again.

Greg moved in for the kill. "Listen, it really wasn't my fault."

"What type of arrests?" Mike repeated. "We don't hang with no pedos."

"Hey." Greg stepped into the men. "Neither do I."

His reaction worked. The men relaxed. With tempers calmed, Greg returned to his explanation. "Anyway," he said, "I lost my job a few months back. So, I go to the bank to pull out some cash, 'cause I know I got at least two hundred dollars left at that bank…when this Jew tries to tell me that I'm overdrawn."

Mike interrupted him. "How'd you know it was a Jew?"

Greg wasn't expecting that question. "What?"

Mike's eyes were icy. "How'd you know it was a Jew?"

The seconds ticked by as he scrambled for an answer, before John decided to intervene. "Duh," John said, practically jumping between them, excited by his own brilliance. "They were working at a bank. Of course she was a Jew. Plus, I bet she had a big Jew—"

"Shut up," Mike said again.

John immediately buttoned up.

"Anyway," Greg continued. "I'm trying to pull out my money, because I know I got money in there, and she's busting my balls, giving me a hard time, and I'm getting pissed off, you know? I start screaming at her, calling her names… It wasn't even a big deal, you know? Just a way to vent my frustration. But I go back after hours, spray-paint some swastikas on the outside sidewalk, break a few windows… Now they got me on hate crimes, harassment, along with a whole other bunch of unmentionables."

"What a scam," Mike said.

"Right?" Greg was relieved to finally be winning him over.

"Actually, we could use someone like you," Mike said, before nodding to his empty glass. "Can I get you another beer, man?"

"That would be great."

Shortly thereafter, John returned with a drink. The three men closed in around Greg, shifting themselves from the pool table to a booth in order to speak more privately. Greg took another sip of his beer. "So, you guys are what," Greg asked curiously, "Aryan Brotherhood? KKK?"

"Hell no," Lewis said, offended.

"Amateur hour," Mike laughed.

Greg waited for a breath. "Paper Boys?"

The men side-eyed each other. Greg had his answer.

"You heard about The Paper Boys?" Mike asked, thumbing a napkin on the table.

"The folks with the flyers, right?" Greg said.

"Not just flyers." John sneered as if insulted. "We do way bigger stuff than that!"

"Seriously?" Mike said, punching him in the arm. "I told you to shut up with all that."

The table settled back into silence. Obviously, they were open to the idea of a new member to their organization… but also, he was still a stranger. They were anxious. Their friendliness shifted into outright distrust at the smallest whiff of trouble.

Greg needed to be careful about what he said next. He took a long drink of his beer, biding his time, before lobbing the only comment he could find. "Well," Greg said, thumping his now empty glass on the table, "if you are The Paper Boys, I should be the one buying you the drinks."

It worked. The men relaxed. Eventually, the decision was made that Greg was okay—trustworthy enough to meet up with again, possibly even garner an introduction to their fearless leader. Greg perked up at the news but didn't press them further. He had just made significant headway. He didn't want to scare them off by seeming overzealous. Beyond all these things, he still needed evidence.

Right now, the only thing he had to take to the police was a lot of talk.

But later that evening, returning to Magic Mud Pottery, seeing that door to Faye's bedroom once again closed and locked tight, he realized something important. Even though he still couldn't remember his past, even though he had no idea who he was or what had brought him to Woodstock in the first place—he had never been a Paper Boy.

TWENTY-NINE

The sun hadn't yet risen when Faye peeked her head out of her bedroom. Down the hall, Greg was still sleeping. Grabbing her purse, she snuck out of Magic Mud Pottery and went to the local train station, where she boarded the first train for Manhattan. Three hours later, she arrived in Greenwich Village.

Finding the address for Rabbi Nachum Solovechick, an expert in Jewish folklore currently teaching at NYU, she made her way to his office. Heading up the stairs of a brownstone, she envisioned an old man, long beard, mumbling words of wisdom beneath a heavy Yiddish accident. He was anything but. Instead, a young man sporting a black kippah and talking on his cell phone waved her inside.

"I'm Faye," she whispered, trying not to interrupt the conversation. "We're supposed to be meeting at ten o'clock...to talk about golems."

"One second," Rabbi Solovechick mouthed back, pointing

to a chair in front his desk, before returning to his conversation on the phone. "It's in the box marked *candles*. I know it's not a candle, but the box was open. I put it inside."

Faye took a seat and glanced around the room. Serious-looking works of Jewish texts exploded from every shelf and corner. On his desk, next to the computer, sat a tiny golem figurine. To the side, a series of boxes, filled with even more books, was still in the process of being unpacked.

"Alright," Rabbi Solovechick said. "I'm sorry. I know… Well, I love you, too."

He clicked off the phone, putting it back into his pocket and turning to Faye.

"Sorry about that," he said, taking a seat across from her.

"Not a problem," she said. "I'm Faye. Faiga Kaplan. Our mutual friend Shulamit sent me."

"Ah, right… Shulamit. How's she doing?"

"Wonderful," Faye said. "I see her almost every week, in some form or another."

He nodded, and they spent a few more minutes talking mutual friends and upstate New York, before Rabbi Solovechick got right down to business. "So, what can I help you with today, Faye?"

An awkward silence filled the room. Despite spending all morning practicing her spiel, it still felt hard to continue. "I'm a ceramicist. I have a business in upstate New York called Magic Mud Pottery, where I make and sell my own pottery…and recently, I've gotten very interested in golems."

He pursed his lips together. "Interesting."

She shifted in her seat, trying to appear logical, an artist just doing research. "Before I begin, I felt it was important to do some research. I asked Shulamit to recommend me someone who would be considered an expert on the matter, and she suggested you."

"She's absolutely right," Rabbi Solovechick said. "Golems are one of my favorite topics to teach. They are also what originally brought me to the world of the Jewish paranormal."

"Really?"

"Of course." He pushed that little clay man across his desk. "There isn't a single creature in all of Jewish folklore that better encapsulates the story of the Jewish people. In many ways, you can say that the golem *is* the essence of the Jewish experience."

"I don't understand."

"Well, let me ask you a question." Rabbi Solovechick had a twinkle in his eye. It was obvious this topic excited him. "What do you know about the golem?"

Faye thought back to all the stories she had heard growing up as a kid, all the movies and TV shows she had seen, too. "I know that they're usually created from clay. And you're supposed to use Hebrew words to breathe life into them."

"Good," Rabbi Solovechick said, egging her forward. "Keep going."

"And I know that they were most often created to defend Jews against anti-Semitic attacks, that there was a really famous rabbi in Prague who had one... But eventually, the golem becomes destructive. Dangerous. He winds up hurting the very community he is designed to protect and often...kills his creator."

Rabbi Nachum Solovechick was smiling.

Faye didn't understand.

"What?" Faye said. "Did I get something wrong?"

"It depends."

"Depends?"

"On who's telling the story..."

"I'm sorry." Faye was really confused now. "I'm just... I'm not following you completely here. Did I get something wrong, or not?"

"Well, to understand that question," he said, "we have to start at the beginning."

"The first golem created?"

"The first appearance of the word." He rose from his seat and, pulling a Hebrew English Tanakh, flipped to a page before handing it to Faye. "Psalm 139, verses 15 and 16. 'Your eyes saw my undeveloped substance.'"

"Undeveloped substance?"

"Or unformed limbs," he said, returning to his seat. "The meaning isn't exactly clear...but this is the verse where the golem legends begin."

"So, that's all the golem story was in the beginning. One word?"

"One unclear word, and then, extrapolation. The rabbis of the Talmud want to understand what this word *golem* means... and so they study it, and eventually, a consensus emerges that the speaker of this phrase is Adam, the first man, and that he is praising God for forming him from this undeveloped substance of the earth."

Faye couldn't help but think back to the way she had created Gregolem. "So that's why a golem is always made from clay and mud?"

"Not always," Rabbi Solovechick said. "You see, for the next few centuries, we start to get these tales of rabbis who successfully create life. Sometimes, they do this through magic. Sometimes, they need the words of an innocent, like a child, to bring this artificial man to life. Usually, this creation is lacking something—he may be mute, for instance, unable to speak, or he can acquire the ability to speak over time. And yet, do you know what word never appears in these fantastical tales of our rabbis?"

Faye swallowed. *"Golem?"*

Rabbi Solovechick snapped his finger, excitedly. "That's it," he said. "Not once do they use the word *golem*. Instead, for centuries, we have these different stories floating around, and we have these stories of rabbis creating men, because creation *is* their primary focus. And this idea of a golem as a helper, or a defender against anti-Semitism, doesn't even exist."

"Huh," Faye said, chewing on her lower lip. "I had no idea."

"Now, something very important also happens during this time. A book called the *Sefer Yetzira* comes into creation. And this book, only about two thousand words long, suggests that letters of the Hebrew alphabet have divine power. *That words, themselves, have power.* And I'm not talking about just the power to hurt someone's feelings, or even change someone's political viewpoint... I'm talking about an actual mystical power to create a new reality. And do you know why we believe this?"

"No idea, actually."

"Because God created the universe with a word," Rabbi Solovechick said, pointing back to the Tanakh she was holding. "Turn to the first page of that. Genesis 1, verse 3..."

Faye flipped to the beginning of the Hebrew Bible.

"'And God said—'" Rabbi Solovechick pointed to his lips ""—let there be light, and there was light.' He spoke, and the world came into creation. *Language.* The thing that separates us from all the other creatures. The ability to name. The ability to communicate, tell stories, transmit those stories to others. *For Jews, language is creation.*"

Faye couldn't help but think back to the anti-Semites operating in her town. They also used words, but unlike with Shulamit and her Say No to Hate Rally, they spread a gospel of hatred in order to do harm.

"I do understand," Faye said, shifting in her seat. "I'm a Jewitch."

"Ah," he said, without any judgment. "So you're familiar with this concept?"

"Words are the most powerful type of magic."

"Indeed."

Still, as much as she was enjoying these larger metaphysical questions on the nature of creation and narrative, she was here for more practical concerns. "But in terms of my project, and the golem…"

"Right," he said, tapping himself on his forehead. "Sorry. I get carried away. Anyway, what I'm trying to explain to you is that, for many centuries, we have a word for golem, and we have stories of the rabbis creating life, but the two concepts haven't merged yet. In fact, it's not until we get to the eleventh and twelfth centuries that we start to see golems being created for utilitarian purposes."

"Utilitarian purposes?" Faye asked. "Not against anti-Semitism."

"Not yet," he said, growing more animated with each stage of history described. "Solomon ibn Gabriol, a Spanish poet and philosopher, has a skin disease, and he makes a female golem to help him with household chores. Unlike later golems, she's not made out of clay or mud…but wood and metal. And we see the golem story shift again. It's not about creating life, but creating life to perform some service. And this continues, in various evolutions, in various transmissions, until we get to the story of Rabbi Judah Loew of Prague. Perhaps the most famous golem story of them all…"

Faye knew that story, too. She had learned that Rabbi Judah had made a golem to defend against anti-Semitic attacks in the ghetto where he resided.

"Except," Rabbi Solovechick interrupted himself, "we have pretty clear evidence that Rabbi Judah Loew did not believe in magic or miracles. Also, historically speaking, blood libel charges were not happening in his community in the sixteenth century, so there would have been no need for him to create a golem to defend against charges of anti-Semitism. In fact, when we line up everything we know historically regarding the real Rabbi Judah Loew of Prague, we come to learn that the entire story is legend, written and developed years after his death."

"Wait." Faye swallowed, her heart beginning to race inside her chest. "So if there was never a real golem of Prague, what

about all the stories I've heard about golems being created to
defend against anti-Semitism turning bad and destroying their
creators?"

"And again—" he leaned back in his chair "—I ask you,
who's telling the story?"

"I don't understand. Jews, right?"

"Take a trip back in time with me," he said, waving his hand
in the air, "to the years between the seventeenth and the nine-
teenth centuries."

"Okay," Faye said, willing to play along.

"Things are not going well for the Jewish people," he said.
"They are living in ghettos. They are experiencing horrible
anti-Semitism. Blood libel charges, accusations that Jews engage in ritual murder of non-Jewish children, are frequent.
Jews are being arrested, forced to undergo sham trials, murdered. In Russia, they are experiencing some of the most violent
outbreaks of organized anti-Semitic violence. Their businesses
are taken away from them, their homes burned down to the
ground. There is a mass wave of refugees fleeing to places like
America. And in the midst of all this terrible, awful, increasing hatred...two heroes appear."

"Golems?" Faye asked, hopeful for the answer.

"Authors."

"Oh."

Faye slumped, disappointed, in her chair. It was not what
she wanted to hear.

"Yudl Rosenberg is a rabbi living in Prague, and to enhance
his income, he's writing books on Jewish law, and midrash, and
kabbalah. But unlike most of his peers at the time, Yudl also
reads secular fiction, and understanding that the Jewish world
he came from would not read such books, he crafts a story.
He makes it look like a tale he discovered and translated from
Rabbi Judah Loew of Prague, and he writes it in a way that

the Jewish world will accept it as a Jewish text. But it is absolutely a fictional story."

Her mouth went dry. "It is?"

"But Yudl Rosenberg gives the Jewish people a hero. He writes this book about a golem, and he humanizes it. He gives the golem a name, feelings. The golem can be hurt, get angry and take revenge. The golem also does chores. He reads and writes. He can follow complicated instructions. He fights for and protects the Jewish people absolutely…and when the golem eventually dies, he dies peacefully. He is surrounded by his community, when Rabbi Judah lovingly removes the words from his mouth."

Faye didn't know what to say. "I've never… I didn't know this story."

"Most people don't," Rabbi Solovechick said sadly. "In fact, poor Yudl almost never gets remembered for the contributions he made in terms of the golem tale, even though that book he wrote went on to become a bestseller in the Jewish community during its time and even inspired other Jewish writers, such as a man named Chayim Bloch, to begin writing their own version of golem stories for the Jewish world they lived in. And yet you can see in Rabbi Rosenberg's version all the golem stories that preceded it, all the history of these various Jewish moments, into one."

It was fascinating. But it still didn't answer one big question. Faye shifted in her seat. "So, when does the golem go bad? When do the stories start changing, and the golem becomes destructive?"

"You ready for it?" he said. "Pretty much at the same exact time."

"I don't… I don't understand."

"Gustav Meyrink, a German language writer, pens *Der Golem* in 1915. And because we are in a time period that is rife with Jew-hatred, his version of a golem reflects his anti-Semitic beliefs…"

Rabbi Solovechick picked up the golem doll on his desk, analyzing it.

"The Jews in his story," he continued, "are not just outsiders, but parasites. They use the blood of Christian babies in their magic rituals to destroy the nations they are a part of…and for creating a golem, they are punished. The golem returns every thirty-three years to wreak havoc on the Jewish people."

Faye didn't know what to say. She couldn't believe that the story of the golem she knew, the one she had held in her head when first creating her golem doll…was inherently anti-Semitic.

"That story," Rabbi Solovechick explained, "would go on to be a bestseller, as well, though amongst a broader non-Jewish audience. It would be translated into multiple languages, get reviewed in the *New York Times*, and go on to serve as the basis for films, which Meyrink himself worked on."

"And what about Yudl?" Faye had to ask. "What happened to his version of the golem story?"

"Largely forgotten, I'm afraid."

Faye stared down at her shoes. "So that's what you mean by it depends on who's telling the story…"

"The thing you need to understand about the golem," Rabbi Solovechick continued, "is that there isn't just one real version. That's why I say there is no better barometer for the Jewish experience, and Jewish folklore, than the golem. The golem is a Rorschach test for what Jews are currently experiencing in their history, in their time, and as times change, the legend of the golem changes with it. It builds, and builds, and builds on the stories that came before it.

"Until the golem is the past, present, and future, all wrapped into one."

She sighed. This had not gone the way she had hoped, or expected.

"So, you don't actually believe that a golem can exist?"

"Oh no," Rabbi Solovechick said resolutely. "I absolutely believe that golems exist."

Her hope reappeared. "You do?"

"I believe in *sheydim*, *mazzikin*, and the power of a *bracha*. I believe that a word can literally change our reality. So, of course, there could be real-life golems out there. Because words create and words destroy. Which means, when we write a golem story, tell the narrative, reclaim what came before in order to make it our own…then somewhere, at least according to our tradition, that golem exists."

"Great," Faye said, pulling her chair in closer. "Staying on this topic for a moment, how would one get rid of a golem that they created?"

"You mean a real golem?"

"Yeah," she said. "If there isn't one version…if you've already tried all the ideas offered up online, and your golem is still…you know, living in your house, sometimes disappearing for hours without explanation?"

Rabbi Solovechick thumbed his lower lip, thinking it over. "I'm not sure."

Faye grimaced. "Could you maybe try and venture a guess here?"

"I suppose," Rabbi Solovechick said finally, "if the golem is an amalgamation of its creator's will and desire, along with the memory of golem stories that came before, then my hunch would be that only the creator can write the story of its destruction. The spell for removal must come from them, from their words and actions—whatever that looks like—because it was their words and actions that created the thing to begin with."

It was something.

Faye thanked the rabbi for his time and, gathering up her things, moved to return to Woodstock.

★ ★ ★

On the train ride back home that afternoon, Faye reflected on her meeting with the rabbi. On the night she had created Gregolem, she had been drunk. She had created him from clay, writing words, a wish list for the perfect man—the perfect hero against anti-Semitism—onto his head and body. But she also had, in the back of her mind, in her memory, the history of all those golem stories she'd heard before.

Perhaps it was a self-fulfilling prophecy that she was losing control of her golem. But then again, Rabbi Solovechick had provided one very helpful piece of advice. *Only the creator can write the story of its destruction.*

Pulling out a notebook and pen from her pocketbook, she began sketching a spell. If Faye had created Gregolem from words and memories, she could certainly get rid of him that way, too.

WHEN SOMEONE YOU LOVE IS HURTING
by Dr. CJ Janowitz

Page 300

It can be difficult to love someone who is hurting. As human beings, we have a tendency to want to fix what is broken. And when we can't fix these things simply, we feel helpless. Sometimes we may even strike out at the one we love, reacting in anger. We just want them to heal so badly. But empathy, and caregiving, is not the promise of making things better, but simply being there.

Your presence counts. In those worst moments, in those times where nothing you can say will change what is occurring, remember that every person needs at least one safe space, a shelter to run to in the storm.

THIRTY

"Faye?" Greg called out early that same morning. "You here?"

Magic Mud Pottery was eerily quiet. Greg checked upstairs, downstairs, the back garden and studio—before finally giving up. She had taken off and, it seemed, hadn't even bothered to leave him a note. Still, he tried not to take it personally. He settled himself on helping her out, opening the store for the day— but then, on second thought, decided to just head to Jumbos.

An hour later, Greg was texting John to come meet him. By noon, Mike had arrived. They were three plates down on buffalo wings when Lewis appeared, and Mike laid another fifty down on the bar.

"Another round on me," Mike said.

John whooped, jumping on Mike's shoulder. Mike pushed him back from the bar. "Seriously, dude," Mike said, scolding him like a small child, "where the hell are your manners? Let the new guy go first."

Greg assumed that by new guy, Mike meant him.

"Thanks," Greg said, taking the beer.

It struck Greg how they operated in a hierarchy. Mike at the top, obviously. Then Lewis. John at the very bottom. Where Greg was fitting into things, however, was anyone's guess. But he was getting the sense that the drinks, like the fact they had all managed to arrive early in the afternoon, meant that they had plans for something.

"I wish I could return the favor," Greg said, returning to his cover story.

"No worries, man." Mike clapped him on the shoulder. "You'll get me back another day."

"Definitely."

"It's what we do for friends, right? And you know, we can help you find a job, Greg. We can help you with a lot of things in Woodstock. Maybe even figure out a way to take care of your little warrant problem."

Now they were getting somewhere. "You would really do that for me?"

"Hell yeah," Mike said. "Our kind has to stick together."

Our kind. It took everything Greg had to maintain his facade. "So," he said, lifting the beer up to his lips, "what are you thinking?"

Mike moved in closer. "We have a little problem."

"A problem, huh?"

"There's this Jew bitch downtown," he said beneath his breath. "She's been getting…well, let's just say she's been getting uppity."

"Uppity?" Greg gripped his beer glass harder. "Uppity, how?"

"Who the hell does she think she is?" John suddenly interjected.

"Don't worry." Mike smiled gleefully. "Big dog has a plan."

"I'm sorry." Greg feigned ignorance. "I'm not sure what you're talking about."

Mike began to explain. "You know, we don't just work to educate the masses. That's only a small part of what we do. Another big part is protecting our communities from Jews. Getting rid of them, you know? Getting them out of our community. So, over the last few months…we've taken steps to help them understand they're not wanted."

"What type of steps?"

"Oh, you know…" Mike said casually. "Graffiti, vandalism, bricks through windows. Nothing too wild. Just a warning that people need to close shop and leave. That we're not gonna sit around and have our communities be destroyed by the Zionist conspiracy."

Greg forced the words out of his mouth. "That's…awesome."

"Right?" Mike nudged him. "So, anyway… We hit this one Jew bitch a month ago. Caught her in the dead of night, tossed a brick right through her window. But instead of taking the hint, she wants to show she's not afraid. She wants to laugh at us, keep operating her business. So tonight, we're gonna teach that uppity Jew rat a lesson. Make sure she closes shop and never comes back."

Greg could feel a rumble building in his chest. *They are talking about Faye. They are talking about Magic Mud Pottery.* He forced himself to maintain his cool, though all he wanted to do was toss Mike across the room.

Greg lifted the beer to his lips once more. "Y'all need help?"

"What do you say?" Lewis nodded at him. "You up for it?"

"Well, hell yeah," Greg said, finishing his beer, slamming it down on the bar. "Count me in, man. You know you don't have to ask me twice."

The news made everybody happy.

"Great," Mike said, pulling out his phone and quickly texting somebody. "Then grab your jacket, man, because we're heading out."

"Out," Greg stammered. "You mean, right now?"

"Yeah, right now."

"But…" He glanced towards the windows. "It's still light out?"

The men looked askance at each other before Mike intervened once more. "Don't worry." He grinned, keeping one hand on Greg's back as he pushed him towards the exit. "We got you. Nothing to worry about at all."

They drove for hours in circles around Woodstock with no clear destination. Mike occasionally texting someone at a red light. John reaching over the front seat to increase the volume on some heavy-metal song blaring on the radio, much to everyone's annoyance. But otherwise, they offered Greg no hints about where they were heading. No escape, either.

He knew this was a bad situation. He was also still reeling from learning that Faye would be the intended target of a hate crime this evening—but he was so close to the truth. He just had to maintain his cool, keep his cover going for a little while longer.

At least until he had evidence.

The car turned, swinging into a neighborhood. He gazed out the window, surprised to find tiny ranchers, set upon manicured lawns decorated for the Thanksgiving holidays.

"This is a real nice neighborhood," Greg said, shifting in his seat to meet Mike's eyes in the rearview mirror.

"Not your type of people?" Mike asked, smirking.

"Not really," Greg lied.

"Well, that's okay," Mike said. "Every war needs soldiers. People not afraid to get their hands dirty. People with few attachments."

Greg forced a smile. "That would certainly be me."

The car swung around another block before finally parking on the street in front of a brown wooden-paneled house. An American flag hung from the side, and a cop car sat in the driveway. Everyone began unbuckling their seat belts, moving to pop out of the vehicle, Mike still texting someone on the phone while he walked, but Greg hesitated.

"Is this some sort of a joke?" Greg asked.

"What?" Mike looked up from his phone, and then, realizing Greg's trepidation, waved his concern away. "Oh, that. Don't worry about it, man. Big dog is cool."

"Big dog?" Greg asked.

"You're about to meet our fearless leader, my friend."

"The man behind the curtain," Lewis continued.

"He says go through the garage," Mike said, looking at his phone. "And straight into the back."

"The back?"

"Big dog is throwing us a barbecue tonight."

"A barbecue." Greg still didn't completely understand. "Is that like…a euphemism?"

Mike laughed, clapping him on the back, but otherwise didn't respond.

The garage opened. A series of work tools hung on one side. A car, covered by a blue tarp, was parked in the center. Another American flag hung on the back wall above a desk. Greg slinked past the car and found himself standing in a beige hallway, staring at a montage of photographs. Chief Eric Myers beamed brightly back at him, one arm slung happily around the shoulder of some elected official, as he received an award for commendation.

It didn't take long for Greg to put it together. Chief Eric Myers was the leader of The Paper Boys in Woodstock. Greg needed to think quick.

"Actually," Greg said, rubbing the back of his neck, "is there a bathroom here?"

"A bathroom?" Mike asked.

"Too many hot wings."

Mike pointed down the hallway. "Last door on the left."

"Thanks."

"Come out to the back when you're done."

Greg wasted no time disappearing into the bathroom. Waiting to hear the men depart to the backyard, the sliding door closing behind them, he attempted to regroup. He had discovered the head of The Paper Boys operating in Woodstock. Members of their cell, too. But if he wanted to bring them to justice permanently, he needed evidence. Something he could give to the FBI directly, since clearly the local police and their investigation had been corrupted.

Greg debated his options. He could use what little time he had to search the house, but he risked Mike and his friends getting suspicious. He could confront Eric directly, but given all that Eric had to lose—and the fact that Greg would be outnumbered four to one in a physical altercation—he quickly scratched that plan.

He debated giving up entirely, leaving the situation without a clear-cut connection to the man and his crimes. But the voice he had heard since coming to Woodstock grew louder inside his mind, egging him forward. *Justice, justice, you shall pursue. Justice, justice, you shall pursue.*

If Greg were an anti-Semite, where would he hide the evidence?

The answer came to him in an instant. A whisper from the universe. *Justice.*

Greg opened the door to the bathroom, peeking out, checking to make sure the coast was clear. Then, slinking back down the hallways, he made his way to the garage and the car that was sitting in the middle of it all, covered completely by a blue tarp.

Greg pulled it off, breath hitching at the reveal. There, hidden away in Eric's own garage, was a blue four-door sedan with the license plate HX3498.

It was the same car he had seen on the night Faye's store was attacked. The same vehicle and number that Faye had given

Eric to run, but Eric had never run the license plate number. He had never had any intention of running it. Because he was the mastermind behind the crimes.

A voice appeared from inside the house.

"Yo, Greg?" Mike called out. "You coming or what?"

There was no time left to spare. Quickly, Greg pulled out his phone and snapped a photo of the car. And then, he took off. Sprinting down sidewalks, he ran as far as he could, as fast as he could, until he found himself a safe distance away. Greg pulled out his phone and texted two different messages.

The first was to Mike in order to buy himself some time: Sorry, man. Too many wings. Bubble gut. Had to go home.

And the second was to Nelly. Chief Eric Myers is the head of The Paper Boys. Contact the FBI. Do not contact the police. They are planning something for tonight at Faye's. Have evidence. WILL EXPLAIN REST LATER.

He didn't have time to wait for a reply. Or call an Uber. Digging the phone into his back pocket, he took off again in the direction of downtown Woodstock and Magic Mud Pottery. The voice in his head, the one that always screamed at him to chase justice, fell into a whisper.

Greg only had one thought on his mind now. He had to protect Faye. He had to get her out of that store, to someplace safe…at least until the proper authorities were notified, and all the guilty parties had been apprehended. He ran, and ran, the thought of losing her an ache, the promise of protecting her his central motivation, until finally, sweaty and out of breath, he rounded the corner and burst through the door of Magic Mud Pottery.

Faye was waiting on the couch in the foyer, her jacket on and at the ready, two backpacks resting on the floor.

"Oh." She beamed, rising from her spot. "You're back. Perfect timing."

THIRTY-ONE

Greg was doing his best to keep up with Faye, currently moving at high speed through the woods towards the cave known as Devil's Cave. It wasn't easy. Despite all his best efforts to get her to sit down and listen to what he had to tell her regarding Eric and The Paper Boys, she had focused her intention *fully* on going caving that late afternoon.

"Come on, Greg," she shouted back at him, "just a little bit more."

"But I need to tell you something," Greg shouted, nearly tripping on a rock.

She waved his words away. "We'll talk about whatever it is later!"

He sighed and gave in to her request again. He also tried to look on the bright side. For now, Faye was out of the house. Away from any danger. He was also hoping that Nelly was working to contact the FBI...

The sound of thunder echoed in the distance. He glanced up at the sky.

"Are you sure this is really the best time to go——"

"It's the perfect time!" she said, without even looking back.

"But it looks like it's going to rain."

"A little drizzle never hurt anybody."

"And it's getting kind of dark…"

"The very best time to make magic," she retorted.

Greg rolled his eyes and sped up. It was only when they came to the opening of the cave, and she had to stop to shift the placement of her backpack, that Greg found his chance.

"I've been investigating The Paper Boys," he said suddenly.

She froze halfway through the entrance. "What?"

"It's a long story." Greg spat out the words quickly. "But basically, since I've come to Woodstock, there's been this voice in my head."

Her gaze narrowed. "A voice in your head?"

"It said *justice, justice*…which, at first, I didn't realize was a whole thing. I just thought it was the word. But I figured out what it meant the night The Paper Boys attacked your store. And then, the words…they became this mantra inside my mind. And I knew that I had to do something to protect you and the entire Jewish community of Woodstock, so I teamed up with Nelly——"

She tsked her teeth sympathetically. "Of course you did."

"Huh?" Greg didn't understand.

"I understand. You can't help yourself. It's part of your nature."

"My nature?"

"You poor thing. You just…have no choice in the matter, do you? You're just this bag of skin and bones holding someone else's wants and wishes."

"I don't…understand."

"Don't worry, Greg. Don't you fret that beautiful, perfectly crafted head of yours. We're going to resolve all this very shortly. You don't have to worry about The Paper Boys anymore. Because I am finally, finally, going to send you back to where you belong."

"Um," he said. "Okay."

"Come on then." She returned to the task at hand, angling her body once again to enter the cave. "We've got a Jewitch ritual to do!"

He sighed, and then, letting it go for the time being, Greg followed her inside. After a short path, they had returned to the womb-like center of the cave.

Above them, through the hole in the ceiling, dusk was setting in. Thick clouds gathered, turning the sky a spectacular shade of purple tinged with pink. Faye drifted to the center of the cave and, kneeling down to her backpack, began pulling out items.

"So," Greg asked. "What exactly is the ritual we're doing tonight?"

"It's a surprise," she said.

"What about setting my intention?" Greg asked.

She glanced over her shoulder at him. "I want you to think about…going away."

Greg grimaced. "Away?"

"Home," she backtracked. "I meant home."

He resigned himself, and his full intention, to being present. Faye returned to her bag and laid out seven candles around the chamber, bathing them both in a soft light. Then she directed Greg to the center.

"Please," Faye said, pointing, "sit."

He took a seat. Faye returned to her bag, pulling out a container of salt, sprinkling a giant circle around him. Next she grabbed a jar of dirt.

"I'm sorry," she said, "but I have to sprinkle this on you."

"Well, I've never been afraid of a little dirt before, so—"

She dumped the whole thing on his head.

"Okay, then…" he said, spitting some out. "Not quite what I was expecting there, but…"

"Sorry about that," she said. "I just…you need to be covered."

"We want this to work, right?" he replied.

"Exactly."

She returned to her bag and pulled out dried rosebuds, tossing them at him. He picked one up, analyzing it.

"Are these from your garden?" he asked.

"They are."

"Huh."

Greg watched while she mixed items together in her small ritual bowl. Oil. Soot. Tiny little shards of pottery. Finally she pulled out her silver knife. "Do you mind if I take some of your hair?"

He considered the question. "Whatever you need, Faye."

She cut a bit from the bottom, tossing it in the bowl, before setting everything on fire. Greg watched the smoke billow up between them.

"Thank you, again," she said, her voice softening, "for humoring me."

"It's never humoring you, Faye."

She opened the red wine and poured it into the silver cup, handing it to him. "If you don't mind…"

"I should drink this?"

"Bottoms up."

He did as she instructed, drinking the whole thing down. She took the cup from him. "And now," she said, circling him, "I want you to close your eyes, Greg…and I want you to clear your mind. Just think back to when you first appeared in my life, what brought you here. And then, go back even further, back to the place you came from…"

He cleared his mind, thinking back on that day when he

had first met Faye. The way she looked, an angel appearing from the heavens. He was so certain that he knew her. It still shocked him to his core that up until that moment, that very second, they had been strangers.

He felt something like a leaf falling on his face. He opened one eye to see Faye tearing pages from the book she had brought.

"Aleph, bet, gimel, dalet, hey, vav," she said, and tore out a page from her Jewish prayer book, tossing it into the air, where it flittered like a feather before landing on the ground beside him. And then, before he could ask a question—before Faye could explain what the hell she was doing—she began repeating the words and motion. "Aleph, bet, gimel, dalet, hey, vav," she said. "Aleph, bet, gimel, dalet, hey, vav."

She went on and on, each round getting louder and more intense—which he might have stopped—but Faye was gyrating on his body. And so, in some attempt to join in her Jewitch ritual, he played along.

Greg began chanting right along with her. "Aleph, bet, gimel, dalet, hey, vav. Aleph, bet, gimel, dalet—"

"Yes," she shouted, her own voice rising alongside his. "Louder!"

He obeyed. "Aleph, bet, gimel, dalet, hey, vav... Aleph, bet, gimel, dalet, hey, vav."

Faye bent down to him on one knee. "Also," she said, "I'm gonna need you to eat one of these pages."

"What?"

"Maybe a few pages..."

He cocked his chin back. "Is that even safe?"

He could see her thinking about it.

"How about I just put them in my mouth?" he said, trying to find a happy medium.

"Perfect!"

Wanting to be a good sport, he shoved four pages of text

into his mouth. Faye continued circling him. "Repeat after me," she said. "I will now return to the chaotic void which I have come from."

"Errgrrr rrrrrr," he grumbled, attempting to get out the words. "Chhhrrr."

"There it is," Faye shouted. "Your true nature."

"Irrr cccrrre werrds."

He was trying to say, *I can't really speak clearly*, but it was coming out all wrong.

Faye lifted from her spot, returning to her backpack. When she returned, she had a mason jar of—well, in truth, he had no idea what it was—but it looked like some sort of black sludge. Opening the jar, she dug her hands in, pulling out a clump of it, chucking it straight at his heart.

She did this ritual seven times in total, putting the sludge on his forehead, arms, and legs before finally dumping all that was left of the stinky, slimy material on his penis.

"Alright," Greg said, spitting out paper, trying to wipe mud from his eyelids, "I think we're good on the mud—"

Faye wasn't listening. Instead, she reached for a candle and, lifting it up into the air, arched her back towards the sky.

"Return to your earthbound state," she said. "Be disassembled, *you golem*. For I, who have created you from dirt and stone, mud and water, fire and air, word and language…revoke my permission. I return you now by the way I have created you. With dirt and stone, mud and water, fire and air, word and language… I destroy you, my creation. I return you back to your original form. Begone, Gregolem. Begone, and may you never return to our human sphere."

And then, much to Greg's surprise, there was silence.

THIRTY-TWO

There was no sound in the cave. No noise. It was like every bird and bug, every living being within a ten-mile radius, had suddenly disappeared. Faye opened her eyes, still cast upwards towards the light of the moon, and took note of the way the energy had shifted around them. She had done it. She had destroyed Gregolem...

And then, the sound of Greg hacking up papers brought her back to reality.

Faye blinked, surprised. "You're still here?"

"What?"

His face was mired with confusion. Also, mud.

"I don't understand," she said. "I did everything right. Everything the AI told me to do. Everything the rabbi told me to do. I created a spell from my own mind and heart...but you're still here. Why are you still here, Greg?"

He squinted up at her. "Because you asked me to go caving..."

Faye shook her head. "I'm confused."

"That makes two of us."

It was then, staring at her creation, that she realized something very important. Greg was not a golem, at all. He was a real live, flesh-and-blood, human being. And she, like always, had made a mess of things.

"Oh my God," she said, dropping to her knees, trying to clean the mud off his face with her own hands. "I can explain. I didn't mean to…well, I did mean to…but I promise, I had a very good reason for everything," Faye stammered. "I… I thought you were a golem."

Greg blinked. "What?"

"A golem," she repeated.

Saying it aloud, saying it to Greg, she realized how positively absurd it all sounded.

She attempted to explain, rambling incessantly, confessing everything. She told him how she had created a golem doll in the wake of those anti-Semitic flyers—how she had molded and shaped the perfect man, giving him long red hair, etching onto his skin all the things she would want in a partner.

"And then," her rambling continued, "the very next day, you showed up. You showed up, Greg, and you were perfect in every way. And we were kissing, and you had a scar on your back, and I remembered that I broke the doll. I broke the doll, and the scar was in the same exact place…and golems always go bad. At least, when I created my golem, that was the story I had in my head, and then you would go on these long walks, and I had no idea where you were…and I had to get rid of you."

His face morphed into sadness. "You were trying to get rid of me?"

"Not you," she said, defending herself. "The golem."

Greg stared down at the spot between his legs. Faye took a deep breath, awaiting sentencing. Because she had done it. Like always. Every relationship she got into she eventually destroyed. Her wrist ached. She was just too damn broken.

"Okay," Greg said.

"Wait." She blinked. "What?"

"Faye," he said, inching closer to her, hands outstretched, "you've been through a lot the last few weeks."

"Haman's hat."

"I mean, really," he said, analyzing the entire affair, "you've been attacked, traumatized… Obviously it's brought up a lot of complicated feelings for you. Plus, this is partly my fault."

She stammered, "Your fault?"

"I can see how my recent actions have increased your sense of feeling unsafe," he said, shaking his head. "This is really all my fault, Faye."

"What…"

Faye could hardly believe what she was hearing. He was too good. He was too perfect. He was so freaking hot, and gentle, and understanding. It made her full-on panic. But Greg did his best. To explain. To tell her the truth. Even though, she couldn't hear it.

Greg continued. "I didn't want to tell you the truth about what I was doing with Nelly because I thought you wouldn't approve. I thought you would stop me…and I wanted to protect you, Faye. At all costs. You said yourself, your whole life, with your mother, with Stuart…no one would ever stand up for you, stick up for you, be there for you in the way that you needed. I didn't want you to have that experience with me."

"No!" she said, covering her ears. "This is not happening."

"Faye…" His voice drifted into a quiet plea. "If you would just sit down for a minute, let me explain to you everything that happened, what I learned about The Paper Boys. It might not make you feel better, but it will be the truth."

"The truth?" she scoffed.

"I promised you once you would be safe with me," he said. "I have never broken that promise."

Time stood still. All her clay memory came crashing up against her present. She didn't know what to do, or say, because this wasn't how her story was supposed to end. Either as a man, or a golem, Greg was supposed to leave her.

"No." She pointed at his head with one finger. "You should be angry at me."

"Well, I'm not."

"You should be furious," she demanded, none of this making sense to her. "You should be storming out of here, telling me that you never want to see me again."

"Because that's what you want, right?" He said it gently, kindly, without any trace of angry accusation. "It's easier to push someone away than admit that you have feelings for them? It's hard to be vulnerable."

"No," she said, tears coming to her eyes. "I demand you leave me now, Greg. I demand, for your own good, that you walk away from me forever."

"Still here, I'm afraid."

"Then call me insane, tell me that I'm too much…*hit me*."

"Never."

This wasn't going at all how she expected. Until finally, unable to deal with her own swirling confusion, Faye took off.

Not waiting for Greg, she slunk back through the opening of the cave, racing as fast as she could down the pathway and towards the parking lot. If Greg wasn't going to have the good sense to leave her, then the simplest thing to do would be to leave him.

She could still hear him calling her name, screaming something about The Paper Boys as she raced through the woods.

She could not stop crying. It came in heaping, uncontrollable gasps, tears blinding her vision. She was so ridiculously ashamed of what she had done, what she had allowed herself to believe, *because Jews were not magical.* She had never been magical. She had never been able to bend the universe to her will, or create men from clay. She didn't have goddamn space lasers, either. She was simply a human being, broken and fallible, caught up in a narrative that had never been hers.

Rain began falling down around her. She crawled into her car and turned on the ignition. With heat cranking through the vents, she attempted to wipe away the steam forming on the windows before ultimately giving up. She just wanted to go home. She just wanted to forget about Greg, and her life, and everything that had happened.

Driving out of the park, tears flooding her eyes, she reached down to the floor of the passenger side, searching for her backpack. Fumbling for her phone, she dialed Miranda's number. Miranda picked up on the first ring, but even before her best friend could say hello, Faye was crying hysterically into the phone.

"I did something," Faye sobbed. "Something horrible."

"What?" Miranda asked, concern filtering through her voice. "What's happened? Where are you?"

"It's terrible," Faye said, shaking her head. "I can't tell you. You'll never forgive me."

"Of course you can tell me," Miranda said. "I'm your best friend. Whatever it is, I'm here to love and support you."

Faye bawled into the phone. "I'm totally unlovable."

And then, Miranda—clearly at a loss over what to do at her best friend's crisis—turned to her wife for support. "Shully," Miranda said, clearly speaking to her wife. "Please get on the line. Faye is having some sort of conniption. I don't know what to do."

"Faye?" Shully got on another line. "Faye, honey…what is it? What happened?"

Faye explained in one loud huff. "I thought Greg was a golem. And then, I took him to a cave…and I tried to get rid of him by making him eat holy text and dumping sludge all over his penis."

Miranda did not hesitate. *"You did what?"*

"Okay," Shully said. "Let's everybody stay calm. Faye, honey, where are you now?"

"I'm leaving," she hiccuped, "Devil's Cave."

"And where's Greg?" Miranda asked, getting more to the point.

"I don't know." Faye bawled some more.

"Holy hell," Miranda said.

The line went quiet. Faye heard whispering in the background. Miranda returned to the phone and spoke more gently. "Okay, Faye," Miranda said calmly, "why don't you pull over somewhere. You don't sound capable of driving right now."

"Maybe you should call an Uber?" Shulamit said.

"I'm fine," Faye cried hysterically.

"I'm calling Nelly," Miranda said.

"On it," Shulamit said.

Miranda returned to the line. "Faye, listen to me, okay? It's not good for you to be alone right now. We're coming over."

"No," Faye said. "I don't need anybody. I'm fine. I'm perfectly fine...*all alone.*"

Her hysterics reached epic proportions, when suddenly, in the glare of her headlights—between her tears, and the fog, and the rain—a lumbering figure appeared, tall and hulking, clearly lost in the darkness, crossing the road completely unaware.

Faye slammed on the brakes. The car came to a screeching halt, and the phone went flying, before a loud thump, followed by a slow and depressing rattle, sounded in the front of her vehicle. She had hit Greg with her car.

"Oh God," Faye said, quickly putting her car into Park. "Oh God. Greg!"

Unbuckling her seat belt, she climbed from the car and raced towards him. Falling to her knees beside him, hands on his chest, she was relieved to see he was still breathing. "I didn't mean to," she said, totally incoherent, checking to see if anything was bleeding or broken. "I swear. I didn't even see you there."

Greg responded with a low moan before promptly passing out.

THIRTY-THREE

It was weird how it came back. His past. His memory. All of it.

Greg had awoken in a hospital room, the sound of beeping machines all around him, overhead lights glaring, and just like that his recollection returned, without issue, as simply as if he had woken up from a long and confusing dream.

He remembered that he was an investigative journalist, often going undercover, currently working on a story for the *New York Reference Daily* about the far reaches of The Paper Boys. He knew that he was the son of a single mother in the military, a woman who had been a JAG military officer, before dying of Parkinson's when he was in his late twenties. He remembered the sign she kept in her office, too. An embroidery, which her grandfather had given her upon graduating from law school, which read, *Justice, justice, you shall pursue.*

His mother was Jewish.

He knew that he been all over the world—attached to combat units in Afghanistan, going undercover to report on human trafficking at the Mexican border. It wasn't that he loved danger, but he had an almost insatiable desire for justice, for truth, for giving voice to the invisible, and telling human stories.

And he remembered that he hated the feeling of being settled down. That anytime he spent too long in one place, he felt itchy. Annoyed. And aside from his daily appointments at the gym, he avoided long-term commitments like the plague.

As for his current life, that came back, too. He remembered that he lived in New York City in a small apartment in midtown Manhattan. He remembered that his brother, who unlike him had settled down, was now happily married and living in Long Island, along with his nieces.

The strangest part, though, was that the memories of his past now sat beside his memories of his time with Faye. He could recall his entire experience of life without the burden of a past. The way he became a new type of man through reading her books, playing Scrabble with her, going undercover with Nelly—but it was like two different movies playing simultaneously inside his head.

It felt impossible to sort through the confusion.

But mainly, he was worried about Faye. After she had hit him with her car and caused him to black out, she had dropped him off at the hospital and absconded. He never got the chance to tell her about Chief Eric Myers and the attack planned for her store. He tried to contact her, but she wasn't answering. His only hope now was Nelly.

Thankfully, she had come through for him. Shortly after he woke up at the hospital, two agents from the FBI had appeared, wanting to speak with him. Now he was desperately trying to communicate everything he had learned to Agent Jones and Agent Diaz.

"So," Agent Diaz said, staring down at his notebook, "you're telling me that you saw a car the night of the attack on Faye

Kaplan's business address and that you gave that license plate number to Chief Eric Myers, but he never ran it."

"Not only that," Greg said, sitting up in his bed. "The car is in his house."

"We saw the photo," Agent Diaz confirmed.

"And?" Greg asked.

"The car is registered to him."

"Of course it is," Greg said, unsurprised. He was eager to put his pants back on and find Faye. "And both Faye and Miranda can corroborate," he clarified.

He tried to rise to his feet, but a dizzy spell came over him. Agent Diaz and Agent Jones rushed to help him back into bed.

"Just relax," Agent Jones said. "We're still trying to get a handle on what's happening here. Now, going back to this Paper Boys cell operating in Woodstock… You said there were three men working underneath Chief Eric Myers, as well."

"Yes." Greg was getting frustrated by his own malfunctioning body *and* how long this all was taking. "I'm happy to tell you everything else I know, in detail, but first, you need to send an agent to Magic Mud Pottery."

The Feds still weren't getting it. "And these three men," Agent Jones continued, "did they give you any inclination of how they had been recruited?"

Ignoring their question, Greg searched for his phone, texting Nelly once again: Still trying to explain all this to the FBI. Please go to Magic Mud Pottery and get Faye. Do not let her stay there. Take her somewhere safe.

Nelly did not text back.

"Sir," Agent Jones said, trying to grab his attention. "If you would just put down your phone and answer our questions—"

"No!" Greg snapped back at him. "You don't understand. Faiga Kaplan, the woman who owns Magic Mud Pottery, is in terrible danger. The Paper Boys are planning something at her store tonight. Now, I'm happy to sit around and keep talking…

I'm happy to tell you everything I know, and have learned, but only *after* you send your team over there and place Faye into protective custody."

The two agents considered his request, before finally, Agent Diaz left the room. Greg relaxed back onto his hospital bed and, leaning his forehead into his hands, realized he had a massive headache. He had been so worried about Faye that he hadn't even noticed.

"I liked your piece on predatory loans in low-income communities," Agent Jones said.

Greg looked up. "What?"

"I read it," the agent explained, "back in college. It's one of the reasons I went into the FBI. It made me want to work conspiracies. I read your piece on trafficking in fast fashion, too. You do good work. Though I never thought I'd actually meet you. I imagine you have to stay pretty on the down-low in real life."

"Something like that."

"Well..." Agent Jones held out his hand. "It's an honor to meet you."

Greg shook the agent's hand, but he didn't feel like a hero. He had simply done what he always did as an award-winning undercover investigative journalist—he had broken the story. *He had pursued justice.* What he didn't expect was to find Faye.

The juxtaposition of those two lives, the person he had been before and the person he had become in the wake of amnesia, banged up against each other like misfitting modular pottery. He didn't know which version of himself would win out, only that he felt changed forever.

Agent Diaz returned. "So, some good news..."

"What?"

"Our guys just pulled over a car with three men matching the description of your guys," he said.

"That's great," Greg said. "What about Chief Eric Myers?"

"We haven't been able to track him down yet. But we have folks watching his house, and the police station…"

It was better than nothing, and yet the way Agent Diaz was looking at Agent Jones told Greg that something was still very wrong.

"What?" Greg said, glancing between them. "Tell me."

Agent Diaz shifted nervously. "They found gasoline in the trunk."

Greg stammered, "They were planning to burn down her store."

"It appears that way," Agent Diaz confirmed.

His whole stomach churned with disgust. He thought back to his night with The Paper Boys, the way they had joked about planning a barbecue—because they were planning to burn down Magic Mud Pottery. His entire body prickled with anger. All this violence and destruction, for what? A window. Because Faye was Jewish. No, the window was just an excuse. Blaming it on the Jews was just a justification, too. These people would always find a reason to live inside their hatred.

He suddenly didn't care about the headache, or his inability to stand. He needed to get to Faye. He needed to reach her, keep her safe, protect her. But when he tried to launch himself off the bed, he fell again.

"Just keep her safe," Greg said finally, desperately. "Please. Whatever you do…just make sure she's protected."

THIRTY-FOUR

She was all out of tears.

Faye stepped inside Magic Mud Pottery and breathed a sigh of relief. She was home. After the disaster that had been her night—*perhaps, also, her entire life*—all she wanted was to disappear back into reality, and a world that was familiar. She couldn't believe she had ever thought that Greg was a golem. But the accusations Greg had lobbed at her that evening, before she both ran away *and* nearly killed him with her car, sat inside of her. *It's easier to push someone away than admit you have feelings for them. It's hard to be vulnerable.*

Ignoring the giant turd that Hillel had most surely, *and deservedly*, left by the threshold, she tossed her bag down on the counter before remembering that her cell phone was completely dead. Pulling it out of her bag, she plugged it into a socket on the wall, waiting for it to charge enough to be able to turn on once again.

"Hillel?" she shouted, peering around the store. "I'm home."

Hillel didn't respond. No doubt he was snoozing on the windowsill behind the couch upstairs, waiting for Greg to return. Of course, Greg wasn't coming back. And it was all her fault. Faye had pushed him away. She moved to comfort herself with a snack.

Opening the door to the fridge, she found a brand-new hard kosher salami waiting. Pulling it out, she gathered up all the necessary items—a bread knife, a cutting board—laying them on the counter to begin slicing off pieces, when someone knocked on the door. Eric was standing outside. Leaving her hard kosher salami, she went to open it up.

"Eric," she said, confused. "What are you doing here?"

"I'm sorry to bother you," he said. "Do you mind if I come in for a minute?"

She hesitated. She really wasn't in the mood for visitors.

"I'm sorry," Eric said apologetically. "I know it's late, but I was in the neighborhood. I swear, I won't be that long."

She looked down to see his foot, and his chest, were already past the threshold. Not wanting to be rude, she let him come in. Eric put his hands on his hips and glanced around her store curiously.

"Where's Greg?" he asked casually.

"Gone," Faye said simply.

Eric arched one eyebrow, surprised. "Gone? Like...forever?"

"Yep."

She didn't want to explain it more than that.

Eric was silent for a few beats. "Well, that's an interesting turn of events."

She didn't understand his meaning. "Interesting? How?"

"I just mean... I'm glad to see you've finally come to your senses."

She scoffed. *No, she had not come to her senses.* If anything, Faye had just survived some sort of psychotic break in a cave.

She returned to the counter and her hard kosher salami. "Well, now that you're here," Faye said politely, "can I offer you a snack?"

"Actually," Eric said, stepping closer, "I was thinking I would take you out for dinner."

"Dinner?" She glanced over to the clock. It was almost midnight. "Now?"

"Or maybe a drink?"

She really didn't feel like a cocktail, either. "I don't think so."

"Please," he said, coming around the counter.

"Eric," she repeated, "no."

He grabbed her by the waist, lifting her up. "Come on," he said. "Let's go out together. Let's have some fun. I promise, you'll love every second of—"

"Eric!" She pushed his hands away from her. "I told you already. I don't feel like going out tonight!"

She came to her feet on the floor, dragging her hands down the clothing he had disturbed. When she looked back at him, his face was a mask. A frozen smile had been plastered across his face. Eric was being weird *and* weirdly persistent. But it was strange the way the universe could offer clues, hint at trouble, whisper danger—because something about the way Eric was acting felt wrong.

She became aware of the tiniest details. Like the way his feet, and chest, were now angled in her direction, trapping her behind the counter. Or his smile—she had never noticed it before, but it lifted all the way up to his eyes, like it was fake. And then, her gaze drifted down the length of his form, to his clothing. He was wearing all black. Black pants. Black shoes. Black shirt.

On instinct, her feet inched back. Her fingers reached towards the phone.

"Actually," she said, thinking quickly, "I'd love to go out for a drink."

"Really?"

She twisted back to her phone, turning it on. "Let me just grab my stuff and powder my nose…"

Eric beamed, but still had her cornered. "Come on, now. You don't need to change anything. You look perfect…just the way you are."

"Oh, Eric." She glanced back over her shoulder at him. "You are always such a boon to my self-esteem."

Thankfully, the phone powered back on. The rest came in a flurry of messages, but the first one—from Greg—was the only one she needed. I didn't have time to tell you. Chief Eric Myers is the head of The Paper Boys. He is planning something for Magic Mud Pottery tonight. Run if you see him. Do not engage. Do not call the police. Help is on the way.

Her hands froze. Her heartbeat sped up as her breathing slowed. Her eyes shifted back to Eric. The man was still blocking her path. And she knew she was in danger. Real danger. She didn't know what he was planning, why he had come to her store dressed all in black, but her body began edging into tremors as her mind went into overdrive, searching for an escape.

"You okay, Faye?" Eric asked softly.

"Fine," she said.

"You seem…nervous." He glanced down towards the phone. "No one is bothering you, right?"

Quickly she moved to click off the phone. It was too late. He grabbed it instead.

Staring down at the message, he tsked his teeth three times, before a long pause drifted through the room. Faye scanned her space for something to defend herself with. She had a backpack. She had mason jars full of herbs and tea. She had a hard kosher salami and a bread knife. She tried to grab the knife… but Eric pulled it back and tossed it down the hall.

Their eyes met, and her lower lip trembled, because this was

Eric. Her friend. The chief of police in Woodstock. A man she had dated. *Perseus, wearing a cap of invisibility, coming to her home with the intent to do her harm.* Perhaps, like convincing herself that Greg was a golem, she had never been good at seeing people for who they really were.

"So, what's the plan?" she asked him directly.

"The plan?" he said curiously.

"You get me out of my store, my business…" Her eyes drifted down his clothing. "And then what? You kill me? Take me somewhere, do Goddess knows what… Will my friends even find the body?"

"Don't be so dramatic, Faye."

"You're a goddamn Nazi, Eric!"

"It's not personal," he said, taking one step closer. "Truth be told, I always liked you. Despite my feelings about you people, you were always…one of the good ones."

"You people?"

"I know it won't bring you any comfort, all things considered," he said, "but it was never supposed to get this far. A few flyers. Some graffiti. Make our position known. Stake our claim back in Woodstock, continue to recruit and grow. But then… you had to go and change your window. I warned you. I told you to take it down, but you didn't listen."

The picture in her mind grew clearer. "So, what? You were trying to get me out of Magic Mud Pottery, because you were planning to attack my store again?"

"Technically," he admitted. "We were going to burn it down. I was going to take you out tonight, we were going to have a good time, and then we would come back, Magic Mud Pottery burnt to a crisp. Of course, all the evidence would point to Greg, the homeless vagrant you were stupid enough to let live in your house…"

"You were going to frame him?"

"*Frame* is such a strong word," he mused thoughtfully. "I much prefer thinking of it as helping justice along."

Faye couldn't believe what she was hearing. She scoffed, thinking back to Greg. "Justice… You don't know the meaning of that word."

"Maybe not," Eric admitted, inhaling long and hard, trying to take all the air in the room with him. "But unfortunately, the plans changed. As it turned out," he said, lifting her phone in the air as evidence, "a large redheaded elephant got in the way of things. Apparently, he was pretending to be one of us, trying to infiltrate my little family, my little cell. And now, I have no choice but to keep my family safe."

He began texting something into her phone.

"What are you doing?" Faye asked.

"I'm telling Greg to come back to Magic Mud Pottery."

"Why?"

Eric didn't answer her.

Faye swallowed. She knew that Greg was in the hospital, but obviously the news hadn't yet reached Eric. She wasn't sure if Greg would get the message. The last time she had seen him, he was still unconscious. She thought back to the text message. *Help is on the way.* She just needed to keep him talking. Or— she glanced towards the door—she could try to escape.

She was still debating her options, watching Eric text a message into her phone, when she heard the pitter-patter of tiny paws coming down the stairs. Hillel had awoken. After tapping his way into the kitchen, he took a place directly behind Eric's ankles, where he waited to get a snack.

Eric glanced down. "Hey there, Hillel."

He picked the hairless creature up.

"Eric." Faye stopped him.

He looked up at her with one eye.

"Don't touch my dog."

Everything moved in slow motion. All those instincts she had learned throughout her life, all that need for survival, kicked into high gear, and she made a choice. A word laid down on this Scrabble board of her life, because Faye was going to fight. She tightened her grip around the meat, and with all the strength inside that she could muster, whacked Eric directly in the head. He wasn't expecting the blow.

The dog dropped from his hands, landing like a cat on all four paws.

"Ow," Eric said, clutching the side of his face. "Goddamn it, Faye!"

She whacked him again…and again…and again…four times in total, all while Hillel circled around the man's feet and began yapping. Eric fell to the ground on one knee, giving Faye just enough time to jump over him. She was halfway through the foyer, her escape only several feet away, when Eric returned to life.

Grabbing her by the hair, he yanked her back, pulling her neck and her body in his direction. She whacked him with the salami again.

"Jesus Christ!" he shouted. "Will you stop doing that!"

She hit him again, and again, and he grabbed her by the waist, attempting to incapacitate her by pulling her down to the ground. Instead, instinct kicked in. Recalling those Krav Maga lessons she had taken in college, she reached for his testicles, twisting and pulling them down as hard she could muster.

He screamed out painfully before releasing her once again.

She was moving on sheer adrenaline now, making her way for the exit. Eric stood up and, lumbering like some scary anti-Semitic monster after her, almost caught her at the door. Instead, Hillel jumped into action. The dog she had always been certain hated her…jumped in to protect her.

Hillel weaved between Eric's feet, barking loudly. Eric tried to swipe him away, but the creature was too agile for him. Instead, Eric tripped. Falling forward, face-first, he landed straight in a stinky mound of Hillel's excrement.

Faye exploded through the front door, only glancing back long enough to see Eric, groaning in the threshold, mucky poop covering his ears, eyes, and mouth. She had just made her way to the street, Hillel trailing closely behind her…when she ran straight into Miranda, Shulamit, and Nelly.

"Faye," Miranda said, catching her. "What is it? What happened?"

"Chief Eric Myers," Faye cried out. "He tried to…he wanted to hurt me!"

"Oh my Gawd!" Shully said, throwing her arms around her. "Faye!"

"Wait here, ladies," Nelly said, sidestepping all of them. "I was made for this moment!"

Faye was beginning to explain what had happened when sirens sounded in the distance. The words she had been saying caught inside her throat. Seeing her friends, seeing the arrival of dozens of federal agents, she knew she was safe. The universe had showed up for her.

Also, her dog.

Faye bent down to pick up Hillel and nuzzled her nose into the crook of his hairless, acne-ridden neck. "You are the best boy," she said, over and over. "You can poop all over my floors…anytime you want, okay? I love you. I love you so much, Hillel."

"Um, guys." Shulamit grimaced, interrupting them. "I'm not really sure what's going on here, but you might want to look through the front window of Magic Mud Pottery."

Faye twisted back towards her store and found a sight most magical, indeed. Eric was still splayed out on the ground, covered in dog excrement. But now, Nelly was standing over him, gleefully electrocuting him with her stun baton whenever he had the audacity to attempt moving or rising up.

"Take that, you Nazi," Nelly whooped and hollered, and with another thrust and zap, cackled wildly into the night.

THIRTY-FIVE

It didn't take long for Chief Eric Myers to be apprehended, and for Greg to hear what had happened. Even though there was a part of him that wanted to check on Faye, she had been placed in protective custody. Until the FBI was certain that all members of The Paper Boys operating in Woodstock had been apprehended, he wouldn't be able to reach her.

He tried to see the forced separation between them as a blessing. As a message from the universe to regroup after everything that happened between them.

Greg stepped into his tiny New York apartment, overlooking midtown Manhattan. It was just as he remembered. Save for the dead plants—even the succulents—everything was just how he left it. The curtains on the large windows were open.

His bed—a sleeper futon—was still pulled out and made up with sheets. Some T-shirts and pants lay in piles on the bed, remnants of his last morning packing before heading to upstate

New York. And of course, as a journalist, his apartment was packed full of books and papers. Photos from his time traveling the globe. Pictures of him with subjects of his stories. And the centerpiece of his mainly unused bachelor pad—a large desktop computer, sitting on a cheap plastic desk.

He threw his stuff down by the door and moved to check the messages on his landline.

He had three messages. As was often the case when he went undercover, or on assignment, his editor had checked in on his home phone twice. Once, wondering if he was alive, as he had missed his monthly check-in. The second time, his editor having found out he was alive, asking Greg when he could expect his article about The Paper Boys.

The third message was from his brother.

His editor and his brother—those were the two people who had called him when he went missing for two months. Those were the only two people in the world who cared about *his* story.

Everything was the same—New York, his career, his apartment—yet Greg felt different. Changed in some way. He had never been a golem, but Faye, and her friends, and his time in Woodstock, had cast an irreversible spell.

And now, all he felt was lonely.

Faye had stopped counting the days since she had last seen Greg—even though she understood now that she was not magical, her spell had worked. After helping Nelly uncover the identity of The Paper Boys, Greg had gone back to his old life. His real life, which apparently was as some sort of bigwig investigative reporter in New York City.

She tried not to spend too much time thinking on it. She also resisted the urge to begin googling, tracking him down herself. What had happened with Greg, what she had worked so hard to destroy between them, was a lesson she needed to learn.

"Aha," Nelly said, laying down a seven-letter word on a triple word score. "Take that."

Faye stared down at the word Nelly had created. *"Killers?"*

"What?" Nelly said innocently.

"Anyone ever tell you that you have a one-track mind?"

Nelly waved away Faye's jab. Faye bit back a smile. Even though she was no longer in the protective custody of the FBI—Chief Eric Myers and the three men who worked with him had all been caught and jailed on multiple charges—she had taken up Nelly's offer to come stay with her for a while.

At first, packing her bags and taking one of the bedrooms on the second floor—toting Hillel along for the ride—she was certain she had made a mistake. Certain the old woman would spend the entire time there berating her for her terrible life choices. But very quickly, she realized she enjoyed living with Nelly. She liked how the old woman fawned over her, and made her chicken soup when she was feeling sad…and humored her obsession with Scrabble.

She was also surprised at how much of her pottery was in Nelly's home. She had no idea that Nelly was such a fan. Or that she had spent so many years buying her pottery under the name Sam Jones.

"I still can't believe you own so much of my work," Faye said.

"Everybody deserves a few secrets," Nelly said.

Faye wanted to understand. "Yeah, but you're always telling me how my pottery looks like *shvantzes* and *pupics*…"

"Maybe I like *shvantzes* and *pupics*?"

"Come on," Faye scoffed. "You have spent thousands of dollars on my work."

"Fine," Nelly said. "I'll tell you the truth. I buy all your pottery because I like it. Because I think you're talented. Because, unlike my grandchildren—who I love, but are unfortunately talentless hacks who would be much better off focusing on the sciences—I actually like your work. No, scratch that. I actually love your work. I like having it in my house."

She shifted in her seat a little. "Why not just buy it direct from me? Why go to all those lengths to hide it under an assumed name?"

"Because," Nelly said, laying tiles on the board, "if I bought it direct from you, you would say, 'Nelly is just buying my art to be nice. Nelly doesn't appreciate my pottery. I'm a talentless hack who doesn't deserve all the good that happens to me.' So that's why I never let you know I bought it. You would ruin it, turn it into something bad, turn it into something ugly. You would never just accept that I thought you were talented. So, instead... I didn't give you the chance."

Faye stared down at the board, comparing how she felt about her art to how she handled her relationship with Greg. Nelly wasn't wrong. "But," Faye couldn't help but ask, "you don't notice all the mistakes in my work?"

"The mistakes?" Nelly squinted.

"The misshapen lips to the vases," she said, pointing out the flaws. "The rough edges, sometimes even the lingering fingerprint."

"You mean because of your finger?" Nelly asked. "Because your mother broke your wrist, and everything you do, all the artwork you've created since then...is a reflection of the experiences that have made you? Because your work will never be perfect."

"Yes."

"Silly girl." Nelly shook her head. "That's exactly why I like your pottery."

Faye stammered. "I... I don't understand."

"You think because you don't create perfect art, that it has no value? You think because your vases don't look like everyone else's vases, that they're ugly and misshapen, broken in some form...that no one will ever love them."

"Yes." Faye could feel the tears coming to her eyes.

"But only you can make those vases," Nelly said. "Only you can make those ring dishes, and jars, and even golems. Because of that broken wrist, and that one disabled finger, and the story you lived...when you create a piece of pottery, it bears the truth of you."

"It's just...so hard."

Nelly nodded. "Because you don't see what I see. You look at the pottery, and you see every flaw. And you think those flaws are bad. I see those fingerprints and bubbles, and I think, 'That's a Faye Kaplan piece. Only she can make it!' All that talent, all that backstory, coming from these two potter's hands. That's your downfall, Faiga Kaplan. You don't see that something doesn't need to be perfect to be loveable."

It was enough. Her words caused a flood to appear inside her. The dam broke, and with it, all the feelings of the last few weeks—of an entire lifetime—came flooding to the fore. Nelly left her Scrabble tiles and, rising from her seat, hugged Faye.

"Faiga," Nelly said, stroking her hair. "My dear, sweet, beautiful child..."

Faye cried, the words falling from her deepest places now. "He didn't ever protect me."

"I know."

"All those years," she said, the words finally coming, "why didn't my dad ever once stop her? All those nights, he could have just intervened. He could have left my mother, and taken me with him. But instead, he just hid. He hid...and he let her hurt me. No one ever, ever protected me. And I'm so tired. I'm so tired of being strong all the time. It's not fair."

"It's not," Nelly said, still stroking her hair, kissing the top of her head, the mother Faye never had growing up. "What happened to you is so unfair."

"I need...help."

It was the first time in years that she considered going back to therapy. Not because she was broken, but because she deserved to live a life that brought out the softness in her. Her mind wandered back to Greg, to the way he had been there for her at her worst moments, to her friends, and Nelly—her chosen family. They were people who cared about her. They were people who fought for her, too.

No, she didn't have to be perfect to be loved.

But she wanted to be better. She wanted to feel better, too.

"So, you've been hurt by the past," Nelly said, shrugging her shoulders. "Okay? You've been shaped by the past, too. But when we live in the past, my dear sweet Faiga-la, we never get the chance to write our own story."

"Like the golem?" Faye reflected quietly.

"How so?"

She thought back to what she had learned from Rabbi Solovechick. "The golem isn't one story," Faye explained. "It's actually a whole bunch of stories, layered on top of each other. It started one way, yes. But each generation added to it and supplemented it, until it became a new type of story for each new creator. I guess that's the beautiful lesson of the golem... We can hold on to memory, bear the things that shape us, but also...write our own story going forward."

Nelly nodded. "So, perhaps this whole journey was for good, after all?"

"You know what, Nelly?" Faye felt her tears drying. "Going forward, that is absolutely the story I plan to tell."

That night, Faye couldn't sleep. It wasn't due to her nightmares, or to the half pound of kosher salami she had downed for a snack with Nelly. It wasn't even because the old woman kept the house the temperature of an igloo. Rather, it was this strange type of energy bubbling away inside of her. A sensation, not of magic...but rather, of hope.

She wandered about Nelly's house in her robe and her pajamas. And whenever she came across some nightstand or desktop where a piece of her pottery was laid out, she took a few minutes to analyze it. She picked it up, turning it in her hands, analyzing all those missteps and mistakes that made her art uniquely hers.

Of course, the instinct was there—to tear herself apart, to notice each flaw and each mistake, to allow that voice in her head, the voice that belonged to Stuart and her mother, to penetrate how she saw the world. But she resisted the urge. Instead, she told herself a new type of story.

In this story, the fingerprint was the mark of a survivor. The misshapen lip on the lid of a jar was her ability to craft a new type of life, despite a past filled with trauma. And she told herself that all the rough edges of her vases, all the missteps and mistakes that made her, were beautiful. *She didn't have to be perfect to be loved.*

When she had finally finished walking through the house, she found her way to a computer. She wasn't a writer, but she felt the need to explain herself, to write her own story, to craft a new narrative.

She told her truth. She poured her whole life into a twelve-page story. She wrote about her mother who was mentally ill, and the father that didn't protect her from emotional and physical abuse, and how that experience led to her shutting down emotionally, mired in her own trauma, constantly believing the worst about herself—a self-fulfilling prophecy.

She wrote about how these self-destructive patterns, and an anti-Semitic attack in Woodstock, led her to believe that a man with amnesia—*the best man she had ever met in her entire life*—was actually a golem. She admitted her mistakes. The way she pushed him away, the way she so adamantly was determined to get rid of him, until finally, she dragged this human being to a cave and dumped sludge all over him.

But there was a happy ending to her story. For the first time in

her life, she could walk around a room and look at her pottery—
and see that it had value. That it was beautiful. That it deserved
to be loved, and respected, and honored. Finally, exhausted by
memory, but also possibility, she titled that essay:

THE ART OF IMPERFECTION

She left it on the coffee table for Nelly to read. And then,
she found a therapist in Woodstock who specialized in post-
traumatic stress disorder, and booked her first appointment via
their website. She was just about to head back to bed when she
swore…she heard four wolves, howling together.

Her ears perked up. She shifted towards a window, peering
out into the woods. She pressed her lips into the shape of an
O—and quietly, so as not to wake Nelly—howled right back.
Jews were not magical. But somewhere, beyond the environs
of Woodstock, in those dark spaces where both the caves and
the forests welcomed magical creatures, a lone wolf had found
its way home.

THIRTY-SIX

"Uncle Greg!"

Greg had barely stepped out of the cab and made his way up the driveway to his brother's house on Long Island, when he was attacked. His eight-year-old twin nieces sprinted from the house where they had been awaiting his arrival, and threw their tiny arms around him. Greg dropped the bag of presents he was carrying in order to pick them up.

"Oh," Greg teased, holding one beneath each shoulder, "you two have gotten bigger."

"Uncle Greg!" Lisa, the redheaded one of the fraternal duo, wriggled inside his arms. "I grew two inches."

"Two inches, you say?" He put both girls on the ground, bending down on one knee. "You know what that means, right?" Greg reached into his bag and pulled out a gift for each of them. "Presents!"

His nieces wasted no time. Grabbing the items, they began

screaming, racing into the house. Greg watched them depart, past their mother, Maggie, who was still waiting on the front porch. "Mags," Greg said, giving her a hug before entering the house.

"Good to see you," she said, warmly, before letting go of him.

He nodded. It had been far too long. Moments later, his older brother, Tom, emerged from the house. "Well, look who finally made it to Thanksgiving." His brother held out his hand before pulling him in for a warm embrace.

An awkward pause in the conversation drifted between them, before his niece Lisa reemerged from inside the house. "Dad!" she shouted, waving Greg's now unwrapped present in her father's face. "Look what Uncle Greg got us. It's a set to make our own pottery."

"I thought they would like it," Greg explained. "It's designed for kids."

"Oh," Tom said, "great. That'll certainly keep the girls entertained while we're working on dinner. I hope you brought your appetite."

"Always."

"Good," Tom said, leaning in to whisper, "'cause I'm deep-frying the turkey this year."

Maggie rolled her eyes. "God help us all."

Inside the house, Greg wasn't surprised to find a Thanksgiving party already going in full swing. Friends gathered together on couches, eating hors d'oeuvres, drinking beers, while watching a football game. Maggie drank wine in the kitchen with her sisters. They periodically put their glasses down to check on the food or kids. Greg took a seat beside his nieces, Lisa and Jules, now each pulling out clay and tools to begin making pottery from their new arts and crafts sets. And yet, sitting among his family—seeing all the friends and loved ones gathered for Thanksgiving—he couldn't help but feel like a stranger.

The prodigal brother returned home.

"Uncle Greg." Lisa dug her fingers into the clay excitedly. "This is so cool."

"Isn't it?" he said, leaning over to make sure that the two girls had all the required items. "What are you going to make?"

Lisa pressed her lips towards one side. "I don't know... What do you think I should make?"

"Well," Greg said, taking the clay in his hands, rolling it around a little as he had seen Faye do ten thousand times. "You can make anything you want. You can make a bowl. You can make a puppy dog figure. You can make a dish to hold things, like rings and earrings. You can even make a doll."

Lisa's eyes went wide. "A doll?"

"Yep," Greg said, handing the clay back to her. "That's the beauty of clay. You can shape it to become anything you want."

"Whoa."

Lisa delved back into her task. Greg watched the two girls playing, and seeing the way they so passionately and diligently dove into their arts and crafts project, he couldn't help but smile. His mind drifted to Faye and Magic Mud Pottery...until his brother appeared from the basement, an extra-large deep fryer between his hands.

"Here she is," Tom announced. "Here is the machine that is finally going to deep-fry our Thanksgiving turkey into perfection."

Most of the men, nursing beers around the football game, broke into shouts of joy and applause. Maggie and her sisters, however, were less than thrilled.

"Outside," Maggie said, pointing towards the backyard. "That was the deal."

"I love you, Mags," Tom said, dragging his deep fryer out the back door.

"If you burn down the house, we're getting a divorce," she shouted back.

Tom was still smiling when he nodded towards Greg. "Come and help me, will you?"

Leaving the girls, Greg followed his brother outside. They spent the next half an hour reading instructions, gathering up items—grabbing their jackets and two beers, too—before finally getting to work on the turkey. When the thing was safely bubbling away in the deep fryer, Greg knew that it was time to talk.

He had a lot on his mind.

After Greg had remembered who he was and returned home to New York, he had called his brother back. He had filled in Tom and Maggie on the basics of what had happened, including the amnesia. And though, as an investigative journalist, he had been in all sorts of dangerous and difficult situations, something about his experience with Faye was still weighing on him.

"So, you're back?" Tom said, lifting the beer to his mouth.

"I'm back."

"For how long this time?"

"I don't know, honestly." Greg shifted the weight on the balls of his feet. "I gotta finish this story first..."

"And then," Tom said, finishing for him, "on to the next?"

Greg shrugged.

"I'm wondering if maybe—" Greg wasn't even sure how to phrase it "—maybe it's time to put down roots somewhere. Figure out a way to settle down more."

He could see by the way Tom's eyebrows rose all the way to his hairline that his brother didn't believe him. "You, who haven't stayed in one place for more than three weeks? You, who always needs to go off on the next adventure, the next challenge?"

Greg dug one toe into the soil beneath his feet. His brother wasn't wrong.

"Look," Tom said, pulling back a little on the accusation, "I don't mean to be a jerk about it. It's just... When I think about you, and us, you've always been more like Mom. You've always been needing something to chase. You've always just done your own thing."

His brother wasn't wrong. They were both raised by a single JAG officer in the military, which meant their lives, like all Greg's relationships, were uprooted every three years. Unlike Tom, who craved consistency, Greg was the opposite. He built a career around his passion for justice, never allowing himself to get too close to anybody. And yet something about his relationship with Faye had changed him. He had lived another life while in absentia...and now he was struggling to reconcile his experience with Faye beside the person he had been.

"It's why—" Tom choked on the admission. "It's why when I didn't hear from you for almost three months, I didn't think much about it. I just figured you were fine...off on another adventure. If there was a problem, your editor would call me. But I mean—"

Tom stopped himself. Greg wanted him to continue. "It's fine," Greg said, waving him forward. "Say it."

"You often go months without calling, Greg. You go months without visiting, too. I love you, 'cause you're my brother..."

"But I'm like Mom?"

Tom shrugged. "Yeah."

Another round of uncomfortable silence settled between the two men. "I met this woman while I was in Woodstock," Greg said finally. "Faye."

"The woman you were staying with?"

"Yeah," he said. "We had a bit of a romance, and... I don't know. I don't think it can ever work out between us—" He left out the part about her thinking he was a golem, doing everything possible to push him away. "But I guess what I learned from that experience is that settling down, building a life for yourself, making efforts to be part of a family and a community...maybe it's not the worst thing in the world?"

Greg's eyes drifted towards the house, where Maggie was

peering through the window, clearly making sure they weren't getting into trouble. Tom noticed and raised his beer at her. She made a dramatic huff, throwing her hands up in the air—he was clearly teasing her.

"You want the truth about settling down, Greg?" Tom asked. "About spending the rest of your life with one woman, raising a family...about giving up the adventure sometimes, just for quiet boredom?"

"Yeah."

"It's awesome," Tom said.

Greg laughed.

"I'm serious," Tom said, his whole face turning red as he spoke. "Every single day, I wake up and go to bed with my best friend in the world. When I'm having a hard day—shit, when I needed neck surgery—she's there for me. When I'm having a good day, when I want to watch a game or a movie on Netflix with the kids, there's no one I would rather spend time with more than her. It's not just that she busts my chops, or has fun with me, or makes me better...it's that I can't imagine how there was ever a me without her."

Greg swallowed. *I can't imagine how there was ever a me without her.* It felt accurate.

"Well, whatever you need," Tom said, finally, "we're here for you. If you need to stay with us for a while, you know Mags is always happy to have extra help with the girls."

Greg laughed. "I bet."

"But really," Tom continued, "we're on your side, okay? We want the best for you. And do me a favor in the meantime. While you're trying to figure out how you can live your adventures, while simultaneously settling down in some form... call us more than once every three months."

Greg offered his hand. "Deal."

Tom's eyes drifted down to the red string still knotted around Greg's wrist.

"What's that?" he asked.

"Oh," Greg said, "it's Jewitch magic."

"Jewitch magic?"

"It's supposed to keep the evil eye away," Greg explained. "Faye gave it to me."

"Interesting," Tom said, before adding, "Clearly, there are some aspects of your time with this Faye woman that you're not telling me."

"That would be correct."

Tom laughed again, before getting serious. "And you're still wearing it? You haven't taken it off yet?"

"Oh," Greg said. "You're not supposed to. You wear it until it falls off."

"Ah." Tom finished his beer. "No other reason then?"

Greg stared down at his wrist, and a pang of longing reappeared in his chest. He had thought about taking off the red bracelet a dozen times since returning to New York. He stared at in the shower, and even once found his scissors. But every time he went to cut it off, he couldn't do it.

"Truth be told," Greg said, shifting in his spot, "I miss her."

"So why not just go back to Woodstock and tell her that?"

"Because." Greg thought back on their time together. "I'm not sure she's the relationship or settling down type."

She was too mired in her past to ever reenvision her future. Still, when night settled over Manhattan, and his dreams wandered back to Woodstock, he couldn't help but set a focused intention for some sort of reconciliation. Greg was just about to explain these things when the scent of something burning caused him to sniff the air.

"Do you smell that?" Greg asked, confused.

"The turkey!" Tom took off the lid, waving away billows of smoke in the process.

Maggie did not hesitate. Opening the door, she shouted from her vantage point on the porch. "I told you," she said, yelling in both their directions. "I told you that deep-frying the turkey this year was a terrible idea."

"It's fine, Mags," Tom shouted back. "The turkey is fine."

"You're sleeping in the bathtub tonight."

She slammed the door behind her. "Like I said." Tom beamed in his direction, his voice dripping with love. "Marriage is awesome."

It had taken him longer than usual, but Greg finally had a rough draft of his article. For the last two weeks, he had been working on a larger exposé—not only on what had occurred in Woodstock, but on the dangerous interplay between problematic personal ideologies and those in power.

It was an important article. As it turned out, Chief Eric Myers was not the only person in law enforcement to have ties to a virulent hate group. Before heading to Woodstock, he had done the research—uncovering dozens of names, including political officials, judges, and more. His hope was that by exposing these people, bringing light to the dangers posed by racism and anti-Semitism, he would make the world a safer place.

The printer came to a pause at his feet. Greg decided to take a break before doing one final read-through. Picking up his phone, he called his brother.

"Greg," Tom said. "Let me get the girls."

Seconds later, he was being regaled with all the adventures of fourth grade. Greg took a seat on his couch and listened to the girls jabbering on sweetly. He was making changes. Unlike in the past, head down at the exclusion of everything else in his life, he was trying to heal relationships, make new friends, build connections. He was trying to find his community, too.

Between writing spurts, he would head to the gym. Normally a weights guy, he joined a pickleball league. He prioritized time for interests, and hobbies, joining three different book clubs at the library, including one for romance lovers.

And at night, he set his intention—making magic cakes, infused with honey for sweetness and whole wheat for grounding.

As for Faye, he missed her. Every time he looked down at his wrist and saw that red bracelet, his heart ached, and he had an urge to contact her. To go back to Woodstock. To try one more time to make it work, especially now that he knew who he was and had full return of his memory. But Faye had been clear. In both words and actions, he knew the truth. She wasn't ready. Maybe she would never be ready.

Greg had no choice but to move on.

"Will you come and visit us, Uncle Greg?" Lisa asked.

"I'll be there this weekend."

The girls responded with simultaneous whoops and cheers, and after taking a few moments to speak with their parents, Greg hung up the phone. The quiet of his New York apartment once again irked him. His eyes trailed down to his feet, where he was half expecting some hairless creature to be waiting... And then, he considered getting a dog.

In the meantime, he went back to his article. Picking up those pages and a pen again, he began to read it through—noting where the flow was wrong, making changes, highlighting things to add or any mistakes. He was three pages in when the sound of an email arriving on his computer brought his attention up.

It had come in to his work email. Greg stared at the name of the sender. *StunningForFunzies.*

Strange. He had no idea who that could be. He opened the email, and a whoop of delight escaped his lips. It was a message from Nelly.

Baby Bird,
How the hell you been? We've missed you here in Woodstock. Chief Eric Myers is gonna spend a looong time in jail. But I got a damn parade! Wish you had been there. Anyway, thought you might be interested in this article. Hope to see you soon, Baby

Bird. Goddess knows, whether you're a golem or not, you have earned a spot in our coven.
Nelly

He laughed reading her words. And then, with shaking hands, he clicked on the link, opening it up.

The Art of Imperfection:
What a Jewitch Learned about Craft from a Golem
By Faiga Kaplan

Emotion bubbled up in him as he read the article, coming to the end:

For six weeks, in the wake of an anti-Semitic attack, I—a Jewish potter in Woodstock, New York—believed I had summoned a golem. I thought I had crafted this perfect man out of clay, breathed life into him with words and magic…never realizing that I was the one who had been created.

All of us start out as clay. We begin soft and unformed, bendy and malleable. We look for gentle hands to guide us, shape us into form. More often than not, we are stretched taut, spun around on a wheel, pounded and battered, placed in a kiln where a fire is raging. From there, we harden. The stress to take shape bears its marks in bubbles, scratches, and tears. As a ceramicist, the instinct is always to patch the cracks, fill the lines in with gold and metal…but what is broken is not ruined.

This is the art of imperfection. The ability to look at your life and see the beauty in the blemishes. To make a mistake, sometimes many mistakes, but see your worth anyway.

I thought the only way to be loved was to be like modular pottery, two perfect pieces, snapping together and unhinging apart, but I am learning to shift my perspective. To tell my own story. To shape my own narrative. Because as a man—not a golem—

once told me outside the entrance to a cave, there's no real differ-
ence between a monster and a goddess.

It was beautiful. *She was beautiful.* He could feel her heart reaching through the page, and it touched him. Greg took a few seconds to bite back his own wellspring of emotion. He chewed on the bottom of his lip, debating next steps, if he should reach out to her, contact her…when his eyes wandered back to that email, and the word *REPLY.*

Quickly he began typing out an email. When it came to getting things done correctly, knowing the inside scoop, setting up a plan of attack—there was only one octogenarian in the world that Greg would ever trust.

THIRTY-SEVEN

Faye placed her newest modular design, a rust-colored Havdalah set painted with swaths of metallic gold, in the window of her storefront. It wasn't perfect, but stepping back from the ledge, careful not to trip over Hillel in the process, she was proud of it.

It had a unique kind of beauty. In the faded sun of a winter afternoon, she liked the dark undertones at the edges. She liked the weird lip of the kiddush cup, the slanted ring that, when it sat on a shelf, looked as if it were in the middle of melting. The design had been a mistake, the result of overfiring during the coloring process, but Faye had been working hard in therapy to silence the negative voices that lived in her head.

Things could be imperfect and still be loved.

It had been almost three months since her article, "The Art of Imperfection," had been published—and in the wake of her writing, things had changed. Her Etsy orders had increased.

Her vases and pottery were finally garnering some critical

acclaim, with one of her pieces even being featured in a local folk museum. The Paper Boys operating in Woodstock had all been caught, and though life was never going to return to normal, she was finding a way to be happy.

The only thing missing was Greg.

She thought about him, of course. When she did her Jewitch rituals, eating magic cakes alongside scrambled eggs in the morning. When she went caving, lighting candles in the spot where she had once attempted to banish him—focusing her intention on full healing instead. When she snuck downstairs at night and struggled to slice her own hard kosher salami. He was gone, but it felt as if there were still pieces of him everywhere.

Faye moved to her storefront window. Outside, the blizzard that had fallen over upstate New York had come to a standstill. Now, a thick layer of white blanketed the sleepy off-season town, causing a complete standstill when it came to customers. Thankfully, there were still good reasons to keep the front door unlocked and open to visitors.

The bell above her business rang out. Nelly shivered in the threshold, shaking off the snow from her jacket as she entered.

"Wooooooo," Nelly said. "It's freezing out there. I swear, my diabetes medication is gonna turn to popsicles in my car."

"So you're finally moving to Boca to be with the grandkids?" Faye teased.

"With all that humidity?" Nelly scoffed. "I'll take the freezing cold." Nelly reached into her pocket, pulling out her car keys. "You ready? The hot Jewish men of Single over Tu B'shevat won't wait forever."

Tu B'shevat marked the beginning of a New Year for trees, and coincided with the time in Israel when the trees were just beginning to emerge from their long winter sleep. In the States, however, it was still freezing—the dead of winter, early February. And yet, the celebration of life, of things that take root and manage to grow again, felt wholly relevant to her current life.

"Hold on," Faye said, grabbing her lipstick. "I just want to reapply some makeup before we go."

"Ooooooh." Nelly beamed. "Going for extra sultry tonight. I like it."

Nelly edged her way beside Faye, and then, staring at herself in the mirror, pushed her own sagging breasts up in comradery.

"Honestly," Faye said, pressing her lips together into a heart, "you would think Shulamit could come up with a better title for these things."

"I suggested Get Wood on Tu B'shevat, but Shulamit didn't like it."

Faye turned to the old woman, mouth open, somewhat aghast, before bursting into full hysterics. Shaking her head, she tossed her lipstick into her purse. After grabbing her jacket, she closed up Magic Mud Pottery and followed Nelly towards the car. They were halfway to her vehicle, another round of snow flurries appearing in the sky, when Faye suddenly remembered that she had forgotten something.

"Oh, crap," Faye said, racing back down the street. "I promised Shulamit I would bring wine for tonight's event. Just start the car. I'll be right back."

Nelly waved her off, and Faye returned to Magic Mud Pottery. Opening the door, moving to the front hall closet, she stared down at that last box of red wine—the one she had saved all these years, which had originally been purchased for her wedding to Stuart. Bending down, she grabbed that box, hoisted it up, and carried it down the icy road, where she got it situated safely in the trunk of Nelly's car.

Faye returned to the passenger side of the vehicle and, out of breath from the haul, took one deep and cleansing breath. Nelly smiled wryly at her over the console—that twinkle of love, and friendship, and often, motherly concern, evident in her warm blue eyes.

"You ready?" Nelly asked.

Faye nodded, certain now of the future she was writing. "I'm ready."

Okay. It was still pretty much a disaster.

Faye couldn't help but think it. Despite shifting her focus to being open to love, it was one missuited, and sometimes misguided, five-minute match after another. Still, she had promised herself that going forward, she would be open. She had survived so much in her life—abuse, anti-Semitism, a violent criminal attack—but she was tired of letting all the bad harden her. And though most of the bachelors she was meeting didn't exactly inspire her to consider romance, she was having a good time.

The conversation was pleasant. She had good friends, a chosen family of women, to keep her company. Glancing back towards Miranda and Shulamit—standing by a table set up with nuts, dried fruit, olives, cheeses, and an array of baked goods—the universe felt good. Magical, even. She didn't even mind that Suitor Number Six was regaling her with a lengthy story about his love of taxidermy.

"You would be surprised," Number Six droned on, "how many pet owners want their dogs stuffed after they die. Not just dogs, you know? Sometimes birds, cats, snakes... I once had a request for a pigeon. All very fascinating. Different anatomies, you know?"

Faye didn't know. But she couldn't help but think about Hillel sitting stuffed one day in a corner of Magic Mud Pottery.

"Do you have any living pets?" Faye asked, trying to politely change the topic.

"Nope," he said proudly. "Just dead ones."

She was happy to humor him. Clearly, the man had a passion—which, as an artist herself, she could respect. But she also couldn't bear the thought of spending the rest of her life with a man and his ten thousand stuffed animal carcasses.

"Have you ever tried it?" Suitor Number Six asked.

"What?" Faye said, returning from her thoughts.

"Stuffing an animal," he said, using his hands to demonstrate. "What most people don't realize is you have to break all the bones in—"

Faye drifted off, her chin in her palm, her mind wandering out the window and towards the snow. And Greg. She didn't want to do it, but she constantly found herself comparing every man she met to him. She knew it wasn't healthy—but the memory of him sat etched upon her heart all the same.

And then, a sight at the entrance of the room caused her to sit up. An extremely large man, with long red hair, covered in a fine mist of snow, was standing in the threshold. She blinked three times, just to be sure she wasn't experiencing some new type of delusion…and then she nearly fell off her chair in shock.

It was Greg.

THIRTY-EIGHT

Greg scanned the crowd. Faye was sitting at a table, her entire body pressed in his direction, and he couldn't help but smile. She was exactly as he remembered.

A bell rang out. All the men at the tables stood and quickly shifted to another seat. Shulamit ran over to him. "Thank God," she said, attaching the number eighteen to his chest. "You made it."

"I wasn't sure with all the snow," Greg explained. "But I found a way."

Miranda smacked him on the chest. "That's the spirit."

"Hurry," Shulamit said, pushing him forward. "You only get five minutes."

He nodded. It was a short walk to the table where Faye was waiting, but an old man in a puffy jacket was trying to get there first.

"Sorry," Greg said, trying to be polite, "but if you don't mind—"

The old man stuck one finger behind his ear. "What?" he shouted. "What did you say?"

"I said," Greg attempted to shout back, "if you don't mind, I'd like to take this seat."

"What? You'd like to have sex?" He shook his head at the offer. "Sorry. You're not my type."

Greg glanced down to see Faye hiding a smile behind one hand. All of a sudden, the old man slapped him on the arm. "Ha!" he laughed. "I'm just kidding."

"Very funny, Ruben," Faye said.

Ruben leaned into Greg, whispering, "I'm only here for the little one, anyway." He turned towards Faye, offering her a tiny salute. "Thanks for the heads-up, too."

"Of course," Faye said, her chin folded into her palm. "Good luck."

With that, the old man adjusted the belt of his pants and skipped his way over to Nelly.

Finally, Greg and Faye were alone. This was his chance. He slid down in the seat across from her. Another bell rang out. Shulamit raced back to her microphone. "Five minutes," she said. "Starting now."

There wasn't any more time for hesitation.

"Faye," Greg said suddenly.

She pointed to the sticker on her chest. "Number Three."

"Right," Greg said, offering his hand. "Nice to meet you, Number Three. I'm Number Eighteen."

"Nice to meet you, Eighteen."

It made sense to begin this way. They were starting over, after all, meeting for the first time as their full and truthful selves. Despite all they had experienced in their past together, it was only the present that mattered.

"So," Faye said, "tell me a little bit about you, Number Eighteen. What do you do for a living?"

"Believe it or not," Greg said, relieved to be able to introduce himself properly, "I'm an investigative journalist. I go undercover to various places and locations…and attempt to uncover the truth."

"That sounds very exciting," she said, before adding, "Also a little bit dangerous."

"It can be," he admitted. "But I do it because I believe that truth should be pursued, and that stories can change the world. My mother always used to say, *justice, justice, you shall pursue.*"

"Your mother?"

"She was a JAG military lawyer…so justice was very important to her."

"Your mother was in the military?"

He nodded. "Whole life, up until she retired. We moved every three years as kids. I suppose you could say she instilled both a sense of righteousness and adventure in me. I didn't want to go into the military myself, but I've spent a lot of time attached to units while doing investigations. And, obviously, I've had a good deal of training to do the more difficult and physical work."

She angled her chin. "That actually makes so much sense."

He nodded. "Good."

The table drifted back into silence.

"And what about you?" he asked, wanting to hear her story.

"Me?" Faye said, returning to her role as Suitor Number Three. "I'm a ceramicist. I own my store right in downtown Woodstock."

"Wait a minute." Greg leaned in dramatically. "You mean that amazing little pottery store right in the middle of town? The one they call Magic Mud Pottery?"

Faye laughed. "That's the one."

"I've always—" Greg swallowed. "I've always wanted to check that place out. Maybe take a class there, too."

"We're registering for our spring session right now."

"Spring," he mused thoughtfully. "I think I can make that happen."

"Well, then…we look forward to seeing you."

One side of her lips ticked upward into a soft smile before her eyes drifted down to his wrist.

"That's an interesting bracelet," she said quietly.

"Actually, a good friend gave it to me."

"A good friend?" she inquired curiously.

"It was kind of a complicated situation."

She laughed. "I know about complicated."

He inched closer to her. "The truth is," Greg continued, "I really liked her, but I also couldn't pursue those feelings…because I didn't really know who I was at the time."

"That does sound difficult."

"But she was, and still is, one of the most remarkable women I've ever met. She's got this fiercely independent streak, but she'll put her whole life on hold to help someone in need. She's also this incredibly talented artist. And writer, it turns out. She doesn't just believe in magic…she is magic."

"She sounds lovely," Faye said.

"She is," Greg said, meeting her eyes directly. "And that's why I'm still wearing this bracelet. Even though things didn't work out between us, I feel really honored that I got to spend a few weeks of my life with her. I got to see the world through her eyes, and whether she knows it or not…that experience with her changed me for the better."

"For the better?"

"I think I had trouble committing before I met her, and her friends. I think, because of the way I was raised, always moving around and not really ever being able to establish roots… I just followed that pattern. But being with her made me reevaluate those aspects of myself that I took for granted."

Faye cleared her throat. "I had a similar experience once. I had this friend. He was one of the most interesting people I've ever met. He was incredibly smart. He read all my books… which really, when I think about it today, is its own special and unique type of love language. He was this huge behemoth of a man, but he had the gentlest spirit. He was always so open to experiencing the world beside me…whether it was hanging out with my friends and eating hard kosher salami, being willing to explore my spiritual beliefs, or playing Scrabble—"

"Scrabble?" Greg interrupted. "I love Scrabble."

"Me, too." Faye laughed. "He was really good at Scrabble," she said, her eyes dipping downward. "He was also just…an extremely special human being. Caring and protective. And I needed a friend like him. He taught me a lot about accepting myself. He taught me to believe that I was worthy of good things. Whether he knows it or not, our friendship—the time we spent together—changed me, as well."

Greg found it difficult to continue. "It sounds like," he said, clearing his throat, "we both had friends who appeared at a time when we most needed them."

Faye met his eyes directly. "The universe has a tendency to do that."

"Baruch Hashem and Blessed Be."

He was caught in her gaze, and they lingered like that—the world disappearing around them—before finally, she wiped one tear away from her cheek.

"So," Greg wondered aloud, "speed dating?"

Faye arched one eyebrow up. "Truly, the very best way to get to know someone."

"I'm not sure," Greg mused playfully. "I heard that slamming into them with your bike, giving someone amnesia, then bringing them home during a series of anti-Semitic attacks works wonders in finding true love."

"I barely even know you, Gregolem."

"Gregolem, huh?"

"It seemed appropriate."

"Well, in case you were wondering, you can pour mud on my groin any day."

Faye defended herself. "If you must know, I was placing on the ten sefirot of the Kabbalah. Very accurate in banishing a soulless Jewish demon back to whatever unformed and messy void he came from."

"Unless he has a soul." Greg felt the need to point this out. "Then you're just dumping mud on someone's genitals."

"True," she teased him back, "but if we are slinging mud here, I think it's important to note that all the things you were doing—running around with Nelly to stop The Paper Boys, hunting down anti-Semites, attempting to bring them to justice—was, in fact, very golem-like."

Greg laughed. "Fair point."

The table fell into silence once more, their eyes latching, their hands drifting closer and closer as each second ticked by.

"And you?" Faye asked. "What brings you to speed dating tonight?"

"Well," he said, shifting in his seat, "to tell you the truth, I'm actually new to the area."

Faye blinked. "Wait… What?"

"The thing is," he said, very casual, "like I said, I'm an investigative reporter, so I travel a lot. I've been keeping an apartment in New York, but rent is expensive, and I don't know, maybe I'm getting old…all that noise and congestion. It's hard to write an article with the constant honking of horns."

Faye laughed, disbelieving. "Come on?"

"I'm serious," he said, laying down facts for her. "I had visited Woodstock a while back, and what can I say? I totally fell in love with the woods, the people…the community. Plus, there was this nice old lady willing to give me a deal."

"No…" Faye said.

Her mouth agape, Faye twisted with her whole body in the direction of Nelly. The old woman responded with a knowing grin and two thumbs-up. From there, her eyes darted to Miranda and Shulamit, until finally Faye put it together. Yes, her friends—her coven of chosen family—had worked their magic on his behalf. Clearly, they were rooting for this Jewitch and golem to have a happy ending.

"I just moved in this morning," Greg said.

"No…"

She kept saying that.

Greg had to fully bite back a smile.

"Truthfully," he explained, "it's a win-win for both of us. I can continue feeling out Woodstock, seeing if it's a place where I want to lay down roots, save a ton of money in the process, and she can have someone help around the house with any miscellaneous chores. Plus, just based on some past experiences with her… I can't help but think she'll be helpful in any upcoming investigations I take on."

Faye laughed aloud at that one. The table quieted once more, before she pushed a curl behind one ear. "I'm actually really glad to hear that you're moving in with Nelly. Beyond the fact that you seem like an interesting guy—" her eyes flicked upwards "—I happen to know Nelly. She's a good friend of mine. Almost a second mother. And I've been worried about her. Ever since her husband died, she's been living in that big house all alone. Plus, her hip has been acting up."

"Good thing I've been told I have a very protective nature," Greg said playfully. Faye rolled both eyes to the ceiling, while Greg continued playing coy. "Like I said, she's an old lady. A little eccentric. Her basement is also all types of weird…but I'm gonna help her renovate it back to some sort of livable space.

And I'm happy with the choice I've made. Even if it doesn't work out—" It was important he explain this part to her. "Even if it turns out that Woodstock is not the place for me, and I decide to go back to Manhattan—I needed to make this change. Actually, I've started going to therapy to help me break some of my own negative self-beliefs and patterns."

"You have?"

"I've read a lot of self-help books," he explained. "And now that I can really analyze what hasn't been serving me, I see where I would like to make changes. So, I guess what I'm trying to do here…is put down some roots. Still be the guy who pursues justice and enjoys adventures, but also has a home, people who love him and miss him when he's gone…people he loves and misses, too."

Faye nodded. "I can understand that."

"Really?"

"Yeah," she said with a small smile. "I've started therapy, too—and one of the things I'm working on is not allowing the past, including negative thinking, to control me. I think I've always been okay with change because it's impermanent, and impermanence makes me feel safer. But I want more consistency in my life. I want to be able to look at myself, imperfections and all, and say that I'm worthy of good things."

Shulamit picked up her microphone. "Two minutes."

He didn't have much time.

"Faye—"

She cut him off. "I'm sorry."

"No," he said, not allowing her to take all the blame for what happened. "I'm sorry. I should have told you what I was doing. I should have told you what I was up to. I thought I was protecting you from The Paper Boys, but the truth was… I was just protecting myself. Because the whole time, I was afraid to lose you."

"I understand." Tears formed in the corner of her eyes. "I

do. And I think I just convinced myself you were a golem because I couldn't believe someone so perfect, so unattainable in my mind, would ever want me. It just seemed easier to push you away than risk falling in love…getting hurt all over again."

Greg leaned across the table, and finally took her hands.

"I've missed you so much," Greg said.

"Me, too." She swallowed, gripping him, refusing to let go. "I just…there is so much more I want to explain to you, so much more that I want to say, and it kills me that we only have like…thirty seconds left."

"Then let's not make it thirty seconds," he offered. "Let's get the hell out of here, Faye. Let's start, right now and at this very moment, to get to know each other. In the present. Without Paper Boys, and missteps, and lies. Hell, let's go to therapy together."

Faye didn't hesitate. "I'd like that very much."

"Good," he said, his voice lowering. "Because I want to get to know you, Faye. And I want you to get to know me…in every single way."

The bell rang out, signaling the end of their five minutes together. The room began to shift, strangers searching for lovers, but for Greg and Faye, the journey wasn't over. Instead, it was only just beginning.

Greg rose from his seat and offered Faye his hand. She took it, and he led her out of the room. Outside, a gentle snow fell down around them. The end of winter. The start of spring, and new beginnings, hopefully.

Unable to resist the urge any longer, Greg kissed her. He kissed her with his full and honest self, and his whole heart. He kissed all the imperfections that made her unique, and whole, and funny, and strange. He kissed her, because in so many ways, he and she were the same. And he couldn't remember who he had been without her.

★ ★ ★

Faye pulled back from the kiss, her heart and her mind reeling. Greg hadn't left her. He wrapped one arm around her waist, nuzzling his lips into her neck, when her feet stopped.

"You came in on a snowmobile?" She blinked, surprised.

He rubbed the back of his neck. "To tell you the truth, I was actually planning to catch a ride with Nelly. But she left for this shindig without telling me, and when I went to the garage, this was the only vehicle there. Weirder still, she left the keys and a note telling me to have fun…so, there you go. I took the snowmobile."

Faye rolled her eyes up to the moon. Clearly, Nelly had never planned to take Greg. Faye was always supposed to be getting a ride with the wily octogenarian. It seemed that, even with The Paper Boys apprehended, the old woman's antics were far from over.

Faye shook her head. "That woman is playing 3D chess when all the rest of us have checkers."

"Anyway—" Greg frowned, concern etching his brows "—I hope you don't mind."

"Not at all," she said, before raising one eyebrow at him. "Though, I have to ask… Did you like it?"

He considered the question. "Truthfully," he said, after a beat, "I loved it. I think snowmobiling may be my preferred method of travel going forward."

Faye laughed again.

Of course he did.

She had spent so much of her life believing that people— along with their love—were unreliable. But staring at that snowmobile, and Greg, thinking back to her friends, and Hillel, the journey they had all taken together—her heart expanded. She had always been open to the magic of the universe, but tonight, she felt it.

Greg helped Faye onto the snowmobile, and together, they

took off—Faye driving, Greg wrapping his arms around her. And it felt remarkable, the wind whipping her hair, the safety of his grip as they journeyed over hills and beside highways together. And all the bad of her life suddenly seemed worth it… for it had led her to finding her person.

Finally, they arrived back at Magic Mud Pottery.

They parked the snowmobile outside, stepping off the vehicle and onto the street. The snow flurries swirled around them, decorating their hair and jackets. Faye lifted onto her tiptoes. Wiping one single flurry off his nose, she kissed Greg again fully. Love was not, and had never been, an avalanche. It was more like a snowflake—imperfect, impermanent—but worth standing in the cold for, anyway.

"I should warn you," Greg said, his lips trailing up her neck, whispering in her ear. "In the time we've been apart, I've been reading *a lot* of romance novels."

Faye pulled back. "I'm actually…okay with that."

He grinned, and then kissed her again. She met his passionate touch with her own heady desire. Despite the cold, her entire being flushed warm. She was ready for this—not just a new beginning, but to take control of her narrative.

Her body caved to his touch. Her back arched, and her hips moved forward, as her hands found his belt. She groaned into his neck as he dug into the fleshy bit of her buttocks with his fingers. She gave in to the aching in her heart, and the need in her body, not allowing the past to destroy the good in her present, while they scrambled to the front door of Magic Mud Pottery.

Suddenly, Faye stopped. The strangest thought occurred to her.

"Actually," she said, placing both hands on his chest, "before we go inside, I have a very important question for you."

"Oh." Greg dipped back, concerned. "Okay. Lay it on me."

"What's your real name?"

He laughed, sweet and adorable. "I guess we never covered that, huh?"

"We did not."

Greg rubbed the back of his neck. "Well, Faye, you're never going to believe this...but my real name is Greg."

She scoffed. "Are you serious?"

"Yeah." Greg shrugged simply. "Greg Stoneman."

The image of that golem, the one she had buried in her backyard, returned. It couldn't be...could it?

But then, catching the glint of his eyes twinkling in the moonlight, seeing the way he looked at her, so full of care and concern—*so full of desire, too*—Faye shook whatever trepidation still lingered in her heart away.

Whatever his name, whether it was magic or some element of nature that had brought them together, no longer mattered. Greg was perfect for her. And she was perfect for him. And together, they would craft a story that would be totally and wholly their own.

ONE YEAR LATER

EPILOGUE

On the first floor of Magic Mud Pottery, Hillel strutted past Faye and the three boxes of pottery she was packing up for a gallery in Miami. Sitting down on the ground beside her, he attempted to scratch an itch, but the diaper he was wearing was blocking him.

"Oh," Faye said, reaching below the material. "Let me help you out."

Hillel happily accepted the offer, before strutting back upstairs with his hairless tail proudly pointed to the sky, to return to Greg. Hillel may have started out as her familiar, but it was clear that the dog was always meant for Greg. Since he'd moved back into Magic Mud Pottery with Faye six months ago, the two had been inseparable.

Greg appeared on the staircase.

"He seems sad," Greg said. "Do you think he seems sad?"

"He'll be fine," Faye said, adamant. "We'll both be fine."

"I know," Greg said, taking a deep breath. "I just... I want to make sure I'm not leaving you with any problems."

"I have all his pants packed up," she said, "and I haven't given him any hard kosher salami in three days. We should be good for the trip."

In fact, the diaper had been Greg's idea. Somehow, he had figured out that Hillel only got diarrhea *after* eating hard kosher salami. Since neither of them wanted the little guy to have to forgo his favorite nighttime snack, they had settled on the extra help of a wearable puppy pad. Greg had also taken the initiative to read a book on sewing, and after joining a local sewing club had made Hillel all manner of adorable pants.

"Go pack, Greg," Faye said, returning to her boxes. "And also, eat that magic cake I made you. It's loaded with lavender and valerian root for anxiety...and sprinkled with sea salt for protection."

"Right," Greg said. "Magic cakes. I'm so gonna miss your magic cakes."

"Pack!"

He nodded, and walked back up to the second floor.

It was strange that Greg was the one who was having so much difficulty with leaving. But she reasoned it was the by-product of them both being in therapy—confronting their demons. Greg had learned that he needed to set down roots if he wanted true and meaningful connection with others, and Faye had learned that she could let someone go—allow them to leave her—and still feel safe in their love.

Not that therapy made either of them perfect, but much like in her pottery business, it turned out things didn't need to be perfect to be loved.

The bell above the front door rang, announcing a new visitor. Faye turned to see the mailman shaking off snow.

"Quite a bunch of boxes today," he said, loading them up.

"Believe it or not," Faye said, moving to help him, "these are for a gallery showing in Miami."

"A gallery showing," he said. "That's impressive."

She nodded. It would be the first major exposition of her work, and she had Greg, Nelly, Miranda, and Shulamit to thank for it. They were the people who pushed her to send her work out, to contact galleries all across America, including her article, "The Art of Imperfection," with each piece she sent. Eventually, an offer from a gallery in Miami came, and she figured, with Greg going away, she might as well use the time to take a vacation.

Faye finished helping the mailman load packages into his truck before signing all the necessary documentation for a safe journey. Returning to her store, she flipped over the Open sign to Closed. She was planning to spend three weeks with Nelly in Florida, dividing their time between Boca Raton, Fort Lauderdale, and Miami.

Followed by one week with Nelly, Miranda, and Shulamit at a Healing Trauma with the Hebrew Priestess Retreat at the Isabella Fellman Center.

As for baby Jules, born healthy and over the holiday of Passover, she would be spending the week being doted on by loving grandparents.

Heading upstairs, Faye felt a mixture of emotions. Excitement at getting a break from work, and for finally having her work displayed in a gallery, opening herself up to new fans and a new market. Worry for Greg, that he would be safe, that he would be okay, while taking on another dangerous undercover assignment. And of course, the most prescient feeling of all, a sense of loss. The sense that she was losing him again. Even though it was just for a few months, she would miss him.

It made walking into her bedroom, seeing his open suitcase lying on the bed—still not packed, because Greg was, once again, obsessing about something on the computer—difficult.

"Honey," Faye said. "You're never going to catch your flight if you keep delaying finishing packing."

Greg turned around. "I know," he said, looking back at the bed. And then, the truth: "I just didn't think it would be this hard to leave you."

Faye came closer. Greg wrapped his arms around her waist, pulling her to him. Of course, she felt the same way. And yet, what she had learned from her experience with the golem, and from therapy over the last year, was that letting go was also a part of love. Allowing someone to be themselves, pursue their dreams—*take up space and be too much*—were all the hallmarks of a relationship that was worth fighting for.

"It's two months," she reminded him.

"Two months," he moaned, and placed his head on her stomach. "I'm gonna miss you so damn much."

"I'm going to miss you, too," she admitted. "But I remind myself that this is what you love to do. This is your passion—following leads, pursuing justice, telling a story. Plus, after what happened with The Paper Boys, I'm excited to see them all finally getting taken down."

Greg nodded. The piece he had written on The Paper Boys, their involvement and infiltration into local government, had sparked not only wider concern and a massive investigation from the FBI—but accolades, as well. His latest undertaking would be an extension of his previous work—an exposé on anti-Semitism at the highest levels of American education, with a possible connection to Iran. It was one of his most dangerous articles ever, but like all the stories he took on, the pursuit of truth was important.

"You have the number to reach me if there's any problem?" he asked.

Faye tapped on her head. "All three of them. Memorized."

"And the number for my editor?"

"Got that, too."

He nodded, and looked towards his suitcase.

Faye took the opportunity to tease him. "Oh, come on," she said, slapping him playfully on the arm. "I know you. I know you can't wait to get back into things. Don't tell me you're not just a teeny bit excited."

The corners of his lips edged upward into a smile. "Maybe just a teeny bit excited."

Faye laughed. "Truthfully," she admitted, "me, too."

"Really?" Greg raised both eyebrows.

"I never thought I would be saying that about a three-week trip to Florida with Nelly…*but oh my Goddess, Greg*, my first ever gallery showing!"

"I just wish I could be there."

"Me, too," she said sadly. "But thankfully, Nelly has promised to film every minute."

"And I—" he grabbed her by the waist, pulling her closer "—am going to watch every single second of it, over and over."

"Over and over, huh?"

His hands drifted up her back. Her chest, like her heart, pressed into him. It was more than love, really. It was the knowledge that you could be completely yourself with someone, and that your love, like your heart, would still be safe.

"I love you, Faye Kaplan."

"I love you, too."

He kissed her again, held her there against him—and she committed every moment to memory. His scent. His eyes. The way his arms felt around her body when she needed a hug. There was so much to Greg, and her love for him, that was good and memorable. It didn't erase the wounds of her past, but it was healing all the same.

Her eyes wandered over to the floor. The red string bracelet he had been wearing for a year had finally fallen off.

"Nooo," Faye said, pulling away from him and picking it up.

Greg frowned, concerned. "Is this a bad sign?"

"It could be," she said, sitting back down beside him on the bed. "Or, it could just mean we need something more permanent."

"Permanent?"

She nodded resolutely. "In fact, I would say this is an excellent sign. As if the universe is telling us that one part of our journey is over and another is about to begin. I think we should listen to the universe, Greg. She's not always perfect, but...she does tend to have our best interests at heart."

"Faye—"

Faye reached into her cardigan pocket and pulled out the ring she had made for him. A simple silver ring, crafted by her own hand. The words *I am my beloved, and my beloved is mine* etched onto the inside. After all, it wasn't just hate that could be built and created on words...it was love, too.

"Wait," he said, blinking three times, shaking his head, before seeking clarity. "Are you asking me to marry you?"

Faye shrugged casually. "I mean, really, what's the big deal? I'm perfect for you. You're perfect for me. We don't have any plans to break up, right?"

He answered with a happy, and wordless, scoff of disbelief.

"Well, there you go," she said. "Since we both see no possible way for this to end, we may as well get the tax benefits that come along with love and a long-term relationship."

The question lingered in the air between them.

Greg rose from his seat and, taking Faye by the waist, spun her around the room. "Faiga Kaplan," he shouted, lifting her off her feet, "I thought you would never ask."

It was the most remarkable type of magic—falling in love, finding your person, crafting your own life, writing a story where you deserved to be valued. And then, taking the ring and putting it on, he kissed her. And she kissed him. They folded into each other's arms and made their way to the bed.

★ ★ ★ ★ ★

ACKNOWLEDGMENTS

About two years ago, I approached both my editor and publisher with a kernel of an idea. I wanted to write a witch romance from a Jewish worldview. I'm so happy that they were as excited by the idea as me. Part of the fun of *Magical Meet Cute* was delving into the rich history of Jewish myth, magic, and mysticism. Also, golems. And I'm pleased to tell you that almost all the spells used in this book, from the baladur cakes to the divination ceremony in the cave, are sourced from original Jewish texts.

As the idea for *Magical Meet Cute* developed, I knew I couldn't write a golem book without exploring its specific connection to anti-Semitism. Once again, I returned to the source texts and to the scholars who had studied this topic. The information contained within *Magical Meet Cute*, including the history of Yudl Rosenberg and Gustave Meyrink, is also based in fact and scholarship and not the product of my own imagination.

That being said, it can be a nerve-racking task to write a book that might surprise the expectations of readers. For many in the book world, a witch romance looks a certain way. A golem always goes berserk and becomes destructive. It should also be noted that this book was completed, and deep into copy edits, when October 7 happened. Point being, there is a lot about this book that would have normally scared the heck out of most editors, agents, and publishers.

Which is why I am going to start this letter of acknowledgment by thanking my editorial director, Nicole Brebner; my editor, Dina Davis; my literary agents at Transatlantic, Carolyn Forde and Marilyn Biderman; my publicist, Laura Gianino; and the entire amazing team behind the scenes at MIRA Books.

Thank you for your constant and unwavering support over four books, for investing your time and energy into making these books a success, for your courage. Thank you all for allowing me to be fully myself in my storytelling, whether that self be disabled or Jewish…or simply a Bible nerd who wants to do a year's worth of mainly unnecessary research into ancient Jewish text for a rom-com about a Jewitch and a golem.

Thank you for making space for these stories on our shelves.

There is so much that goes on behind the scenes of writing a book, and so, I would be remiss to stop my acknowledgments there. In editorial, thank you to Evan Yeong, for every email and update letting me know about a promo and filling in for questions when others are away. Thank you also to Jennifer Stimson, and her awesome copyediting eye. Thank you also to Tamara Shifman and Gina Macdonald, and all the work you do on my behalf behind the scenes.

In marketing, thank you to Ana Luxton, Ashley MacDonald, and Puja Lad. In channel marketing, thank you to Randy Chan and Pamela Osti—and I loved spending time with you both last year at ALA. In digital marketing, thank you to Lindsey Reeder, Brianna Wodabek, Riffat Ali, and Ciara Loader.

Thank you also to everyone in the sales department. Thank you to the subrights team, Reka Rubin, Christine Tsai, Nora Rawn, and Fiona Smallman. In leadership, thank you to Loriana Sacilotto, Amy Jones, Margaret Marbury, and Heather Connor. In managing editorial, thank you to Katie-Lynn Golakovich.

I was absolutely blown away by the cover of *Magical Meet Cute*, and full-on sobbed at the sight of that perfect tallit so beautifully and lovingly wrapped around my main characters. Thank you to Alexandra Niit, the art director in charge, and to Ana Hard for (once again!) crafting such a beautiful illustration. Thank you also to Erin Craig and Denise Thomson for your creativity, hard work and talent.

I am so beyond appreciative to you all.

One of the things that has happened four books in is that I have become exceptionally busy. Thank you to my mom, Leslie Meltzer; my sisters, Evelyn Meltzer and Danielle Chesney; and to my favorite little people in the world, Elissa, Jared, Rose, and Jules for being so understanding. Thank you for loving me, and being proud of me, and never making me feel guilty about missed phone calls, or events, as I learn to manage an increasingly hectic schedule. Thank you also to my friends Rabbi Aviva Fellman and Rabbi Aaron Weininger for the same love and understanding. And to Karen Maskuli, my mother-in-law.

I could not have gotten through this year without the love and support of so many author friends and readers who became friends. Truth be told, I spent a long time wondering if I should attempt to list your names…but honestly, there is just no way I could do it. I would most certainly leave someone out.

So, let me just start by saying thank you. If we met up for a phone conversation, shared a drink over Zoom, texted each other our fears and concerns in the wake of October 7—thank you. If I roped you into founding a Facebook group, or a Jewish Joy Book Club, or begged you to get involved in an auction, either as a founder or a volunteer…thank you.

If you wrote me a letter, shared your story with me, took the time to write a review, thank you. If I met you at an event, or if you invited me to speak, if you listened to my podcast, if you read my Friday Shabbat posts, if you helped me create community and access points through my books and through groups and chats on social media—thank you. If you chose my book, bought my book, read my book, talked about my book to friends or on social media, through Bookstagram or Jewish Bookstagram, thank you. If you chose my book for your own book club, or bookstore, or library, if you reviewed this book, or considered it for an award, thank you. If you chose to showcase this book in your publication, or on your television show, or on your personal page, thank you.

I started this letter talking about my gratitude to my publisher, but at the end of the day, books like *Magical Meet Cute* exist because of readers like you. For me, as a Jewish author, writing proudly Jewish rom-coms in a time of increasing anti-Semitism, these stories feel both timely and necessary. Or, as Faye Kaplan says at the end of *Magical Meet Cute*, it's not just hate that can be built and created on words…but love, too.

Thank you to everyone who has helped me craft a more loving and whole world.

MAGICAL
MEET
CUTE

JEAN MELTZER

Reader's Guide

/||MIRA

1. Faye was raised Jewish, but also considers herself a Jewitch. What did you learn about Jewish magic and folklore while reading this book? Did anything surprise you? Have you ever explored or participated in the more esoteric traditions of a faith or culture?

2. In *Magical Meet Cute*, Faye believes she has summoned a golem. What did you know about golems before reading this book? Did anything about their history surprise you? If you were going to create a golem, what would they look like? What would you name them? What special skills and talents would they have?

3. In the wake of an anti-Semitic incident, Faye creates a golem for protection and support. What did you learn about anti-Semitism by reading *Magical Meet Cute*? Have you, or someone you know, ever been targeted in an anti-Semitic attack? What happened?

4. Greg begins reading Faye's books in order to stave off confusion and help aid his memory. Yet, with each book he reads, he takes on the traits of the characters within the story and learns a valuable life lesson. Name one book that has left a lasting impression on you. Do you believe that books are capable of changing people? Why or why not?

5. Faye feels saddled by memory and a history of abuse. Greg is dealing with amnesia. How can memory be

both an asset and a detriment? In addition to individual memory, *Magical Meet Cute* deals with collective memory. What sort of collective memory do the Jewish characters in this book share? What are some other examples of collective memory in your own life?

6. At one point, Nelly says, "We Jews are a storytelling people." What do you think she means by that? How is storytelling used by cultures to transmit and maintain traditions? How is the golem tale a story that has shifted, and been shaped, by the teller over time? How can a story be changed, or distorted, by the person telling it? Give one example.

7. At the end of the book, Faye learns that her pottery doesn't need to be perfect to be loved and valued, and pens an article called "The Art of Imperfection." How is Faye's pottery a metaphor for her own life? Have you ever loved something that was imperfect?